THE BRAIN BUILDER

SUE HANSON

ISBN 978-1-64079-468-9 (Paperback)
ISBN 978-1-64079-469-6 (Digital)

Christian Faith Publishing, Inc.
296 Chestnut Street
Meadville, PA 16335
www.christianfaithpublishing.com

Printed in the United States of America

This novel was written in 1991. Things were very different then. At that time, the inventions that are described in this book were way ahead of anything we had. I was a business broker in Grand Rapids earlier, where I met this genius inventor, and Part One of this book is based on his life and work. I took it into fantasyland in Part Two. I had given up on having it published (back then, publishing was a lot different than it is now), and then gradually technology started catching up with what my friend had invented. So I decided this story was past its time and had kept only one printed-out copy for my own pleasure. Then a good friend read my manuscript and convinced me to publish it. On rereading the book, I decided perhaps he is right. It may not be cutting edge anymore, but I think it is entertaining, and I hope you enjoy it. I lost contact with my friend a few years ago, and I think he may have died, but he did read the first manuscript and said he liked it. I have changed all the names to protect his family and anyone else involved in his life and business.

I hope you enjoy the story.

PROLOGUE

In the main laboratory, Perceptor One raised his head. Something was wrong in the building, he sensed it. His eyes searched through the gloom and fixed on a vague movement at the far end of the complex. A second later, he perceived another movement, a mere shifting shadow in the cavernous manufacturing plant. Even as the thought crossed his mind, Perceptor units sprang into action and in a moment, surrounded the intruder, who crouched behind some storage barrels. Swift and silent, the nearest Perceptor unit grasped the thief by his neck and lifted him high into the air, where he thrashed and writhed to no avail, until at last he gave up and dangled helplessly. The interloper was secured and would keep until morning. The other units moved silently back to their stations. Satisfied, Perceptor One eased back into his place and waited.

PART ONE

1967

CHAPTER 1

The heat was a force that seemed to shape and mold the whole country, shimmering before his eyes to trick his mind into seeing things that weren't there. Mud oozed up around Chris's belly, tickling as it seeped through his shirt, creeping higher and higher up on his back. He was sure his feet were rotten from being wet so long, and his boots smelled like something had died in them. He had stopped counting the endless, mindless, identical days and nights he spent slithering through mire on his belly or hacking through jungle, dodging bullets, sneaking through tall grass, sweating out booby traps, shooting at whatever moved, and killing, killing, killing. He felt as though his own soul was slowly, slowly dying in the jungle and being buried in the mud.

Month after month, through torrential rains and strength-sapping heat, with one narrow escape after another, he had learned to block out thought and function like a machine. Chris was as good a soldier as any of the men, but it often seemed as though they used his outfit in the worst action, as though they were expendable. One perverse pleasure of his life was picturing the gory details if Officer VanSlyke were the Viet Cong's prisoner. He shifted his heavy gun from one shoulder to the other. *If I get out of here alive, I'll give Judge Lamb an earful!* he thought.

Bone weary, he staggered through the mud and moved on with the others, covered with dirt that would never wash away and a whole lot older than he had been just a year before. Could it possibly have been only a year?

The day his life ended started out the same as all the rest. Hot, clammy, stinking troops made their way through the jungle to destroy a bridge and cut off the road south. One minute he was thinking that if they weren't careful the VC would smell them coming, and the next minute Johnson, up front, stepped on a mine. Johnson was blown to bits right in front of them. It was horrible beyond belief. Chris froze for a second before from long training, his feet took over, and he dashed for cover in the tall grass. Blood surged in his head, numbing his brain. *Hurry…get out of here…Quick, down behind that clump…Don't move. Don't even breathe. Oh, God, please hide me!* He lay still, fear pounding through him with every loud heartbeat.

A gun barrel jabbed hard between his shoulders. He swore and, with great reluctance, rolled over and looked up at the enemy. The gun motioned him to get up, accompanied by loud jabbering by its excited owner. He obeyed, getting shakily to his knees and then to his feet as he looked around. His heart sank as he saw they'd captured his whole outfit! He counted them…there was nobody left to help them escape.

The prisoners moved in a lead-footed line along the narrow trail through thick wet jungle, their hands bound behind their backs, unable to dodge the branches that whipped their faces and legs. The gun jabbed regularly into Chris's ribs, urging him along faster. He grimaced from the pain. *These Cong are merciless little bastards…I wonder what torture they have planned.*

Up ahead, he saw another bunch of VC squatting around a small hole in the ground. He stared at it. They must've come out of that…*Oh my God! They can't expect us to go in there!*

No. They all gestured and jabbered, and then the loudest one, an officer, made his decision. Again the gun jabbed him in the ribs… move…move at a jog now farther, farther along the trail. He saw a clearing ahead and guessed they were headed for that. Tall grass grew over the whole open space except on the far side. Over there was a high muddy bank, as though there must be a big hole on the other side. The gun prodded him over to the bank, along with the rest of his outfit, and they lined up.

Suddenly, Chris realized what was coming, and his heart pounded in his ears so loud it was hard to hear what was going on.

God, help me! he screamed inside his head as he watched the guns swing up to enemy shoulders. He heard the first shots before his world exploded into…peace.

****

It had all started simply enough…Grand Rapids had enjoyed a typical day in late May with sunshine and warm breezes that promised a long sweet summer. Trees in the large yards wore glorious blossoms of purple, pink, and white. Tulips and daffodils with their bright colors and intoxicating scents were everywhere. Chris's senses were on overload as he strolled down Bridge Street minding his own business, basking in the warm sun, and hungry as usual. He glanced ahead at the donut shop. *I wonder if I can sweet-talk Florence into a free sample…*

The thought of warm, doughy pastry made his saliva run. He breathed its heady aroma as he neared the shop, and swallowed in anticipation. Then within a few seconds, his life changed…

"Carson, your sister's a stinkin' whore!" He spun to face Jerry Sharnowski, who laughed, one arm hanging out of a beat-up hot rod. Chris jammed his fist through the open window. Jerry screamed in pain and rage as blood spurted from his nose. Theron Frezewski leaped out the passenger door, shrieking, "They'll getcha for this, Carson!" And right on cue, Officer VanSlyke stepped out from the shadowed entrance to the drug store across from them.

"Ya never learn, do ya, Carson?" That raspy voice grated on Chris's ear. "Let's see what the judge has ta say about this." VanSlyke grabbed Chris's arm and steered him around the corner where a squad car waited. Chris cradled his throbbing right hand in his good left one and submitted to being pushed into the backseat.

Jerry's gang had been out for revenge ever since he'd beat up Bud Wisinski for stealing the tip money from his busboy job at the Red Hot Inn. Chris slouched down, hoping nobody would recognize him in the squad car. What rotten luck! How in heck did VanSlyke happen to be right there, anyway?

Then with a sinking feeling, he understood. *Oh, brother…how stupid can I be? They set me up, and VanSlyke was in it with 'em. I'm gonna find a way to make those rats pay!*

Chris had left home at fifteen after a showdown with his Dad, who came home drunk again, ranting at the kids. He never went back home to live, only stopped by on occasion to see his sister and two younger brothers.

What Chris subsequently called home was a scantily furnished second floor room in a decrepit store building on Bridge Street. It had a lumpy bed and a broken chest of drawers and mice. A torn rag rug partially covered the floor, and the barely usable bathroom was just down the hall. Sometimes he had to share that with another tenant, but other tenants never stayed long, so he usually had the place all to himself. It was cheap and handy to his jobs. Now he knew it was all coming apart.

"Yer hot temper ez caught up with ya at last, Carson. Maybe this time ya'll end up in jail! Boys shud be home with ther famlies, not out on the streets. Pity yer dad didn' discipline ya better." VanSlyke pushed him into the station, where he endured the routine. When his turn came, Chris stood before the bench, fists clenched behind his back, and waited to hear his punishment.

"So, Christopher, you're in trouble again." Judge Lamb looked over the file, rubbed his chin, and thought a few moments. Then he sighed and turned to look at the defiant boy. He said it kindly, "Son, you've been here once too often, and now you're headed for a life in prison sooner or later, unless something changes. You're eighteen now…you're out of school, and you have no particular skills…" He paused, took off his glasses, and wiped them as he looked down at Chris standing there before the bench. Then he put the glasses back on and handed down the sentence. "Here's your choice, Christopher. You either join the army or spend time in jail. Which will it be?"

VanSlyke escorted him to the recruiter, a too friendly toad named James Buzz, who had grown up not far from Chris's neighborhood. Sergeant Buzz often came around when the local teens were hanging out on street corners or in the pool hall. Mostly he just shot the breeze, telling them how great the army was and all that bull about what great education and training and travel they'd get if they joined up. So maybe he was right; at any rate, Chris no longer had a choice. Judge Lamb had made the decision for him. He fell into the chair Buzz offered and filled out the forms, while VanSlyke watched to make sure he didn't skip out.

They gave him three days to "get his affairs in order," so he had time to see Betty. She cried when he told her what happened and wiped her eyes on the bottom of her old T-shirt. When she could talk without weeping, she said, "I sure am gonna miss you, Chris…but I'm glad you're getting out of here…hey, maybe this'll turn out good for you!" Her eyes widened, and she looked up at her big brother. "Gee, maybe that's what I should do too…join the Army soon as I'm old enough. Chris, you think I could pass for eighteen?"

He eyed her skinny frame and shook his head. "Naw, Sis. Anyway, there's gotta be a better way for you!"

She knew he was dead serious the way he said, "But make sure you stay away from Jerry Sharnowski and his gang. They're out to get you for some reason, and they'll do anything they can to hurt you. They already did it to me." He put his hands on her shoulders and looked into her face. "You understand me?"

She nodded and gave him a teary smile, and he thought of something else. "Say, Betty, maybe you should go talk to Judge Lamb. Maybe there's someplace you and the boys could go to be safe from them…and from Dad too!"

"Yeah, but what would that do to Dad? I sure like the idea of finding me and the boys a safe place, but I don't want to wreck Dad's life entirely doing it."

"You're way too loyal, Betty. I don't know how you can feel that way about Dad when he hurts you so much. You're just like Mom used to be." He put his arm around her shoulders. "Didn't help her much, did it?"

"Oh, Chris, why did she have to die?"

He swallowed hard, his throat hurting from the lump there, and hugged his little sister, feeling her thin body shake while she wept a brief weep for their mom and for Chris and for herself. His eyes were wet too.

Later, with pretended bravado to cover the apprehension that burned in his belly, he had said good-bye to his childhood and boarded a bus with other recruits for the trip to a different life.

****

Boot camp was hell. Chris had lived through it one day at a time, one hour at a time, one minute at a time. He hated the drill sergeant; the man was a sadist! Sometimes Chris had felt he was probably going to die, as they ran mile after mile in the rain or tried to swim while loaded down with all their gear, or struggled through yet another grueling obstacle course, and sometimes he didn't care if he did die! But all the while, he was growing up and learning to cope, while his boy's body and mind developed into those of a man.

When their ordeal was over at last and the Army considered them soldiers, the survivors had shipped out for Vietnam. As a group, they were hard-bellied, tough-muscled, and shaven-headed, and they were thankful down to their bones to have made it through their training and out from under Sergeant Stratton's boots. They laughed and sang and told jokes on the plane during their long trip to cover the nervousness and fear that filled them in the quiet and the dark. The trip was a welcome break from the misery they'd just experienced. Then they had found that compared to boot camp, Vietnam was the epicenter of the hottest fires of the pit!

CHAPTER 2

How strange…there was no noise anymore. The battle seemed to have disappeared, and the pain was gone from his feet! He felt pleasantly weightless and airy. He looked around in surprise and realized he was floating high over the countryside. From up here, Vietnam appeared peaceful and colorful, like a patchwork quilt far below him, all lovely green and brown and delicate colors. Funny how he could see and appreciate the colors; he'd always been color-blind. The war hardly showed from up here. He gazed in every direction. *I seem to be alone up here. I wonder what's next. I guess I must be dead, but is this all there is to it? It can't be…*

He enjoyed floating for a while, even practiced moving up and down, turning and diving, before panic began to form again. *I don't want to die! I'm not ready for this yet! I'm too young…there's so much left to do! I wonder where my body is. Oh my God, I've gotta find my body and get back into it somehow…where did those gooks put it? Where is that clearing? Where are all the other guys?*

He was frantic to find and reclaim his body—his shell—his anchor to the earth. There! A whole stack of bodies lay just below him! He descended to search, but it was hopeless…they all looked alike, were all dressed alike, all had the same short haircuts. They were all young, too young to be lying there dead! He raced back and forth above the poor broken corpses but couldn't locate his own. He realized he had never seen himself from the outside before, never three-dimensionally, only in flat mirror images. At last, he gave up in frustration and drifted, feeling helpless. *I wonder what happened to the enemy. What should I do now?*

He was floating up again…up and up until the earth was far below him.

Wait, there was something, someone, moving toward him from a long distance. He stared. This person…so bright and shining… hard to look at! As the light came closer and closer, finally all Chris saw were his eyes. He had never seen such eyes before. There was absolute peace and deep, compassionate understanding in them.

Chris was overwhelmed with love such as he had never felt before. It seemed to flow over him like a warm liquid. He sensed that this being knew him thoroughly, knew everything he'd ever done, the few good things and all the rotten ones. And then Chris realized this incredible, indescribable entity was Jesus, although not a word had been said.

Chris had heard about Jesus when he was a little boy and his mother took him to Sunday school, but he never imagined Jesus to be like this! They'd always made him seem like a wimp, but this was no wimp he was facing. This being was strong and powerful with white light streaming from him and that great, awful love in his eyes!

Jesus gestured, and Chris became aware that his whole short life was on display all at once and all around him, like on large movie screens. By rotating, he could see himself as an infant cuddled by his mother, and at the same time as a small boy in school teasing Ronnie, the class nerd. He watched himself raise his hand in a church meeting when they gave the invitation to be saved, and saw himself later hanging out with the guys on the street. It was weird.

Chris didn't feel any judgment from Jesus, only love, but Chris certainly did judge himself! What a rotten life he had led. His heart was broken. Why didn't he do better at life, and what would happen now? He didn't have to speak, as Jesus obviously knew what he was thinking. But then he did speak anyway, although there was no sound. "Please," he asked. "I know I've blown it! Please can I have one more chance to do better?"

"Yes, my son. It is not yet your time. I will send you back. And if you yield to me, I will use you as an instrument to change the world." Chris didn't hear the words with sound, but they were clear in his mind. "You will use the intelligence I have given you to help my people. Learn all you can and use what you learn for good. Above all, love my people because with love, you will be greatly used for good. Without it, you can be deceived into using your knowledge for terrible evil. Study my Word. It is a guide for your life."

Jesus turned his eyes fully on Chris's own, and immediately ideas flooded into his mind—such ideas as he had never known were possible; things he was not capable of thinking before, intelligent as he was. Suddenly, he understood physics principles that he had never learned in school. He reveled in knowledge, soaking it into himself like a sponge but at the same time wondering, questioning. Where was this place? Well, wherever it was, it was unbelievable. Peace enveloped him and love beyond his understanding. What euphoria! He opened his mouth to ask some questions, but Jesus was gone. There was only a bright dot far in the distance.

And then before he could protest or change his mind, it was over.

****

Bang! His world exploded into pain, intense pain! He cried out and then moaned as the pain surged over him in continuing waves until he felt his head would burst with it. He was aware of running feet and voices calling for help, and then several hands lifted him from a hard tile floor. They laid him on a soft surface and covered him with a clean sheet and blanket, and he realized with amazement that he had just rolled off a hospital bed!

No sooner had nurses settled him into bed again than doctors appeared, poking him and asking questions. They seemed amazed he was awake. They gave him a shot. He had a hard time getting his voice to work, and he had difficulty making words form and make sense. He had so many questions. He wished they would stop asking him questions and start telling him some answers, but he was so tired. He just closed his eyes for a minute to rest, and he was asleep.

They let him sleep, marveling that the coma ended so abruptly. This was good refreshing sleep, sleep that would help him to heal, so they waited until he woke again to ask more questions. He could give them no answers, anyway. Chris had no idea what had happened to his body after the enemy shot him.

Gradually over time, Chris comprehended his condition. They told him the headache was because he took a bullet in the forehead, and he hurt in the middle because they also shot him in the back. (Thinking about that later, he figured his body must have spun around when they hit his head.) He raised his left hand to feel his forehead and stopped it in midair, staring. *Oh my God, my fingers are gone!*

Numbly, he felt the scar on his forehead with his right hand. This is incredible! How could anybody live through this?

Then he remembered…*Jesus! But I know I was dead…wasn't I? And how can I live when they shot me in the head and in the back and shot off my three fingers?*

He waited for the doctor to return and asked, "How many other men from my unit survived?"

The young intern shook his head. "I don't know how in the world you made it either! You must have angels all around you!"

"Yeah, I guess so." Chris closed his eyes again, thinking. When he asked the date, he realized that he'd rolled off that bed six months later than the day they lined up before the firing squad! Where had he been, and who had rescued him? How did it happen that he escaped being buried with the rest? What miracle was responsible for his being in New York, not Vietnam? How could it possibly have been six months ago, when he had spent such a short time in that marvelous place with Jesus and he wanted to stay there a lot longer and ask him so many more things? He never found out those answers. He pondered and meditated and prayed. *Show me, Jesus. Show me what to do. Don't let me blow it again!*

"Good morning, sport!" Jean, the nurse with the beautiful brown eyes and the smiling voice, shook down a thermometer preparing to shove it in his mouth. "It sure is good to talk to you," she confided. "We weren't sure you'd ever be able to talk to us. Looked like you might just be a vegetable." She stuck the thermometer under his tongue. "I wondered what color those eyes were…thought they might be brown, but now that I see them, I know they couldn't have been anything but blue."

He smiled as well as he could around the thermometer. He liked Jean. She was a gentle one, and he knew, he thought, what a miracle it was that he was in this place and able to think, talk, and feel again. "Hi, Jean," he answered when she took the thermometer out again. "Do I get a real breakfast today?"

"Be here any minute. If you're lucky, you may get oatmeal."

"What, no bacon and eggs? And wheat toast and black coffee, please."

"Uh-huh! You wish! But if you're good and keep on getting better, it won't be long before they'll let you. You're the talk of the hospital, you know."

Day by day, he mended and began to regain all his functions. As his mind cleared, he asked for books and read them voraciously. There had to be answers somewhere for the things he had experienced, or at least he thought he had experienced. He wanted, and needed, some answers. They provided him with a Bible where he found answers, along with a lot more questions. He read and studied with great interest while an idea formed in his mind and took root. One day, he decided to talk to Jean about it on her next shift.

"The army recruiter promised me an education," he said to her the next morning as she prepared to help him shave. "If he was serious, I wonder how I go about getting it."

"I suppose you apply to the Veteran's Administration. At least, that's what I'd do. Want me to ask at the office?" He raised his eyebrow. "The hospital office?"

"It is a VA hospital, you know."

Understanding dawned. "Oh yeah, I should've known that, sorry! But back to the college thing, guess it wouldn't hurt to get started, would it? I need someplace to go from here anyway, and Michigan State would probably be as good as anywhere else."

"Why Michigan State?"

"I guess because it's close to home…or what used to be home. Michigan's my home state. I had some friends who talked about going to MSU once. Seems like a place to start, anyway."

Jean nodded and smiled. She was busy all day, but she took the time to inquire about veterans' benefits regarding education. She couldn't help liking the strange young man who seemed so old sometimes. There was often a look in his eyes that she couldn't understand, though he was beginning to laugh now and then, and even make jokes. He had a "different" sense of humor. She supposed that was logical considering all he'd been through.

She arrived at his room the next day armed with booklets and applications for every program the Veterans Administration had to offer, even to backing for real estate loans, as if he were interested in settling down! He grimaced. *Fat chance, I can't even imagine buying a house and taking root. There's so much to learn and so much to see and so little time to do it!*

But he was surprised and grateful, and he let her know it. "Hey, Jean, I know that was a lot of bother! I can't tell you how much I appreciate it. It would've taken me a long time to get all this stuff." He started filling out the forms immediately, and she mailed them for him.

Endless weeks dragged on in the hospital. He met other men with a variety of wounds—some physical, some mental. Chris talked to them during physical therapy sessions, asking what had happened to them, trying to find out if other guys had gone through an experience like his. He couldn't find even one. He didn't talk about it, though, not to anyone. Some things are too private and special for a person to share with others!

The thing with life is, you never know what a day will bring. This special day started the same as all the rest, with no warning that he was nearing a milestone. His doctor checked him over and then casually asked as he checked the chart he was holding. "Chris, how do you feel about going back out into the world? It looks like we can't hold you here much longer. In fact, we can release you next Thursday if no complications arise."

Panic and rejoicing fought in Chris. This was news he had longed for one minute and feared the next for months! There was just time to enroll in school for the fall semester. He had six months Army pay for the time he was in a coma and seven months more pay he'd saved while he was in the hospital. He had a discharge and a Purple Heart and life! Now he figured he needed a car.

"Hey, Jean, want to go shopping with me Thursday?" He smiled so she wouldn't see how much he needed her to say yes. She raised an eyebrow at him. "That's the day I get out of here, and I feel like celebrating! Go with me to buy some new duds and a car, and I'll buy you a steak. Deal?"

"Deal, sure." she agreed. "But you'll have to wait until I get off work at three o'clock."

He felt weird being out on the streets again. The world teemed with people, traffic, and noise, and Chris wasn't sure he was ready for this. He'd never been in New York before the hospital. It was a lot different from Grand Rapids or Vietnam! Jean knew the ropes, though, and she took his arm and whistled for a taxi. She gave the driver directions and had Chris into a store and outfitted with a wardrobe sooner than he would have thought possible. She was great! He felt good in new jeans, sport shirt and sweater, new socks, and Reeboks. The other things were in big bags.

"Okay, now to find a reasonable car." He looked at her gratefully. *She's a knockout*, he thought. Funny how different she looked out of uniform. Her blond hair caressed her shoulders, she wore a soft blue sweater and gray skirt, and she smiled and laughed easily. He appreciated that, and he loved her voice. He wondered if she sang. He said, "We need a good used car lot. Know any around here?"

"Hardly anybody I know owns a car. They take the bus or a taxi. It's too hard to find parking in the city. Anyway, it costs a fortune, but my dad buys his at the Motor Mall."

"Sounds good to me. Is it far from here?"

"Not by taxi, but I wouldn't want to walk it!"

They managed to get another cab and found the Motor Mall. They looked over several cars and picked out and haggled over a blue Ford with 52,000 miles and new tires. He parted with $1450 more, and finally they were riding down the street in New York City traffic in the first car Chris had ever owned. He had never had much driving experience either, and for a few minutes, he was nervous, but gradually he got used to the pace. He glanced at his watch. It was seven o'clock already!

He looked over at Jean. "I'm starving! How about you?"

"I thought you'd forgotten you promised me a steak. I'm so hungry I could eat two by now!"

"Well, lead on. Where do they serve the best food in town? Somewhere that's close by, that is? I guess I don't want to drive any farther in this city than I have to!"

She laughed. "I guess I don't want to ride with you any farther than I have to!"

It wasn't far to The Great Steak-Out, a medium-sized, medium-priced restaurant where the steaks were great, and they enjoyed themselves over a leisurely dinner. Too soon to suit Chris, Jean insisted she must get home. "Some of us have to work in the morning."

"Gosh, I forgot that," he teased. "Maybe we should just go and get married, and then you could come along with me."

"I suppose if you were a Rockefeller and this were a limousine, we could talk about that." She laughed. "Let me know when you have your education behind you, then we'll talk."

He drove to her apartment as she gave him directions. He stopped at the front steps. "I suppose your roommate's home?"

"Yes, afraid so."

"Oh…that's what I thought." He kissed her and held her close for a minute. She smelled good, and he felt as if she belonged in his arms. He wanted to stay with her and not have to face the world yet. He kissed her again. "Thanks for all you've done. You've been so good to me. You're as close to an angel as a person can be." He swallowed the lump in his throat. "I hope it won't be long until I can come back again. I'll miss you so much, Jean!"

It took a long time for him and the blue Ford to get out of New York City and longer after that to find a cheap motel with a vacancy, and Chris thought about Jean all the way.

CHAPTER 3

He steered the Ford slowly down Grand River Avenue to Michigan Street and pulled into the MSU entrance. To Chris's eyes, it was a stereotypical college—old buildings covered with ivy, new glass-and-metal buildings, dormitories, and other buildings that didn't easily reveal their purposes to the uninitiated eye. Lofty trees shaded the walkways, giving this school an aura of established learning that somehow newer schools with smaller trees can't convey.

He surveyed the campus with interest, watching fresh-faced students walking along the paths and sidewalks or riding bikes, their books in backpacks. Some sat under the trees, laughing, talking, and just going about being students. In a way, he envied them, so young and carefree and most with parents to love and support them. Then he straightened his shoulders. *Hey, you wouldn't trade places with them even if you could, and you know it!* he said to himself.

He found his way to the registration office, pulled into the closest parking space he could locate, and walked a block back to the building. Chris was almost twenty-two years old and looked older with his wise eyes. A lock of wavy hair over his forehead usually covered the round scar that gradually faded to the same color as the rest of his skin. A freshman could easily mistake him for a faculty member, especially when he spoke. His voice was a clear baritone that exuded confidence and authority, though he wasn't aware how he sounded to others. He entered the office and registered for the courses he would need to major in Philosophy.

From there, he found the Campus Bookstore and wandered among the stacks, selecting the best used textbooks he could find. He inhaled the bookstore smell deeply, as though he could "breathe in" the knowledge packaged in all those pages. As he surveyed the many books in the Philosophy section, he could see this was a study he'd enjoy. He picked up the Plato and flipped through its pages.

"Are you taking Professor Phillips' class too?" The voice had a nasal tone as though its owner had a sinus problem.

He turned to face a rumpled fellow whose round wire-rimmed glasses had slid down on his nose so they no longer covered his friendly blue eyes. He appeared a little older than most students. His straight, straw-colored hair had not seen a barber for too long and hung down in his face, which obviously bothered him as he impatiently brushed it back while trying to retain his hold on the stack of books he carried.

"Yeah, I guess I am." Chris liked the guy's looks. "I'm Chris Carson" He put out his hand, and the fellow set the books down and gave it a hearty shake.

"Fred VanDam. You been here long? I haven't seen you in any of my classes, and you don't look like a freshman."

"Just arrived. Afraid I'm one of those Vietnam veterans people seem to dislike so much. Just out of the hospital and ready to get serious about life." He waved his hand across the Philosophy section. "I decided this is a good place to start to figure things out."

"I'm in grad school myself, and they call me a professional student," Fred responded with a rueful grin. "Learning is my favorite thing, and there's so much more to know that I simply can't decide I've had enough and go out into the workforce!"

Chris laughed. "I can relate to that. I'm here to learn all there is to know and preferably as fast as possible." They finished their shopping and stood in line at the cash registers. The store was crowded by then, and people pushed, shoved, and tried to cut in line. Student cashiers did their best to cope with the pandemonium. It was time to get out of there and look for a place to live!

"Say, Fred, do you know of a good small apartment close to campus?"

"You mean you bought books before you even found a place to crash? Man, you're something else!" Fred hesitated a moment, eyeing Chris critically, and then admitted. "In fact, I could use a roommate if you're interested. Gordy's gettin' married, so he just moved to married housing. I'm not the neatest housekeeper, though."

Fred's apartment was great. It was messy, as Fred said, but with two good-sized bedrooms, decent living room, minuscule kitchen, and a bathroom featuring a big old-fashioned tub with claw feet and a strange circular shower curtain. Chris moved his stuff in and in no time felt right at home.

On Sunday, he figured he'd find a church and begin to learn more about Jesus and what he expected of his followers. After reading the Bible himself, Chris wanted to discuss the things he'd been thinking with someone who could give him fresh input. He had noticed an imposing stone church not far from campus. It sat back from the street on manicured grounds, shaded by ancient oaks and maples. It was obvious this was a place where the person in charge would know something about God's Word.

Chris walked up the long front walk along with other worshipers and stepped through massive doors into the dim and lofty interior. Light filtered through richly colored stained glass windows, giving the sanctuary a hushed and holy feeling. He moved with proper reverence along the dark red carpet and found a place toward the back where he could see and hear easily without being conspicuous. He settled on the velvet-cushioned pew uncertainly.

So this is one of your houses, Lord. I'm impressed! He talked to the Lord in his mind a lot and always said what he thought. Anyway, he knew from experience Jesus could read his mind and heart. People quietly took their seats, and soon the church was nearly full. The choir filed into place on either side of the platform below the impressive organ pipes that had been making soft music for the last few minutes. They wore white robes with red satin scarves, and they were as elegant as everything else about True Trinity Church. The organ sounded a chord, and the choir sang "Praise God from Whom All Blessings Flow." At that signal, a door beside the platform opened, and Pastor Conrad Braxton made his way to the pulpit.

As the choir finished their praise, the minister raised his hands and his head dramatically to invoke the Lord's blessing on the service. Chris enjoyed the music and the prayer. Pastor Braxton's eloquent sermon was based on the parable of the lost sheep. His voice was resonant, his face earnest and concerned, and his wavy blond hair, touched by the light from the windows, made him seem to have a halo. He frequently stretched his black-robed arms toward his "flock" as he made them weep with the story of the Shepherd who cared so much for his sheep.

The sermon touched Chris. He felt as though he himself were that one lost sheep Jesus had searched for and found and given another chance for life. Pastor Braxton stood at the door shaking hands after the service, so Chris introduced himself. "I'd like to talk with you sometime. Do you have a special time for meeting with people?"

Pastor Braxton looked Chris over, sizing him up on the spot. *A student…this one is a little different, though. There's something about him. Probably needs help with a drug problem, or he's gotten a girl in trouble or something.* "I'll be in my study Tuesday afternoon at one o'clock, if you can be here then?" Chris nodded and was pushed on by the crowd behind him.

The Reverend Dr. Conrad Braxton prided himself on his humility. If anyone were humble, certainly it was he. He would meet with anyone, no matter how poor or strange or weird they were. If they sought help, he would guide them. The world was filled with people who needed the Lord, who needed to be told how to live their lives righteously according to God's laws, and Conrad was available to teach them what God required.

At forty-five, Braxton was at the peak of his career as a minister. He had started in a small church in Northern Michigan, where the membership had doubled within two years under his care. From there, he moved up through a series of progressively larger churches until he was offered the pastorate at True Trinity, one of the most successful and influential churches in the state. He enjoyed this position. He felt satisfaction in knowing how well he had served the Lord, and he enjoyed prestige among his fellow clergymen as well as the whole city. He was often asked to speak at special events at the university, where he was popular with the students. His beautiful wife, Lenore, encouraged his work and graced his impressive home with tasteful entertaining. She also worked to help the poor by directing a group that collected and distributed used clothing and household goods. His two children were handsome and intelligent, and they were, as far as he knew, good upstanding Christians, who were leaders in their classes. Yes, the Lord had greatly blessed Conrad Braxton, and he was grateful, feeling that he had earned those blessings.

Chris looked forward to their meeting on Tuesday. He had never talked with a minister before, hadn't been to church for years… not since his mother died. And that church wasn't anything like True Trinity! It was just a small group of dedicated people like his mom, led by a shabby but sincere older man who sometimes wept as he preached. That had been embarrassing, but Chris remembered raising his hand one time when that preacher—he couldn't even remember his name—asked who wanted to be saved. There'd been a lot of water under the bridge since then, and now Chris had many things to discuss with a man who obviously must know the scriptures as well as Doctor Conrad Braxton did.

The pastor's study was on the building's south side with a separate entrance. Chris stepped into the outer office, gave the attractive middle-aged receptionist his name, and waited while she disappeared into the study. She came back in a moment and beckoned him, then as he walked into the room, she closed the door quietly behind him. Dr. Braxton rose from behind his massive mahogany desk, extending his hand. Chris shook it, noticing the firm grasp, and then took the chair the pastor indicated. After some preliminary chitchat about nothing significant, Doctor Braxton asked, "And what was it that you wanted to discuss?" He settled back into his comfortable chair, ready to hear the typical student problems.

"Well, sir, I've had an unusual experience, and I'd like to discuss it with you." Chris hesitated a moment and then decided to go ahead and bare his soul. "I've never told anyone about it until now." Braxton raised his eyebrow inquiringly, so Chris continued, "It happened in Vietnam." He began to describe his being shot, meeting with Jesus and how he had felt while with him, waking up in the hospital, and then studying on his own. "It's hard to reconcile some things I've read with what I hear and see around me, and I'm not sure just what I should do with the things he's showing me about new technological techniques." Chris stopped talking and looked up at the older man, waiting to see his reaction.

Conrad Braxton sat astounded. He had never heard anything like what this odd young man had just told him, yet he couldn't doubt Chris's sincerity. Either the fellow was telling the truth or he was a complete mental case. If this was truth, it was far from anything Conrad had ever imagined. He cleared his voice, then stood up and walked to the door. "Judy, will you please get us some coffee?" he asked and then used the time to gather his thoughts while Judy brought cups and asked Chris whether he needed cream or sugar. By the time she left again, he was ready to pursue the conversation.

"You're a most blessed young man," he told Chris. "I hope you realize that. There are precious few people who've had experiences such as you have described to me." (He was privately somewhat disgruntled that the Lord had seen fit to speak to a nobody like Chris rather than to himself.) He eyed Chris across the desk. "All right, I believe we need to start at the beginning. Have you asked Jesus for salvation?"

Chris hesitated then admitted he had not formally done so. "I raised my hand in a church service when I was little and would have done more if anyone had pushed me, but no, I guess I haven't asked to be saved." He shrugged. "I guess I just took it for granted that I'm saved after my meeting with the Lord."

"Well, Chris," the older man said wisely, "it can't hurt to make it official between you and the Lord. Let's take care of that right now, shall we?"

Chris nodded assent, and Pastor Braxton led him in a prayer of repentance while he asked for and received the gift of salvation. As he looked up after the prayer, it seemed good and right, and he was grateful to the pastor. He appreciated this man.

"The next thing you need is to be baptized, Chris." Dr. Braxton opened his Bible and pointed out the scriptures to Chris, showing him verses that clearly tell the need to be baptized into Christ's death and raised up in the likeness of his resurrection to walk in newness of life. "The old things have passed away—behold, all things have become new."

"I read that but wasn't sure how it applied to me. Now that I see the need, I'd like to be baptized right now and get that settled. Is that okay?"

"Why, we usually baptize on Sunday, Chris," Dr. Braxton began and then he stopped and reflected. "But you are a somewhat unusual case. Let's see if we can take care of it now." He called his secretary again and sent her for robes and towels. When she came back with them, he took Chris into the small anteroom adjoining the baptistery, where Chris undressed and put on a long white cotton robe.

After a few moments, Dr. Braxton came in, wearing his own baptismal robe, and opened the door into the baptistery. It was above the altar, high up between the ranks of organ pipes. A beautiful scene on the wall behind them made it seem to a watching congregation that the person being baptized was in a wide river bordered with trees, with the light of heaven shining down on it. Of course there was no congregation now, and Chris looked out over the empty church, where sun streamed in through the lovely stained glass on the right side, making soft red, blue, and gold patterns on the wood and velvet of the pews. Chris felt peace in his soul. What they were doing was right. He bowed his head. *In the likeness of his death, in the likeness of his resurrection, Lord, help me to walk in newness of life.*

They stepped down into the cool water together. Pastor Braxton turned Chris around so he could hold onto him and prayed a brief prayer. Then he said, "Christopher Carson, I baptize you in the name of the Father and of the Son and of the Holy Ghost. Amen." Holding one hand behind Chris's head, he tilted him backward under the water, raising him up again the next moment and giving him a soft cloth to wipe his face.

Chris felt good as he dried and dressed. He felt clean and as though now Jesus was walking right beside him. He was grateful to Dr. Braxton for showing him the right way to go, and he told him so as they settled once again in the doctor's study. "Now what do I do?" he asked.

Dr. Braxton leaned back in his chair. "It seems to me you have some responsibility on your shoulders, considering the things Jesus showed you. It is obvious you need to learn all you can while you're here at school. I shall be glad to teach you privately each week to further your understanding of the Lord and what he requires from you now." He rose and put his hand on Chris's shoulder, looking into his face. "I'm glad our Lord sent you to me, Chris. It will be my privilege to guide your search. Now I think we should pray." Chris bowed his head, while Pastor Braxton prayed for God's guidance in his life and for wisdom to use the new knowledge he was receiving to further God's will on the earth.

Both men had a lot to think about as they parted. Chris felt he had found a mentor who could help him understand his purpose in life. Pastor Braxton thanked the Lord for sending Chris to him so he could "guide the boy aright" and keep his feet on the narrow path.

They met each week after that to discuss scriptures. Chris came up with many disturbing questions Pastor Braxton had trouble answering. In more than one instance, his answer was "That's a mystery for now. We just have to take it by faith. Someday, though, we'll understand!" meaning when we get to heaven. Chris wanted to understand now! Where did Cain get his wife? And how did he build a city if there were no people? How does it happen that there are different colored races, even after the flood, if only Noah and his family survived? Why would God tell his people to obliterate another race and judge them so harshly when they saved some alive? Where did the other ten tribes of Israel go after God divorced them? The Bible clearly says that they'll be joined again to the two tribes of Judah and Benjamin called the Jews, so they must be somewhere in the world now.

He had many other questions too, and as he read his Bible, unencumbered with having been taught someone else's theology, he found some answers revealed. When he pointed them out to Pastor Braxton, the good reverend-doctor was horrified. "You can't believe that, Chris," he would often say, or "But that's not for today!" But when Chris would ask him to point out when and where it had changed, there was no good answer. Over time, Pastor Braxton began to dread their meetings and to dislike Chris as a troublemaker! He would never have admitted that to himself, though, and certainly not to anyone else!

****

"I suppose it's odd for a freshman to live with a grad student, but I like this arrangement," Chris remarked to Fred one evening after they'd been sharing the apartment a few weeks.

"Yeah, me too. I'm glad we have Professor Phillips' class together. Makes it more challenging to have you to discuss things with. You have a different slant on things than the other guys in that class. What is it about you that makes you so different, anyway?"

"Someday I'll tell you about that, Fred, when the time is right. First, I have some things to figure out for myself."

They discussed Plato's ideas for a whole term and then explored Aristotle, Kant, and others. And Chris kept studying the Bible, and even read Confucius. Over the course of three years, he studied many religions—Buddhism, Taoism, Islam, Judaism, and the Indian religions. In the end, he realized that although all those religions held grains of truth, the only real answer was in the Bible, in Jesus, the one he had met—he was sure he had met him—and not in any religion.

"As a matter of fact, Fred, I'm more and more convinced that religion has been the underlying cause of much conflict and trouble in the world. Most wars were caused by religious differences of one kind or another, and religion was the prime cause of the dark ages. When you think about it, the Bible shows that religious people were the ones who killed Jesus. Jesus was righteous, not religious."

"You didn't get that from any course here!" Fred pushed his glasses back up on his nose and surveyed Chris critically. "You sure are a strange one! I don't know anyone else who takes that attitude, but you know, it almost makes sense to me too."

"That's scary, you know." Chris laughed. "Nothing ever makes sense to you, at least nothing I've ever said. That's what makes you a valuable asset to me. You're a good sounding board for my wacky philosophies." He changed the subject then, and they continued studying.

When he expressed the same ideas about religion to Dr. Braxton at their next session, he found he had opened a serious rift between them and had to sit through a lecture on pride and thinking he was better than other people just because of one experience. Dr. Braxton waxed eloquent as to how he should be more humble and not make judgments about things he obviously didn't understand! "God gave shepherds to his flock to teach them the way they should go. None of that flock must go ahead of the shepherd, for fear he'll be terribly lost...a casualty out on the craggy mountains...dashed to pieces in a fall to the rocks far below him!" Dr. Braxton prayed that Chris would be humble and take his proper place in the order of the church and understand the Lord's reasons for instituting rules, regulations, and religious requirements for his flock.

As he left the pastor's study, Chris's mind was boiling with conflicting feelings. His feet crunched on the snow, his face glowed red in the cold, and Chris covered the ground unseeing as he thought and prayed. "Lord, show me the truth. Help me to be what you want me to be and not listen to anyone who would turn me aside from your truth. Oh, Lord, please don't let me be proud and puffed up as Dr. Braxton said, but Lord, don't let me be sidetracked from you by anyone else." He walked and prayed and thought for an hour before he realized how cold he was and turned quickly for home.

Chris never went back to Dr. Braxton's study, and he avoided the church services, preferring for the time to study and pray on his own. Spring arrived, and as the weather began to warm and the first bright yellow forsythia burst into bloom, Chris was increasingly restive. One evening, he turned to Fred as they shared a can of tasteless stew for their dinner. "I've been thinking...you know, all this stuff we're learning is pretty doggoned interesting, and I think it's important and all, but how are we going to earn a living with it? You intend to be a teacher? I sure don't. I'll have a degree as an epistemologist, a knowledge engineer, but what will I do with it to earn a salary?"

"You know, I've wondered about that sometimes myself. I just figured you were planning to write books or be a professor somewhere. For myself, I guess I'll have to take my 'old man' up on his offer to let me work in his parts-manufacturing company. I took enough business courses during my first years here that I can easily finish a BA in business administration. That might impress him."

Chris nodded. "I can relate to that since manufacturing is basic to our whole economy. What interests me more, though, is research and development. I'd like to get into that. I have some radically different ideas on knowledge engineering, relating to artificial intelligence…some things I'd like to try. I'm afraid Professor Abbott thinks I'm weird though. He's so sure the laws of physics he teaches are absolute. I wonder why people are so careful not to try anything new or radical just to see if it might work. It seems to me you can't put God's creation in little boxes and categorize them neatly. Anyway, I intend to spend a lot more time experimenting with some ideas I have—that is if he'll let me use the lab without his direct supervision all the time."

They talked on into the night, discussing their futures. Fred was turning over an idea in his mind, but he wisely decided to discuss it with his father before mentioning it to Chris. He had another idea too that he didn't mind talking about. "Say, Chris, it's been a long time since we had any social life. What say we look up some women and invite them out for dinner or go dancing or something?"

"Are you kidding me? What with? My pockets are empty, as usual! Anyway, who would we invite?"

"There's this girl I've had my eye on…works in the bookstore. She's great-looking. I mean, she's not beautiful, but she looks like she'd be great to get to know."

"Oh, I didn't know you'd been shopping around." Chris kidded. "Okay, there is Linda King from my physics lab class. Maybe I could ask her. But I don't know what we'll use for money!" Then he brightened. "I think I know how to make Beef Stroganoff, and you make that good salad. We could get some French bread or something. Do you think they'd come here for dinner?"

"Hey, that's a great idea…except we'll have to clean up the place."

"I guess it's time we did that, anyway." Chris looked around at the general mess and clutter and noticed the dirt accumulating underneath it. Dust curls moved gently on the floor in an occasional breeze from the open window. A layer of grit coated the furniture, and dirty clothes and dishes adorned tables, counters and chairs as though used for the latest decor. "Phew, guess I hadn't really looked at this place lately, but it could sure use some spit and polish. Let's do that first, and if we can make it look good enough, then we'll ask the girls, okay?"

They worked all day Saturday and Sunday sweeping, dusting, polishing, and even cleaning out the refrigerator. Chris washed the windows, while Fred took all the dirty clothes to the Laundromat. They were remarkably pleased with themselves when they considered the apartment clean.

"My mother wouldn't believe this," Fred remarked as he surveyed the new surroundings. "I didn't realize we were living in such a pit."

"Yeah, maybe it was worth thinking about women to get us to clean up our act. No sense shopping for the food until we see whether or not they'll come, though."

They did come! Chris and Fred outdid themselves in the kitchen, even adding a cake and ice cream to the feast. They spent a pleasant evening eating, talking, and enjoying each other's company. Watching Fred and Callie together made Chris grin. But Chris, while he was attentive to Linda King, remembered Jean. He missed her ready wit and her soft beauty. They had written occasionally at first, but it was a long time now since Chris had heard from her, and he suddenly realized how much he missed Jean.

Saturday he took time off from his studies to call New York. Jean's lilting voice answered. "Chris Carson! I gave you up as lost." She teased. She sounded wonderful; he could picture her standing there at the phone, smiling and beautiful with her lovely brown eyes and long blond hair. He wanted to see her again and tell her how much he missed her.

"How about if I come out to New York? It's been a long hard grind here, and I miss you."

She was quiet too long before she said softly, "Chris, you need to know I'm being married in June."

His heart felt as though she had stabbed it with one of her hypodermic needles. Why hadn't he called her more often or written more often or gone to see her before this. Damn! "Oh," he said. Then after giving her his congratulations and making some stupid small talk, he hung up. He was sure his heart would never recover from the wound. It must be bleeding inside his chest. He grabbed his jacket and got out into the fresh air as fast as he could. It was hard to breathe indoors.

He walked, not noticing where his feet took him, along the Red Cedar River, down sidewalks that crisscrossed the campus, past some dorms, past fraternity houses, not paying any attention to people or places he passed along the way. Eventually, he found himself standing in front of Dagwood's, so he turned in there and sat at the bar, where he indulged himself in melodramatic thoughts and drank beer. As the bartender set a third glass before him, he realized what he was doing and faced up to the situation.

He shoved the glass away and stared at his own face in the mirror behind the bar while giving himself a mental lecture. *Okay, come on now, you know you had no hold on her. And you surely couldn't expect her to just wait around for you. She's too pretty and too nice not to have guys hanging around her. How could you even think she might be interested in a guy like you with no money, no job, nothing!*

He shook his head to clear it and headed for the door. It was time to move on and see what work there was for him to do. Besides, God spared his life for a reason, and he knew it was time to try to find out what that reason was; the world was waiting for him!

CHAPTER 4

Chris enthusiastically accepted a job in research at Mason-Masters Corporation in Orlando, Florida. After their mass graduation party, he said good-bye to Fred and his life at MSU and headed south in the now ancient blue Ford. It was 1974, the aerospace industry was booming, and Chris was eager to start work on something to challenge his theories.

Chris had never been to Florida. He found the air a bit muggy, and the trees were different from those in Michigan or Vietnam—short and scrubby, some with moss hanging from the limbs—except for the palm trees, of course. He drove around the city to get the feel of the place. It surprised him to find several small lakes within the city limits. Disney World was a huge complex at the edge of town. He drove past the Mason-Masters plant to see where it was, then he located a seedy motel that rented rooms by the week. The proprietor let him take the key to check out a vacant room.

Chris nosed around, taking a quick survey. A kitchenette off the bedroom held an ancient refrigerator, teeny table and two matching chairs, half a gas stove, and an old-fashioned white enamel sink with the drain board built right onto the sink opening. Some small cupboards held plates and cups for two and a couple of cheap aluminum pans. The bathroom had a rusty stall shower with a rubber-backed curtain, no tub, and the double bed had seen better days a long time back. A metal stand with some hangers served as the closet. An overstuffed chair covered with a flowered slipcover waited in the corner. Two ugly pictures featuring flamingoes hung over the bed, and a double dresser with mirror and a squatty lamp completed the furnishings. The price was right; this would do fine.

He hung his few clothes on the rack, put his personal things in the bathroom and the drawers, and was settled. Since it was late afternoon, Chris elected to wait until morning to go to the plant. He found a diner nearby, where they had hot beef sandwiches (not too greasy), what they called homemade pie, and good hot coffee. He was happy so far.

In the morning, Chris reported in at the personnel office. "You'll be working with Charlie Morse and his team," the attractive secretary told him. She put him through the routine, filling out forms and getting his badge made, assigned him a time card, and gave him a copy of the company rules. Then she showed him around the plant and finally turned him over to a skinny, hawk-nosed man with piercing dark eyes. Charlie Morse's menacing appearance changed dramatically when he smiled.

He shook Chris's hand. "Glad you got here, Carson. We're 'up to our armpits in alligators' right now, trying to work the bugs out of our latest project." Charlie turned to his team, who had gathered around when Chris appeared. "Meet the guys you'll work with, Chris." He turned to a fat, red-bearded man who appeared to be about forty years old. "This is Don Blair." Chris extended his hand.

"Glad to have you aboard, Chris."

"Jim Myers, meet Chris Carson, our new member." Jim's handshake was as firm as he expected it to be. Jim looked tough and capable, dressed like a truck driver.

"Hope you like it here!" Jim boomed. Chris nodded and grinned.

"Here's our 'movie star,' Frank Berman." Frank had wavy blond hair and a beautiful smile. He wore a suit and tie. "He likes expensive cars and women too," Charlie teased. Frank's handshake was soft, and Chris felt a momentary doubt, but he shook it off as they met the last team member.

"Mick McKinley, our comic. He has a joke for every occasion." Charlie winked. Mick was big, black, and jolly. He engulfed Chris's hand in his huge grip.

"They've been putting all the stuff they don't want to work on on your desk, Carson. Good thing you finally got here!"

Chris grinned. "I'm looking forward to working with you!"

Chris soon found out how intelligent they were. He told them right off how he lost his fingers and showed them the scar in his forehead to save more questions later. They were fascinated with the little Chris told them. He didn't elaborate, merely saying that he woke up six months later rolling off a bed in New York.

Chris fit right in with the team, and after the first few days, he began to try his ideas. At first, Charlie was skeptical, but gradually, as he discovered that Chris's unusual approaches to problems actually had merit, Charlie turned into a special friend. Together, the team solved a major design problem on a piece of the space shuttle, just then being developed.

New ideas and different ways to do routine things occurred to Chris. He constantly asked the group, "What if we tried this method for that?" or "Why wouldn't this system work for that application?" Don and Jim were always skeptical of his ideas. Frank thought he was "just weird." Mick cracked jokes about the bullet in his head affecting his brain. Charlie began to admire his capacity for original thinking and kept an open mind. Working together, the men managed to complete their assigned projects on time and with exceptionally good results.

The months passed with Chris absorbed in his work, as usual. He took no time to socialize, even if he'd had someone to socialize with. His teammates were married, except Frank, with families who took up their time. Chris never asked where Frank spent his off hours. Once in awhile, when he stopped to think about it, Chris was lonely. Sometimes he took in a movie on a Sunday afternoon but spent most evenings with paper and pencil, thinking and rethinking about his main obsession—artificial intelligence.

It was close to Christmas, and lights, Santas, and wreaths were everywhere, but Chris was feeling especially grumpy and "out of it." He stopped in at the diner for his usual several cups of black coffee and some dinner, and there she was! His heart seemed to stop beating for a moment.

"What can I get for you?" she asked in a soft, sweet voice, pencil poised over her order pad. She was young and curvy, with short brown curls tied back in a blue ribbon. Her blue waitress uniform, cut above her knees, showed off shapely legs, and when she brought his coffee, he saw she had deep hazel eyes and a smile that hurt his heart. Her name was Diane; he knew because it was on the nametag pinned on a lace-edged hankie in her uniform pocket.

"Whatever you want, anything you like...oh, bring me the meatloaf special." He ate the meal, hardly tasting it, while he watched Diane work. After that, Chris spent even more time at the diner. He always took his notepad with him to work on a project while drinking coffee, though truth be told, he spent most of the time looking at Diane.

For her part, Diane was flattered by Chris's obvious interest in her. She was young and pretty and ready for adventure, and this older man fascinated her. "Whatcha doin' for Christmas?" she asked one evening as she set his Swiss steak and potatoes on the table.

"I don't know...I haven't planned anything. Why?"

"Well, you know the diner's closed on Christmas?" She eyed him sideways as she said it.

"Oh? Rats! I hadn't thought about that." He frowned and then wondered. "What are you going to do? Do you have family?"

"Oh no! My family's back in Michigan. I just live with my roommate, Judy. We came down together to get away from home and 'seek our fortunes.' Thought we could get jobs at Disney World. So far we haven't had much luck." She grinned wistfully.

"No kidding! I'm from Michigan too!" He couldn't believe it. "My hometown is Grand Rapids."

"Get outta here! I mean, that's where I'm from too. Rockford, I mean, right near Grand Rapids."

They talked about hometown things, between her business with other customers. Chris was jubilant. "How about us having dinner together on Christmas since neither of us has any family in town? There must be someplace nice that stays open for people like us."

Diane happily agreed. She looked forward to spending time with Chris. He was different from any guy she'd known before. He treated her like somebody special. She liked that!

They had a great time together. The restaurant Chris picked cost way more than he was used to spending, even though now he could afford it. There was white linen and crystal and silver and waiters in black tuxedos. Diane was overwhelmed, and it was obvious neither of them was accustomed to such luxury. She told him she was just through high school and had decided against college. She had a good sense of humor, and she made him feel macho. He liked that feeling and the woozy sensation he got when she came too near, or when she leaned toward him and he could smell her special fragrance. He'd never felt such desire before, not even with Jean.

Diane wore a silver dress trimmed with a silky bright blue scarf. It showed her soft curves. She looked young and fresh and gorgeous. He gave her a present—two shiny combs to hold her curls back.

"Oh thanks, Chris!" She lifted them carefully from the tissue and put them in her hair, then turned so he could see. "I love 'em!" Then she pouted her lips at him. "But you shouldn'ta bought me anything, you know!"

"I'm glad I did. They look great on you."

Soon after Christmas, Diane seemed upset. He watched her with rising concern and finally asked, "Is something wrong? You aren't smiling tonight."

"Yeah…It's just that Judy says she's goin' back home, so I won't have a roommate, and I can't pay the rent alone. We're paid through next weekend, and then I don' know what I'll do!" Her eyes shone with unshed tears. She'd do anything not to go back home. She'd just gotten free from her folks. They were strict and old-fashioned and unreasonable. She just couldn't go back there!

Chris wanted to put his arms around her and tell her not to worry because he would take care of her, but what he said was "Hey, that's no problem. Why don't you move in with me?" He surprised himself as much as Diane, and he didn't even think to pray about the decision first. He simply loved her and wanted her.

She looked at him with a strange expression he couldn't read, but he thought he could. "That's okay. I mean, I meant we should get married!" Why didn't he tell her he loved her? He didn't know, except he had never said that to anyone, and it was a hard thing to say for some reason. But he knew how he felt inside.

Diane had no other choice. It was either marry Chris or go home to her parents. She did like Chris a lot, and he seemed sincere and honest. She would have felt a lot happier if he loved her, though. But some marriages worked out ok, anyway, and if it didn't, she could always get a divorce later! She nodded and gave him her hand. "Okay," she whispered. He pulled her down to the seat beside him and kissed her soft cheek. Then she stumbled back to the kitchen for another order, her head in a whirl, while he made some quick plans.

They were married Friday afternoon (he took time off work) in a simple ceremony at a little church Chris found. He explained the situation to the pastor, and the pastor found a couple from the church to stand up with them. Afterward, Chris could never remember for sure what denomination it was. They drove down the coast and found a little pink motel on the beach where they spent the weekend.

Chris couldn't remember ever being so happy before. It was such a good feeling to go home, knowing there was someone to share the evening with, someone to hug and kiss, hold, and love…someone to pour out all his stored-up passion on. Diane seemed happy too. She even made their drab motel quarters seem homey. But they started at once to look for an apartment more suitable for them since Chris was now earning a good income. He didn't realize what a miserable hovel the motel was until Diane moved in. Then he saw his "home" as it looked through her eyes. Before they had a chance to move, the phone call came.

CHAPTER 5

*F*red stood in the doorway of his father's office at the plant. Plans, blueprints, and specifications spilled over the desk and the drawing table behind it. Mr. VanDam ran his fingers through his thinning hair impatiently. "There's no good reason I can see why this design won't work. Yet we've tried every possibility we know, and no matter what modifications we make, it still isn't right! How are we going to fulfill this contract on time?" He glared at Fred. "Why in the world would you tell them we could do this project? Even if it is a six-million-dollar job, if we can't produce, we end up looking stupid and inept."

Fred brushed his unruly hair back and peered earnestly over his glasses.

"I didn't think it would be difficult, Dad. We've done similar jobs before, and it didn't seem as though changing the size and the material would be that serious a problem." Fred had tried hard to fit in at the plant and for the most part, had been an asset, but all his good work seemed forgotten now with this huge mistake.

"We should have done some research first to see what effect the heat factor would have on this type of metal."

Research! In a flash, Fred remembered his friend, Chris Carson, whose big interest in life was research and development. He told his father about Chris's talent for figuring out unusual problems and about the things he had talked about at college. Fred was convinced Chris could solve the problem, so with some reservation on Mr. VanDam's part, they decided to contact Chris, lay out the situation, and offer him a job at VanDam Metal Parts.

"He's a real genius, Dad! He thinks in a different dimension than most people!"

"And you're convinced he'll be able to fix this mess?"

"I sure think it's worth at try! If we can get him to come back to Michigan…"

Chris answered the phone, surprised to hear from his friend. "Fred! Hey, I'm glad to hear from you. How are you? What's up?"

Fred explained the situation and made his proposal. "And we'd like to have you come as soon as possible, Chris. Do you think you could help us?"

"Sounds right down my alley, Fred, and yeah, I'd be interested in the challenge." Chris winked at Diane. "But I can't make the decision alone. I'm married now."

"No kidding! When did that happen? Who's the lucky lady?"

Chris proudly told his friend a little about Diane, including the fact that she was from Grand Rapids. "So I'll have to get her approval before I can even think about taking her back there again. Say, tell me the problem you're working on again?"

They discussed the problem at the plant, the salary they could offer Chris, and the fact that they needed him "yesterday." The challenge intrigued Chris, and Diane could see he wanted to try his luck with the new venture. Grudgingly, she agreed to move back to Grand Rapids. It seemed she couldn't get away from that place no matter what! She sighed a resigned sigh and gave her new husband a wry little smile. "At least I won't be under my folks' thumbs any longer."

"We'll find a nice place to live, and you can rule our roost." He promised her.

It was hard for Chris to say good-bye to the team at work. They were used to working together, used to each other's ways to approach problems. They fit together well, and breaking in another man wasn't an exciting prospect to the others. Charlie was especially sorry to see Chris go.

"This place won't be the same without you, Chris. I even thought we might get in on some big breakthroughs in the artificial intelligence you're always talking about. But hey, I guess if you did discover something like that, you wouldn't want it to belong to

Mason-Masters, huh!" He grinned hugely at the joke. They constantly teased Chris about his preoccupation with AI.

Don and Jim arranged for a farewell get-together, and the team and their wives all had a good time at Don's house the evening of Chris's last day on the job.

In what seemed like no time, Chris and Diane were on their way North again. This time they were in a red Chevy since Chris wasn't at all sure the old Ford would make it. Chris felt this new opportunity was sent from the Lord, and he looked forward to new challenges. Diane decided to make the best of it since Chris seemed so happy. She did like him a lot. They stayed with Diane's family until they found an apartment they both liked. Diane's parents weren't thrilled that their wayward daughter had married someone she had known for only a few weeks, but they tried to make Chris welcome, anyway. Ed Portland stuck out a pudgy hand and shook Chris's heartily. "Welcome to the family! Hope you'll fit in with our bunch and be happy!" He hugged Diane hard. His wife gave Chris a quick hug and told him, "I always wanted a son, and now I have one." Chris was embarrassed, but he returned the hug and gave her a peck on the cheek.

The Portlands were an oddly matched couple. Ed was round and easygoing. His belt had a hard time deciding where his waist was supposed to be, and he kept having to hitch up his pants. He was mostly bald with a fringe of graying hair above his ears and a tuft on top of his head. (He reminded Chris of the Kewpie dolls he used to try to win for Betty at carnivals that had come to Grand Rapids from time to time.) Jane, Ed's wife, was as skinny as Ed was round. She was a little taller than her husband and was constantly in motion, her hands patting a head, straightening a pillow or a chair, or tucking a wisp of hair back into place.

Chris liked Diane's folks. He couldn't help thinking about his own parents. His dad died of a stroke while Chris was still in college. Chris had come home to the funeral mostly for Betty's sake. His dad's family was better off without him, and their prevailing feeling had been relief instead of grief. Now as he interacted with Diane's family, he thought *maybe they'll be like real parents.*

Ed and Jane Portland were Christians, who belonged to a small nondenominational church. They insisted that Chris and Diane attend with the family on the first weekend in town so they could introduce Chris to their friends.

"You may not like this," Diane told him. "It's different, not like the churches you're probably used to. Sometimes they do things like speaking in tongues and interpreting. It's pretty weird if you're not used to it."

"Hey, now I'm curious, Diane. I've heard about those things, but I've never been in a service where they were practiced. What should I do?"

"You just be quiet and behave yourself, Chris Carson!" She shook her finger at him. "Don't you dare disgrace me."

"Who, me?" he asked innocently. "I can't imagine what you mean."

They spruced up in their best clothes, which for Chris were pretty casual, and filed into the church together. They found a pew near the middle of the small sanctuary and had just settled down in their seats when a woman took her place at the piano and played a beautiful chorus. The congregation sang with love and joy in their voices such harmony and praise and worship, a whole different kind of music than the stately music they used at True Trinity back in East Lansing. The whole congregation knew these songs, and their worship flowed from one song to another, the pianist following the song leader without benefit of a music book. Chris joined in as best he could. He had a feeling this was how Christians should sing!

Pastor Sam Early was a man about Chris's own age with an earnest tone to his voice and a serious look on his face. He spoke with a slight accent Chris couldn't place. He wasn't particularly handsome, but there was a glow that came over him when he began to speak about Jesus, and Chris soon felt that this man would understand his experience with the Lord.

Sam Early knew the scriptures well, quoting the Bible easily and fluently, and Chris noticed that he spoke without referring to notes. He based his message that morning on Acts chapter 1, and he touched on some questions like how to receive the Holy Spirit. Chris had wondered about that, and it was one thing he'd questioned Dr.

Braxton about, receiving a vague, unsatisfactory answer. Chris was absorbed in the message and sorry when it ended, with the piano playing again softly while people prayed. Some went forward and knelt for prayer, while others joined the pastor and prayed quietly over each one. Then they sang again, and the service was over. There was a basket on a table near the altar, where people dropped their offerings on their way out.

Chris shook hands with Sam at the door. "You gave me a lot to think about," he commented. "Maybe sometime we can discuss these things further? I have some questions."

"I'd like that," Pastor Early responded with a smile that made his face look almost handsome. "There's nothing I enjoy more than talking about the Lord and his Word." Ed Portland pushed forward and introduced Chris as his new son-in-law. Sam responded with an even warmer welcome, and the Carson and Portland families moved along, making way for others to shake hands with their pastor.

"I'm disappointed there wasn't any speaking in tongues and stuff, but it was a good service," Chris said to Diane afterward. "I intend to talk to the pastor some more. He seems like a person who'd make a good friend."

Sam Early was a humble man of prayer, a man who talked regularly with Jesus and who was open to his leading. When the following Tuesday evening Jesus laid it on his heart to call on Chris, Sam rose from his knees, put on his coat, and drove to the Portlands' house without asking why or what he should say when he got there. Chris and Diane were home and welcomed him, surprised at the promptness of the visit but happy to see him. They sat around the kitchen table and talked for hours over fresh coffee and rolls that Diane provided. They delved into the Bible at length, first Chris asking a question that Sam answered with a verse and then Sam asking a question that Chris supplied scripture for. Both men learned things they hadn't seen before.

Chris gradually became convinced that he needed to be baptized in the Holy Spirit. Once convinced, he put action to his belief and emptied himself out before the Lord and then prayed for Jesus to fill him with his Holy Spirit. The Lord answered his prayer, flooding into his heart, soul, and body, overwhelming him with his presence so that Chris lay flat on the floor, completely and wholly given to the Lord, washed with waves of pure joy. He was alone at the time, and it was a solemn, serious transaction between Chris and Jesus. Deep peace and love filled his soul. It was like his out-of-body meeting with the Lord.

Next day, Chris called Sam Early to tell him the wonderful news; he could hardly keep it to himself. Sam was thrilled to hear about Chris's experience and rejoiced with him, but Diane was not so happy with this new situation. She'd always thought her parents were weird, and now her husband was just like them! Sam and Chris became close friends, studying the Bible together as often as they could fit it into their busy lives, while Diane watched TV in another room.

Chris and Diane settled into an apartment in the suburb called Wyoming, and Chris quickly fit in at VanDam Metal Parts. Together they worked out a solution to the heat problem, and they were able to manufacture the special parts and get them out almost on time. The whole department celebrated with a special luncheon at Sayfee's, an excellent Greek restaurant on Grand Rapids' East Side.

"I want you to know how pleased I am with your work." Mr. Van Dam pushed aside his plate. "The reason for this lunch is to thank you for helping us get that order out. It meant a lot of extra income for the company, Chris." He signaled the waitress for more coffee, pushed his chair back a little, and studied Chris's face. "We've decided to add on to our R&D department, and we'd like you to manage it. Of course, there will be a raise involved. What do you think?"

"I think that's a great idea, sir! Best idea I've ever heard!" He couldn't wait to tell Diane. This would give him a perfect chance to keep working on his own projects after hours.

Diane had found a job as a waitress in a family restaurant on 28th Street. She worked days, so they were together in the evenings. Altogether it was a happy time.

They saw Chris's brothers and sister on occasion. Betty was married to a press operator named Bud Jones, and they had a new

baby. She seemed happy. The boys were in business together selling industrial cleaning products and were doing well. Chris's family
weren't close. They had no good memories to bind them together. It
was better just to make their own lives.

CHAPTER 6

*D*iane was pregnant! Chris was jubilant; he was going to be a father! He would be a good father too. He'd be the opposite of his own father. He'd pay attention to his child and care about what happened to him. He'd love his child!

Chris expected a boy, so when the months of morning sickness, waiting, and preparation had passed and he found himself looking through the viewing window at his daughter, he was dubious. But watching her with her tiny button nose and dark shadow of hair, hands closed into tiny fists as if to defend herself against the world, his heart seemed to soften and then expand a little, and from then on, Teresa was her daddy's girl. "Thank you, Lord," he said as he stood there feeling blessed indeed.

A few months later, Chris came home to find his favorite dinner waiting, candles on the table, and Diane in a dress, looking especially lovely. "Chris, I've found the greatest house!" Diane told him earnestly as he enjoyed his steak. "It has lots of room, and there's a big front porch. Honey, the kitchen is all remodeled, and there's a bathroom upstairs and a half-bath off the kitchen."

"Oh?"

"Yes, and it's been redecorated, and it's clean and nice, and I bet you'll like the garage, Chris. It's two-stall with a workbench in the back."

"Where is this wonderful place?"

"Oh, it's in Rockford, not far from my folks but not too close either. Dad looked at it, and he says it's a good solid place."

"What can I say then? I'll take a look, but it sure sounds as though you've found yourself a nest."

They settled in the new place happily. It was a great house for them with room enough and to spare. Diane stayed home and looked after Teresa.

"I want us to reserve some special time every day, Diane, when we can talk." Chris's blue eyes shone earnestly. "I don't want our marriage to fail because there's no communication." (Chris had read articles about things that cause trouble in marriages.) So early each morning, they talked. He told Diane his thoughts about creation and the purpose for life and about the high-tech work he was doing, and she talked about the baby and the house and when they would take a vacation. They were in two different worlds intellectually, but Chris loved and cared for Diane.

Work at VanDam Metal Products was going well. Chris made some real breakthroughs for them in new ways to treat special metals for use in aircraft engines, as well as computerizing their operations to make them much more efficient. That gave VanDam an edge over their competitors, so the company grew at a great rate. Fred was a good friend to both Chris and Diane. He had a new girlfriend, Violet Grover, who became a regular visitor to the Carson home with Fred.

"You're so different than anyone I've ever known, Violet, and you're so beautiful! Is your hair naturally curly?" Diane asked her one afternoon as they talked in the kitchen over coffee. Violet nodded. They were complete opposites in looks. Violet, with her long dark hair, white skin, sky-blue eyes, and gorgeous figure, could have been a fashion model, and she was always dressed in the latest styles. Diane, on the other hand, still looked like a teenager, slightly plump, and her shorter brown curls needed a good cut. She wore jeans and T-shirts like a uniform. Secretly, Diane suspected that Violet only liked Fred for his money, but the two women were friends despite their differences, and Violet treated little Teresa as a loving aunt would.

One day, as they discussed life in general and their own places in the world, Violet confided in her affected way. "I plan to be rich someday, Diane. I promised myself when my mother died, I would never be in that situation myself."

"What situation?"

"Well…" Violet got a faraway look in her eye, and she leaned over the table, holding a spoon between her hands as though she were trying to bend it. "We were so poor that sometimes supper would be crackers soaked in warm milk, sometimes in warm water. Dad left us when I was three. We had to move into a hot little apartment, and Mom worked cleaning office buildings at night. She often took me along. Some of those offices were like palaces to me with soft couches and thick carpets. While Mom polished the furniture and swept the floors, I would pretend I was a princess in a castle. On lucky nights, we found parts of sandwiches or stale donuts in the waste baskets."

Violet stopped for a moment, thinking back on those times. Then she continued, "Poor Mom. She must have been tired all the time. She worked days too at a dry-cleaning plant. It must have been exhausting work, but she still tried to spend time with me, reading to me about glamorous movie stars and their lives. She used to tell me that I could be a movie star someday if I was lucky and if I applied myself."

"So where is your mom now?" Diane thought about her own mother, so busy all the time but so ready to drop her own projects to help her children.

Violet shrugged. "She was probably sick a long time but never admitted it. We couldn't have afforded a doctor anyway. I was only twelve when I came home from school one day and found her on the floor. She was white as a sheet, and I didn't know what to do. I ran to the neighbors, Mrs. Horton came over right away. She revived Mom and got her into bed and made some hot tea. She wanted to call an ambulance, but Mom wouldn't let her because we didn't have any insurance or any money. Mom said, 'I'll be fine. I guess I need to rest for a day or two.' But when I came home from school the next day, I found her dead."

"Oh, Violet! You poor thing!" Diane was crying now, but Violet's face hardened again.

"After the funeral, some woman from the state put me in a foster home. It wasn't too bad at first, but then I began to grow up, and my foster father started to pay too much attention to me. When he began feeling me in the wrong places, I was scared. And the day he tried to force me to have sex with him, I got away from him and ran. I guess they never reported it. I was fifteen then, and I managed to get some part-time jobs. Thank God for McDonald's. Between them and a messenger service, I managed to keep from prostitution. Later on, one of my messenger service customers had an opening for a receptionist, and he said they would train me, and that got me started with a different life. I learned to be tough, Diane. There's no other way to survive on the streets!"

Diane couldn't believe it. "But, Violet, where did you live after you ran away?"

"I spent the first two or three weeks sleeping sitting up in the bus station or the movie theater. You learn fast where the restrooms are that have hot water and soap and where you can manage to bathe in the sink. I had a few bucks saved up, so I could eat. When I got the job at McDonald's, I ate there. Then I met another girl who worked at McDonald's, and we managed to find a room to share. Sharon and I bought fashion magazines and learned how to dress and fix ourselves up, and we both ended up with pretty good jobs. It isn't the usual story for kids on their own. I guess if there is a God, he was watching over us."

She sighed and smoothed her hair. "Anyway, I swore that some way I would get enough money, so I'd never have to be dependent upon anyone again...enough money that I could live in luxury! There's a lot of wealth in the world, and I mean to have my share and some more besides!"

Diane could see that she meant it. "Well," she said matter-of-factly, "if you marry Fred VanDam, you'll have plenty, won't you?"

Violet smiled enigmatically.

CHAPTER 7

Things settled into a comfortable routine for the Carson family until a fateful Monday afternoon in early March. It was a rotten day in Michigan—snow had been falling for a day or two, and now the wind came up and blew it in sheets across the roads and fields. Chris felt the cold penetrating to his bones as he ran across the office parking lot, head down against the wind, hands over his ears. He zigzagged to avoid the worst drifts since as usual he had not worn boots. When he saw the stake truck backing toward him, it was already too late. He woke up in the hospital, swathed in bandages and with fluid dripping into his arm from a hanging bottle. Diane was there beside the bed, looking forlorn and stricken.

"What happened?" his voice croaked. He felt strange, disconnected.

"Oh, Chris!" Tears welled up and rolled down, and she gave way to sobs. He tried to comfort her, but he could hardly move and seemed to drift in and out. Finally, she began to calm down and between gasps, told him how the big delivery truck had backed over him. The driver hadn't even seen Chris because of the snow and wind.

He took a deep breath. *Oh, Lord, not again!* "Don't worry," he whispered to Diane. "I'm too tough to kill. I'll be up and around again soon." But the injuries to his back and legs were serious, and Chris could not go back to the plant.

"There has to be a reason for this. God must want you to do something else. I don't know what, but we have to trust him. He doesn't let things like this happen to his children unless there's a plan behind it. I guess when Joseph's brothers sold him into slavery in Egypt, it looked pretty black for him too, and then just when things

53

were looking up, he got thrown into prison for a few years. Imagine! But without that, God couldn't have used him the way he did to help Israel. There's undoubtedly some blessing ahead for you too," Sam Early told him.

"Sure hope you're right, Sam! I don't see it now, but I suppose Joseph didn't either. I'll try to make the most of this like he did. As I recall, he was put in charge of the prison before they finally let him out!" He eyed his friend gratefully. "Thanks. That gives me something to think about, and I'll try to keep positive."

It turned out they had enough insurance money to keep them going for some time. Chris was never one to sit around, and as soon as he could hobble, he resumed work on his Artificial Intelligence. He drew formulas and plans for a working brain from radical ideas based on the things he was shown back in Vietnam, or wherever he had been with Jesus. And the ideas he had worked on over the years since then began to come together.

He spent hours thinking, reading, planning, drawing, and formulating new and foreign plans. Chris had been obsessed with designing an intelligent computer, and now he had time to devote to such a project. He also had time to play with Teresa and teach her to count and to read simple words.

It had been a month since Chris came home from the hospital, and one morning, Diane was on the warpath. "Papers and pencils, erasers, clipboards, rulers, notebooks, reference books…everywhere I look there's something you're working on cluttering up the house! You either find yourself another place to work on this stuff, or I start cleaning it up myself!" She threatened as she tried to make things presentable for her mother, who was coming to take Diane and Teresa to lunch. Chris looked around with new eyes and realized how his mess did make life difficult for Diane.

While she was gone, he had a brainstorm. He grabbed the cane that served as his prop and ventured slowly outside. The April air that filled his lungs felt almost like helium in a balloon. He was light enough to float. Sun had taken the snow, leaving mud behind it. Daffodils and tulips bloomed around the house, and in his deep breaths of air, he smelled spring. He hobbled out to the garage to appraise the situation. Yeah, I could make this into a pretty good office.

He poked cautiously around amid the stored snow tires, old oilcans, and seldom used yard tools. Two sturdy cardboard boxes from some new stereo speakers were the right height. When he had maneuvered them to stand on end a few feet apart, he could put that old closet door over there in the corner, across them to make a desk. He dragged it out and stood it up with much difficulty. The door was bashed in on one side, which explained why it was here in the garage. He turned it upside down with the doorknob hole in back, pushed it against the wall, and it worked fine. When he put a paper cup in the hole, it was a convenient pencil holder.

He pushed the hair back off his forehead, looking around him. *Whew, what this place needs is a good cleaning up and throwing away!*

It took a long time and hard work, and it wasn't the best thing he'd ever done for his aching back, but when he finished and dragged his tired and sore body back to the house to soak in the tub, the garage had turned into a reasonable office and work area.

"I don't even care that the car has to sit outside! I'm so much happier with your stuff out there!" Diane exclaimed when she saw it. Then she looked at him closely. "You didn't hurt yourself, did you?"

A few more cold days kept him working in the house, but spring came on fast as May's blossoms filled the trees, wafting their fragrance on the air. Baby robins chirped in the nest in the big maple tree beside the house. He showed them to Teresa, holding her up so she could see.

Now with a separate place to work, Chris was more and more engrossed in his research. It was theoretically sound, he felt, though it was an entirely different approach to artificial intelligence than anyone else was taking. He envisioned a genetic DNA model and used that double-helix spiral as his basis to design a brain that could function as human while not having "life." He divided each spiral image into segments and defined each segment in terms of characteristics. He logically defined the relationship of one segment to another and linked each segment dynamically to all related segments. The idea was to have an interactive system that allowed changes in any separate aspect to ripple throughout every part of the whole. It was a brilliant concept, but so far it was only on paper.

Diane was pregnant again. Chris helped her as much as he could, taking time out from his work to take Teresa for walks or make her lunch, so Diane could shop or work on baby projects. They were all relieved and happy when little David was born. After the upheaval over the new baby died down again, Chris worked harder than ever to finish his invention, spending more and more time in the garage.

"I'm at a point where I must have hardware for the brain so I can test my theory." He explained to Fred VanDam. "Trouble is, I don't have the engineering skills to build hardware, and I certainly can't afford to hire someone to do it!"

"Say, I think I might have just the fellow for you!" Fred exclaimed, looking around for the phone book. "This guy is a genius with computer hardware design. He works for an aerospace subcontractor down near Forty-Fourth Street, but I'll bet he'd love to get his teeth into this!" He paged through the book. "Here he is, name is Jonas Barnes, but everybody calls him Red." Fred wrote down the name, address, and phone number for Chris. "Want me to set up a meeting for you?"

"I guess so, sure." Chris agreed. "If you think he's that good, I can at least talk to the guy. I wonder if he's adaptable to new and different ideas."

"He's an oddball, eccentric and moody sometimes, but you should be able to relate to that!" They both laughed.

They called Jonas and set up a meeting in the conference room at VanDam Metal Works. Fred introduced them, and after some talk about Jonas's current work, Chris tentatively began to outline his project. Jonas grew more and more excited, asking questions, making suggestions, until finally they were just naturally working together. By the next week, Chris had drawn up an agreement setting out the partnership conditions. Jonas would get one-third of the company profits when they got into production or sold their inventions. Until then, they toiled without pay. Jonas signed, and the deal was made.

Red, as they called him, fit right into the routine. His wife, Gloria, was a self-sufficient, hardworking secretary at Steelworks, and fortunately she was also tolerant and understanding. The men worked nights in Chris's garage because Red had to work at his regular day job. Chris became used to working late into the night, but he still always made sure to spend some time with Diane and the children each day.

He fell into a routine, and the months passed hardly noticed, so involved were he and Red with their revolutionary ideas, except that new little Carson babies arrived regularly. Martha followed David, and then Kathie. Money was running out, and Diane began to nag Chris about it. When she shared her concern with her parents, they came over to talk with Chris.

"You know, son, you have big responsibilities here with the children and Diane, and you need to think about how you'll keep on eating and making house payments and all. The kids will need college educations one day, and there are other things they should be doing too, like taking piano lessons and going to summer camp like the other kids do." Mr. Portland's kind face showed concern for his grandchildren. "I know you feel this invention you're working on is important, but there are some more immediate needs you should be thinking about."

"Chris, we can't go on like this much longer!" Diane added, "The insurance money is running out, and your puttering around isn't bringing anything in, and it doesn't look like it ever will either." Diane was putting her foot down. She was so pretty, he thought, and she hadn't had an easy time these last few years.

"You're right, honey. You're right, Dad Portland." Chris ran his fingers through his hair, pushing back the lock that covered his scar. It flopped back into place as soon as he removed his hand. "I'll get a part-time job, at least. I'm certainly well enough now to hold down a job. But it has to be something that won't keep me from working on the project. We're getting near the breakthrough." He looked at Diane, wanting her to understand, willing her to. "Honey, if this works out like it should, you'll be a millionaire! You won't ever have to worry about money again. We'll live in the style we've always talked about and travel and have a place in the islands. The kids can go to the best schools. It'll be so great, Diane! Just hang in there with me until we get through this, can you?" He pulled her into his arms and held her close.

He went job-hunting the next week and found work right away. "I'm going to be an investigative paralegal for Jones, Haines, and Bickel, Diane," he told her. "I'll be responsible for developing cases for the firm. I won't have as much time to spend with you and the kids now, though."

"I'm so proud of you, Chris! I know you'll do a good job there." Diane kissed his forehead. She felt more secure and encouraged him to work hard at this job and get ahead. This was a regular job, after all, with a paycheck, not some pie in the sky idea. She had begun to hate his invention, that artificial brain or whatever it was! Sometimes she wished she hadn't married Chris, but you can't go back and relive your life unfortunately!

The new job was tailor-made for Chris, and he learned lessons that later turned out to be valuable to him. Being the person he was, Chris studied the law, and each case he worked on gave him more knowledge. He was the best paralegal they'd ever had. The legal processes interested him; he got a kick out of the cloak and dagger detective work, and he earned enough to keep his family going.

Baby number five arrived—another boy. "Let's name him after Fred, shall we?" Chris suggested. They had the baby baptized by Sam Early the next week. Chris loved his children and spent as much time with them as he could with all the other things on his mind. He thought he tried to make up for all the things his father had not done for him and his siblings.

But Diane became more and more restless. She watched soap operas in the afternoons, and she read *People* magazine and the tabloids. The housework was undone, and dirty dishes overflowed the sink. Chris was too busy with his job, his inventions, and the kids to pay attention to Diane's needs. She convinced herself he didn't love her, and had only married her out of pity, and Chris never said anything to make her change her mind about that. It became her hobby to feel put-upon and neglected, and the soaps and the magazines fueled her imagination even more. Chris didn't notice, so he didn't think to pray about the situation.

As it happened, Chris and Diane were having coffee in the kitchen on the Saturday afternoon when the news came on TV. "The owners of a local manufacturing plant were killed this morning when their small plane crashed in a cornfield a mile short of the airport where they attempted to land. They had reported an engine problem, and though they tried to glide the plane in, they couldn't make it to the airport. Rescuers at the site say that the two men, Albert and Fred VanDam, owners of VanDam Metal Parts, were killed on impact." The picture showed the smoking ruins of the plane with rescuers picking up the pieces.

They could hardly believe it. "I talked to Fred just yesterday, and he was happy and excited about his business and asked about our progress with the AI. Oh, Lord, I'll miss him so much!" Chris stood at the kitchen sink, pounding his fist on its edge, while he stared out the window, swallowing hard against tears. "He was a friend, Diane, and those are hard to come by." He thought of his own "death" and how beautiful it was there with Jesus and knew he wouldn't grieve long for Fred, but he felt worse for himself having lost his best friend.

Diane was already dialing the phone to talk with Violet, but Violet was out of town and could not be reached. Sam Early came to visit and grieve with them over their loss. "It's okay, Sam. I know where Fred is, and I know he's happy there, but I can't help wishing he'd had a longer time here! I guess that's selfish on my part, though."

They attended the funeral, still hardly able to believe it was true, and Fred was gone forever. Violet moved to New York right after that, so Diane lost a close friend too. Life went on with a large hole in it for a long time. The VanDam Metal Products factory was sold to a large company from Chicago, who merged it with their own manufacturing plant. Now Chris no longer had access to their facilities, and that put another crimp in his plans. He managed to find other ways to accomplish his work and continued the project, but now had no prospect of financial backing.

Diane was expecting again. This was the eighth year Chris had been working in the garage on the AI project. It seemed forever to Diane, who only vaguely understood what Chris told her about his work. She privately thought it was all a crazy dream, and the longer it dragged on without any tangible results (at least, that she could see), the less she believed in it. Of course, her husband couldn't be inventing anything that would change the world. There was no way he would be earning millions on his crazy ideas. She humored him, but he was just a nice, sort of weird, ordinary guy. All she needed now was another baby! She was depressed and felt helpless. How could God do this to her?

But Chris was happy. The baby was a plump, blond little girl, whom they named Angela. This made six children in their eleven-year marriage. It was difficult to make ends meet, even with the paralegal job.

Diane was more restless and resentful than ever. She laid her feelings out for him one day while they had coffee in the cluttered kitchen. "I'm tired of taking care of kids all the time, Chris. It's different for you. You have other things you're interested in, but I haven't anything but kids and laundry and diapers and cooking and cleaning. I feel like I've been pregnant forever! Life is passing me by, and I'm not getting any younger, Chris. I'll be thirty soon!" She looked closely at him to see whether she had gotten the message through and decided she had. "I really need to get out awhile every day." To Chris, she looked as pretty and young as the first day he saw her. He still couldn't refuse her anything, so he agreed to babysit evenings while she worked as a waitress at King Vic's on Plainfield Avenue on the north side of Grand Rapids. "It will help us out with the finances." She assured him. And so a whole new chapter of their lives began. Looking back on it later, Chris realized they hadn't prayed together over the decision. They didn't pray together over anything lately.

CHAPTER 8

In winter of 1983, Chris and Red at last succeeded in building a working model of the artificial brain. They could demonstrate its capability in a primitive way. It didn't have a voice yet, and so far it was just a black box; but they could question it, and it would answer on a computer screen or ask questions for more information. They could put coins down in a row and ask the brain what the differences were or what the amount was, and the brain would ask questions and give answers. They could put objects such as pens, pencils, and paper clips on the desk, and the brain could describe them and learn their names. The camera they used for the eyes was simple, but the system worked. They needed money for development to the next stage.

"What we need is a promoter to raise funds for the project." Chris was discouraged by his own failure to get backing.

Red answered without looking up from his work, "I know a guy who does stuff like that. He'll probably want part of the action for doing it though."

"You know we're going to run into a whole lot of that before we get this project off the launch pad. If it looks like this will make money, we'll have a hard time hanging onto it." Chris's words were prophetic. "Who is the guy?"

"Name's Joe Donner. Lives over on the west side somewhere. He's a strange fellow but seems to be a good promoter."

"Can't hurt to meet him, and see what he thinks he could do with this. See if he can meet us at Denny's for coffee tomorrow, and let's talk." It was to be the first of endless meetings over coffee to "talk."

Joe Donner was, as Red had said, a strange fellow. He was tall and gangly with owl eyes behind large horn-rimmed glasses, and his straight black hair stood out at odd angles from his head. It looked as though he'd forgotten to comb it when he got out of bed. Chris suppressed a grin. The fellow was likable in spite of his looks. Joe seemed interested at first, and he grew more and more excited as they unfolded their hopes, plans, and dreams for this new "intelligent machine."

Chris envisioned a whole new society that would eventually come to pass with his new technology. "Computerized intelligent robots will do all the work." Chris painted a vivid word picture now with such an interested listener. "People will have time to do the things they like to do, and we'll hardly need money anymore once there are enough robot helpers. But getting the new system into place will be traumatic at first. It'll make the existing computer businesses obsolete, for one thing, and that's a powerful lot of money we're talking about!"

Joe's dark eyes were shining behind the horn-rims, and he kept rumpling his hair with his big hands. Chris could see why it looked that way. "We should be able to get backing from any one of the big companies. Think what Imperial Engines could do with this! Think what it would do for companies like Lockheed or Boeing. How about nuclear power plants and places like that?"

He started jotting down notes. "Now the first thing to do is write a prospectus. We'll get it all down in good readable form, and then we'll start sending it out to the Fortune 500 companies. That should bring us some backing without going any further. But if it doesn't, then we can talk to the state and local governments to see if they will fund the project. When they understand how big a company this will be and how many jobs it will create to manufacture these things, they should jump at the chance to have the facilities in their jurisdiction!"

Chris looked at Red and grinned. He felt elated, as though they already had the backing they needed. Enthusiasm like Joe's was catching, and Chris knew how exciting his product was. "So we have a marketing department." He looked back at Joe Donner. "You realize we have no money? We can't pay for your work until we get funded, so you'll have to build your fee into the amount we need to get started."

Joe nodded. "I'd like to be an officer of the corporation when we get underway. With a product like this, it shouldn't take long. I'll keep track of expenses and bill the company as I go, but I won't expect to be paid until we're up and running, okay?"

"Deal!" they agreed, and they all shook hands on it. Chris had a contract drawn up the next day.

Joe got right to work, writing long, tedious business plans that he accompanied with long, wordy letters to the heads of a great many companies. He heard back from one or two with polite rejections. This stunned Joe. "I can't believe it," he moaned at one of their coffee meetings. "I thought they'd be fighting over this!"

"Maybe they just don't understand it...or more probably, they don't believe it."

"Okay then, how can we get them to believe it?" Red was disgruntled, and it showed.

"I guess we have to show them."

"Sure, and how do you propose to do that?"

Chris hesitated. "How about having a demonstration? We could invite them here and show them what the brain can do. What do you think?"

Red was agreeable. "If you think they'll come on a weekend?"

"It might work. I can get the word out again and see whether anyone would like to take a look at our brain in action." Joe sounded positive again. They discussed the plan and how it could work and agreed it was worth a try. So Joe sent invitations to fifty companies he felt should be both interested in their project and capable of backing it. Chris and Red cleaned the garage and prepared a demonstration.

"We need a name for the brain, guys." Chris patted the black box. "What do you think of 'Perceptor'?"

"Great!" They agreed.

"I hereby christen thee Perceptor." He tapped the box lightly with his coffee cup. "It's still a baby, but we know what it can grow into if we can find it enough food."

"Yeah, and the food it needs to eat and thrive is money…lots of it!"

They received a few replies to the invitations, but they hoped others would show up without replying. When the fateful day arrived in April 1984, they were ready and waiting. There were coffee and cookies on the corner table. They had covered it with Diane's white tablecloth and decked it with a small vase of flowers for the occasion. Perceptor was ready for action. Chris, Red and Joe were uncomfortably presentable in jackets, ties, and slicked-down hair.

Two o'clock came and passed. By three o'clock, they began to lose hope. Three-thirty, they drank some coffee and ate cookies. At four o'clock, they faced the fact that nobody was coming! It was a terrible letdown.

"So much for that great idea." Chris threw his clipboard on the workbench and looked around at all the work they had done for the occasion. What a waste! Momentarily, he was crushed and disgusted. He glanced over at Joe, who looked near tears, and then another idea hit him. "What do you think of this?" He stood in front of Perceptor belligerently. "If they won't come to us for a demonstration, why don't we send the demonstration to them?"

"Are you completely out of your tree?" Red asked angrily. "What do you mean send it to them?"

"We'll borrow a video camera, put the demonstration on film, and send it to them. Maybe they'll spend a few minutes to look at a tape."

Joe and Red agreed without enthusiasm. It was better than nothing, and that's what they had right then, so they worked on making the tape. They showed how Perceptor could distinguish different coins and how it could tell the size, shape, and positional relationship of several objects and how it would ask questions until it had all the information needed to make a determination and come up with an answer. Chris gave a long-winded explanation for the things they showed, explained what they wanted from an investor, and said the investor could expect at least a triple-digit percent return on his money. It was a badly done tape, and after they made twenty copies, the quality was so bad it was hard to watch. They sent it out with their hopes high again.

Joe did receive a few inquiries and traveled to different places across the country to pitch the product to various CEOs. Sometimes Chris met with them too. Anytime Joe felt he had sparked some interest, he had Chris go along to explain properly. On rare occasions, Red accompanied them.

It was a discouraged group who met at Denny's a few weeks later to discuss their situation.

"We've spent money we don't have without any tangible results. Oh, sure, there's been some interest, but when investors realize that we'll only sell the results and not the rights to the technology, they lose interest." Joe's tired dark eyes were discouraged behind the horn-rims.

"It's proving to be true, what I've always observed. Inventors of the most important things throughout the world have died in poverty, while the people with money cashed in on their discoveries. I don't intend to let that happen to me and Perceptor. Chris vowed. "I won't let Perceptor's secrets get into the wrong hands, not if I can help it. It could even be a matter of national security." Red and Joe had heard it all before. They wandered home, completely dejected.

Then came the break-in. One evening, Chris found the side garage door ajar. He knew he had left it locked. On closer inspection, he saw the wood beside the doorknob was badly splintered where someone had forced it open. "They must have used a crowbar," he said to Red on the phone. "I guess we should have known this might happen! I don't think they got anything important, though. They obviously don't know exactly what they're looking for. And anyway, I had most of the files with me in the house last night, so I could do some figuring while I watched the kids."

"We've gotta do something to keep this from happening again!"

"You sure got that right! I'll work on that today!" The first thing he did was repair the door and install new dead bolt locks. But he knew that wouldn't be enough. Sam Early stopped and surveyed his work, and after talking over the problem, they prayed about it together. Chris relaxed a bit after that.

It seemed sometimes new and unusual answers to problems just dropped into Chris's mind when he needed them. In less than a week, he had developed a simple method to protect Perceptor or anything else he wanted to protect. The result was that if anyone tried to take Perceptor apart to see how it worked, the new device would implode and melt down.

"I certainly hope nobody ever sets this thing off because we sure can't afford to build another one!" Chris said to Red after he had shown him the device and explained how it worked. He was pleased himself at its simplicity and efficiency.

"Yeah, but it sure is an effective way to keep the technology from getting into the wrong hands!" Red whistled as he looked over Chris's newest invention. "You know, we could patent this and sell it too! There must be other people who want to protect different ideas or products."

Chris was sarcastic. "Sure, all you have to do is patent something, and anyone can copy it easily. Just change one little thing, and the patent doesn't apply. If we were to patent Perceptor, we could kiss the technology good-bye in a hurry. It'd be like handing the plans out to the public and inviting them to just have at it!"

They were more careful after the break-in. Obviously, someone who'd heard about their work (possibly as a result of their invitations) was more than casually interested. They began to realize more fully how important Perceptor might be. Of course, they had talked about that, but it was all surreal…a dream. Now they got nervous about it. Chris asked the Lord about his reasons now and then but didn't seem to get any answer, just more new ideas.

Joe came up with the next step for him. "I guess it's time to take our case to the government. That's where all the money is, and they've been trying to make this breakthrough for a long time themselves. They might want to fund us when they see what we already have." Joe showed them some letters he was ready to send to President Reagan and several other key people in the cabinet and to the chairman of the Committee on Foreign Affairs.

"I hate to get them involved." Chris hesitated. "We could be getting ourselves into a whole barrel of snakes here."

"We've tried everything else now with no luck."

"Yeah." Chris took another drink of coffee, then set the mug down almost too hard. "Okay, go ahead and see what happens. We may be getting in a bit deep, but I guess that's inevitable. The government will certainly have a say about this technology because it'll make serious changes in the economy and in every other facet of life as we know it now. It's hard to realize how much impact Perceptor will have on the world."

There was no reply from the letters, but a month or so later, Chris got a strange phone call. The man on the other end introduced himself as Jack McCall and asked Chris to meet him at the airport on Wednesday.

Jack McCall wore a gray trench coat and navy blue suit with regulation striped tie. He flipped his billfold open to his ID card— FBI! Chris almost laughed out loud at the stereotype. But one does not laugh at the FBI, not if one has good sense! A man Jack introduced as Bill Williams appeared from nowhere, it seemed to Chris. Jack's partner.

At the Hilton on 28th Street near the airport, they found a quiet corner of the dining room. The men ordered lunch and then got right down to business. It was obvious they were extremely skeptical about what Chris told them regarding Perceptor's present capabilities and future potential, but they listened and took notes, and Chris was sure he was being recorded. He was pretty careful with what he said. After lunch, he was glad to take them back to the airport.

"Thanks for the information, Mr. Carson," Jack McCall said as he shook Chris's hand. "We'll be in touch, sir!"

They started up the concourse toward the gate then turned, and Bill Williams said, "You be sure to keep us abreast of any new developments! And be careful what you do with that invention…if there is such an invention!" Chris simply waved his hand at them. He was glad to see them go.

He and Sam laughed about it later as Chris described the scene in graphic detail for his friend. "Maybe you should be more careful though, Chris." Sam cautioned him. "This must be more important than we know!"

Joe called on Thursday morning all excited. "We have a meeting with the State of Michigan's Economic Development Committee! They've looked over our prospectus and want to interview us next Tuesday at nine thirty." Joe was more optimistic than Chris was, but enthusiasm is catching, and by the time they arrived at Lansing for the appointment, Chris was mentally making plans as to the best place for building their first plant. Developing and manufacturing products such as theirs would obviously be of great benefit to the state, providing a great many jobs as they got underway and generating high revenue. How could the committee possibly turn down such an opportunity?

They met with a woman named Wanda George, newly appointed to her job with the EDC. Wanda put them through their paces, asking pointed questions about the product they had and if they could demonstrate their claims on a prototype. She wanted to know what the costs would be and what the profits would be, how many jobs they expected to generate, and where they planned to locate. It turned out that Wanda was the "committee."

"Your obvious buyer for the technology is Imperial Engines." She sounded absolutely positive that her opinion was correct. "The first thing I want you to do before we go any further with this project is take the prototype to the IE Labs near Detroit for testing. Then you'll have something concrete to work with when you talk with investors." Wanda reached for the "phone," flipping her Rolodex until she found the number she wanted. She watched them over the rims of her glasses as she waited, and then proceeded to set an appointment for them with Jim Foxx at the IE Lab. "Is next Wednesday all right for you?" Her palm covered the mouthpiece as she waited for their response. They looked at each other, then Chris shrugged and nodded.

"They'll be there Wednesday, Jim," Wanda told the phone. "We'll be interested in the results here also," she added. "Okay, Jim, and thanks." Wanda indicated the meeting was over, so they gathered up their papers, along with their dashed hopes, and departed.

Carefully, they got Perceptor ready for the trip. They would borrow a camera from IE for the eyes, and they would hook up to

IE's computer for the printed interface with the brain, so all they needed to take with them was the black box, the brain—Perceptor.

They were especially careful to explain several times to every person in the lab just what would happen should anyone try to take the black box apart to examine it. They even put it in writing. The only purpose at IE was to test Perceptor to make sure that it could perform as promised. Chris's last words on parting with Jim Foxx were, "Now don't forget that it will melt down if anyone tampers with it. We won't allow anyone to steal this technology."

Jim nodded. "Of course." He agreed.

They waited a week, with no response. They waited another week and called the lab. Nobody was available who could answer their questions. Finally, they drove to Detroit. Jim Foxx saw Chris coming and tensed; his complexion looked green, and he frowned as he ranted, "You should never have done that to us! We ought to sue you! Someone could have been seriously hurt!" He was shaking, he was so angry, or was it guilt that made him so defensive? At any rate, Perceptor, the first brain with real artificial intelligence, was dead! All that remained was a mangled lump of melted components. Chris carried it as though it were the lifeless body of one of his children.

Chris grieved for Perceptor more than for a person. He felt as though he were in shock. This was a serious setback, a tragedy in more ways than one. There was no money to build another prototype. They had no borrowing power. They thought seriously about trying to sue Imperial Engines but quickly realized how futile that would be. Anyway, they had no money to hire attorneys. "Why, Lord? What do we do now?" he asked, but there was still no answer.

All they had left were a few demonstration tapes and a whole lot of dashed hopes.

CHAPTER 9

While driving home from the testing lab, Chris thought about Diane. It seemed forever since he had spent any time with her. He wanted her. He needed her. He pictured her silky curls, her shining hazel eyes, and the freckles sprinkled across her nose. He could hardly wait to hold her soft body close to his and to have her hug him and comfort him. He forgot that she wasn't home evenings anymore. When he got there and found the kids with a babysitter, he felt cheated. But he hugged the kids and spent some time with them, asking about their day and talking about their problems and their projects. Then tired and hungry, he went looking for Diane.

From a booth in Diane's section at King Vic's, he watched her wait on a couple across the room. She hadn't seen him yet. She was friendly and efficient, and he knew she was a good waitress, but that didn't make him happy. He was jealous of the time she spent with all those people. She was so lovely; motherhood and maturity had only made her more graceful and self-confident. The young innocent girl he had fallen in love with was gone, but in her place was this beautiful woman—still trim and curvaceous with that same smile that had caught his heart so many years ago.

He'd missed the smile lately. She was giving strangers the smile that should have been his! He suddenly realized that in his preoccupation with Perceptor, he had neglected Diane and the kids. *Oh, God, forgive me,* he breathed. *You know I didn't want to do that! I didn't mean to do that.*

She was standing at the table with coffee pot in hand before she looked at him. "Oh!" she exclaimed. She recovered quickly. "So you got back safely." She poured him a cup of coffee automatically. "What are you doing here?"

"I missed you. I want to be with you." He took her hand and held it for a minute before she pulled it away again. "I need you." Why didn't he ever say, "I love you"? Why was it that he never could seem to say those words?

She pulled the order pad from her pocket, looking businesslike. "What can I get you?"

He sighed. "Just bring me some dinner, Diane, will you, please? You pick it out. I'm tired of thinking."

She nodded and walked away, stopping at another table to pour coffee on her way past. It dawned on him, watching her, that he was tired right down to his bones. Losing Perceptor after all his hard work and great hopes was a bigger blow than he had realized. His body and mind just wanted to turn off and rest. No more thinking. He ate the food she brought, hardly tasting it, then somehow drove safely home, paid the sitter, got into bed, and sank into oblivion.

Chris slept for almost two days, off and on, but finally he was ready to face the world again. The sun was shining. It was a gorgeous day, and he knew that somehow things would work out with Perceptor. He and Red still knew how to build another one, and somehow they would get the money to do it. After all, the Lord was in it. He walked downstairs to look for his family. In the kitchen, he picked Diane up from behind and swung her around. "Honey, let's take the kids and go over to Lake Michigan for a picnic. Let's get out of here for a while and be together, can we?"

"Are you serious? It's a school day! Of course they can't go on a picnic. And I have work to do. They've been calling you from the office too, wondering when you will be well enough to get back there."

He raised his eyebrows, and she answered, "I told them you were sick." She was indignant and hurt. She turned her back on him. *This is just typical! All he thinks about is himself and his own needs, never mine or the kids!*

71

Reality set in again. Chris knew he had neglected the attorney's office. He'd be lucky if they didn't fire him. He dressed quickly and headed downtown to find out what poor jerk he had to follow around today. It turned out to be a woman, the wife of a prominent businessman in Grand Rapids, who thought she might be having an affair. She was. Chris got through the day somehow.

Sam Early, on his knees in his small office, was moved to pray for Chris and Diane Carson. The Lord impressed him that there was a great need in their lives and that Chris would go through even deeper trials ahead. Sam prayed long and earnestly for his friend. It seemed as though he felt evil forces opposing him. He wrestled the enemy in prayer until peace came, and rose from his knees much later, exhausted and wet with sweat.

****

The partners gathered over coffee at their regular table at Denny's that evening. It was a far from cheerful group, but they had to decide on their next step.

Chris voiced the obvious, "We have to raise some money somehow to build another prototype."

Joe retorted glumly, "Sure, and just how do you propose we do that?"

"We still have the videotapes. Do you think anyone would finance us with just that evidence if we tell them what happened at Imperial Engines?"

"I suppose we'll have to try it and find out. Right now that's all we have." Joe poured a little plastic container of cream into the coffee and stirred it, sloshing into the saucer. "Sure wish you had the stuff to build another one, though!"

"All we need is a fully equipped factory, and we're in business." Red was sarcastic, but he gave Chris an idea. He started talking as he thought it out.

"If we could take over some small manufacturing company, we could use the place to build another intelligent computer while we made some money manufacturing their products. You know, like if a man wanted to retire and didn't have anyone to turn the place over to, or maybe the business wasn't doing too well, and he just wanted to get out or something."

Joe jumped on that with both feet. "Great idea!" His dark eyes began to take on the familiar shine they always got when he was excited. "Let's look around and see what we can come up with." He thought a moment. "First place to look is the newspapers. Maybe someone is advertising to sell."

Red went out in front of the restaurant where a row of newspaper dispensers offered papers from New York, Chicago, Los Angeles, and even the USA. He brought back a Grand Rapids Press, and they proceeded to spread it on the table looking for the business opportunities section. They read the ads carefully. There was nothing that looked like exactly what they needed, but one ad for a tool and die shop caught their eyes. It was advertised by a woman from a local business brokerage.

"Why don't we call this gal and ask about that place? Maybe they'd have something else for us if this one doesn't work out." They agreed to that idea, and Joe headed for the pay phone. Soon he came back to the table, grinning. "She'll see us tomorrow morning at ten thirty. Can you both get away, or do you want me to handle this first?"

It was almost a chorus from Chris and Red. "You handle it, Joe!"

Falling leaves blew in swirls on the streets as Joe drove into downtown Grand Rapids and looked for a place to park. He finally gave up hope of street parking and pulled into the city parking ramp. That meant he had to walk two blocks against the wind to the address on Monroe Street.

When Joe got off the elevator at the fourth floor, he was right in front of the double entrance doors of Commercial Enterprise Business Brokers. He stepped through the doors into plush offices with rich dark wood, mirrors and brass, and soft mauve carpeting. Joe smoothed his wind-blown hair and straightened his tie. The efficient secretary took his coat, showed him into the glass-walled conference room, and brought him coffee in an expensive cup and saucer. Joan

Nelson appeared almost immediately and introduced herself, giving him a firm handshake. Then she seated herself opposite him, her yellow notepad in front of her. She was a trim, middle-aged woman with short dark hair and a bright smile. She wore a gray flannel suit and silk blouse. She looked like a business broker.

Joan put Joe at ease right away. They chatted about the weather and about the general situation with business sales before getting to the point. Then Joe asked about the advertised tool and die business, and Joan asked him to sign a confidentiality agreement. She wanted to know how much money he had and where it was now, so Joe spilled the whole story. He told her about Perceptor first and elaborated about how they had lost the prototype and how they thought maybe they could get into a manufacturing company without much upfront money.

"Oh. Then what you're really looking for is venture capital."

"Yeah, that is what we need. Do you people, do that?"

"Not often but in this case, I'd be glad to try for you. This project sounds exciting. There are some people I'd like to present this to and see what they think. Grand Rapids is a conservative town, however, and investors here are unusually careful. Before we do anything further, I'd like to meet the inventor and talk with him."

They set up a tentative meeting for the next week and shook hands. Joe was optimistic about the meeting. He made Chris wear a suit for the occasion. "This might be the contact we've been needing! They seem to know what they're doing, and they have a whole range of businesses for sale. This Joan Nelson says she'll try to find us some venture capital, though."

Chris wasn't so sure this was a good idea, but he kept his reservations to himself and sat through one more meeting to tell the Perceptor story one more time. At least, this time the audience was receptive. Joan was excited about the project. She called another broker into the conference room to meet Joe and Chris and explained a little of what they had told her. John Shafer asked even more questions, then promised to help Joan find them an investor. Joan took a copy of the demonstration videotape to show her prospects. They shook hands all around, and she showed Chris and Joe out.

"What do you think?" Joan asked John. "Are they for real?"

He shrugged. "It's hard to tell. It's such a fantastic story it's hard to believe, but if it's true...wow!"

"What do you think?" Joe asked Chris. "Do you think they can help?"

He shrugged. "It's hard to tell. They sure seem to have the right setup for it, don't they? Guess we'll have to wait and see. I don't intend to leave it in their hands, though. We have to keep on trying ourselves!" Joe nodded his agreement.

Joan Nelson called every company she could find that worked with robotics in any way. She contacted all her buyers with over two hundred thousand dollars cash to invest and tried to talk them into going into a new venture instead of buying an existing business. She called every tool and die business Commercial Enterprise Business Brokers had on the market and approached them with the various possibilities.

Several buyers and companies met with Chris and Joe and asked them about the technology. It was too much for any of them to swallow. The project was too big; they talked in terms of millions and billions in income not far down the line. It sounded like a rip-off scheme.

"It's too big for Grand Rapids investors." Joan looked at Chris and raised an eyebrow. "If we could cut it down in size somehow into chunks that wouldn't choke people, it would be easier to sell. It's hard to make people believe what you're telling them. And even if they do believe it, Grand Rapids buyers are so conservative they won't take a chance of losing two hundred thousand dollars, not even if they stand to gain millions!"

"Yeah, I see what you mean." Chris nodded. "We're spooking them. Maybe that's been our trouble all along. We're offering them a deal that sounds too good to be real." He thought a minute. "I have an idea, but I'll need some time." He looked at Joe. "There are several smaller products we could start with. Maybe we can sell one of those and use the money from the sale to start our main venture. I'll work on it."

Chris never expected to hear from Imperial Engines again, so he was completely unprepared when he got their letter saying they'd like to meet with him again. "Again! We've never met once. They only wrecked our prototype!" Chris wasn't sure what he should do but finally decided it couldn't hurt to find out what they had in mind, so he made the appointment and called Joe. On the appointed day, they drove to Detroit to meet with William J. Smith, the vice president in charge of acquisitions.

Chris and Joe sat on big leather chairs opposite William J. Smith's desk and eyed him warily. They weren't sure whether this had to do with the destruction of their prototype and, if it did, just what their response should be. Mr. Smith rubbed his manicured hand, over his bald head then leaned back in his even-bigger-than-theirs leather chair and smiled fatuously. "Imperial Engines is prepared to submit an offer to buy your new AI technology."

Chris was taken by surprise and didn't respond immediately. Joe couldn't stand the silence and said stupidly, "You are?" Then he recovered himself and asked, "Just how much are you prepared to offer?"

"Our offer is for twenty-five million dollars." Smith fingered some papers on his desk.

Twenty-five million dollars! Joe got so excited he almost jumped up off his chair. Chris's heart jumped too, but he was calm on the outside. He gave Joe a warning glance. "We are prepared to sell you the rights to manufacture and sell our products, but we must retain the technical knowledge. We feel it is of such a nature that we would not be willing to lose control of the basic secrets for our intelligent computer. You can arrange to handle all manufacturing and sales of the products."

He could see that William J. Smith did not understand, so he elaborated. "This technology could have a vast array of uses, some of which may not be for our country's good. Consider, for instance, a nuclear missile you could instruct to hit a particular target, and it would go and find that target unerringly. It could see and identify the target you specified and could go around, over and under anything in its way, and that's only one possible use."

William Smith leaned forward over his desk. "Imperial Engines would not be interested unless we can buy the technology." He smiled again. "Think what you could do with twenty-five million dollars.

You could invent anything you could imagine and have the money to develop it yourself! Nothing could stop you then!"

"If this technology gets into the wrong hands, money won't mean anything to anybody!" Chris countered. "I cannot sell it to you, but I can let you have the manufacturing rights, and I know those are worth a great deal more than twenty-five million dollars. If I could get the money I need to manufacture Perceptor myself, I could make billions. It's the power that goes with the technology that I will not sell to you."

Joe couldn't believe it had happened. He bit his lip to keep from yelling, or worse, weeping. Belatedly, he realized he didn't understand Chris at all, and now all his hard work was for nothing. They were silent the first part of the trip home. Then Chris began to talk about some products he knew they could develop from discoveries he had made on the way to perfecting Perceptor. "Some things I've discarded as not right for the intelligent computer could still be used for fantastic new products. If we could make one smaller product and sell the rights to that, we could earn enough to develop and manufacture Perceptor ourselves."

Joe grunted and stared out the window. He wanted Chris to know just how irritated he was at the entirely unreasonable inventor.

Chris lived in the lab for weeks while he came up with a design for a new color television screen. He changed the concept for the color guns completely. His guns would rotate on a flat disk device. He gave the screen four million pixels for the guns to color, making a much, much clearer picture than anything currently available, and the whole thing could easily be built only about two inches thick. It was a great idea, but they had no money to build the prototype. It would take at least two hundred fifty thousand dollars to develop, build, and test, but when perfected, the market would be unbelievable for such a product.

Joan called the giant Matshustha Company to see if they would have any interest. "We would be extremely interested, yes. When can we see the prototype?" the man asked. When Joan said they needed funds to build the prototype, the answer changed to: "When you have something we can look at, please call us again."

Joe wrote up another endless business plan, and they tried every investor they thought might possibly part with two hundred fifty thousand dollars in venture capital. Dead ends all around. As they met to regroup yet again, Joan sighed tiredly and put down her cup. "I don't believe that there is any such thing as venture capital in Grand Rapids. What they call that is a complete misnomer since investors here will only back a sure thing with an established track record."

At a meeting in Joan's office later on, she was chatting about how busy she had been and happened to mention a new business listing that was "an excellent opportunity for the right buyer. The sellers are motivated, and the products are salable. This is ripe for somebody with vision." She had no intention of selling that kind of business to Chris and Joe's company, though. It made screen prints and related products, not metal products or computer-related things.

But Chris thought about that overnight. He called Joan in the morning. "I'd like to take a look at that company you were talking about. I think we could use something like that to get us started, and we could go on from there little by little."

"If you really think so, I'll be glad to set up a meeting for you to take a look at the business and talk to the seller. Let's make it at ten o'clock tomorrow, if that fits your schedule. We'll need to meet at about nine fifteen, though, to get to Grand Haven by ten o'clock. I'll drive."

Chris agreed. It was one of those times you look back on later and know God had it planned. Chris and Joan had never been alone to talk before. She turned the radio on, and they began to discuss music, and somehow that led into religion.

"Personally, I hate religion, I love the Lord with all my heart, but I feel that religion is responsible for most evils in the world now. And if you look at the Bible, religious people were the ones who persecuted Jesus and finally put him to death," Joan commented and waited for his reaction.

"I couldn't agree more. That's exactly how I feel." Chris looked at her curiously, wondering what the Lord had in store next.

"No kidding? Well, how do you feel about Jesus?"

"I know he's the Son of God. I feel God himself came into flesh in the form of Jesus and lived life so that we could see his example and then died on the cross for us himself to redeem us. He had pronounced judgment on man, and there was no other way to save us, so he came himself. The very one who created us came in flesh like ours and gave his life for us. It took a long while before I understood that, and when I did, it changed my whole outlook on life."

"I understand what you mean. That's the way I feel too. The thing is, we should be living like he did as much as possible. And contrary to popular opinion, he wasn't a 'religious nut.' He loved people, and he met their needs. He didn't try to separate himself from them by setting up rigid rules and regulations. All they had to do was ask him in faith, and he granted whatever they needed. And then he died to set them free!" Joan grinned. "It doesn't take much to get me up on my soapbox."

"I'm curious, what do you think about Israel and the situation over there?" He pushed her further, wondering just how much they did have in common.

"I think we are Israel, at least a part of it. All the evidence points to our being part of the ten lost tribes. We fit all the biblical descriptions of the latter-day Israel. Not that it matters as far as salvation is concerned. We still each need to be saved, but as far as prophecy for the nation is concerned, it makes a great deal of difference!" She glanced at him to see how he was receiving what she'd said then added, "It took me a long time to accept that truth, but then the proof of it came to me from so many different sources that I had to know the Lord was showing it to me. And it's been proved more and more to me ever since."

He nodded. "I know what you mean. It's hard to buck the prevailing and accepted beliefs. It's so much easier to fall in with generally approved doctrine, even though it doesn't fit what the Bible says. But there comes a time when you have to make a choice whether to believe what the Lord shows you or what people want you to believe. I experienced that a long time ago with Dr. Conrad Braxton. He never forgave me for rocking his safe boat!"

"I can't believe this. Finally, I am talking to a kindred spirit!" Joan was so interested in the conversation she missed the turnoff to Grand Haven, so she had to go around by Muskegon, and that took an extra fifteen minutes. That gave them time to go into some other topics. They found endless interesting subjects to discuss, and they agreed on almost every point.

"By the way, since you mentioned Dr. Braxton, and speaking of religion," Joan commented, "did you hear him on TV Sunday? He's certainly an impressive speaker!"

"No. You mean he has his own TV show now? Huh! I guess I'm not surprised. He's just the type for that ministry. He likes having people depend on him for their spiritual guidance. He calls himself a shepherd and thinks the sheep should follow him so they don't 'die alone out on the mountains.'" Chris was quiet a moment, remembering. "I really do owe Pastor Braxton a debt of gratitude. He helped me cement my relationship with the Lord, and he opened my eyes to the difference between legalism and freedom in the Lord. He doesn't know that last one, though." Chris laughed. "He'd be pretty upset over that."

In fact, Dr. Braxton, in his study in Lansing, thought about Chris Carson often over the years. He wondered what had happened to Chris and whether he had pursued his work on the technology he'd talked about. Conrad had aged over the years; his once blond hair was turning gray, lines showed in his forehead and around his mouth, and jowls were beginning to form, but he was still a handsome and imposing figure. He sometimes thought about the questions Chris had posed to him and was troubled. He preached against those things now and again, as much to reassure himself as to keep his flock from danger. People like Chris were dangerous. They could cause one to lose the blind faith one needed to follow Jesus. There were certain rules and regulations Christians must follow, and there was no way around that! Dr. Braxton was glad he himself had always followed those rules!

He radiated self-confidence and consecration to the Lord as he preached on television each Sunday, and bit by bit his congregation expanded until it reached the whole country on a national network. Conrad Braxton was a successful servant of the Lord and sometimes a pretty troubled one.

CHAPTER 10

*D*iane was not herself lately, but Chris didn't seem to notice. He still tried to spend time with her each day, though lately their talk was strained. It upset Diane that Chris wasted so much time on a 'dead-end' dream. She wished he would get a proper job and quit fooling around with all those big ideas. Since she said these things to him more often lately, Chris was all the more determined to prove himself to her.

But when one day Chris woke from his preoccupation with Perceptor and his other projects, he realized his kids were neglected, and the house was a mess, while Diane spent more and more time at the restaurant. Angela, who was only two, cried easily and clung to Chris like a little vine. The other children were not doing well either. Chris supposed it was his fault, so he resolved to make up for it. He got a babysitter and drove to King Vic's to see Diane.

"Diane's not working tonight." The manager was cool. "Are you staying for dinner?"

"No, thanks, I guess not." Chris wasn't sure what to do. His thoughts were in turmoil. Diane wouldn't go somewhere without telling him, would she? Anyway, where would she possibly go? He returned home and waited for her. She usually came home at around one in the morning. Sure enough, at 1.05, he heard her car pull into the drive.

She opened the door softly and stepped carefully into the room. He thought he saw her jump when she saw him sitting in the big chair waiting for her, and she was instantly defensive. "What are you doing down here? Why aren't you upstairs at your desk? Don't you have work to do?" She was different somehow, not his beautiful lady now. Her eyes were strange and dark, her cheeks flushed, and she pulled away when he reached for her.

"Diane, what's wrong?" He was genuinely concerned for her at that moment.

"What do you mean, what's wrong? Nothing's wrong!" she almost snarled.

"Well then, where have you been?"

"Where do you think? Where do I always go?"

He reached for her again and held her hands in his. "Diane, I know you weren't working tonight. I went there to talk to you."

"You had no right to check up on me like that!" She was indignant, and she was scared. He could feel her shaking.

"Diane, tell me what's wrong, won't you? Is there something we need to talk about? I know I haven't paid enough attention to you lately, but please don't shut me out, honey!" He squeezed her hands and held her tight. *Dear Lord, please help us!*

"Why not? You always shut me out! You spend all your time with Red and his wife, Gloria, and with Joe, and that Joan person, and who knows who else!"

"But that's just business, Diane, and I'm trying so hard to build and market Perceptor. When I get the financing, we'll be worth millions and soon! Then we can live like kings, Diane, and you can have anything you want. The kids can have anything they want. It'll happen soon, Diane, I promise!"

"I don't believe you anymore, Chris!" Her eyes looked anywhere but at him. He held her fast as she tried to pull away from him. She couldn't get away, so finally she stopped struggling and faced him defiantly. "Yes, there is trouble, if you want to know!" She fairly spit it at him. "I'm pregnant!"

"Oh!" He relaxed, thinking he knew how she felt and understood the problem. "Honey, that's not such a major trouble, is it? We already have six, one more won't make such a great difference, except you'll have to quit your job after a while." He tried to pull her into his arms to comfort her, but she evaded him, stumbled, and dropped to her knees. He tried to help her up, but she scrambled away toward the stairs.

"You don't understand! You never understand!" She got to her feet and turned to face him, her eyes wild. "It's not your baby, Chris!"

"Not mine!" She might as well have plunged a knife into the depths of his heart. "Whose is it then, Diane?" As he looked closely at his wife, he suddenly realized why she looked as she did. She was on something. "Diane, you're doing drugs, aren't you? What is it, cocaine?"

She nodded as though that were not at all important. "It's Jim Morton from work." She looked to see his reaction and was suddenly afraid of him. Chris's eyes turned to steel. His face was white with shock. This was more than he could bear, he was sure. The knife turned and gouged in his heart.

"A black baby! Diane, how could you do this to me…to us?" If Chris had not been a Christian, things may have spun out of control. At that moment, he wanted nothing better than to choke the life out of Jim Morton. He was afraid what he might do to Diane. He balled his hands into tight fists at his sides. His voice was deceptively calm. "I suppose if it had been a white child you wouldn't have needed to tell me?"

She stood glaring at him defensively. "It's all your fault, anyway! You never loved me. You only married me because you felt sorry for me. Admit it! Jim loves me. We have a good time together."

Chris shook his head, unbelieving. "Doing drugs and having sex? You call that a good time? You call that love? Diane, I have loved you with all the love that is in me. I loved you the first time I saw you. I would have done anything for you! Yes, I have trouble saying those words, and I'm sorry I haven't said it before, but I thought you knew after all this time. How could we have gone through so much together if I hadn't loved you?" Then a new thought struck him. "Diane, do you love me?" he asked her, looking into her drug-clouded eyes.

The defiance faded, her eyes fell, and she hesitated a long time and then admitted. "Yes, I guess I do." She gave a despairing, sobbing sound. "But I love Jim too." She was so confused, her mind was in such turmoil she couldn't think. She turned, stumbling against the arm of the big chair, and almost fell.

"Go to bed. We'll discuss this in the morning." His voice was tight and cold.

Diane left willingly. She couldn't look at Chris any longer. She suddenly knew that he did love her and through her fog, realized what she had done. His eyes looked almost black instead of blue, and there was an expression there Diane had never seen before.

Chris grabbed his jacket and left the house. He got into the pickup and backed out into the street. He knew Jim Morton was not at the restaurant, but he drove there, anyway, looking for him. The place was closed and dark. There was only one car in the lot, way at the back. He continued to drive around aimlessly, while the anger slowly drained out of him. Then he pulled off the road beside the Rogue River and sat there in the dark thinking, praying, regretting, and trying to relive their lives. It wasn't possible, of course, and finally, he turned back for home, where he fell asleep on the living room couch.

Things didn't look any better in the morning. Chris woke before Diane and made breakfast for Angela, David, and Martha. When Teresa got up, Chris left the little ones with her and went out to the garage. He tried to work on his latest project, but he couldn't think at all this morning. He had to talk to someone. He called Joan Nelson and asked her to meet him at Denny's for coffee.

Joan looked up when he came in and smiled. "Hi." Then she took another look at him. "What happened?" She half-rose from the booth.

He slid into the seat and grabbed the cup of coffee she had ordered for him as though it were a lifeline. "Thanks."

"What's wrong?"

"It's Diane. She's pregnant...by somebody else!"

"Oh, Chris!" Joan felt his grief like a heavy hand weighing her down. "Oh, Chris, I'm so sorry."

"I needed to talk to somebody, and there isn't anyone else I could think to call. Sorry to do this to you..." His voice faltered.

"That's what friends are for."

"Yeah...thanks. I don't know what to do. If I had gotten my hands on the guy last night, I probably would have killed him!" He paused, looked out across the parking lot at nothing, and sighed a deep shuddering sigh. When he spoke, it was as though he were talking to himself. "It's gonna take work or maybe a miracle…but I'm going to do all I can to put things back together. The kids need her, and so do I."

He closed his eyes and sighed. "She says it's my fault. Maybe it is partly. I thought she knew how much I love her and that I'm working hard to make things better for us, but I never could tell her. All of a sudden, it's easy now when it's almost too late." Privately, he thought, *And how will we explain the poor little half-black child in the family?* But he wasn't willing to tell Joan that yet. He didn't mention the drugs either. He was trying to protect Diane. He did love her, and somehow he'd get things put right again. He was grateful to Joan for just being there when he needed to talk.

Later he returned to the house, ready to face Diane and try to put their lives back together. They sat across from each other at the kitchen table, while Chris tried his best to understand what was going on in Diane's mind and in her life and how she had gotten into this situation. He kept pushing her about Jim Morton. "How do you feel about him?"

"I love him, Chris," she said it miserably, looking sick and scared and lonely. He wanted to take her in his arms and comfort her, but at the same time, he was furious with her.

"Then how do you feel about me?" He demanded.

"I love you too."

"You can't love both of us in the same way! Life doesn't work that way. You have to make a choice, Diane. Can't you see that?" Chris was desperately unhappy, but he held his hand out to her. "We can try to put our lives back together. We'll treat the baby as another of our children, but you have to be true to me, Diane. You're my wife, and I love you in spite of this mess. Somehow we'll put all this behind us and go on with our lives. I'll try to be a better husband and spend more time with you." He sighed tiredly. "But you have to work at it too, Diane. I want you to quit that job and stay at home with the children and me."

She pulled her hand away and turned her head. Tears filled her eyes. "I can't, Chris." Then softly, she added, "Just let me think about it, will you? Can I have some time to think?"

Diane left the house the next morning, asking Chris to stay with the little ones until she got home. "I have some shopping and things I need to do." Her head was high and her back straight, and she walked out the door purposefully. He played with Martha, Kathie, Freddie, and Angela and fed them lunch. They were napping when she came home. She looked flushed, feverish, and sick.

"What's the matter?" He was afraid she would fall, so he helped her to the couch. "What is it?" he asked again.

"I took care of the problem for you," she retorted defiantly.

"Took care of it? Took care of what?" Then he knew. "Diane, what have you done?"

"I had an abortion."

He took a deep breath. *Oh Lord…help!* "You had an abortion?" He was sick at his stomach. "You killed the baby?"

"I did it for you! I knew you wouldn't want it. I knew you couldn't love it. It's your fault!" She fell onto the couch. She couldn't stand any longer.

Chris would never have believed he could be so angry with Diane. He felt cold, detached, bitter. Had God left him? Had the Holy Spirit completely deserted him? *Why, Lord? Why this?*

He looked straight into her clouded hazel eyes—eyes he had once thought so beautiful. "I can't believe you could kill a child and that you could blame me for the murder! Diane, I thought we had a chance to make things right again." He turned away from her. He couldn't look at her any longer. He reached for the door, and as he slammed it behind him, she rolled off the couch and crawled to the kitchen, reaching under the counter for a bottle hidden there.

Over the next few weeks, Chris used his training as an investigator to watch his own wife. She promised to stay away from Jim Morton. She promised to be a good wife and mother to him and the kids. But at night, she left for King Vic's, and he found her with Jim Morton again and again. The first time he caught them together in Jim's car, he pulled Morton from the seat and belted him in the face and then proceeded to beat the tar out of him in an all-out fistfight. That only made Diane feel sorry for Jim, but it made Chris feel a lot better, at least temporarily.

He tried for months to keep the marriage together. He forgave Diane again and again, and they agreed to stay together, and then he'd find her with Morton again, anyway. She was on cocaine sometimes, and she was on alcohol the rest of the time. He couldn't believe his beautiful Diane, the love of his life, could change so much. She looked hard and tough. He hardly knew her anymore. Days and weeks dragged by while he tried to find a way to save his life, his family, but finally, inevitably, it came to an end. A man can take just so much and still keep his sanity and self-respect.

He couldn't work anymore, with his mind so filled with the problems. He prayed until he couldn't pray anymore. He read the Bible looking for an answer and found the place that says the only reason for divorce is if your mate is unfaithful. It occurred to him that even God got a divorce—from Israel, his wife, whom he loved, because she was unfaithful, 'playing the whore.' He prayed about his situation one more time with Pastor Sam Early, and the answer still seemed clear, so he faced the fact that his marriage was dead. It was over. His heart broken, he filed for a divorce.

He found himself a small apartment, and he had a long talk with each of his children, telling them how much he loved them, and that he would try to take them to live with him as soon as he could make a place for them. They cried and clung to him and didn't understand. How could they? It was the worst year of his life, even counting the war years. His wound was deeper than those the Viet Cong had inflicted on him, but he survived by burying himself in his work, and slowly, slowly, over time, he began to heal.

CHAPTER 11

*C*hris met many people in his work for the attorney's office, and some of them he found fascinating, such as Billy Rodini. He'd never met anyone like Rodini before. Billy was an entrepreneur who at first gave Chris the uneasy feeling he might be involved with the Mafia. He constantly flirted with danger and was often in trouble with the law because his purpose in life was to become filthy rich, and he didn't seem to care how he did it. One of his past activities had been gun-running in South America. Just now, he was operating a "clean" distributing business in Grand Rapids. It was a beautiful sunny day, bursting with the feel of hope about to be fulfilled, when Chris called on him in June 1986.

"Chris Carson, just the man I want to see!" Rodini's shifty black eyes sized Chris up as he snuffed out his cigarette in the overflowing ashtray on his cluttered desk. He balanced back and forth on his expensive pointy-toed Italian shoes. Chris instinctively went on guard.

"I may have found the answer to your financial problems." Billy paused for effect, then reached for his leather briefcase on the floor next to the filing cabinet. He swung it onto the desk and opened it with a flourish, spilling out some fancy documents. "All we have to do now is cash these babies in."

Chris picked one up and looked it over. "German war bonds! Where did you ever come up with these? How many do you have? Are they even any good anymore?"

"I don't know, but they look good, and there are more worth millions of dollars where I got these. All we have to do is figure out how to cash them in!"

"Where in the world did you get these?" Chris asked again. He was skeptical but fascinated.

"A guy I know in the Cayman Islands. He'll give us half of these if we can cash them in for him. Doesn't dare try it himself. He's in some hot water with the government. He's giving me until the end of next month to see if I can cash them, and he'll go halves with me on all the cash I can get from them!"

"So where do I come into this?"

"Let's face it, Chris, I don't have the best reputation. Some people don't trust me." He chuckled cynically. "So I need someone like you to interface for me in this. I'll split my take with you fifty-fifty. What do you say?"

Chris knew better than to fall for such a get-rich-quick scheme, and he was less than thrilled over making a deal with Rodini. On the other hand, he was getting desperate to find financing and start the projects. He didn't consult the Lord. He held out his hand. "Let's go for it."

Chris decided not to involve Joe and Red with this particular enterprise, but he did share it with Joan Nelson. They sat in her office and read the bonds carefully. They seemed legitimate, all right. Some marked "1000" in each corner, said "Province of Hanover, State of Prussia, Republic of Germany." Further down, they said "Harz Water Works Loan, 6 1/2% Gold Bonds Due February 1, 1949." On the back, they read, "Principal and interest payable in the Borough of Brooklyn, the City of New York," or some said in the City of Boston, Massachusetts, or in the City of Chicago, Illinois. At the bottom, some said, "Botchkins Trust Company." Some read, "Payable at the office of Dilton, Huey & Co. in the Borough of Manhattan, City of New York."

Chris called different banks, trying to locate someone who would know if the bonds were real and how to cash them. Chain Brooklyn Bank in New York told him that indeed some authentic German war bonds were still in existence, and asked him to send a sample for the bank's expert to look at. They waited what seemed like forever to hear back from that lead. While they were waiting, Joan made a trip to Ann Arbor to look for some documentation of the bonds in the University of Michigan Library. She found it. They were real! The only question was, could they be cashed? They were bearer bonds, and for a while, it looked as if this was going to work! They were finally on the way!

Then one day, Rodini called to say the FBI had picked up his friend in the Cayman Islands! Seemed he'd stolen the bonds.

"Oh well, I guess that was too good to be true." Joan struggled to recover from the disappointment when Chris told her the news. They sat in the booth at The Big Boy on Pearl Street, where they often met for coffee during the day to compare notes.

"Yeah, but we sure put a lot of valuable time into those bonds. What a waste when we could have been doing something more constructive."

"When you come right down to it, that didn't seem to me to be the way the Lord would answer your needs. There has to be a better answer to the money problem."

"Well, I do have another idea for the flat screen." Chris was never one to sit around and wait for something to happen. "Manufacturing companies need CAD-CAM systems." He looked at Joan. "That's computer-aided design and computer-aided manufacturing." She nodded. "The system Hewlett-Packard sells is priced at over two hundred thousand dollars for a workstation, so most smaller companies can't afford it, and they're still struggling along with horse and buggy systems. We could build an excellent workstation with a better and faster computer than they have, and build the flat screen into the system so the operator could draw on it with a special pen and print it out. Our system could be expandable to work with artificial intelligence systems later on, and we could sell it for about twenty-five thousand dollars a station."

This was not major new technology, just an improvement over what was on the market now, so they felt it had a better chance of being accepted and backed by an astute investor.

The workstation fared no better than any of their other ideas. It seemed as long as you needed money, nobody would lend you any. If they hadn't needed it, Joan found they could get all they wanted. If the prototypes were already built and operational, they would sell easily.

They decided to form a corporation to work on getting the workstation financed and manufactured. Joan would be president of the new company, and Chris would own all the technology. They finished the paperwork in no time and were officially in business as Autoplan, Inc., only the address was Joan's home, and there was no business being done yet.

"I have another idea." Chris and Joan were at the Big Boy again. "This one might pan out, because it should be popular and would be a cinch to sell!" He signaled the waitress to bring more coffee. "Do you have any idea how many people are sitting with home computers they have no idea how to run? Many people who buy computers get them home and try to make them do something and can't figure them out, so they give up, and the expensive equipment sits there gathering dust. Now if those people could buy a video tape for under twenty dollars that would teach them how to use their computers, wouldn't you think they'd be running right down to the store to grab one?"

She put a napkin in her saucer to sop up the coffee the waitress spilled. The coffee was fresh and smelled good. She took a sip while thinking. "That sounds logical. Who would you get to do the demonstration on the tape?"

"We'd have to hire an actor and train him or her how to run the computers, unless we could find someone who knows computers who wouldn't be too boring to watch. It would be tricky, but I think it could be done, all right."

They spent hours discussing how they would go about starting such a company. Joan volunteered to find a place to produce the tapes and cost out the production to see whether they could make a tape that would sell under the twenty-dollar limit. They were convinced they could sell tapes in major stores such as K-Mart, Sears, Meijer, etc. It was a good idea, and it was one that might have worked, but just when they were getting all their ducks in a row, Joe came up with an investor for some of the other technology, so they put the tape company idea on hold.

"No kidding! That's wonderful!" was all Joan could say when Chris told her. "You mean you'll be working in Arizona? That's really big for your family, isn't it? What do Diane and the kids think about this?"

"I won't be moving until the investors find a suitable building for the business. And Diane's probably glad to have me gone. The kids know as soon as I get settled and earn enough money, I'll try to take them with me."

"I hope that happens soon for all your sakes." Joan knew this marked the beginning of success for Chris, and most likely the end of her involvement in his plans. "Someday I'll be telling people I knew you when you were getting started."

Sam Early was sorry to hear Chris was leaving, because he'd be losing a good friend, but he was glad for Chris's sake. "I'll look in on the kids once in a while for you, and I'll try to keep them in church. Between me and their grandparents, we should be able to manage that much, at least. Ed and Jane Portland haven't had any luck at all with Diane either, though. She's skidding downhill fast! It's such a shame, but I know God will reach her someday. I just hope it isn't too late!"

"I'll try to get the kids as soon as I can!" Chris could hardly stand thinking about the life his children had these days, but the court wouldn't give him custody until he had a place to live and a proven way to support them. He shook Sam's hand and then gave him a hug instead. "And I'll miss you too! I can't thank you enough for all you've done for me and my family, and especially for being my friend! I know there's a reason for all I've gone through, but I sure can't see what it is right now! Don't stop praying for me, will you?"

"You know I won't!"

Chris turned and left quickly to hide the tears that welled up in his eyes and threatened to overflow.

CHAPTER 12

As it turned out, Chris didn't leave Grand Rapids right away. His investors were businessmen from Detroit. They bought only a small part of the technology with the understanding that they would buy more as they could afford it. Chris had enough experience from his years with the attorney's office to know how the paperwork should be drawn up. He made sure that he retained control of his technology. Finally, he had found investors who were happy with the opportunity to manufacture and market its products, at least for now.

They named the new company Stellar. Chris hated the name, but it was Molly Herman's idea, and her husband loved it. The others agreed with him. They struck the deal in August, but funding didn't come through until November, so Chris remained in Grand Rapids while he waited. They rented a small building on the South Side for him to work in, knowing he was never one to just sit and wait. They were right—he came up with several more ideas for products made from his technology.

One impressive invention was an entirely new form of communication he called an Amplitude Variation Circuit. It was a revolutionary concept in that it had virtually unlimited data transfer rates and could transmit live continuous color video signals over standard telephone lines. Within weeks, he and Red were able to demonstrate a 20,000 hertz signal on a 1700 hertz channel using a 1 hertz bandwidth and no sidebands!

It was another "impossible" invention that any well-educated engineer knew could never work. It would allow three thousand or more broadcasts on the same channels using a microprocessor to sort between them. Its most important characteristic was that it was completely secure. He put the AVC under Autoplan Corporation, along with the flat screen technology.

It was easy to modify the flat screen idea for use on a telephone, along with the new AVC. When some funds finally came through in November, it took Chris only five weeks to develop and test a new modem that had a baud rate thousands of times faster than anything on the market. The first time he tested it, he completely wiped out the protection devices on the Bell lines.

"You know," he said to Joan, "this modem combined with the AVC makes a system that's virtually impossible to break into. Most computer transmissions can be tapped into, so they're not confidential." He waved a screwdriver in the direction of the contraption on his workbench. "This moves so fast that by the time they manage to figure out the code, the transmission will be finished, and it will take a lot longer to break the code when the modem is using the AVC system."

"Wouldn't you think a big bank would grab this? I don't understand why companies aren't clamoring for your products!" Joan shook her head. "I can only think it hasn't been God's time yet, but then why has he given all this stuff to you? I just don't understand it!"

Word inevitably got out about the new secure modem, since it belonged to the investors, and they were excited about its possibilities. One day, the FBI showed up again. His modem would be vital for banks and government work, and they didn't want to take any chances on its being grabbed up by enemies of the United States. They asked some hard questions, and Chris tried his best not to answer them too clearly.

After that, Herman, Pike, and Pooler, Chris's investors, decided to have a professional business projection done on just the modem. They hired Simon and Simon, Inc., who did a thorough research job, and came up with a projection showing that the modem would earn a billion dollars in the first five years after it was put on the market. That was mind-boggling considering that this was only one little side product of the technology!

"They need the AVC to go along with the modem, so I've been thinking about the best way to handle that. What do you think of this?" Chris sketched out a diagram on the pad of paper. He turned it toward Joan and pointed as he talked. "Let's form a subsidiary corporation to be held by both Stellar and Autoplan to produce the flat screen. We could take that public to raise some badly needed cash."

Joan nodded. I suppose it's the only way now to get Autoplan off the ground." She wrinkled her nose. "I just wish we didn't have to deal with Ken Herman. I'd a whole lot rather do business with Mr. Pooler!"

"You know the situation better than that, don't you?" Chris grinned at her distaste. "I'll set up a meeting for you. Now here's the way I think it should go..." He sketched on the pad as he talked. "We'll use Autoplan as a research and development facility with all its products manufactured and marketed through Stellar. We can let Stellar use the AVC technology on a royalty basis." They hashed out the details privately, and only a day or two later, Joan Nelson and Ken Herman met to "make up an agreement as to the terms."

Herman was charming and slippery as a snake. Joan was smiling but firm and stubborn. The agreement was signed without giving Stellar any more control.

"Stupid woman! Why isn't she home cooking and cleaning, where she ought to be?" Herman fumed to himself and anyone else who would listen. The dislike was mutual.

"What does he think I am, a doormat?" Joan asked indignantly as she talked to Chris later.

"No, he thinks because you're a woman, you don't know anything, and he can take advantage of you."

"Well, he has another think coming!"

"I gathered he was fond of you too."

In November, the investors were ready to move their operation into a facility in Phoenix. The three investors were a strangely mismatched group. Ken Herman was a smooth-talking, high-powered, money-loving type that Chris instinctively distrusted. John Pike was a straight-laced, poker-faced banker. Delton Pooler, round and jolly, was the former owner of a manufacturing company and other businesses.

Of the three, Chris trusted Pooler over the others, but having waited so long for financing, he was ready to take his chances with anyone who would put up some cash. He tailored the amount and type of technology he would sell to fit the resources his investors had available.

Ken Herman bought himself a million-dollar home in Phoenix, and he and Molly moved there right away. Delton Pooler prudently rented an exclusive condominium. John Pike stayed based in Detroit and traveled back and forth. Chris Carson drove out to Phoenix with all his possessions in his pickup truck and rented a small apartment. Red and Gloria Barnes found a small house they could afford not far from Chris's place. Joe Donner got a housekeeping room in a seedy motel and flew back and forth to Grand Rapids to visit his family on weekends when no meetings were scheduled.

Ken Herman was instrumental in finding the location and setting up operations in a vacant building in an industrial park, conveniently near some major microchip manufacturers. Stellar's products would need microchips, and they planned to work out a mutually beneficial deal with one of them. The problem was (as Chris suspected at first and as was confirmed to him continually) Herman was greedy as sin.

Herman's attorney friend, Maxon Kidd, drew up the corporation papers, and Chris examined them thoroughly with his own attorney, Bob Haines, from the Grand Rapids firm he had worked for. Chris prudently inserted a clause that specified if any partner should try to cut any of the others out of the company, then the offending partner would automatically lose his own partnership share. He never expected to have to use that clause but for some reason, he felt it a good idea to spell it out. "I don't know these fellows that well, Bob, but I have a gut feeling about them. Let's not take any chances with the 'greed factor.' I've seen what it can do to people."

Bob nodded. "And we're dealing with the prospect of a great deal of money here."

Herman, Pike, and Pooler had plenty of money to put into the company, but they worked on the philosophy that it's always better to use somebody else's cash than one's own, so they were looking for outside investors to back the company. They found some interest among the microchip manufacturers and were arranging with Chris to sell one of them Autoplan Company, the workstation with the flat screen that was compatible with AI for later use with Perceptor. Then the inevitable happened, or at least, looking back at it later, Chris could see that it had been inevitable given the personalities of the players.

Ken Herman surreptitiously made contact with an offshore investor, an unsavory character who couldn't get into the country, the authorities already having him under surveillance for drug dealing. But he had a pile of cash to invest, and he was ready to put it into what he considered a "sure thing." He offered Herman twenty-five million dollars for a share of the company, provided Herman could get rid of Pike and Pooler.

A few days later, as Chris walked out of the conference room after a regular board meeting, Ken fell into step beside him. "Need to talk to you alone, Chris. Got some important information for you." They stopped in Ken's office. "I've got all the money we need to get us set up and rolling for sure! All we have to do is shed John and Delton, just buy out their interest. I can talk them into letting us have it for a song, and then this new investor will step in and take their place. He's got deep pockets, Chris, and we won't lack for anything we need with him on board." He went on to paint a glowing picture for Chris, telling him what a great situation they'd have if they just replaced Pike and Pooler with this new investor.

Chris stood quietly, his thoughts in turmoil. He didn't reply, so Ken came over and put his arm across Chris's shoulders like a fellow conspirator. "What do we need them for? They shouldn't be a part of this project, anyway. They're small-time guys with small-time ideas. Let's ease them out, and that will give us a clear path with this new backer. This guy has a ton of money, and that's what we need to get moving on the development," He squeezed Chris's shoulder. "Of course you know, Chris, I'd never try to ace you out! It'll be just you and me and the new backer. I can't tell you his name yet because he doesn't want anyone to know what he's doing."

Chris squared his shoulders under Ken's arm. *Of course, you wouldn't ace me out. Without me, you don't have the technology to sell!* Chris felt his stomach tighten the way it had done back in the jungles when danger was imminent, but he was noncommittal. "Let me give it some thought, Ken. How about if we talk again next week?" He could hardly stand to have the man touch him, but he moved out from under the arm casually and strode off down the hall to his office. *Lord, what next?*

He waited until the others had gone to lunch and then took the minutes of their business meetings and the copies of the signed contracts from the main files. He wanted to check the wording of his protection clause, along with other details he wanted to look over. To his great surprise, there was no mention of the protection and penalty clause he had made sure to include! Quickly, he scanned the minutes of the business meetings. They had been changed, with key parts of the agreements and details of the plans left out or altered.

Chris replaced the files, hurried into his office, where he closed the door, and called Bob Haines in Grand Rapids. "There's no doubt what he's been up to, Bob." He quickly filled Bob in on the plot. "You remember that extra clause we wrote referring to what would happen if anyone tried?" Bob did remember it clearly. "Well, it isn't even mentioned in the copy of the contract that's in the file here, and several other things in the minutes have been changed."

"You were certainly right about keeping copies of all that stuff, Chris! What do you want to do about this? I suggest we give him enough rope to hang himself, before we tip him off as to what your attitude is."

"Right on." Chris tilted his chair back and then leaned forward again over his desk. "I want to know who changed the papers and how they managed it."

"I have a feeling Herman's attorney friend, Maxon Kidd, may hold the answer to that. He's just the type for that sort of play, and Herman probably promised him part of the company for his trouble! And say, Chris, did you know Kidd sold his house here in Grand Rapids and bought a big place in Phoenix?"

"What a coincidence!" Sarcasm dripped from Chris's voice. "Is he still with the same law firm?"

"Firestone and Bond, among the biggest in Grand Rapids. Not the kind of place to want their name dragged into a fraud charge!"

"Sorry about that…if we can prove he altered the paperwork, they certainly will be in a fraud charge right up to their necks! Will you start the ball rolling on your end?"

"Glad to. I'll get right on it."

Chris hung up and dropped his head in his hands on the desk. *What now? I was sure we were on the way this time!*

He was tired, but more, he was angry. He knew he'd have to talk with Red Barnes about the situation, but he wasn't eager to do it. When Red stopped in at his office that afternoon, Chris got up and closed the door again. "Sit down, Red, we have to discuss something." Red sat, and Chris collapsed into his own chair and started pushing at a paper on the desk with his little finger—the one finger remaining on his left hand.

"Oh no, what now?" Red had known Chris long enough to realize that there was a problem. "Did something else hit the fan?"

Chris quickly outlined the problem, telling Red what he had told Bob Haines. "So here we are again, right back where we were before! Does everyone in the world have to be so greedy?"

Red took it even harder. "That dirty SOB! I'd like to get him right where it hurts!" He was up and pacing the carpet. "Chris, I don't know how long I can hold on without more income! I was counting hard on this deal coming together right."

"We all were, Red. You know my situation too, but we can't let Ken get away with this! It's rotten and crooked he'd probably sell out his own mother for a couple of bucks. I'm sure hoping that we can just drop him, like it says in the protection clause he had removed. Maybe the other investors can carry us without him." He pushed the lock of hair off his forehead; it flopped back again. "Don't say anything to the others until we hear from Bob, okay?"

"When are you going to tell them?" Red put his foot up on the chair opposite Chris and leaned his elbow on his knee, bouncing it back and forth absently, nervously.

"We'll need to have a meeting soon, but I want to make sure where we stand legally first. I haven't let on to Ken how I feel about this yet. I figure to give him a little more rope and then hang him with it!" Chris smiled grimly. "We'll make it sooner or later, Red. We have to!"

As it turned out, it wasn't that easy to get rid of Herman. He was like a rattlesnake, slithery and fast and dangerous when cornered. When Chris and the other partners confronted him with their accusations, he coiled to strike rather than slither away. What he did was have Maxon Kidd file bankruptcy for the company.

"He has us stopped effectively for now, the crook! I don't know how a guy like that can stand to live with himself!" Pooler was more generous than most men in his situation would have been.

"But the company is not bankrupt. There are no grounds to file bankruptcy, are there?" Even Chris hadn't seen this one coming, and he usually covered every contingency.

"Maybe not, but he'll keep us in court for years if he can to stop us from being able to do anything with the company or the products."

Chris fought hard to keep Ken Herman from gaining control of the company, and he must have been getting to someone. One evening, he stopped at a phone booth to call Haines, since he had a feeling someone had bugged the office phones. He ended the conversation, stepped out of the booth, and was headed across the parking lot toward his car when a bullet whizzed past his ear! Instinctively, he ducked and ran zigzagging for cover. Another bullet zinged over his head. There was no mistaking what it was—it brought back vivid memories of Vietnam! You never forget the feeling of being shot at! Apparently, the out-of-the-country would-be investor was not happy! Chris made it to the car, crouching down to start it, and tore out of the lot. He thought about calling the police but decided against it. He was shaking as he drove home. *Maybe I'd better move...*

Afterward, he figured they'd tried to scare him. They did scare Pike and Pooler. They'd both had enough, and they pulled up stakes and moved back to Michigan. Red had had enough too. He walked into Chris's office one afternoon spoiling for a fight. His voice was defiant as he demanded his due. "Look, Chris, I've put a lot into this invention. I don't feel thirty percent of the take is fair for me. I deserve at least fifty percent for all my work!"

"Red, now isn't the time to talk about money. We haven't any to talk about, anyway." Chris took a closer look at Red—he was drunk! *Just what we need now! Doesn't it ever stop?*

He pointed toward the chair opposite his. "Sit down, Red. I know it's a blow to you. It is to me too, but after all this time and work, let's not make things worse now, okay?"

Red wasn't about to sit. "It's fifty percent or nothing." He insisted, his voice loud and slurred. "You know good and well it's owed to me!"

"Red, think about this for a minute, buddy. I only get thirty percent myself with Stellar. How can I give you fifty percent? We sold to Stellar, and you signed the papers as well as I did, and you agreed to thirty percent."

"Well, now I want fifty percent! I've earned it, and I want it!"

"Let's face it, Red, fifty percent of nothing is nothing. But, Red, if you want out, I'll be glad to buy your interest from you. You'll have to wait until we get some money in the company, but if you want to sell me your interest in the inventions we've worked on, *all* your interest, for, say, ten million dollars, then I'll have Bob Haines draw up the papers."

"You got it!" Red swaggered to the door and grabbed the handle. His face matched his hair and his name, and his eyes rolled back. Chris worried about him, but Chris couldn't handle any more stress right now. "You got it, and you'd best get the dough!" Red repeated as he slammed the door behind him.

Chris decided he'd better call Gloria. He sighed deeply as he picked up the phone and dialed. When she answered, he told her, "Red was here, and he's in bad shape, Gloria. He's drunk, and he's mad, and I don't know what he might do."

"Thanks, Chris, I'll go find him. He's been doing this a lot lately." Gloria hung up the phone and picked up her jacket and purse resignedly. She was pretty sure she knew where to find Red. He'd taken up hanging out at the bar near Stellar's building.

Gloria had put up with a lot lately. She'd been working extra time to support both of them for too long. Red was waiting for the millions to start rolling in, and he couldn't be bothered working for small wages anymore. He was important, a necessary part of the major invention of the century, and he was worth millions!

Gloria Whitney Barnes was as loyal a wife as you could find. She worked hard and waited through all the evenings Red was with Chris putting Perceptor together. Red had been preoccupied with the project and with his other job for so long that now he hardly knew Gloria anymore. It was lonely for both of them, but their communication lines had broken down a long time back. She couldn't reach him anymore.

Gloria was tall and slender with light brown shoulder-length hair that she sometimes pulled back in a ponytail or twisted into a topknot. Her style of dress was casual, bordering on sloppy, as though she didn't have time to pay attention to such trivial details. She was strikingly attractive with large green eyes, a small straight nose, and a smile that grew slowly from a slight curve at the corners of her mouth to a full revelation of even white teeth. She didn't smile much these days, though.

She pulled her little Cutlass into the parking lot at the bar and looked around for Red's Blazer. It was there, taking up two spaces down at the end of the lot. She got out, slung her purse over her shoulder, and took a deep breath as she started for the door. Dank air from the bar came out to meet her as she pushed the heavy wooden door open. She paused a moment to let her eyes adjust to the dimness. Then she saw a few small wooden tables and chairs and a long wooden bar with a polished top and a brass rail along the bottom. A row of high-backed, padded red stools was occupied by a motley group of patrons. A large TV set blared away at the far end.

Several men, along with two or three tough-looking women, sat at the bar. Red had his back to the corner and was talking to a brassy blonde in a tight top, short skirt, and spiked heels. Gloria figured her for a hooker. "I thought I might find you here," she said flatly, waiting to see what his response would be.

"Oh, hi, Gloria. Whatcha doin' here?" He turned to the blonde. "Mindy, this is my old lady. She keeps tabs on me." He laughed drunkenly as he swung the stool all the way around to face Gloria. "I'm busy, babe."

"Yeah, I can see that." She reached for his hand. "But it's time to come home now, Red."

"I'm not ready yet, babe. I got me some drinkin' and some thinkin' to do."

"Why not do it at home with me?"

He laughed that strange laugh. "You gotta be kiddin'! Listen, Gloria, I'll be along in a little while. Then I've got things to tell you, kid. Things are gonna change around here!"

Mindy slid off the stool and patted his arm. "Gloria's right, Red. Why don't you go along home with her now?" She grinned at Gloria. "You gonna have your hands full tonight." She moved on down the bar and took another stool.

Gloria pulled at Red's hand, and he gave in and followed her out the door. She left the Blazer there and helped him into her Cutlass. Before they cleared the parking lot, he was leaning back in the seat with his head cocked against the window, in a stupor.

CHAPTER 13

There was nothing more he could do in Phoenix. That deal was dead! Chris decided to move to Colorado, where Mason-Masters Co. had transferred Charlie and the R&D team. Red and Gloria moved north also, and they found apartments in Longmont near Boulder. The climate was wonderful with clear, bracing air, and rugged mountains towered in the distance. Chris loved it immediately. Somehow, he felt as though he had come home, and he knew within a few weeks this was where he wanted to spend the rest of his life.

When he made the long trip to Michigan to see his kids, it tore his heart to see how they lived now. Diane was usually either drunk or stoned. Even Jim Morton had lost interest in her long since. She neglected the children, and his daughter Teresa was being mother to them. She was only thirteen, and he knew it wasn't fair to her. He remembered his sister Betty, and what her life had been like. "Teresa, honey, I promise as soon as the courts will let me, I'll take you to live with me," he told her.

She hugged him hard. "Why can't you stay here with us, Dad?"

He was quiet for a few moments as he smoothed her long brown hair. "I just can't, honey. You know how it is with your mom and me. You're old enough to know some of what happened. She doesn't love me anymore, and now I have a new place to live in Colorado. It's beautiful there, Teresa." He told her about the mountains and the skiing and the lakes and how clear the air was.

"But Michigan is beautiful too, Dad, and we have lakes. I love it here. Oh, Daddy, why can't you come back here with us? We need you so bad! Maybe if you were here, Mom would change and be nice again!" She was crying, and his eyes were moist too. He held her close and promised again to take her with him as soon as he could.

"We have to pray for your mom. We have to pray a lot, Teresa. Does Pastor Early come to see you sometimes?"

She nodded. "He says the same thing you did, that things are different now, and we have to pray for Mom. He says God has a reason for all this to happen to us, but I can't see any reason, Dad! It's horrible now, and things used to be nice when you were home."

David came into the room in time to hear the last remark. "Yeah, Dad, why do we have to stay here, anyway? Why can't we go with you to Colorado?" David was eleven now and 'nearly grown-up.' Chris promised David too that as soon as he could take him, he would. But Freddie, Martha, Kathie, and Angela would stay with their mother. Chris knew he wouldn't be able to get custody of the little ones unless he could prove Diane was an unfit mother and that he could provide a more stable home life for them, and how could he do that with all the uproar going on with the investors and Stellar Company and Perceptor and Red Barnes and on and on...

Chris and Sam Early had a long visit, getting caught up on all that had happened since Chris left Grand Rapids. "The whole church is praying for you, and especially for Diane and the children, Chris. Diane is farther away from the Lord than ever and into some pretty nasty stuff, I'm afraid. Her parents are brokenhearted over her, but we know that when she was a child, she gave her heart to Jesus, and he promises he'll never leave us or forsake us. We're just holding on and believing that she'll wake up one day and turn back to him before it's too late! And we're all doing what we can for the children, Chris. It's been hard for them, but they're strong little people, and with all the prayer and attention from their grandparents and the other folks in the church, they'll be okay. I know the Lord wouldn't let them down!"

"Thanks, Sam. Thanks more than I can say!" They prayed together before Chris left, putting it all in Jesus's hands and asking for guidance and help for each of them.

****

They all got together at The Raintree Plaza Hotel in Longmont—Charlie Morse, Mick McKinley, Frank Berman, Don Blair, Jim Myers, and Chris Carson. It was like old times. The others were glad to see Chris and fascinated with the story he had to tell them. They were disgusted as he told them what happened to his prototype, and could hardly believe the mess he'd gotten into with the Stellar group. Finally, he trailed to a stop. "So…"

"So you really did it?" Charlie asked again, cocking an eyebrow at Chris as though to make sure he wasn't just making a huge joke at their expense.

"Yeah, Charlie, I really did it." Then Chris came out with his idea. "How'd you guys, like to help me build Perceptor again and finish the development?" He looked around at the group and waited.

"Sounds like fun to me. I'd love to get a look at the plans!" Mick laughed, and his big brown eyes gleamed. "We need a hobby, anyway."

Don and Jim nodded agreement and grinned. "Sounds good to me," Jim boomed in his gruff way.

Frank Berman smiled his beautiful smile and said, "I hear you, man. I'm in."

"What I have in mind is to make you guys into a separate corporation to do research and development, and then whatever company I sell to or go with, I'll make sure all the R&D is done through your corporation. That should give you a pretty good income somewhere down the line. But I want to make it clear right now that only I personally will always retain the rights to the technology." Chris's face was hard. "This is an extremely important breakthrough. It will change the world someday for better or for worse, depending upon who controls it and how it gets used. I plan to use it to make the world better, like Jesus told me to a long time ago."

He began pacing, hands in his pockets. "When Perceptor gets rolling a few years from now, life should be a lot easier. People won't need to work at most jobs anymore because Perceptor will be able to do anything we can do, and do it a lot faster and better. It can be your doctor since it can see and think better than he can. And since it won't demand an income, everyone can afford medical treatment. It would be worth all the trouble for that alone! It will make technology better because, for one thing, it can operate in an entirely airless atmosphere, so real clean rooms can be maintained. It can do micromechanics easily or, at the other extreme, heavy manufacturing, and it can do that twenty-four hours a day if needed."

He warmed to his subject, waving his arms as he spoke. "Perceptor will make life enjoyable for everyone, not just rich people! As a matter of fact, we won't even need money someday! We'll all live on the same social level, and we'll all enjoy life. Perceptor will be able to work in a toxic or contaminated environment, so it will take over all the dangerous jobs. Perceptor will change the computer industry entirely since we'll no longer need any software or programming. Once we get Perceptor units built and operating, we'll only need to talk to them just as I'm talking to you now, and they'll understand and obey the instructions. Offices won't be necessary anymore because Perceptor can make the decisions, answer the phones, and keep all the records. Therefore, we won't need large cities to house office buildings anymore. That should make for a better standard of living for everyone, right there." He paused to make sure his audience was still interested. They were.

"We can turn office skyscrapers into housing developments someday. Perceptor can grow our food and take care of distribution. All our needs and wants will be supplied, leaving us to do the things we want to do. We can play golf all day or paint or study or travel or sail or whatever else we might like." He turned serious, and a frown crossed his forehead. "But if Perceptor gets into the wrong hands, it could be used to make life hell on earth for most people. It would give ultimate power to whoever controlled it."

He stopped, took a drink of water, wrinkling his nose at the chlorine taste, and added slowly, "Sometimes, I'm afraid of it. Already I've seen what greed will do, and we haven't even started on Perceptor yet, just the AVC and modem!"

They all started asking questions and making suggestions, and the meeting lasted into the wee hours. They had a lot to think about, but they were excited over the project.

****

Ken Herman kept things hung up in the courts for years, so Chris couldn't use the AVC or modem technologies the way they had been, but had to make some changes to them. The changes turned out to be even better than the original inventions, but still he couldn't lure an investor. People were even more wary after the word got out about Stellar Company. Ken Herman was bitter and vindictive and vowed to get even with Chris. Chris ignored Herman for the most part and figured out a way around him when he got in the way.

Red Barnes hung around, checking in now and then to see what was happening with Perceptor. He took a job designing hardware for a large aerospace company and promised to stop drinking. Gloria found work as a secretary for Honington Electronics Company. She surprised Chris one day when she stopped to talk with him. He was a friend, and there weren't many she could talk to. "I hardly know Red anymore." She admitted to Chris. "I want to be close to him, but he shuts me out. I don't know what to do about it."

"Maybe you could see a marriage counselor?"

"That's a laugh, but don't think I haven't tried. He won't even let me talk about it. He won't admit anything's wrong, and if you won't admit there's a problem, how can you fix it? And then, I know he's drinking again. He comes home late and smelling like a brewery. Maybe I should take up drinking too. At least, we'd have something in common!"

Chris could relate to the feeling. It brought back bitter memories. He tried to comfort Gloria. "At least, he's not running around with somebody else!"

She shrugged. "Sometimes I wonder."

Then one Saturday afternoon in early fall, she walked into his small office at the lab and dropped into the chair beside his desk, not even noticing the stack of his papers she sat on. Her face was white, and her eyes were dark, and she looked like she was in shock.

"Gloria! What's wrong? Are you sick?" Chris got up and came around the desk to her side.

She shook her head. "I found him in our bed with another woman, Chris. It's over now." She spoke woodenly, numbly.

"Oh, Gloria, I'm so sorry!" He got coffee from the pot he always kept on the warmer. "Here, drink this." It was all he could think to do for her right at that moment. What he wanted to do was find Red Barnes and punch him out! The guy had to be nuts not to appreciate Gloria. She was a real winner in Chris's eyes, and she'd stood by Red through more than most women would put up with.

She took a sip of the bitter coffee and then another. It seemed to melt something inside her, and she began to weep quietly. "How could I ever trust him again?" She sounded like a lost, hurt little child. Something happened to Chris's heart, and he swallowed hard. She searched her pockets and found a tissue.

He cleared his throat noisily. *Come on, man, do something to help her, will you!*

"Listen, Gloria, why don't we go somewhere and have some lunch. Maybe you'll feel better when you've eaten. I know I always think better when I'm fed." He took her cold hand and pulled her up from the chair. Then he hugged her briefly and patted her shoulder. "Come on, I'll drive."

Chris served as Gloria's listening post as they sat in a small fast food restaurant, where they could refill their cups as often as they liked. She sipped part of a bowl of soup and pushed it aside. When she was all talked out, he took her back to her car, and she drove to her apartment, ready to deal with the situation.

What Gloria felt now was rage. She was so angry she could hardly think straight. She grabbed his things from drawers and closets and shoved them into his suitcases and into paper bags and put them all out in the hall. Then she ripped the sheets off the bed and took them to the apartment's laundry room, where she dumped them into a washer and added lots of soap and hot water. Then for good measure, she dumped in half a bottle of bleach. When she got back upstairs, she wrestled the mattress off the bed and managed to turn it over. She wanted nothing to do with any trace of his betrayal of their marriage. It turned her stomach when she thought about walking into the bedroom and finding them there. She scrubbed and cleaned the apartment until it shone, and every trace of Red must have been erased. She wanted nothing left of him! Gloria had put up with a lot over the years, but blatant infidelity was beyond the limits of what she would bear. Late in the evening, she heard Red come and take his things from the hallway. She held her breath for a few seconds, afraid that he'd make a scene, but he just carried his belongings out to the Blazer and drove away. Gloria breathed again.

She felt better after that, but when she lay down in her clean bleach-scented bed late that night, she began to weep again. She cried softly at first, but then the months and years of her life with Red began to flash through her mind like a bad movie, and she was torn with deep, racking sobs. She cried as she had never cried before in her life, rocking and gasping with tears that cleansed her soul of grief and pain, until finally, the tears slowed, and she fell into an exhausted sleep. When she woke late on Sunday morning, she felt different. She was free, yet not sure she wanted to be free. It seemed strange not to have someone to cook for and clean up after, but she realized now that there hadn't been any love between her and Red for a long time.

A few days later, Chris called and asked her to dinner. That happened often during the next few months. They were just good friends, and they enjoyed each other's company. Over the weeks it took to go through the divorce though, there was a subtle change, a new awareness of each other. This was an exhilarating experience for both of them. Each had been lonely for a long time, and they were happy being together, going places and doing things that they wouldn't have done alone. They even attended church together. Chris was able to help Gloria through the divorce procedure since he'd already had that unhappy experience and he knew the pitfalls. It took some time, but the day finally came when she was legally free.

"You realize you've just divorced a man who will have ten million dollars one day?" Chris teased her as they walked out of the courthouse.

"I suppose I blew that one, didn't I?" They laughed together.

"Maybe so." He sobered and looked down at her. Her hair was soft and curled just under her chin, and her clear green eyes looked happier than he had ever seen her. "Maybe not," he added. "Gloria." He put his arm around her and pulled her close. She didn't resist. "Oh, Gloria," he said, and he kissed her. She kissed him back, and they forgot all about where they were and who might be watching. All their lonely years dissolved into that kiss. This was right. It was what should have been all along. They both felt it, and neither one fought it. Why should they? Chris didn't want to stop kissing her. He had never kissed anyone this way before. Gloria's head was reeling.

"Chris…Chris, stop." She gasped.

"I love you, Gloria! I love you," he murmured it tenderly, his face in her neck.

"Oh, Chris, I love you too! But we can't…it isn't right. It just isn't right!"

He turned her around and started back toward the courthouse. "We'd better get a license then and make it right! What are you doing on Saturday?"

"I think I'm getting married." She laughed. "But you'd better stay away from me until then, or who knows what may happen!" She sobered. "I do love you, Chris, so much! I think it would be wonderful to be your wife!"

"It's funny," he said. "When I married Diane, I thought I loved her, and I did in a way, but I didn't know her at all. We married only a few weeks after we first met. I think now it must have been something else, although I did learn to love her dearly, but we never had anything to talk about. With you it's different, Gloria. I feel like we know each other…we're friends. I feel a different kind of love for you. It's fresh and new and unbelievable as though I'm in love for the first time!"

"It'll seem like forever until Saturday, Chris, but it will give us both time to be sure what we're doing is right. I wouldn't want you to move too fast again!"

"It's okay, the Lord seems to be leading me this time. I've asked him about it, and he seems to be telling me that we're supposed to be together. Last time I didn't ask, and I'm sure sorry I didn't! But I appreciate you more because of all we've been through." He kissed her again.

On Saturday, they walked out of the courthouse into the sunlight after the brief ceremony, holding hands tightly. "Look…" Chris pointed across the street to the Holiday Inn. She nodded, and they walked together with their arms around each other, touching even as he signed in, and when the door closed behind them, they didn't even look at the room. In the morning, when they came out looking for some breakfast, they felt like life was starting over again. They were meant for each other...they were one.

She moved in with him the next day. Her things were all packed, so he helped her carry them to his place. They were together. Their loneliness was gone. They had finally found each other, and with what each had been through in the past, they would be careful to nurture their love.

CHAPTER 14

*C*hris had been working on the modem design, to change and improve it so that he could use it without infringing upon any Stellar agreements. It was now at the stage where, using a modulation technique he called frequency key shifting, he could send information at the rate of 56,000 bits per second. That was 500 percent faster than the industry standard at the time. He managed to interest a Canadian company in refining the technology into a manufacturable product and marketing it; however, they wanted proof that it actually worked before they would invest.

He decided the best way to come up with working capital for the testing process would be to interest some limited partners. These would be able to realize a fantastic return on their investment in a short time, provided the modem could pass the tests required. He was all but positive that it could. Nobody else seemed to be so optimistic, though, and he wasn't able to sell the partnerships, so he couldn't close on the Canadian deal. It was another in the seemingly endless chain of disappointments.

"I guess it just isn't the right time yet for this technology," he told Gloria. "But it sure is discouraging. It is so miserably frustrating to have this technology ready to be tested and used and not be able to get anyone to back me, especially when I know that so many companies are working their hearts out trying to come up with what I already have! Not only that, but the government is spending billions on the same kind of project! And besides that, the president recently said in his State of the Union speech that he was trying to encourage new developments in technology!" He pounded his fist on the table in frustration. "Why won't they believe me?"

"It isn't so much that they won't believe you. It's more that they won't pay you for it, isn't it?"

"I guess it's a combination. I think what it gets down to is they don't want me to have it. This technology wasn't supposed to be discovered by any individual person, at least in their opinion. It was supposed to come from some big corporation! Oh, I'm sure in God's good time he will make a way for this invention, but it's mighty discouraging in the meantime! You know, there are hundreds, maybe thousands, of guys out there trying to come up with the answers to artificial intelligence, and some have had promising results, but there's nothing remotely like mine yet from what I can determine."

Gloria came up behind him and hugged him around the waist, then began to gently rub his back. He continued to talk as she rubbed. "The difference is that the others are all scientists and engineers, and they come at the problem from a purely scientific slant. I know it takes both science and faith for the real answer. It's because they deny God and his creation that they can't come up with this technology. Maybe the secret is that in order to be able to create artificial intelligence, you have to know the power who created the original intelligence and gave it life!" He sighed deeply then turned and took her in his arms, and they held each other.

****

Chris and Gloria worked together to get custody of Chris's two older children, Teresa and David. They had Bob Haines working on it in Grand Rapids, and it wasn't too hard to prove that Chris could now make a better home for them than Diane could. Gloria fixed rooms for the kids, and when they arrived, she tried her best to make them feel comfortable, welcome, and loved.

They entered the Longmont school system—Teresa in high school and David in middle school—and Chris spent time with them in the evenings when he could. They seemed to be happy, popular students and made friends quickly. Chris would have liked to have his other children as well, but there was no way he could manage that yet. He planned to try to get custody of all of them as soon as he started making enough money to prove to the courts he could provide for them better than Diane could. He knew Diane was still drinking and doing drugs, and his heart was sad for his children. All he could do was hope Diane's mother and dad would be able to watch over them as much as possible.

The day Bob Haines called with the news about Freddie, it almost broke Chris's heart. "He's going to be fine," Bob said. "But they'll probably take the kids away from her now. Freddie was alone, and the police found him riding his bike on Ten Mile Road with all that traffic!" Freddie was six years old.

Chris flew to Grand Rapids immediately, but there was nothing he could do. Freddie, Angela, Martha, and Kathie were wards of the court now. He made sure Freddie was going to be all right, and he had a talk with the little boy. "Grandma and Grandpa Portland will probably be able to come and see you there too." He gave Freddie a hug. "At least I hope so!"

Freddie started to cry. "But I don't want to live with somebody else. I want to live with you and Mom!"

"I wish more than anything that I could take you to live with me and Gloria," Chris told him, "but the courts won't let me. I know it's hard for you to understand. Hey, it's hard for me to understand too, but that's the way it is. And your mom is sick. She can't take care of herself, and she can't take care of you either. We can't help it right now, Freddie, but one day things will change. You'll see, son." He returned home resolved to get his children with him whatever he had to do.

****

Chris's old friend, Billy Rodini, had started a marketing company in Florida. He was still trying anything he could do to get rich quick, so he was still interested in Chris's projects. The only problem was that Rodini didn't have any more money than Chris did, so they kept finding companies who would be interested in manufacturing the products "after we see a working prototype." But since it still would cost $250,000 to build the prototype, they were always sent back to square one.

Charlie and the crew were as helpful as they could be, building bits and pieces of equipment as Chris supplied them with the ideas and explained his theories. It was hard to explain his technology to engineers since engineers are trained to know that certain things just will not work, and Chris was proving the opposite to be true. He gave them little bits of information at a time so they could get used to the new ideas slowly. He missed Red sometimes. Red was able to go with Chris's "wacky" ideas and had gotten used to seeing things work that everyone knew absolutely couldn't work. It had saved time and explaining.

Joe Donner surprised both Chris and Red by remaining loyal to Ken Herman. Chris told Gloria, "I'll bet he likes working with someone who has money for a change. He probably thinks Herman will win this fight, and then Joe will be in position to have an important job with a big corporation." Chris pushed the lock of hair off his forehead and grinned ruefully. "I wish him luck, though. Even if Herman were to win—and there's no chance of that—he wouldn't have any loyalty at all to Joe! Ken Herman only worries about Ken Herman!"

"Isn't it too bad?" Gloria agreed. "It may take longer with you, but he'd have been a lot smarter to stay with the brains than with the cash!"

"Is that why you stay with me?" He cocked an eyebrow at her and grinned.

"Of course! I'm no dummy!" She teased back.

He pulled her close to him and kissed her neck. "I guess I wouldn't even care if that were true. I love you so much!" Seemed these days he never tired of saying those words he hadn't been able to say for so many years.

Chris had always been full of energy, up all hours of the night working on plans and doing several jobs during the day. He was inventor, promoter, business plan writer, attorney, and anything else that was needed, along with working at the lab with Charlie and the guys, but now he noticed he was beginning to tire early in the day. He shook himself to wake up. *Guess I'll get some vitamins or something.*

These days he often worked with Frank Berman. Frank wanted to know all about Chris's projects. He asked even more questions than the others. Frank was the one he was least comfortable with and the one who seemed the slowest to grasp new concepts, but Chris didn't complain about it; he just worked steadily along. Frank often talked about how much money Chris would make on Perceptor when they got it built, as well as all the other inventions. Chris could almost see the dollar signs in his eyeballs. Frank smiled his beautiful smile and kept asking questions.

Chris had trouble keeping up his schedule these days. He was tired—tired to the bone. He'd always lived on black coffee, but now even that didn't have much effect. When finally one day he couldn't get out of bed, he realized something was seriously wrong. "Gloria, will you find a doctor for me?" he called to her. She was in the kitchen making breakfast for the kids. In a moment, she was at his bedside with a thermometer. "It's more than a virus, honey," he told her. "I can't move out of bed. I'm just so tired."

Dr. Hockstader at the clinic took some tests, and after ruling out several major problems, he diagnosed chronic fatigue syndrome, which was probably brought on by stress. It would take a long bed rest as well as medication. What a blow to a dynamo like Chris, who usually could hardly spend six hours in bed at a time. The first few days, he was so tired he didn't care, and he hurt everywhere, but when he started thinking clearly again, he became irritable at being trapped in a body that couldn't function. Gloria was taking classes at the local business college, working toward a degree in Business Administration, so she was gone for hours at a time. The kids were in school and busy with other activities. Gloria provided Chris with a ream of paper and a handful of pencils; he had a computer...and lots of time.

Gloria and Delton Pooler, Chris's old partner in Stellar Company, had both been bugging him for some time to write a book about his discoveries and experiences. Now Chris decided to give it a shot; he couldn't do anything else for the time being, anyway. So one windy Tuesday, when he was frustrated because he couldn't be outside moving and working and breathing the fresh air, he opened the computer and wrote "Chapter One" at the top of the screen. He began with the common assumption that the world was headed for a climax he called an apocalypse. Then he explained why the apocalypse was inevitable and who was causing it, the probable results without Perceptor, and then the possible results with Perceptor. A month or so later, at the end of the book, he explained what his technology was and how he built the brain using spirals similar to DNA double-helix spirals.

It was an excellent book except for the grammar. Unfortunately, like so many of his generation, Chris had not been interested in English in school. Grammar, spelling, and sentence structure hadn't seemed important to him. (After all, he was never going to earn a living by writing!) So the book badly needed an editor. Delton Pooler was the person who had encouraged him to write the book, so Pooler undertook the editing and publishing of *Perceptor*. Unfortunately, Pooler wasn't any better in English than Chris was. The book was published with many errors in word usage and spelling, although Chris's superior vocabulary shone through, and all the big and important words were spelled correctly.

Pooler had never tried to market a book before, and he was not terribly successful at it. However, Joan Nelson read it and was impressed enough to send it, along with a letter explaining something about this unusual man and his life and trials, to Mack Willis of the TV exposé show, *This Hour*. Several weeks later, the phone rang at Chris's apartment.

He put down the article he was reading and picked up the receiver. "Hello," he said shortly.

"Is this Chris Carson?"

"Yes."

"The author of Perceptor?"

Chris's interest was piqued now, and he became friendlier. "Yes, what can I do for you?"

"This is Mack Willis from *This Hour* show. Do you have time to talk?"

"You'd better believe it!" They did talk for a few minutes, and when they hung up, Chris had an appointment to meet with Willis the next week. *This Hour* paid for his flight to New York City. Chris was optimistic again. "Maybe this is the break we've been waiting for," he said as he kissed Gloria good-bye at the airport. He had a new suit for the occasion and a fresh haircut. He looked a little out of his element but respectable.

Gloria was proud of him. "I'll be waiting to hear from you. Don't forget to call and tell me about the meeting. I wish I could go along!"

"Me too, honey, but if this works out, there'll be lots of other times when you can go. Just pray this opens things up for us!"

They put him through the wringer at *This Hour*, asking him so many questions, he couldn't believe they could possibly use all the information he gave them. Later, when he said as much to Mack Willis, Mack laughed and said, "We wanted to make sure you're real. We get people who would like to use this program as a forum to proclaim some weird belief or sell some product. We have to weed them out."

He talked with the *This Hour* staff and Willis for hours, and then they all flew back to Colorado with him and did more interviews, took pictures, and made everyone nervous. When the segment on Chris and Perceptor finally aired, Chris and Gloria had a small party at their apartment. Charlie Morse, Mick McKinley, Frank Berman, Don Blair, and Jim Meyers were there as well as Delton Pooler and his wife, Emily.

They watched as Chris talked with Mack Willis about Perceptor and the things he experienced with the Stellar bunch, and the years he'd tried to get financing for any one of his many inventions. If he could only get a prototype built of any one of them, he would be on the way, on a course that would eventually change the world. They showed the book and told how to order it. (Joan Nelson had arranged with Pooler to have it professionally edited and reprinted— costly but necessary.)

The clock ticked the *This Hour* theme, and Chris switched off the TV. "Well, what do you think? Will this do us any good, or will it work the opposite?"

"I'm impressed!" Charlie's dark eyes shone with enthusiasm. "I don't know how you could have any better publicity than that! I was worried they'd make you out to be some kind of kook, but you only came off as a little eccentric, and that's true to life, of course." He grinned and slapped Chris on the shoulder.

The others were equally enthusiastic, and they partied on as they celebrated all the expected results of his instant fame. When the guests were gone, Gloria held Chris close. "I'm so proud of you!" she murmured in his ear. "Honey, I do think we have a chance now for something good to happen for a change."

The kids were already in bed. He swept Gloria off her feet and carried her into their bedroom. Chris was on top of the world tonight. Let tomorrow happen as it would. It had taken months, but it seemed the CFS was finally gone, and the world was waiting for him. For tonight, he had love.

****

In Lansing, Michigan, the Reverend Doctor Conrad Braxton watched the program with great interest. He switched off the set and leaned back in his big chair. *So that's what Chris Carson has been up to over the years. I can't believe this robot thing is in God's will for man!*

He reflected on the conversations that he and Chris had in the past—a long time ago it seemed. He remembered again his frustration at Chris's refusal to accept sound doctrinal teaching and how he always brought up disquieting questions about the scriptures. Conrad purposed to get a copy of the book as soon as possible and read what this rebellious and restive man had to say. He ordered the book and waited impatiently until it arrived.

It was Friday when the brown delivery truck stopped at the Braxtons' imposing address, and the driver deposited the package at the door, rang the bell, and drove on. Dr. Braxton was busy with his ministry all weekend, but on Monday, he took the book with him and retired into his private office with instructions to the staff not to disturb him. He read with great interest the strange ideas of this "deranged genius," and as he progressed through the book, the seed of an idea began to form in his mind, taking root and flourishing rapidly. By the time he reached the final page, Conrad Braxton had no doubt this could only be the work of the Antichrist or, at least, the direct agent of the Antichrist! He fell on his knees and began to tell the Lord about it.

The television ministry had grown rapidly under Doctor Braxton's spellbinding oratory and heartfelt invitations to the lost for salvation. His flock increased by the day, and the coffers were beginning to overflow. They would soon be in position to build the college and seminary that Conrad was sure God would bless. He had the plans displayed in his large and comfortable new offices. Conrad felt the Lord would not have him go into debt to build, so he invested the money until there was enough to pay for the school as he built. He rose from his knees and looked again at the account books. The balance was satisfactory; it was time to start. He must hurry if the Antichrist was already knocking at the doors. He must train his flock to withstand the deceptions ahead. There was no time to lose.

Conrad reached for the phone to call the head of his building committee, who called the contractor, and set a meeting for that same week. Braxton had bought a huge tract of land located between Lansing and Jackson—an easy drive to Detroit. He would build the ultramodern campus there. It would be an inspirational place for learning with its gentle hills, large trees, and private lake. In the meantime, Pastor Braxton would begin to warn people by way of his telecast!

The first sermon against Chris and his inventions was mild, only suggesting the possibility that Antichrist might exist somewhere in the world already. With each succeeding sermon, however, Pastor Braxton depicted Chris more clearly as that "evil one" coming as an "angel of light" while being controlled by Satan himself. He warned his audience that the world was in grave danger from the invention of the brain so like a human brain. Braxton even lost his integrity so far as to tell the world about Chris's so-called meeting with Jesus. He said that was a meeting where Chris had sold his soul to the devil, who was now using Chris as his agent to bring chaos into the world. With this diabolical machine, Chris Carson could conceivably set out to conquer the world, enslaving all the people and causing them to worship him!

As always with human nature, the more Dr. Braxton preached against Chris, the more books sold. Soon there was plenty of money to build Chris's first prototype, the modem, which sold immediately when it worked exactly as Chris had said. From then on, money started to flow in, and in short order, there was enough to form Cognition Tech Company and begin to build Perceptor One. The rest was history! When Chris stopped to think about it, he was amazed at how the Lord worked. It was obviously God's will that Chris himself should manufacture Perceptor technology.

"I don't understand it, Father, but I appreciate it so much. Just keep me on track and don't let me fall from your will for my life. Lord, let me stand true whatever comes," he prayed often.

PART TWO

2015

CHAPTER 15

$\mathcal{M}$ohammed Karadshie strode into the conference room, his robes flowing behind him, his dark eyes taking in the details of the scene instantly. He smiled coldly, sending a chill through the group assembled there upon his order. The room was large enough to accommodate a conference table with twenty chairs. Dark blue paper with strange red, gold, and white twisted and swirled figures covered the walls. The woodwork and table were light ash wood, modern in design. Two large gold-framed paintings of horses graced one wall, while the other was bare of other decoration than the wild wallpaper. The far end of the room was all glass with a city view, except now the blinds were closed, and the heavy white and blue draperies were drawn tight. Recessed lighting around the room and over the table revealed all those details.

A diverse group graced the few occupied chairs. There was a short fat man with no neck, straight black hair, and large morose eyes; a tall, muscular black man with a mustache; and a mean-looking older man with scraggly gray hair and a long scar on his right cheek. A beautiful dark-haired woman, who might have modeled once, sat next to him, and a handsome man with graying, wavy hair and a lovely smile completed the group.

Mohammed Karadshie took his place at the head of the table and glared around at them. "Himes has not returned. We must, therefore, assume that he has been captured or killed. It will be better for us all if he has been killed." He pulled at the short pointed beard as if to pull it off his chin. "It seems this Perceptor is capable of many things. We must find another way to get to it. So far, nothing we have tried has worked. There is only one answer left—we must make Perceptor submit itself to us!"

"But, Great Master, it is impossible!" The words exploded involuntarily from the short man, who instantly regretted his indiscretion, his dark eyes betraying his fear.

Karadshie turned a piercing gaze upon his unfortunate underling. "Are you losing your nerve, Karl? Do you want to back out of the deal?" Karl shrank back under the cold scrutiny and shook his neckless head dumbly.

The dark master turned from him scornfully, continuing to regale the others with his powerful speech. "This great power must belong to Islam! With it we can eliminate the infidels once and for all! Allah would want us to steal it from them. And yes, there is a way to get to this Perceptor. I have a plan." He smiled wickedly and leaned forward with his hands outstretched on the table before him.

"I understand that you, Violet, my dear, are personally acquainted with Chris Carson and his family, that you were even close friends." Those evil eyes seemed to probe Violet down to her soul. She squirmed but returned his gaze.

"I knew them many years ago, Great One, when he was only beginning to work on the invention. I was friends with his first wife more than with him."

"And you were the close friend of his friend. He will remember you?"

She nodded. "I think so, yes."

"And you will tell him something that will move him to give you a job with Cognition Tech, a job in the offices where the plans are kept. Then we will have two agents on the inside. Between you, you will find a way to take Perceptor." He shifted his gaze to the wavy-haired man, who nodded nervously. "Then go, both of you, and report back to me when Violet is employed there."

Violet and Frank rose and left the room, bowing to Karadshie. The gray-haired man shifted in his seat as though ready for action too. "You, Louie, keep an eye on them and see that they are loyal to our cause. Those two are useful because they know Chris Carson, but that also makes them dangerous to us." Louie left swiftly, bowing as he went.

"Abdul, you will discover what has happened to Himes. If he is captured and not dead, you will make him dead. See that you do not fall into the same trap!" Abdul rose, bowed, and made his graceful exit. That left Karl alone with Karadshie, a situation Karl did not relish in the least. "And you, my timorous friend, will continue to watch Chris Carson. I want to know where he goes, whom he talks to, what he does. We will meet again soon. I will get word to you."

With that, Karadshie rose from his chair and strode from the room, robes rippling majestically behind him. Karl sighed with relief as he slid from his own chair and took a large hankie from his pocket to wipe his damp brow and palms. Then he carefully turned out all the lights, made sure the room was locked, and waddled away to find Chris Carson.

****

In another part of the city, seated in a long gray limousine, agents McCall and Williams held a strategy meeting with their superior. Benedict lectured them, his voice tight with urgency. "We must get through to Carson whatever it takes! War could break out any minute. Things are at the boiling point now. We can't take the chance that the Muslims will control Perceptor. No, it is imperative that we ourselves get control." The moment was solemn; they all felt the import of his next words. "The President is depending on us."

"He's adamant about not selling the technology. We've offered him everything." McCall ran his finger back and forth across the soft leather armrest. "He will sell us some Perceptors, though."

"Not acceptable! We have to own the technology to keep anyone else from controlling it. Let's face it, whoever owns Perceptor can control the world! We can't take a chance on that being the Moslems! They'd wipe us off the map in a minute and feel they'd done the world a big favor!"

McCall had researched Chris's life, looking for a chink in his armor, some lever he could use to move that stubbornly set mind. He had found what he considered a pretty good bet. He cleared his voice and decided to go for it.

"Okay then, I have an idea, sir. Carson has a weak point, an enemy, his ex-partner, Jonas Barnes. Jonas—they call him Red—used to be a close friend of Chris. He helped develop the hardware for the brain, but the story is he got impatient and sold his interest to Chris for a fraction of its present value. He's bitter now that he sees Chris about to become a billionaire. Thinks he should own half of Cognition Tech. He makes no bones about it, but he's drunk most of the time."

"We can likely use that to our advantage. Let's discuss this situation. How do we get to Chris through Red Barnes?" Benedict leaned forward eagerly.

"Sir, as it happens, Chris is now married to Red's former wife, and I think we can get to Chris through her, using Red." He laid out his thoughts, and Williams and Benedict added their own ideas, until when the limousine dropped the two FBI agents at their beat-up 1999 Lincoln, they had formulated a plan. It wouldn't be hard to find Red. He hung out at Porky's Place down by the warehouse district.

Red had turned into a bitter alcoholic bum. He'd spent the ten million Chris paid for his interest in the technology long since, and had a pretty good time doing it. He played the horses and spent time gambling in Atlantic City at the old Trump Villa. He joined the jet set and saw the world's glitter and the world's dregs, and he knew the wrong kind of women. It didn't take him long to go through his fortune until one day he woke up broke and friendless, with no job, no home, and nothing to live for…except his bottles.

Porky's Place was attractive from the outside; a chalet-style cedar-sided building with a large gravel parking lot on the right, where a heavy wooden door topped with amber glass window panes welcomed the customers in. Geraniums bloomed in several half-barrels along the sidewalk. A large sign advertised that 'Skinny Bones and his Skeleton Crew" was the current entertainment. Porky's was the watering hole for engineers and other personnel who worked at the many manufacturing plants clustered in Longmont's industrial area.

Red sat alone brooding over his drink. He told himself Chris still owed him half the company. After all, without Red, Chris would never have been able to build Perceptor. Without Red's genius, who could have understood what Chris was talking about? And who else would have stood by him through all the hard times before Chris got started? (Red conveniently forgot that he had not stood by Chris until he got started.) He felt he had been completely wronged, tricked, aced out of his rightful place in Cognition Tech.

And worst of all, now Gloria had the job that should have been Red's, and Chris even had Red's wife! He had stolen Gloria away from Red! Red drank and brooded, brooded and drank, as he sank lower and lower into his private hell. Then just when things looked darkest, fate handed him an ace.

McCall and Williams, the inseparable team, entered Porky's Place and glanced casually around. Williams took a stool at the bar, while McCall faked making a phone call at the phone center in the corner as he looked over the patrons. Yes, there was Red sitting in a booth alone. The former millionaire was dressed in what used to be sharp white slacks and a navy jacket with a white shirt open at the throat. He had a red scarf knotted around his neck. If he weren't so dirty and shabby, unshaven and uncombed, he might have looked fashionable—for a sailor.

McCall hung up the phone and strolled over to Red's booth. "Jonas Barnes?" He smiled at Red. "Mind if I join you?"

Red squinted up at this well-dressed stranger, sizing him up as a detective or cop or something. "Why not?" he conceded. McCall slid into the seat opposite him. "Who the heck are you?" Red demanded sociably.

"A friend." McCall assured him. "You can call me Jack." He motioned Williams to the booth behind Red. "I understand you designed the hardware for the Perceptor technology. If true, that means Perceptor wouldn't be a reality without you." That got Red's attention, all right. He felt an immediate liking for this man and straightened up, looking interested. McCall took his reaction as yes and continued, "I think maybe we can help each other."

"Help each other what?"

"We both want to see Chris Carson brought down a few pegs, am I right?" Red nodded agreement, eyeing McCall through bleary eyes. "And we can help you get back your position in the company where you belong." Now Red began to feel a strange elation. Whoever this guy was, he sure talked the right language!

****

At the Cognition Tech offices, Fred Carson, the office manager, checked his order for raw materials. He looked up from his desk as the outer door opened, and a woman stepped into the reception area. She was a dish—older, sure, but lithe and shapely with dark wavy hair and sky-blue eyes, he could see from his office, and she knew how to dress! He listened.

Her voice was low and melodic. "I'd like to see Mr. Carson, please. I'm a friend from years back." Fred felt a jealous pang. His dad got all the breaks! But how did he know this fabulous-looking woman? She didn't seem Chris's type!

"Which Mr. Carson?" Cindy, the receptionist asked. "Mr. Chris or Mr. Fred?"

"Oh, I didn't know Fred was working here. I guess that makes sense, though." She smiled a wonderful smile. "I know Chris Carson. I used to be a friend of Fred's mother."

Fred nodded. *Oh, a friend of Mom's! That makes more sense. Sure, she and Mom would get along. Mom's a sharp lady too!*

Cindy asked for her name. "I'm Violet Grover Welford. I'd like to speak with Chris Carson. Is he here?"

"Mr. Carson is busy. I'll have to see whether he can be interrupted." Cindy was efficient. Fred wondered how things would go when a Perceptor unit took over as receptionist. He knew that was in the plans not far down the line.

Cindy disappeared into the office at the far end of the hallway. When she came out, she was smiling. "Please come in, Ms. Welford."

Violet followed her down the hall, trailing a waft of expensive perfume. Fred caught a whiff as she passed his door, and was even more intrigued with this mystery woman.

Cognition Tech's offices were nice but not as plush as Violet expected. The carpeting was a sand color with small red and green flecks. The chairs picked up those colors, as did the abstract artwork on the walls. The windows had sand-colored blinds, and the wood-work was oak. Violet surveyed it all critically. Nice but sadly dated. They could use a good decorator!

Chris's office was big, with room for a small conference table and four chairs as well as his huge desk overflowing, as always, with papers and books. Behind the desk, a large credenza held a coffee thermos and some coffee glasses on a tray. A computer filled a smaller desk at right angles to the big desk, and some filing cabinets lined the wall beside the door. Floor-to-ceiling windows along the left side of the room afforded a view of the mountains. It was a lovely view, useful for resting one's eyes and one's mind on occasion. Chris stood and came around the desk as she entered.

"Violet! How great to see you!" Chris took her hands in his, smiling. "How has life treated you all these years?" He stepped back and looked at her again. "You certainly look great!"

"You haven't changed, Chris, except for the color of your hair. I know how things have gone with you, everybody does!" Violet laughed and then sobered. "Truthfully, things could be better, Chris. My husband, Jim Welford, died six months ago." She paused a moment and sighed and then gave her head a little shake and continued. "I thought he had left me set up for the rest of my life, but now the attorneys tell me I'm broke! I don't understand how Jim could have had so much debt. He never talked to me about finances. I guess he didn't want me to worry. But Jim must have worried himself right into a heart attack." She looked up at him through long dark lashes, her sky-blue eyes tear-filled. His heart melted.

Violet saw him swallow her story. She continued sadly, "I came to you looking for a job, Chris. I used to be a pretty good secretary. I'm sure I could be useful to you here."

Chris hesitated a moment. "It would be easier to simply give you some cash. Wouldn't you prefer that?" She lowered her eyes and let her shoulders droop. "It's only that we won't need office help much longer, Violet, since Perceptor will run the whole business soon. I just haven't taken time yet to pursue that goal. I've been pretty busy working with Perceptor on the Space Station." He watched her while he talked, admiring her beauty, feeling sad that she felt sorrow. "When that is in operation—soon I hope—then I want to get our business shaped up and running completely by Perceptor as a model for other companies."

She looked up again through those long lashes. "I need to earn my way, Chris. I think my help can be valuable to you too, even if only for a short time."

Chris capitulated. "Okay, Violet, but I'll have to talk to my son, Fred. He manages the office. I'll tell him I'd like you to work here, and he'll find you something to do."

She hugged him impulsively. "Oh, thank you, Chris! You won't regret it, I promise!" She dazzled him with her smile. "I'll be glad to talk with Fred for you," she called as she sailed out and down the hall, laughing inside at how easy it was to con a man. Women weren't nearly so easy to fool, at least in her experience.

Chris, meanwhile, grinned and then sighed and sat down again to the pile of problems on his desk.

Gloria and Violet passed in the hall, and Gloria stopped into Chris's office with an update on the situation with the intruder. She turned almost involuntarily to watch as Violet stopped in the doorway of Fred's office.

Gloria Carson had matured into a charming, knowledgeable, and capable businessperson. She was even lovelier now than she had been at thirty-five, and the former tendency toward sloppiness was gone. Instead, she now wore beautifully tailored clothing that fit her age, personality, and station in life as president of Cognition Tech. Her light brown hair was now touched with gray, and she wore it short and pulled up and back at the sides with a deep wave at the side of her forehead. She walked into Chris's office. "Who was that?"

"A piece of the past come back again." Chris teased her a little. "That's Violet Grover Welford. She was Fred VanDam's girlfriend back when I worked at VanDam Metal Works. They probably would have married if he hadn't been killed in that accident!" He paused a moment, remembering, still feeling the loss of his friend. Then he continued, "Violet used to be good friends with Diane. Apparently, she's come on hard times. I gather her husband died and left her without money. She says she needs a job. I told her Fred would find her something to do here for a while, at least."

Gloria wrinkled her nose. "I don't know if I want competition like that. It's hard enough to keep your attention now!" She hugged his shoulders from behind his chair. He swung the chair around and grabbed at her, but she eluded his hand and sat down across the desk from him. "Seriously, Chris, we have a problem. I'm not sure what to do with the intruder Perceptor caught at the plant. He won't talk. We haven't been able to find out who he's working for."

His brow furrowed as he thought, and he felt the frustration pull at his strength again. Sometimes it seemed as though the chronic fatigue syndrome he'd had years ago still had a hold on him somewhere deep in where you couldn't put a finger on it.

"It could be any one of a hundred different outfits. I'd like to know whether it's Myong, though. I turned him down again the other day, and he's super-anxious to get his mitts on Perceptor." Chris considered a moment. "Too bad we can't use the enemy's tactics and torture him. I guess we'll let Perceptor question him."

"I hate to do that to anyone, but I suppose you're right." She sighed and rose from the chair. "I hope it works! I'll get right at it." He nodded. She turned at the door. "Don't forget we're having dinner with the FBI. That should be great fun!"

"Don't be sarcastic, honey. You know they're a bunch of sweethearts with only our best interests and those of the country at heart."

She cocked an eyebrow at him. "Uh-huh. Of course they are."

"Let me know what Perceptor finds out as soon as possible."

"Right." Gloria headed back to the plant. As she passed Fred's office, she saw Violet sitting by the desk, talking earnestly with him. Gloria felt a twinge of something…was it premonition or jealousy? She kept going. There'd be time to meet Violet later.

They had transferred the intruder to a small windowless storage room, where Perceptor kept an eye on him. He sat on a hard chair, hands and feet securely tied, muttering to himself, "Karadshie will kill me! Maybe I should kill myself first and save him the trouble. If he thinks it's so easy to break in here, let him try it himself! This sure ain't no picnic ground."

SUE HANSON

Himes was in black, even to his knit hat. His face was blackened too except around his eyes so that he looked like a negative picture of a raccoon. He had always been good at his job, but these days the rules were changing so fast that Himes wasn't able to keep abreast of the newest developments. He was a giant rat caught in a high-tech trap.

Outside the building, a muscular black gardener carefully edged the grass, but anyone paying close attention would have noticed that whenever he got near a window, he managed to find a reason to look inside. He hadn't found what he searched for and was beginning to get nervous. *Wait, though...what was that?* He glanced again into the nearest window. A woman stood talking to a robot. They opened a door and disappeared. A few seconds later, they came out, bringing with them a man dressed in black—the one he was searching for!

The gardener pulled out what looked like the end of a water hose, pointed it toward Himes, and squeezed. The laser dropped Himes like a deflated balloon. The gardener sprinted toward the gate, jumped into a late-model black sports car near the driveway, and sped away, leaving Gloria and Perceptor with a body but no information.

At Gloria's scream, Charlie and the crew came charging from the lab and Chris from the office, but it was too late. They milled around, trying to piece together what had happened. Chris was furious. "That's it!" he said, staring down at the black-clad body. "We're putting Perceptor on guard outside the building as well as inside! This is outrageous, to think they could so easily eliminate their problem." He paced the plant's cement floor. "I don't want to take time away from the Space Station, what with the Moslems about to drop the bomb, but we can't take chances anymore. They can't break in and destroy our work, but maybe they can do it from outside!" He looked at the body again. "Anybody recognize him?" They shook their heads. "Okay, call the police and get him out of here. Poor stupid fellow..."

Back in Chris's office, he sat for a few moments and thought about his project, his invention—yes, even his friend, Perceptor. At this point, only a few Perceptor units were in general operation. The first, Perceptor One, stayed in Cognition Tech's plant.

It was almost scary how fast Perceptor One learned, even to Chris who knew its potential. As his team produced more Perceptor units, Chris joined all of them to Perceptor One's brain by AVC, so they all learned at once. All the individual units were actually one big brain (a fact that Chris thought prudent to keep to himself, and only he, Gloria, and Charlie Morse knew.) And that brain never forgot anything it learned. It could ask questions, could reason intelligently, and, after he added a body to each of the units, could act immediately.

Perceptor bodies were a marvel of technology. Their silicon retina eyes with infrared lenses could see in the dark. They sent photographs to the brain and remembered any face, map, book, or picture they ever saw. With their anthropomorphic arms and prehensile fingers, Perceptor units could do the most delicate tasks, including microsurgery. They moved about on either a system of rollers, or feet, depending on their intended use.

Surveillance systems for banks and other security systems would only need a "black box" brain. Those were still an integral part of the main brain. And even now robot units were being tested for use in high-risk jobs since being exposed to radiation, toxic chemicals, heat, cold, or even fire did not harm them. They were made with a special super-hard metal Chris had recently developed.

Yes, Perceptor was a miracle of sorts, the breakthrough science had tried to find for years, a new creation of life, and Chris was the creator! He still wrestled, though, with one big problem. Perceptor had no conscience, no compassion, no love, no hate, no feeling! Perceptor passed judgment immediately and without mercy.

Chris sighed and turned back to his paperwork. Business went on.

CHAPTER 16

*R*oy Benedict and Jack McCall of the FBI were already seated at a corner table in Antonio's Restaurant when Chris and Gloria arrived, a little late because of the police reports over the intruder. Chris recognized Williams, who was trying to be inconspicuous in the foyer. They pretended not to see each other.

"Good evening, Mr. Carson…Mrs. Carson." Benedict rose, reaching out to shake Chris's hand.

McCall held a chair for Gloria. "It's good to see you again."

They exchanged pleasantries and chatted about nothing in particular awhile, and then Benedict cleared his voice. "I suppose you know why we asked to meet with you again." He twirled his wine glass slowly between his hands. "The President feels it is of the utmost importance that the United States control the technology you call Perceptor, so he has authorized us to make you a new proposal."

Chris and Gloria waited.

Benedict became nervous. A lot was riding on this conversation, and from the Carsons' response so far, it didn't seem promising. He tried to maintain his cool composure. "Our proposal is this—in return for the rights to the technology, we will pay you the sum of five hundred million dollars." He paused to let that sink in, saw no encouragement there, and added, "And put you in charge of further research and development as well as the manufacturing facilities." Another pause to see what effect that would have on Chris.

As Chris shook his head just slightly and opened his mouth to respond, Benedict hurriedly continued, "You would also receive a good salary and would have a seat on the cabinet. We propose creating a new cabinet seat called the Department of Artificial Intelligence Development and Usage, and you would become secretary of that department! How does that sound?"

They had offered him wealth, prestige, and power; they had nothing more to offer. Now would he react the way they wanted? Benedict and McCall tried to remain calm as they waited for Chris's reaction. This was a proposal unheard of in the history of the country. It was unimaginable that he would turn it down.

Chris's mouth was dry. This was a fantastic offer—hard and quite probably dangerous to refuse. He looked at Gloria. She raised an eyebrow and winked at him. He pushed the lock of hair back off his forehead, briefly revealing the round scar. It flopped back again when he took his hand away. He took a deep breath. "You know I would be happy to sell the United States the rights to the use of my technology. I would like nothing better, in fact. You also know that I cannot, in all good conscience, let anyone buy the technology itself. It would be too dangerous to let any country have it or any individual or company! The world is too oriented to greed and power. We all know they would use Perceptor to try to control the world, and I can't let that happen. I want Perceptor to be used to help mankind, not rule over them!" He took Gloria's hand and held it. "We are honored and pleased at your unbelievably generous offer, but unless you can let me retain the technology and sell you the exclusive rights to the use of it, we cannot accept."

Benedict's face turned red, and his fists clenched. How dare Chris turn down this proposal! His voice shook as he demanded. "What is it? Did Myong give you a better offer? How can you sell your own country out?" He glared at Chris. *Maybe he is the Antichrist like that idiot preacher says!*

Chris sighed deeply. "Can't you hear what I say? Is everyone in the world deaf? Don't you realize there's a lot more to life than money? No, Benedict, McCall, I am not selling to anyone else either. Yes, they have made proposals, but I've answered them the same as I have just answered you. Perceptor technology is not for sale. Perceptor usage and ability *is* definitely for sale!"

Benedict and McCall rose from the table. "I will relay your reply to the President." Benedict was unhappy, McCall was unhappy. "The President will not be happy."

Over in the far corner of the restaurant, a short, neckless man sighed, drained his glass, and reached for his check.

****

Fred Carson was a capable, intelligent office manager. He was a handsome man, tall and slim, with a look of his mother around his eyes and mouth and with some of his father's brainpower. Fred had felt abandoned when Chris took Teresa and David to live with him in Colorado. It wasn't fair! Fred was unhappy in the foster home and just as unhappy later living with his mother once she regained custody of her children.

Fred was fiercely loyal to Diane. He felt, as she had told him many times, that she had been cheated out of what should have been her place in the world. But Fred certainly never said that to Chris or to Gloria. He was friendly and businesslike with them. "Not a normal loving son, unfortunately, but what can you expect from how he grew up?" Chris said to Gloria.

Diane still lived in Grand Rapids, so Fred didn't see her often. It was hard work managing the office for a company like Cognition Tech. It gave Fred a chance to prove to his father he was just as smart and as worthwhile as David! More so, even. David wasn't working with them, after all! (David was in California trying to make his name as a director of holographic movies.) Fred was single and sought-after, an eligible bachelor, the probable heir to many millions. He dated various women but none seriously.

Violet was a revelation to Fred. She often felt him watching her as she filed papers, typed letters, and did other things around the office. Violet was an excellent worker, naturally doing whatever needed to be done. She soon made herself a valued asset to the office. Fred told himself if she weren't so much older than he was, almost his father's age, he'd make a play for the woman. She worked quickly and quietly and was always pleasant. And she was mysterious. He didn't know where she lived or what she did after office hours. She avoided talking about herself, changing the subject whenever anyone tried to find out more about her. She gave a post office box as her address.

Gradually, she became almost an obsession with Fred. Violet was so beautiful with her dark wavy hair and her eyes that told everything and nothing and the way she dressed. She looked like a model, except a little older than most models. He told himself it wasn't out of the question to date a woman so much older than himself, but somehow he never got the nerve to ask her out. Then one afternoon, he saw her talking to Frank Berman from the lab. They stood in a hallway, talking soft and low like close friends. Fred felt a stab of jealousy. He had never liked Frank Berman, and now he began to hate him! He resolved then and there to ask Violet to dinner—soon!

****

The private office of Kim Myong, president and CEO of Kyutu Electronics, was large and impressive. Soft green carpeting underlined the room like a lush thick lawn. The light-toned wood furniture was upholstered in exotic flowered print, further heightening the garden-like feeling. Intricately carved artwork decorated small tables here and there, and rich paintings complemented and completed the exquisite decorating. An imposing desk dominated the far end of the beautiful room. From there, Myong directed his empire.

Myong had worked for years trying to develop artificial intelligence. Kyutu Electronics had come close to success too, but not anything to compare with the kind of results Chris Carson had with his Perceptor. Myong was a proud man, who wanted all the best technology for Kyutu. So far, he had not let ethics or laws stop him from getting the best. He would not let anything stop him now from obtaining Perceptor. Of course, he could simply steal the plans somehow, build the brain, and give it a different name. All he had to do was change it a little here and there, and no one could prove anything.

Myong was an oily type, about Chris's age. He was grossly fat (a condition he blamed on his inordinate love of Western-style cuisine) with slick black hair and dark, inscrutable eyes. He sometimes dressed in the traditional Korean garb and sometimes in the best Western fashion. He was meeting this afternoon with Jong Lee, his right-hand man who handled his "negotiations."

The last meeting with Chris Carson had not gone well. Carson was stubborn and pig-headed and could not be bought or coerced. Too bad. Now Myong would have to steal the secrets and have Chris eliminated.

He laid out the situation to Jong Lee briefly and then gave him the instructions he waited for. "Diane Carson, Chris's first wife, lives in Grand Rapids, a city in western Michigan. She is bitter against him and eaten up with jealousy. I want you to go to Grand Rapids, contact Diane Carson, and win her over to our cause." Myong's eyes narrowed craftily. "If Chris Carson cannot be bought, his former wife can. You must encourage her to feel even more hatred toward him for his success and her failure. Play on all her emotions, jealousy and guilt and loneliness. She can be controlled with money or with drugs and drink. Use what you need but secure her allegiance to us."

Jong Lee understood. He leaped to the challenge, wasting no time. He was on an afternoon plane bound for the United States to find Grand Rapids, Michigan, and Diane Carson. The dapper, well-dressed Jong Lee was experienced at espionage and treachery. Many unwary or unwilling opponents had been victims of his skill at "negotiation" and murder. He looked forward to this assignment.

****

Agents McCall and Williams left their afternoon meeting with Benedict and headed straight for Porky's Place to find Red Barnes. Sure enough, he was at the bar, seated in his regular booth, talking to one of the prostitutes who frequented the place looking for business. He brightened when he saw them coming and signaled her to leave him alone. "Hi, fellows. What's up?" He hadn't had time to get smashed yet today; it was still pretty early for that.

The FBI agents slid into the seat across from him and ordered beers, then McCall leaned toward Red. "Mr. Barnes, what is your present relationship to your former wife?"

That flustered Red. "What do you mean my relationship?"

"Do you ever see her? Does she give you money or anything like that?"

"I haven't asked Gloria for money for a long time!"

"So if you asked her to meet you on the pretense of asking for help, would she do it?"

Red thought about that for a minute. "Yeah, I guess I could talk her into that. Why would I want to do that, though?"

McCall leaned forward, talking low and fast, while Williams kept an eye on the rest of the bar, making sure nobody else was privy to their conversation. Red gave them a long look to see if they were trying to trick him. He decided they were serious, so he listened with growing enthusiasm. After all, he was working with the FBI, what trouble could he get into that they couldn't easily fix? And what a great way to get back at Gloria and Chris! He asked a few questions and made some suggestions of his own. They did some more planning, and finally McCall asked, "Is there gas in your van?"

Red nodded. "Do you have the stuff we need?" he asked in turn. Williams affirmed that. They rehearsed the plan one more time.

At last, McCall leaned back and said, "There's no use waiting any longer. We're ready when you are."

Red felt powerful; he was finally taking control over the situation and doing something to right the wrongs in his life. He straightened his shoulders and raised his stubbly chin. "I'll call her right now." He slouched over to the phone center and ran his phone card through the slot. "I'd like to speak to Gloria Carson," he said to Cindy.

He was able to reach Gloria on the first try, a rare occurrence. She was usually in a meeting or on the road somewhere on business. She sounded confident and in command as she answered, then her voice changed, and Cindy heard her say curtly, "What do you want?" And a few seconds later, she heard her say, "Oh, all right. I guess I can spare you a few minutes if it's that important. Where did you say?"

A minute later, she left the office, carrying her purse and jacket. "I'll be back in half an hour or so, Cindy. If Mr. Erickson from the State calls, tell him I'll call right back." She got into her blue Jaguar and tore out of the lot.

"I wonder what's wrong with her." Cindy remarked, watching through the office door. She shook her blond head. "She isn't usually like that. Something's not right!"

Gloria thought as she headed for Porky's Place, *What a nuisance. I hope Red's not in some sort of trouble with the authorities. I don't need any bad press right now, and you can be sure I'd get it! They never let up!*

She pulled up beside Red's battered van, got out, and turned to close the car door. Somebody grabbed her from behind, covering her mouth with a rough hand, while somebody else pulled something over her head. They yanked her arms behind her back and bound them rapidly. A second later, they pushed her onto the floor of what she supposed was Red's van.

Gloria was furious. *How dare he do this to me!*

She squirmed and struggled to get her arms free, but someone held her still as the van started up and began to move. Gas fumes were suffocating her. The floor she laid on was cold bare metal in the spots where the carpeting was torn, and dirty and smelly in the spots that still had carpeting. She could hardly breathe with the covering held so tightly over her head! *Lord, please help me, she pleaded silently.*

Williams found Gloria's keys where she dropped them and pulled out of the lot in the blue Jaguar a few seconds after the van.

CHAPTER 17

The room was too cold, Violet thought, shivering, as the group waited for Karadshie to make his entrance. Karl, Louie, and Abdul were there, but Frank wasn't able to get away from the lab without raising questions, as work on the space lab was at a crucial stage. She studied the strange swirled design on the dark blue wallpaper while they waited. No one spoke, maybe because they suspected the room was bugged. There was certainly a ton of electronic stuff behind that wall! She fingered the papers in her purse, it wasn't much, and she wasn't sure anyone not clued in on Cognition Tech's unusual technology could read it, but at least she had something to show Karadshie she was trying.

The door opened abruptly. The master entered and took his place at the head of the table. His dark eyes swept over the group and stopped. "Abdul, you have done your job well. They have no idea who Himes was or who he worked for. You got to him in time. It is too bad he failed to accomplish his mission." He turned his gaze to Violet. "Have you been able to obtain information for us?"

She handed him the papers. "They say this is the language code, but I don't know…"

"You are not paid to know. We will do the knowing. You are paid to steal the papers for us to study." He glanced at the papers and nodded as though he understood what they said. "How are you getting along with Chris Carson? Does he trust you?" Those piercing dark eyes turned full on Violet again, making her feel uncomfortable as always.

"As much as he trusts anyone, Great One." She managed to keep her voice steady.

"And Frank Berman, is he able to provide you with any information?"

"He's working on a way to deactivate the protection device on a Perceptor brain in the lab. They use it there for surveillance, I think. Frank feels with the device deactivated, he might possibly be able to steal the whole brain rather than just the paperwork."

"Ahhh…" Karadshie placed his fingertips together. "I see." He considered a moment and then asked, "Does he need any help from us other than what you can give him?"

"Not yet, Great One. If he does, I'll get word to you. He feels he can somehow delude Perceptor into thinking he's repairing the device, and then when it is deactivated, he'll simply remove that brain unit from the plant. You can appreciate how dangerous that is, and he will have to take his time and wait for the right opportunity."

"And you, my dear Violet, see if you can manage to find us the complete plans."

"I think Chris Carson keeps them hidden somewhere in his private office."

"Then you may have to become even closer friends with him." The black eyes glittered. "I am sure you know how to accomplish that. He is only a man and surely is not immune to temptation."

She nodded. "Yes, Great One." *I'm not so sure of that.*

"You are excused from our presence."

She bowed and left, and he turned to Louie. "It seems they are completely loyal to you, Great One." Louie reported. He described how Violet was acting at her job. "I found a place where I can watch her through a window in the office. The telescope works well for that, but we can't bug the building. There's a barrier or something in the walls that prevents our listening devices from working." He shrugged his shoulders. "All we can do for now is watch the office. Violet seems to be doing her job well. We can't even tell that much for Frank. There are no windows in the lab, only in the manufacturing plant. We watch him come and go, and we watch him outside the plant. He seems to be doing all he can for us."

"Stay nearby so if he needs help, you can provide it quickly."

"Yes, Great One. It would help if Abdul could watch the other side of the building."

"So be it." He nodded them out and then turned to Karl. "What have you found out?"

Karl described the meeting with the FBI. "Benedict didn't seem happy when they left, Great One. It seemed that the conversation did not go well for him." Karl's sad eyes seemed even sadder.

"Carson stays true to what he has said, even with his own government." Karadshie pulled his beard gently, thinking. "I wonder how much they offered him," he mused aloud. It is not possible this is the one man I've found who cannot be bought. Every man has his price!" His fingers drummed the table absently, and then he said, "Stay with him, Karl. Let me know of any other meetings."

****

Jong Lee entered The Timbers, the restaurant where Diane worked nights. The host showed him to a small table near the back of the dining room where he could observe the whole room. The place smelled good, and he was hungry. He ordered dinner and then relaxed, surveying the room. He nodded to himself when he saw Diane waiting on a booth by the window. He recognized her from the picture in his pocket.

Diane no longer looked like a teenager. Her hair was shorter, the frizzy curls pinned neatly back as required by the restaurant. It was now dyed a dark auburn color. She had gained some weight, mostly on her hips and thighs, but she wasn't fat by any means; only she looked more matronly, less girlish. Her face showed the ravages of drink and drugs, though she still seemed naive and vulnerable. *A pushover*, he thought.

Jong took his time eating, savoring the excellent Beef Wellington and the fresh, crisp salad served with it. Then he dawdled over a rich dessert and ordered more coffee. It was late, and the restaurant was nearly empty. He waited until all the other diners had gone and then paid his own bill. Jong could see Diane still working, putting things away and setting up for the next day. He waited outside where he could watch the back door.

When she came out, he called to her from a little distance so as not to frighten her. "Ms. Carson!" She stopped, startled. "Please, I'd like to talk with you." She began to run toward her car. "I'm a friend! I want to talk to you about Chris Carson and Perceptor."

She stopped again, turning tentatively. "Who are you? Why are you here at this time of night?"

As he moved toward her, she backed toward her car, which was only a few feet away now. "My name is Jong Lee, and I work for a computer manufacturer." He paused again, a little way from her. "If you will, I'd like to go somewhere where we could talk."

She hesitated. "Well, I suppose I could. All right, meet me at Nick Fink's across the river. You can buy me a drink."

"I'll follow you there." Excellent! She will be easy to manipulate.

They found a secluded booth, away from the bar's few patrons, and ordered drinks. She eyed him warily over her glass. "Okay, what do you want from me?"

"We understand you were the real inspiration for Chris Carson's great discoveries, and we see you are now cast aside without a thought, while another woman reaps the rewards for the work you began." He saw Diane's eyes moisten and proceeded to press his advantage. "We would like to help you regain your rightful credit, and your rightful share of the wealth that has already been realized from Perceptor as well as that unimaginably greater wealth to be realized in the future."

"And what do you get out of helping me?" Diane had been around long enough to know that nobody would help her without helping himself too. But this man knew what she had been through. He understood how terribly unfair it all was! Diane looked into Jong's dark slanted eyes and thought she saw a friend.

"Ah, my dear lady, I see you are an astute person." Jong flattered her. "Yes, we do want something from the deal, of course. What we want is to gain access to the technology. This way, the United States will not have an unfair advantage over the rest of the world. We will avoid wars by being on an even footing." He hoped she would be gullible enough to believe that without his having to elaborate further. She was.

"What do you want from me? How can I possibly be of any help to you?"

"You may know some way to get through the security that surrounds Chris Carson and obtain the plans for Perceptor."

Diane downed her drink as she thought for a few moments. Jong ordered another drink for her and waited. "Well," she finally said, "I know Ken Herman and Joe Donner are both anxious to get back at Chris for what he did to the Stellar Company. Maybe I could get them to help us. And then there's Freddie."

Ahhh…so she is ours this easily, he thought. "Freddie?" he asked.

"Yes, Freddie is my son, and he manages the Cognition Tech office now. I think I could get Fred to work with me on this…if you make it worth his while."

"I am sure we can easily do that, Ms. Carson." Just so easily, the deal was struck, and they stayed on, talking and drinking, until the bar closed. Jong continued to flatter her, making her feel beautiful, intelligent, and terribly mistreated. When they parted, Diane felt she had found a wonderful new friend, who appreciated her worth.

CHAPTER 18

"I've never met any woman as fascinating as you." Fred gazed at Violet across the white linen tablecloth. The silver and crystal artfully arranged on the cloth reflected their faces. "I don't care about the difference in our ages. You're so beautiful, and you're all I can think about lately." He felt like a real man of the world tonight, having finally talked Violet into going out with him.

Violet looked especially lovely in the candlelight, where the little wrinkles around her eyes and mouth didn't show as much. She smiled at him. "I'm flattered, Fred. You're an attractive man too." She studied her menu. "I'm starved, aren't you? It was a busy day. Your dad and Cindy were still at the office when I left."

"I'm more starved for you than for food," he said foolishly. Then he realized how he sounded and retreated, red-faced, behind his menu. "How about the Rack of Lamb for two?"

"Wonderful." She put the menu down and, ignoring his last remark, asked "Have you heard from your mother lately? I'd like to see her again. We used to be good friends a long time back." She watched him signal the waiter. *He's naive, but nice...so easy to lead around by the nose. I wonder how I can use him to get what I want.*

She smiled at him, fluttering her eyelashes a little, keeping him mesmerized.

He shrugged. "She's doing fine. Insists on working at that restaurant, even though she has plenty to live on without working. Dad sends her money, and so do I."

"He still supports her, even after all that's happened?" That surprised Violet, and she felt even more respect for Chris. She guessed what Diane had put him through.

"I suppose he figures he owes her, and I guess I figure he does too."

"Oh, I take it you aren't too fond of Gloria?"

"She's ok, but she shouldn't be married to Dad. She had a perfectly good husband. She only married Dad because she figured he'd be rich and famous, and she saw her chance to get in on it!" The bitterness he felt showed through plainly then, and Violet didn't miss it. Quickly she changed the subject and soon had him once more under her spell.

****

Chris paced the floor. It was after 6 PM, and Gloria had not returned. He knew she wouldn't be gone so long voluntarily without letting him know where she was and whom she was seeing. He stared out the window, trying to think. "Where could she have gone?"

Cindy's innocent blue eyes were wide with concern. "When the man called, she left right away, but she said she'd be back in half an hour, so she couldn't have been going far."

"What place is close enough to us that she could go there and meet someone, talk, and get back that fast?" They thought of it together. "Porky's Place!"

"But who would she meet there?" Cindy wondered.

Chris was already going out the door. "If I'm not back within an hour, or if you haven't heard from me, call the police, Cindy. Better call Fred too and see if he has any ideas." He was at Porky's without knowing how he got there and picked out a friendly redhead to ask about Gloria.

"Nope, she wasn't in here today. Haven't seen anybody like that, and believe me, I'd have noticed! Red? Yeah, he was here earlier with some other guys, but he left about three o'clock. Yeah, they were all together." The prostitute was glad to talk to Chris, especially after she pocketed the fifty.

"What did these other guys look like?" Chris was so angry he could hardly contain his rage, but he fought to remain calm.

"A couple of 'suits.' One sat down with Red, and the other one wandered around checking the place out before he joined them. I thought at the time they looked like some sort of hoods."

"Did the one who sat down have brown hair and glasses, about six feet tall, medium build?" The woman nodded. "The other one a little younger, tall and skinny with black hair?"

"You know these guys?"

"Yeah," Chris nodded. "Thanks." *Those dirty bastards! Wait till I get my hands on them, I'll make them wish they'd never been born!*

Cindy was still waiting anxiously when he got back to the office, so he sent her home, asking her to please pray for Gloria's safety. He knew who he was dealing with now. He knew they'd call. He was pretty sure McCall and Williams wouldn't hurt Gloria, but he wasn't so sure about Red anymore. The guy was a mental case. He clenched his fists. *If he touches her, so help me.*

He paced back and forth in complete frustration, trying to think and plan.

Then finally, he fell to his knees and took his case to Jesus, first apologizing for not seeking his help in the first place. It was hard for Chris to leave his problem in the Lord's hands, though, especially when Gloria was in danger! There was nothing he could do until he heard from the kidnappers. He felt so terribly helpless! "Lord, please keep her safe until you help me find her!" He kept praying.

****

Gloria was mad. She had never been so angry! "Jonas Barnes, how dare you do this to me? And who are these men?" Her eyes flashed fire as she stood with her back to the wall, fists clenched.

Red didn't remember her being so beautiful. "Shut up!" He commanded as he grabbed her arm and shoved her roughly into a soft armchair where it was hard for her to sit straight and look dignified and threatening.

She surveyed her surroundings briefly, noticing the soft carpet, expensive furniture, comfortable-looking bed, and the bathroom beyond it. Then there were the two men in suits and rubber masks— one wore a monster head and one was Mickey Mouse. "I didn't realize it was Halloween already."

"You'll be okay, Gloria." The monster head reassured her. "As long as you don't make trouble for us, you'll be treated like a lady. We only need to talk to your husband, and maybe now we can get his attention!" McCall remembered to disguise his voice.

"He'll never do business with you as long as you're keeping me captive! What do you want from him, anyway?"

"Only Perceptor…just Perceptor." All three men chuckled, pleased with themselves at how well their plan had succeeded.

"Red, I knew you had problems, but I never, never thought you could stoop as low as this!" She stopped to compose herself briefly and then looked up at Red, making clear contact with his bleary eyes. "You know Chris, and you know what happens when he hits a problem. He attacks it, and he solves it one way or another, and he always comes up with an answer that nobody else ever thought of. I hope you're prepared for the results."

"Just shut up, Gloria! This time, I'm in control, and this time, Chris Carson will have to play my way, or he'll never see you again!" His voice grew soft and sarcastic. "And wouldn't that just about kill him?"

Gloria glared at him, but she shuddered inwardly. She knew he was right, it would just about kill Chris if anything happened to her. She prayed again, *Oh, Lord, please help Chris find me, but please watch over him and keep him safe!*

McCall came up behind her. "We won't tie you as long as you behave yourself. If you try anything though, you'll be tied to the bed, understand?" She nodded. "Good. Now we're leaving you for a while, but there'll be a man outside your door." He grabbed a handful of her hair and twisted it, pulling her head back against the chair. "He'll stay outside your door, and we'll treat you like a lady as long as you cooperate, but if you give us trouble…" He let go of her hair. His meaning was clear.

As she heard the door lock behind the men, Gloria immediately jumped up and ran to the window. She seemed to be in the country; there was a big, beautifully manicured lawn below her with a long driveway through it. The lawn ended where woods started, and by leaning her head tight to the window and looking to the left as far as she could, she thought she could see a pond or lake. Doing the same thing on the other edge and looking right, she saw only more trees. The window had no ledge, and she seemed to be on about the third floor. Nothing she could climb down on that she could see. The bathroom had no answers either. No window but a small skylight too high to reach even standing on the top of the vanity. She squinted at it. It doesn't look like the kind that opens, anyway…you might know!

She kept exploring the room, searching for anything that might help her escape. She found nothing.

****

The same evening, Frank Berman was hard at work in the lab, seeming deeply engrossed in his project. "Hey, Frank, it's late. Time to go home!" Charlie was on his way out, ready to turn out the lights for the night.

"Oh, I'll just be a few more minutes, Charlie. I can't quit now. I'm right on the verge of solving this thing." Frank hardly looked up from his computer screen.

"Oh, okay, I guess. Don't stay too long, though, and lock up when you leave. Perceptor is likely to get nervous if you're here too long, you know." He kidded. He walked out through the plant, and the far door echoed back as it closed behind him.

Frank checked around to make sure he was alone. He worked a few more minutes and then said to Perceptor, "I think I've found the problem with your interface with this smaller unit. Looks like a tiny fracture in the second ring that secures the defense mechanism to the frame. I think I can fix it easily, but I'll need to detach the defense mechanism for a moment and take the unit out into the plant where I can use the laser welder on this spot."

He began to loosen the small bolts gingerly, waiting for some sign that Perceptor would not allow him to do so. Nothing happened. Frank took a deep breath. *He bought it! Now if I can just make it all the way through the plant.*

Slowly, carefully, he deactivated the protection device, then removing the other bolts, he lifted it clear, setting it on the bench beside the computer. "I'll only take a minute....be right back." He assured Perceptor One. Casually, he carried the brain unit out into the manufacturing plant, stopping beside the laser welder. He took a deep breath and then a dash for the door only a few feet away.

Yes! He was out free, running wildly toward the black sports car that waited, motor running. The door opened, and Frank and the Perceptor unit were pulled in. Tires squealing, the car careened down the street away from Cognition Tech. Behind, in the factory, Perceptor set off the alarms.

"Oh no! What now?" Chris dashed for the plant. "Perceptor, what's wrong?"

"A traitor, a traitor! Frank Berman has stolen a brain unit. I was deceived! It will never happen again!"

"Where is the unit now, Perceptor?"

"In a black car with three men. Frank Berman, a large black man with a mustache, and an older man with a scar on his face. They are heading toward Boulder now."

"All right, let's wait until we find out where they're going and deal with them after we discover what we have to contend with." He shook his head. "I always had an uneasy feeling about Frank. Seems he didn't know what he was messing with, even after all these years he worked with you. What an idiot!" He pushed the lock of hair back off his face wearily. It fell back again. "I'm a lot more concerned right now with finding Gloria. If you have any ideas on that, let me know, Perceptor." He turned toward the door. "Maybe she drove home and fell asleep."

"She is not at home," Perceptor answered. "She has not been home since eight twenty-two this morning."

Chris's face tightened. "Damn!" He slumped into a chair and buried his face in his hands. "They've got me for now, Perceptor. I can't do anything but wait for them to contact me. It wouldn't do any good to call the police. For all I know, they could be in on it." He straightened up again and got up from the chair. "It's a rotten world, buddy, and lately you and Gloria are about the only friends left in it I can trust besides Sam Early, and he's in Grand Rapids! Guess I'll get back to the office in case they try to call me with a ransom demand." He looked back from the doorway. "When you find out where Frank is with the unit, signal me, and we'll start to deal with it." He headed back to the office. *Lord, please keep her safe. Please help me find her fast!*

Chris finally stopped for something to eat, knowing he had to keep his strength up, but first he called his friend Sam Early. He told him the situation, as much as he felt was necessary for Sam to feel the urgency to pray and to get the other Christians to pray with him for Gloria's safe and quick return. "Oh, Lord," Sam prayed right there on the phone, "give Chris peace now and wisdom to do exactly the right thing in his difficult situation. And please, Lord, keep Gloria safe and let Chris find her soon!" Then he added, "I'll get the prayer circle working on this right away, Chris!"

"Thanks, Sam, I knew I could depend on you! But please don't let anyone talk openly about this. I don't want the newspapers to get wind of it or anything like that! Her life would be in danger then, I know!" They talked a few minutes more, Sam giving his friend what comfort he could. It did help Chris to know that others were praying.

CHAPTER 19

Ken Herman sneered. "Will I help you? You can bet on it!" He listened as Diane talked on. "Sure, I'll contact Joe. I already know he'll go along with us. We're all just as anxious to get back at Chris Carson as you are. When do we meet to formulate a plan?"

They talked for another moment, then Diane put down the telephone and turned to Jong Lee. "It's all set for tonight at your motel room. I'm sorry Fred can't be here too, but I'll tell him what the plan is later. He'll be a key player. He's already on the inside! My daughter Teresa is in Denver too, but she's too loyal to Chris and Gloria. She'll make an extra excuse for me to visit out there, though. I can say I wanted to see both her and Fred."

The group gathered later around a coffee table loaded with bottles, glasses, and plenty of ice. Ken Herman was all bluster and importance, as usual, ready to take charge of the whole plan, but Joe Donner looked sick. He was pale and skinny and coughed a lot. "I spent so much of my time and money trying to help that SOB. I can't believe he aced me out like he did," he whined like a spoiled child.

Diane looked surprised. "Oh. I understood you had sided with Ken against him?" Joe suffered a violent coughing fit and couldn't answer.

"Doesn't matter, he should have cut Joe in on the company anyway, after all they went through together." Ken was as unreasonable and greedy as ever. They were a sorry group, all trying to blame Chris Carson for their failures in life and all deep down knowing he wasn't at fault. Jong Lee took over the meeting.

"What we're trying to do here is obtain the Perceptor plans, blueprint, whatever Chris Carson has for it... or to steal a Perceptor unit if possible. It will keep peace in the world if Korea also has the Perceptor technology. We don't want any one person or any one country trying to run the world, destroying the chances for world peace, and it seems that might happen if everyone else doesn't have the same chance at the technology." It didn't seem prudent to tell them the real plan—to steal Perceptor and get rid of Chris so Kim Myong and Kyutu Company could have all the power.

"At the same time, we feel some people have been seriously wronged by Chris Carson, and we want to help make things right for those people." Three heads nodded agreement at that statement. "So we have to figure out a way to accomplish our goal. Diane seems to think her son, Fred, might join us, and he might be able to locate and copy the plans." His voice was low and conspiratorial, making them all feel like comrades in an exciting adventure. "Joe and Ken, you know Chris pretty well. Maybe you can figure out a way to get hold of a unit that we can break down and copy? Carson must have a weakness we can exploit. The thing is to figure it out, and among us all we should be able to come up with a plan."

They talked and plotted late into the night, feeling kinship with one another in their thirst for revenge on Chris. Diane was solicitous of Joe, trying to make him more comfortable and getting him drinks when his glass was empty. By the meeting's end, Joe was beginning to look at her fondly, feeling something foreign for Joe, something another man might recognize as lust. Her hand remained a little long on his shoulder, her thigh just happened to brush against his when she sat down once or twice, and she leaned over just a little farther than necessary when handing him his drinks, allowing a tempting view down her blouse. Joe was definitely feeling something other than just revenge for Chris.

They decided Jong and Diane would meet with Fred Carson and get his input into the problem. "We'll see he is paid handsomely for his efforts." Jong assured them. "All of you will be well paid. The Kyutu Company is a wealthy business and can well afford to be generous with you."

"Exactly how generous?" Ken was always one to get to the real bottom line.

"I'm sure there can be several million apiece when we are successful."

"If you can get that in writing, you can sure count on me to go way out on a limb for you!" The others nodded agreement, and the meeting broke up.

"I'd be glad to drop you at your place, Joe." Diane smiled at him, her eyes half-closed. "That way, Ken won't have to go out of his way for you and can get right on the road back to Detroit."

"Oh, I don't mind taking him home." Ken protested.

"That's okay, Ken. Why don't I just go with Diane, and we'll talk again tomorrow?" Joe felt giddy somehow. It was entirely out of character for him to make a play on Diane, but he knew he would.

They drove out of the lot and headed toward Plainfield where Joe lived; but at the first dark parking lot behind a small business, Diane pulled in and stopped. Without saying anything, Joe grabbed at her, pulling her close, kissing her passionately, hotly, while he ran his hand up her thigh. They moved to the backseat, shedding clothing in the process. Nothing like this had ever happened to Joe in all his years. He gave himself up to it and lost himself completely. "Oh, Diane, Diane...you wonderful, marvelous woman," he moaned.

****

The call finally came at ten o'clock. Chris grabbed the phone. "Yes?"

"We have Gloria." The voice was muffled, but he could understand the words. "We will exchange her for a Perceptor brain unit, complete with plans and without a protection device."

"Red? Is that you? Don't be crazy, man. You'll end up in prison for the rest of your life! Red! You know you can't get away with this!"

"We have Gloria, do you understand?" The voice demanded. "If you value her life, you'd better do business with us!"

Chris talked slowly and calmly despite his fear for Gloria's safety. He had to keep his feelings reigned in and think rationally. "If you hurt so much as one hair on her head, you will have me to deal with! All right, what are your demands?"

"As I said, a Perceptor brain unit, the plans, no protection device. We want it ready by tomorrow morning at ten o'clock. We'll contact you then to tell you what to do with it." The caller hung up.

"Perceptor, did you get a fix on that?" Chris asked his metal friend.

"It was from a phone center at Fairmount shopping mall near Boulder."

"We better get started modifying a unit. We'll do some small changes before we put it into their hands." Chris called Charlie and rapidly explained the situation. Charlie arrived at the plant fast, and they headed for the lab together.

"I can't believe this, Chris! Gloria's kidnapped, and Frank Berman steals a unit all at the same time?" He shook his head. "Have you called the police?"

"No. I think we'd better handle this on our own!"

"Where is Frank Berman with the stolen brain unit now?" Chris asked Perceptor as they entered the lab.

"In an office building on Baseline Road in Boulder. The unit is on a table. There are five men gathered around it, and one is dressed like a Moslem."

"Oho...so Karadshie is the bold one! I had thought it might be Myong. Well, anyway, now we have him where we can deal with him." He nodded at Charlie. "We have to take care of this quickly before they discover any of our secrets, but we need to keep working on the unit for Red tomorrow too, make its arms even stronger, use more of that new metal."

Charlie's hawk-nosed face was grim. "Leave those adjustments to me, Chris. You go deal with Karadshie! Don't worry, it'll be ready on time." He shook his head again. "I just can't believe old Frank would do a thing like this!"

Chris picked up a small Perceptor unit. "Is this identical with the one they took?"

"Except for the protection device," Perceptor responded.

"We'll have to remove it from this unit too then." Chris began to work on it. "I need them to look exactly alike. It's hard to believe Frank wouldn't think about the possibility the brain unit was in communication with you by AVC. But I guess if you want something badly enough, you can delude yourself into thinking you can get it!"

Chris and Charlie worked feverishly to finish their modifications. Perceptor cooperated with their ideas, adding some of his own. "We can fit a tiny dispensing device in under the bottom edge of the middle section, here where it won't show at first."

"And by the time they notice it, it'll be too late!"

"Yes, unless Frank is a lot more observant than he has been in the past!" The last little screw was quickly put in place, and Chris put the small unit in a case and headed for his car. Chris made the trip to Boulder in record time and pulled his little white solar car into a side street a block away from the office building where Frank, Karadshie, and their cohorts were celebrating.

"What are they doing now, Perceptor?"

"They are drinking something and celebrating with a toast to Frank. The unit is on the table in front of the Arab, Karadshie."

"Can you get me in without their knowing?"

"The shades and draperies are drawn. If I cut the power, it should be pitch-black in there. The table is about six feet from the door, and the unit is two feet from the end of the table. Karadshie stands at the head of the table. The others are moving about."

"Good, Perceptor, as soon as I get to the door, hit the power. Just make sure I'm outside the room again before you turn it back on, okay?"

The elevator rose smoothly to the fifth floor, where Chris stepped out and glanced around him. *Good, nobody in sight. Uh-oh...a guy coming out of the john. Just pretend to study the directory board a minute. Number 510...right...coast is clear now.* "Okay, Perceptor, here we go." Perceptor switched off the hall lights, plunging Chris into the dark, his hand on the doorknob.

Inside the room, Karadshie gloated over the Perceptor unit. "The future now belongs to Allah. The cause of Islam is secured. What a triumph over the puny forces of the infidels!" He paced back and forth, clasping his hands in satisfaction. "You have done well, Frank Berman! For this, you will be well rewarded! Go ahead, drink to our success." He encouraged the others. Karadshie did not drink liquor, but he was already drunk on power. "Drink to the kingdom of Allah!" They raised their glasses, and the room went black. There was silence for a split second and then panic.

Abdul ran into Louie, trying to find the light switches, but Louie moved away quickly. Abdul swore and yelled at him to stand still. Somebody dropped a glass. In a moment, Karadshie found the draperies' edge and pulled them back by hand, letting in a faint glow from the streetlights outside. Then he managed to open the blinds, and they could just make out each other's shapes through the gloom. He checked the table quickly and didn't notice the door closing softly. "It is all right. The Perceptor unit is still here!" The lights came on as suddenly as they had gone off. "Idiots!" Karadshie muttered at no one in particular. Abdul didn't notice that Louie was standing near Frank at the far end of the table, away from the door.

Frank Berman suddenly had a strange sinking feeling about this. "Let's check out this Perceptor unit again." He suggested. "See if it works okay."

Chris sat in a cubicle in the men's room and waited, the case on the floor at his side. He checked his watch, even though he knew Perceptor would let him know when it was time. It had been a close shave in there, running into Abdul in the dark. He grinned. *Thanks, Perceptor!*

The conference room seemed to grow colder. The men were serious now, no longer celebrating, as they began to test the unit. Gradually, the cold became like an evil presence among them, almost tangible. Karl, the shortest one, was the first to notice anything. He began to gasp for air and then sat down abruptly, holding his head in his hands. Louie was next, at almost the same time as Abdul. They quickly turned blue, their eyes began to bulge, and then gasping and choking, they fell one by one to the floor. Karadshie moved from one to the other, shaking them. "Get up!" He ordered furiously, trying to ignore his own growing discomfort.

Frank Berman, traitor that he was, understood at last, even as he himself began to lose consciousness. "Perceptor," he croaked as he fell, clutching at his throat.

Karadshie pulled his robe over his mouth and nose, crawling, stretching toward the door, frantically determined to escape this foul "spirit thing." He fell with his hand almost touching it.

"Now!" Perceptor said. Chris picked up the case and moved quickly back into the room where the Perceptor unit waited for him. He retrieved the unit, slid it into the case alongside the other, and then closed the door on the cold, cold room with its dead bodies and left the building by the stairs, making sure nobody saw him.

Later, Chris couldn't remember the trip back to the lab. His mind was in turmoil, but he felt he had done what he had to do. They would have killed him in an instant if the roles were reversed. He felt some pleasure at first. This was a whole different way to deal with his enemies than when he'd used his fists back in another lifetime.

Then he remembered Jesus's warning. "Oh, Lord," he groaned, his mind and soul in an agony of regret. "Please forgive me! What else could I do? What else could I do?" Tears flowed down his cheeks unchecked as he somehow guided the car safely down the highway. The emotional stress was almost too much for him, and the tears provided an urgently needed release.

As Chris continued to pray and seek forgiveness, the Lord spoke to his heart, bringing to his remembrance one instance after another from the Bible where God had dealt just as severely with his enemies. "You're in my hand, Chris. As long as you trust in me, I will guide your way."

Chris was overwhelmed with love for Jesus and thankfulness for his forgiveness. He asked one more question then. "What next, Lord?" He knew what next—find Gloria!

CHAPTER 20

Fred was glad when his mother arrived for a visit. What a nice surprise! But he was curious when she introduced him to Jong Lee. His first thought was that his mother planned to marry this slim-hipped Oriental, and he tried to prepare himself for their announcement. As he spent time with them, however, he felt she'd be making a real mistake. There didn't seem to be much feeling between them. He sensed that Jong was a cold, selfish man. Diane didn't need any more grief in her life!

The three of them had dinner at Fred's favorite restaurant, at Jong Lee's expense. They spent the evening talking about old times and about how different things were in Korea where Jong Lee grew up. When Diane came to the point at last and told him what they were planning, Fred was dubious. But the longer they talked, the more sense it made to Fred that the plans should be shared with other countries and with the United Nations so no one country could rule over the others. Besides, this was his chance to help both Diane and himself get rich overnight. "Dad is awfully stubborn about sharing this technology with others," he parroted. "It makes a lot more sense for all people to have the same chance to benefit from all the good things Perceptor can do for them." They each conveniently forgot about all the bad things Perceptor could do for everyone; so Fred agreed to steal the plans for Jong Lee and Korea.

****

Now with the uproar over Gloria's disappearance, everyone was out searching, and Fred was alone. It was a chance in a million to quickly copy some crucial files. He didn't bother with the computer, as he knew Perceptor wouldn't allow him access to that information. He slipped into Chris's office and tried the file cabinet. Locked! He pulled open Chris's top desk drawer, searched briefly among the paper clips, rubber bands, papers and debris, and came up with a set of keys. Great! He checked the front offices again, assuring himself he was still alone.

The key stuck in the lock and wouldn't turn! He pulled and pushed and twisted it, sweat beginning to break out on his upper lip. Finally, it turned, and he had the drawer open in an instant. Yes, this must be part of the plans, but he sure couldn't read them. Looked like they were written in a whole new language or something. He quickly set the whole stack from the first file folder into the copy machine and pushed the button.

Just as he turned the key in the lock again, he heard the outer office door open. "Hi," Violet called. "Anybody here?" He threw the keys back into the desk drawer, tucked the papers into an empty folder, and stepped out of Chris's office hurriedly.

"Oh, Violet, good that you're back. There's so much to do, and nobody else here to help. They're all out trying to locate Gloria."

Violet was pretty sure she had caught Fred at something. He looked like a kid with his hand in the cookie jar, but she said nothing about that. "I hope they find her fast. Poor Gloria! I hope the kidnappers don't hurt her!"

"Dad's sure torn up about it. I haven't ever seen him like this before over anything!"

"Yeah, I know. I guess we can do our part best by being here to answer the phone in case they try to contact him again." She took Cindy's chair. "I'll be receptionist until Cindy gets back. She had to go on an errand for Chris earlier." She glanced out the window as the white solar car pulled into the lot. "Oh, here's Chris now!" They watched him go directly into the side door of the plant, carrying a large brown case.

****

The conspirators celebrated Fred's copied information. They didn't know what it was, but they felt pretty sure it was important. "You're every bit as smart as your father." Diane sat on the arm of his chair smoothing his hair. "They'll probably want you to run the business for Kyutu Company!"

Fred grinned, blushing. "It wasn't too hard to get. The others were out looking for Gloria, so that left me a clear field. If this is the stuff you want, I think I can distract Violet on some errand again and get more."

They planned what they would do next, deciding to wait until Fred got more files copied before they turned the information over to Jong Lee. "We ought to have enough to impress him with first." Ken looked over the papers again. "This looks different from the plans for the modem I saw before. This must be for the brain itself. I think you've struck pay dirt!"

Joe came and stood next to Diane, wanting to touch her but knowing it wasn't a good idea. He looked different than at their first meeting. His skin had a pink tinge now, his eyes were bright, and he smiled a lot. Life had taken on a whole new luster for Joe. "Maybe I can lure Violet out of the office for you." He volunteered. "I could pretend I was a friend of her husband's or something…or no, I could tell her I'm an old friend of Diane's. She doesn't know Diane is here in Longmont. I'll get her to meet me for lunch. That should get her out of your way for an hour or so."

"Hey, great idea! Just don't get any ideas about making a play for her!" Fred was serious, but they all laughed, thinking it was a joke. "She's mine. Just don't forget it!"

****

Gloria had searched the entire room top to bottom without finding anything to help her escape. It was a plush prison they held her in, but a prison, nonetheless. Finally, she gave up and, exhausted from her ordeal, lay down on the bed to rest. *I'd better save my strength for later. Maybe I can get away from them when they open the door or something.*

164

Then while she prayed for strength and for Chris to find her, she fell asleep in spite of herself.

It was morning when she woke. She couldn't believe how long she'd slept, but she felt stronger now. She spent some time in the bathroom getting as presentable as possible with only the materials she had in her purse, and making another check for any avenue of escape. *I wonder what Chris is doing*, she thought for the hundredth time. She checked the window again, but there was nothing new to see there either.

The door rattled as someone unlocked it, and "Mickey Mouse" came in, carrying a breakfast tray. She looked at him carefully this time so she could describe him later if needed. Dark blue suit, neat white shirt and striped tie, and well-polished brown wingtip shoes. Wait, those shoes reminded her of someone. Now who was it? *Think, girl!*

"What's going on? Why are you keeping me here?" She tried to get him to speak so maybe she could recognize his voice. "Who are you, and why are you helping Red steal Perceptor? You should know you'll never get away with this!"

Mickey Mouse simply set the tray down next to the chair and left, locking the door.

Gloria inspected the food. *I suppose I may as well eat and keep up my strength. Oh-oh, I wonder if they put something in this stuff? No, I don't think so. I guess if they wanted me dead, they would have shot me by now.*

She ate some fruit and toast and drank the coffee, all the while thinking about those shoes. *Where have I seen those feet before?*

She pictured each man she knew, one by one, and rejected them one by one until she thought of dinner with the FBI men. Then she paused. *I think that's it! That quiet one, the tall skinny dark one. But why would he be here with Red? Oh no! Not the FBI! Oh, Chris, be careful. Please be careful!*

****

Chris paced, waiting for the phone to ring. He brushed the lock of hair off his forehead. It flopped back down. "It's ten o'clock, Charlie!" He complained. "Why doesn't he call?"

"He'll call," Charlie returned grimly, his dark eyes even more piercing than usual. "He'll call, and we'll have him right where we want him! I can't believe the people who worked with you so long on Perceptor would be so gullible. Don't they realize what they're dealing with?"

"It's greed. It blinds people like nothing else I know. It is good of them to let us put a Perceptor unit right in their hands, though." Chris shook his head, thinking of the old days with Red. "If he weren't a drunk, Red would never make a mistake like this. He's lost his thinking ability, and Red was a sharp engineer in the old days. It's sad, you know?"

"Anyway, we'll be careful not to kill this bunch, at least as long as they haven't hurt Gloria!" Charlie ran water into the coffeepot and poured it into the old machine. Coffee started running out the bottom before he stuck the pot under it again. "Darn!" He began wiping up the mess with a paper towel.

"If they've hurt her…" Chris's face was dark.

The phone rang, and Chris grabbed it. "Carson…yeah!" Charlie stood holding the towel.

"A Perceptor brain unit without a protection device and a set of plans!" the muffled voice recited.

"Yeah, yeah…I want to talk with Gloria first!"

"She's okay. We'll give her back to you as soon as we have the stuff."

"If you don't, you'll wish you'd never seen the light of day!"

"Bring the stuff to Mountain Park at two o'clock, and you'll get your precious Gloria back! Put the unit beside the tallest pine tree near the west hiking trail and then go back toward the restrooms and wait."

He hung up. "Funny they didn't warn me to come alone!"

"Sloppy kidnappers!"

"Or maybe they don't care and didn't think of it!"

"But who…" The light dawned on Charlie. "The FBI?"

Chris nodded. "I'd bet on it!"

The phone rang again, and Chris picked it up.

"Carson?" came the same muffled voice. Chris affirmed. "If you bring anyone else with you, if we even suspect that you brought anyone else with you, consider Gloria dead!" The caller slammed the phone down.

"Sloppy kidnappers is right!"

CHAPTER 21

Violet had her own problems. She hadn't heard from Frank for two days, and she couldn't reach Karadshie or any of the others by phone. Maybe they'd decided to cut her out of the deal! If they had, her life wasn't worth much. They'd happily kill her, her good friends! She stayed hidden in her apartment, her imagination going wild. Chris had not been in the office since Frank got away with the Perceptor unit, so she didn't know what he was up to either. He spent all his time in the lab.

Just in case, Violet packed her bags and bought a plane ticket. She figured she could disappear before anyone could find her. This was why she'd been careful not to let anyone have her street address. She looked in her refrigerator for something to eat and found some eggs and bread and a little strawberry jam in the bottom of a jar. She turned on the television while she ate her toast and eggs. It was almost news time; maybe there was word of Gloria.

She ignored the usual commercials. Then the news team came on, the beautiful tough blonde reporting the top news story of the day: "In a bizarre case, police have found five bodies in a locked conference room in Boulder, Colorado. There is no evident cause of death. No poison was in their systems, no sign of foul play except the bodies." Violet listened with mild interest until they showed the office building, and then she leaned forward and held her breath as the blonde continued. "Police broke into a conference room at the offices of Mohammed Karadshie, an executive of Iran Oil Enterprises at 1540 Baseline Road after a secretary reported him missing. The four other men apparently worked for Karadshie, whose operations are a mystery to the authorities. The FBI is investigating the case, as it may have some connection to the Moslem war threat."

Violet ran to the bathroom and got rid of the toast and eggs. She sat on her bed, shaking. No wonder she hadn't heard anything from Frank! What should she do now? Should she leave town using the ticket? No, maybe they didn't know about her involvement with Karadshie, and that would make them suspicious. She stared out the window, unseeing. *I guess I'll take a chance and keep working there and see what happens next. I wonder how Chris did it. This Perceptor is scary!*

Then it dawned on her—the news report didn't mention any machine or black box or anything, so they didn't know about the stolen Perceptor unit! Chris must have gotten it back somehow. She sat down, breathing deep, trying to calm herself. Nobody could know about her involvement with Karadshie…could they? She thought back, *No, I can't think of anything that would give me away.*

When Violet got to the office in the morning, wearing more makeup than usual to cover the ravages of her sleepless night, Fred and Cindy were already there. "Hi, Cindy. Sorry I'm so late." She headed directly for her desk and put her purse in the drawer.

The usually pert Cindy gave her a wan smile. "That's okay, Violet. Nothing is normal around here today anyhow."

"Any news of Gloria?"

"Don't know. We're waiting to hear from Chris. He was supposed to get a call from the kidnappers at ten o'clock, but we don't know yet if he did. He and Charlie have been spending all their time out in the lab." The phone rang, and Cindy answered, "Cognition Tech, may I help you?" Then she said, "Mrs. Carson is not in the office just now. May I take a message for her? No, I don't believe she will be in the office today, but I'll be glad to have her call you as soon as she contacts me for her messages…Fine…I'll tell her you called." To the outside world, it sounded like business as usual at Cognition Tech.

Violet poured herself a cup of coffee to calm her nerves. Fred watched her from his office, imagining what it would be like to make love to her. She felt his eyes on her and smiled wanly at him, calling, "Morning, Fred."

"Morning, Violet. I think we'll go ahead and work on the arrangements for Dad's meeting at Houston next week. When Gloria gets back, she'll want things to be running smoothly, and we certainly don't want word to get out she's missing. Dad would blow his top!"

"Be right with you, Fred." Violet began to relax. So far so good. Nothing seemed out of the ordinary regarding her. The focus was all on Gloria and Chris and business.

****

Gloria was plotting various ways she would like to capture and torture Red and the "masks" when she heard the key in the lock again. Red blustered into the room, reeking of liquor, as usual. He wore the same dirty clothes, and he talked louder than necessary. "Come on, babe, time to trade you for the real goods!" He laughed rudely at his cleverness. "Chris must be nuts to make a deal like this! What does he see in you, anyway?"

He pushed her toward the door. The "masks" were waiting for her. They "helped" her into a blindfold and then down the stairs and into a car. "Where are we going?" She demanded.

"Pipe down, or I'll gag ya too!" Red threatened.

Gloria could hardly believe how he had changed. It was hard to imagine she had actually been married to him once! She remembered back to their newlywed days. He was nice then, sweet and kind. It was just that he'd started working so many hours, and they were never together anymore. Then he began to drink, and now look at what he had become! The thought made her slightly nauseated. What if she were partly responsible? She prayed, *Oh please, Lord, forgive me if I caused any of his problems.* Then she became angry again.

They drove for what seemed an eternity but in reality was just nearly an hour before the car finally bumped to a stop. When they took her blindfold off, Gloria blinked, closing her eyes against the bright sunlight. They were in a wooded park on a mountainside. The small road they parked on was a two-track high above the main picnic area. She could see the park restroom building below them to the right and picnic tables here and there among the trees and trails leading up the mountain. It was a beautiful place, and under other circumstances, she would have loved to be there. Her shoulders ached from having her hands tied behind her so long, and she was glad to stand up again.

The "masks" paced back and forth, looking down at the picnic area and muttering to each other. Red stayed near Gloria, making sure she didn't try to run. "There he is!" The monster head pointed toward a white solar car driving up to the restroom building. They watched Chris get out and reach back into the car for his briefcase. Then they saw the Perceptor unit. "He's brought us a whole robot!"

Red was skeptical. "Why would he do that?" Then he shrugged. "It's our gain, his loss!"

Chris and the robot walked toward the West hiking trail, looking up at the treetops. Chris carried the briefcase. He handed the case to Perceptor when they reached the tallest pine tree. "Okay, Perceptor, now it's up to you," he said to the robot and through him to Perceptor One, back at the lab. He started back toward the restrooms.

Red slid into the driver's seat of the old Lincoln. "Come on, let's get it!" Williams and McCall jumped in as he started down the steep road. They left Gloria up on the mountainside, her hands still tied behind her back.

"Chris…Chris!" she yelled as loud as she could. He heard her faintly and searched with his eyes until he saw her far above him. The FBI car was coming up the road toward him now. He recognized the Lincoln as it passed him, and watched as the two "masks" got out and grabbed the robot, one on each side. With hardly an effort, Perceptor picked them up, one in each hand, sailing them into the brush one at a time with great force, as though they were no more than rag dolls. They landed hard and didn't move again right away. Perceptor started toward Red, who waited in the car.

Finally, much too late, it dawned on Red what he was dealing with. As memory came back, panic took complete control of him, and he wet his pants as he jammed his foot on the accelerator, roared away across the grass, careened around two picnic tables, and bounced back onto the road heading east. He sobbed as he realized his situation, taking the corner on two wheels, a piteous caricature of the man he had once been. All he wanted now was to get away as far and as fast as possible!

The next corner was sharp, and Red's reactions were slow. The ancient, immovable pine felt the impact of cold hard metal on its trunk and shuddered. Then there were only echoes of the terrible crash and the sound of a hubcap bouncing down the gravel beside the road.

Chris and Perceptor made the trip up the dusty mountain road to Gloria in record-breaking time, and Chris pulled her into his arms, holding her close, while Perceptor undid the rope. She wept with relief, pain from her arms, anger, and frustration all at once. He held her and caressed her, rubbing her arms and shoulders to soothe the ache. "Did they harm you?"

She knew what he meant. "No, they treated me all right, except for the ropes."

"Thank God!" he exclaimed, hiding his face against her hair.

"Amen!" She agreed as she clung to him.

Below them, they saw Williams and McCall slowly pick themselves up and limp about, so they knew the men would be all right. They drove away, leaving the FBI's inept operatives to fend for themselves.

Chris skidded his car to a stop when they came upon the accident and ran to the mangled heap of metal to pull Red out. But when he checked the body, he knew it was too late to help Red. They left him there and quietly drove home as Gloria wept for her former husband, whose life had once held so much promise and who had wasted it so badly. There seemed no point in telling anyone else what had happened.

****

Tension was high at the office. They jumped each time the phone rang, hoping to hear good news about Gloria. So far, they'd heard nothing. They kept themselves occupied with the usual business. Violet and Fred were deep in planning details for the Houston meeting when the phone rang, and Cindy indicated the call was for Violet.

She reached for the phone. *Who in the world can it be? Anyone I might have expected to hear from is dead!* That thought shook her, so her voice was tight as she answered.

"Violet Grover? This is Joe Donner. I'm a friend of Diane Carson."

"Oh! Oh, how is Diane? Have you seen her recently?"

"Yes, I had a nice visit with her a few weeks ago" (understatement of the year, he thought). "If you have time, why don't we have lunch, and I'll tell you about it."

"I'm not sure…things are in turmoil in the office today, but maybe I can get away." She shot a questioning look at Fred, who nodded. "Yes, okay, I'll be glad to meet you, or you can pick me up here at Cognition Tech. Fine, see you then."

Fred managed to find an errand for Cindy too, and when he was alone, he hurried to Chris's office to retrieve the key from his drawer. It was easier to open the file this time, and he removed several folders and ran their contents through the copy machine. The telephone interrupted him four or five times, so it took him longer to finish than he would have liked, and the last papers had not made it through the copier when he heard Violet saying good-bye to Joe Donner.

He grabbed the remaining papers out of the machine and jammed them into the file folder, then hid the finished copies hastily under his desk. The files were barely back in the cabinet when she came into the outer office. He managed to lock the file, throwing the keys back into the drawer, as she came through the hall. "Anyone here?" she called.

"Be right there," he answered. He stepped into the hall, closing Chris's door behind him. "Just putting some mail on Dad's desk," he told her as he returned to the front office, trying to look as though he'd been playing receptionist for Cindy.

Violet noticed he was breathing heavily, and he wiped his forehead and upper lip with his hankie on the pretext of blowing his nose. *That's strange…I wonder what he's been up to?*

She put it in the back of her mind for future consideration as she told Fred what a good time she'd had talking with Joe Donner about Diane and old times. But later on, she noticed the papers under Fred's desk. Unlike his father, Fred was usually neat, so it seemed odd to see clutter in his office. She began to pay more attention to Fred's activities. She wasn't sure why; it was just a feeling she had. Later she struck her palm to her forehead as she realized: *I know that feeling. He's acting like a spy!*

She didn't want to admit, even to herself, that Chris's own son might be plotting against him. It seemed terribly wrong to her, even though she, supposedly Chris's good friend, had done the same thing! Still, she tried to convince herself she was wrong and invent some other reason for Fred's behavior

****

Ken Herman felt good. They were accumulating the information Myong wanted faster than they had hoped, thanks to Chris and Gloria's long absence from the office. The conspirators gathered at Ken's hotel room where they could be sure of privacy. Ken riffled through the papers and put them in order in a neat stack. "Is there more stuff you can get your hands on?"

"Yeah, the file is chock-full. I'm afraid it'll take a long time to get another chance like the last one, though. Dad's getting ready to put Perceptor units into the office now, and then it will be next to impossible to get anything more."

"Then you'll have to move fast before that happens! Maybe you can get in at night." It was as much a question as a statement.

"I don't know. I'd have to have a pretty good explanation for why I needed to work late." He brightened. "Dad'll be in Houston next week, though, for at least two days or more. If I can get alone again, I'll try to copy the rest of the files then."

Diane was proud of her handsome son. He was on her side and would fight for her rights, and she appreciated that. She hugged him. "You be careful though, Freddie. I don't know what would happen if you got caught, even though Chris is your father!"

"Don't call me Freddie, Mom! I'm not a kid anymore!" He pulled away from her impatiently.

Joe Donner (who hardly ever coughed anymore) said, "Want me to try for another date with Violet?"

"No! No, that's okay, Joe. I'll get her and Cindy to do something for me together…something that'll keep them busy for a long time! It takes awhile for the copying, and you never know who might call or come into the office!"

"Hey, why don't we come in and help you when we know they're gone?" Ken suggested. "That way, you can tend the front office when you need to, and we can keep right on copying and putting things back."

They all thought that was a terrific idea, so they arranged to be close by the office on Tuesday and Wednesday so they could act fast on Fred's signal. Diane had been thinking and now put in, "But maybe I can call Violet and see if we can get together. I can just 'happen' to be in town to visit with Fred and Teresa." She smiled. "Now that Joe's broken the ice with Violet and told her all about me and all, it should come naturally that I call her. Besides, I would like to see her. She was a good friend once."

They all agreed Diane would be the one most likely to keep Violet busy for a long time. "Cindy will be a bigger problem, but we'll think of something to get her out of our way." Fred picked up the sheaf of papers. "I'll put these in a safe place until we get enough to give to Jong Lee."

Ken could already imagine the money in his hands. He scowled at Diane. "He'd just better be ready with our cut!"

CHAPTER 22

Chris and Gloria took a day for themselves. It was a long time since they'd spent a whole day and night ignoring Perceptor and the intrigue surrounding them. The Colorado sky was bright blue with fleecy white clouds scudding before the breeze. The mountains looked closer than usual, and trees were rapidly changing their green for more exotic colors. They took a long walk in the fresh September air.

Later they ordered and enjoyed champagne and a delicious dinner sent in from Antonio's and then soaked in their luxurious whirlpool tub. Chris picked up a movie they wanted to see, and they watched it from the comfort of their big bed, propped up on a heap of pillows. It was a wonderful, restful escape from reality, and they thoroughly enjoyed it, though they felt guilty as kids playing hooky. But they badly needed the break, and they came back to their work refreshed and renewed after the unusual stress they'd just gone through.

So it was the next day at breakfast before Chris told Gloria about the Karadshie episode with Frank Berman. "Frank? Not Frank! I can't believe he sold you out!" Gloria was indignant.

"Well, he certainly paid dearly for it. He's dead now, along with his fellow traitors, the poor miserable wretch!"

She nodded with tears in her eyes, thinking about Frank and his wasted life and misguided loyalty. Then she realized what he'd said. "How in the world did you pull that off without anyone finding out?"

"You know that new gas we discovered while we were processing the special metal for Perceptor's strongest robot units?"

"You mean the gas that nearly wiped out the lab group?"

"Yeah, that's the one. It leaves no traces behind. It simply combines with all the oxygen from the air unbelievably fast, turning it into an odorless gas much like carbon monoxide except much more lethal. The process makes the air extremely cold. We must think up a name for it soon. Anyway, we simply substituted a Perceptor unit rigged with a certain amount of that gas in a device Perceptor could trigger and waited."

"You simply substituted! How could you do that? Never mind, don't tell me!" She pushed her cup away, suddenly no longer hungry. "But it seems so heartless, Chris! Can this possibly be God's will?"

"Would you prefer they had a Perceptor unit to dismantle, along with an engineer to explain it to them?"

"No, I guess not. But poor Frank! When is his funeral?"

"Should be today, I guess. I haven't taken time to read a paper. Charlie and the lab boys'll know. If it is today, we'd better go. I don't think he had many other friends, did he?"

"None that I know of." She glanced at his casual slacks. "Maybe you'd better put on your navy blazer then!"

Frank's funeral proved to be exactly the break Fred was looking for, the perfect excuse to have the office to himself. "I'll be glad to stay and run the place while the rest of you go to the service," he said. "You all knew him longer than I did."

Diane phoned Violet at almost that same moment. "Oh, Diane, I'm so glad to hear from you! Where are you? Oh, dear…I can't meet you today. A friend died, and his funeral is this afternoon. We plan to attend that. But how about tomorrow? Let's meet for lunch! How great that you could make the trip to Colorado!" They set a time and place for the next day, and Violet hung up and turned to Fred. "You didn't tell me your mother was coming!"

"I'm sorry. In all the excitement around here, I just forgot. I think she plans to stay a couple of weeks." Fred flushed guiltily and turned away from Violet. A few minutes later, he found a chance to call Diane, and they quickly changed their plans to meet at the office during the funeral. It was perfect.

Violet finished her work, delivered the letters to Cindy for mailing, and filed the copies she had made on disk. She shut down the copy machine, noting the number of copies and thinking that it wouldn't be long until she'd need to put in a new toner cartridge. The others were ready to leave for the funeral, so she was the last one out of the office and into Mick McKinley's station wagon. As they left the parking lot headed toward downtown Longmont, a blue sedan passed them going the other way and turned into the lot, but they were all talking about Frank Berman, and nobody noticed.

Fred already had the file open and the first few folders on the desk by the copy machine when Ken, Joe, and Diane walked in. They had parked their car at the far end of the lot near a clump of trees, hoping it wouldn't be noticed. They got right to work. Joe ran the machine, Diane handed him the papers in order and put them back into the proper files when finished, and Fred made sure they were back in Chris's file cabinet where they belonged. Ken bossed the procedure and kept saying, "Hurry up, can't you?" until they were ready to strangle him. The telephone only rang once or twice, so the work progressed faster this time.

They managed to finish the whole cabinet, but Fred became concerned at the amount of paper they used. He hoped Violet and Cindy wouldn't notice! He made sure things were back in their original state in Chris's office. Then he closed the door again and gave each conspirator a stack of papers to carry and all but pushed them out of the office just before the others returned. It was close, but they made it, and Fred was in his office, deep into the monthly accounting when Violet, Cindy, Gloria, and Chris returned. "How was the funeral?" he asked, looking up from the books.

"There were piles of flowers. Frank's parents were there as well as his sister from Cincinnati," Cindy told him. "She looks like Frank, same smile."

"Funny, I never thought about Frank having parents. I mean, I know everybody has them, but you know what I mean." Violet gathered some reports to copy for the lab. She carried them to the machine and then stopped, staring at the copier, her hand on the switch. That's funny! I could have sworn I turned this thing off before I left!

She put the stack of reports into the rack. Then she noticed the number on the counter—it was over eight hundred higher than when she had looked before they left! She changed the toner cartridge and went on with her copying, saying nothing but doing plenty of thinking.

****

"What's the latest on the situation in the Middle East?" Gloria asked Chris.

He looked up from the plans he was studying. "Doesn't look good! There's a good chance the Moslems in Russia are collaborating with Iran and her allies." He sighed and stood up to stretch. "Ever since the USSR dissolved back in 1991, Russia has been a real problem! They act like good friends, yet we know they're all set to launch a neutron bomb strike at us and at England and Europe at the same time. Several South American countries will probably support them too, along with Mexico. The situation's getting more critical every day! We just have to get the space station up and operating, and fast!"

"It would help if people would leave us alone and let us work on it!"

"Fat chance! And I haven't heard from our main plotter lately. I don't know what he's up to, but I'm sure Kim Myong hasn't given up. Keep your eyes open all the time, Gloria. I hate it that you're always in danger, but that's the nature of what we're involved in. I plan to give you a Perceptor robot as a body guard as soon as I can get one specially made for you."

"You know," Gloria mused, "it would be easier to accept the Perceptor robots if they looked like people. It'll look pretty strange to have a robot following me everywhere, but if it looked like a person, it might just be my secretary or a friend or something." She laughed. "Oh well, maybe I'll put the robot into a dress, or better yet, slacks and blouse!" She glanced at Chris. He was staring at her with a strange expression. "What?"

"I can't believe you do that, but you do it so often! I know I've never mentioned it to you. I'm still only in the what-if stage!" He eyed her closely. She cocked an eyebrow quizzically.

"How did you know that I'm trying to devise a way to give our Perceptor units humanoid bodies?"

Wide-eyed, she shook her head slowly. "I didn't know! But Chris, it's a great idea. Can you really do it, do you think? I'm sure people would accept them much more readily if they didn't look so creepy!"

He nodded. "I'm almost sure we can use some new advances in biological engineering, along with my own discoveries, to turn Perceptor into an android you could hardly tell from a human. That does get pretty scary if you think of all the ramifications, though. It would be possible someday for Perceptor and the androids to run the Earth! Then who knows, at some point in their development, they might think humans were unnecessary? On the other hand, I too have been thinking that they might be more readily accepted if they looked like people."

Chris tapped the plans on the desk with his pencil. "For instance, NASA might not make so many waves if they saw a normal-looking space crew going up in the Carson II. Guess it will take some time yet before we can accomplish that, though." He pushed back his chair and brushed the hair back from his forehead. It stayed back for a few seconds before flopping down again. "I'm hungry. How about some dinner?"

Next day was lovely and clear with the late summer sun shining on the city and a feeling of fall in the brisk breeze blowing down from the mountains. Violet and Diane met for lunch at the new President's Dining Room at the Hilton. They talked and laughed, compared notes, and remembered old times. It was a little strained on occasion when they remembered things that concerned Chris and Diane together, but on the whole, they thoroughly enjoyed themselves. They had finished their salads and were lingering over coffee when Violet decided to bring up what was on her mind.

"Diane, I'm worried about Fred." She stirred her coffee, even though the coffee didn't need stirring, as it was black.

"Really? What is it that worries you?" Diane stiffened, waiting.

"You understand I have no proof, only a gut feeling and a few little things." She looked at Diane to see what reaction she was getting. Diane's expression was unreadable, but Violet plowed on anyway. "I'm afraid Fred is stealing information from the files! I have no idea what he's doing with it, Diane, but I'm pretty sure he's copying it. He could be on dangerous ground, you know. I wouldn't want him to be hurt, but I wouldn't want him to hurt Chris and the company either."

Diane's face paled noticeably. She wadded her napkin into a ball and then smoothed it out again as Violet waited for her to say something, but she was silent. "Oh, boy, I guess I've blown it. But I thought maybe you could talk to Fred, Diane, and help him see what he's doing, get him to stop before it's too late!" Violet's face was as pink as Diane's was white.

They sat a few tense moments, while Diane managed to get herself together. "I appreciate your concern, Violet. You didn't mention this to Chris or Gloria?"

"No, I was hoping it wasn't so, and now I'm hoping you can talk some sense into Fred, and we won't ever have to say anything to Chris about this. Fred's such a nice young man, and he loves you, Diane. I think if you talk to him, he'll try to please you." She lightened up and added, "You know, if he were just a little older, I think I could go for Fred!"

They finished and paid their bill. They hugged, and then Violet asked, "If you're going to be here for a while, let's try to get together again, Diane. It's been good to see you, and besides, I'd like to know what Fred tells you."

"That'd be great. I plan to spend some time at Teresa's, but I'll call you later on and see if we might have lunch or dinner again, and I'll let you know what Fred says. Thanks, Violet, you're a real friend!"

After they parted, Diane headed directly for Joe's hotel room. She was pretty sure Ken was there too, planning how to get the papers they had in order and present them to Jong Lee. When Joe answered her knock, Diane rushed into the room and threw herself into a chair. "We have a real problem now. Violet is on to Fred!"

"What do you mean?" Ken grabbed her shoulder and shook it. "What do you mean 'on to' him?" He demanded.

"She suspects he's copying Chris's files! She doesn't have any idea what he intends to do with them, but she asked me to try to stop him!"

"That's ironic, isn't it?" Joe paced the small room, running his fingers through his scraggly dark hair. He felt panic start to rise, causing the adrenaline to flow and his heart to pound. "Hey, this is a real problem, guys! We have to do something about it before Jong Lee finds out, don't we?"

"We certainly don't want him to think we botched the job! And we can't take a chance that Violet will talk to Chris about her suspicions." Ken turned from the window to face them. "This is getting a whole lot more serious. You realize what we have to do, don't you?"

Diane stood up to pour herself a drink from a bottle on the dresser. She said it for him, her voice hard and cold. "We have to kill Violet!"

CHAPTER 23

On Tuesday, Chris left for Houston, taking Jim Myers from the lab with him and leaving Gloria to run the business. At the airport, he told her, "Remember, if you need my input, just consult Perceptor. He's always in touch with me! Charlie and Mick and Don, along with Perceptor, should finish their modifications to the specially designed robot for the space station soon, and when they do, I want to hear from you. We may need that information as a final trump card in getting the government okay."

She hugged him tight. "You be careful, Chris! There's been an awful lot of trouble lately. Who knows what'll come next! Just please stay on your toes, honey!" She let him go, squeezed Jim's arm, and waved as they disappeared into the plane.

Chris settled into his window seat and carefully slid the case holding the Perceptor brain unit under the seat in front of him. Jim sat next to him. They looked around at the other passengers, studying each one while trying not to be obvious about it. Nobody seemed suspicious, so they relaxed and fastened their seatbelts.

Chris knew it was a risk to fly on a commercial plane, but it could have been just as risky, or more so, to charter a flight or to buy a company plane. That would be even easier to sabotage, at least until Perceptor units could take over the maintenance and pilot the planes. He hoped that would be soon. One reason he'd picked Jim to accompany him was that Jim looked even tougher and more rugged now than when he was younger. That may or may not deter anyone, but it couldn't hurt.

They still built Perceptor units one by one in the lab, but Chris dreamed of the time when there would be enough of them to fill the big manufacturing plant with Perceptors building more Perceptors. As it was, there were only twenty-four units, and half of those were in Chris's buildings being tested for various uses. It was still extremely expensive to build each unit, and each took a long time to perfect. Perceptor One had recently begun to help reproduce himself, so now the process was going a little faster, but each unit cost a fortune.

The FBI had borrowed one unit to test for various national security uses and quickly discovered how useful Perceptor could be. That was when they began putting the pressure on to get control of the technology. Chris wondered when the next attempt would come. He wasn't naive enough to believe one little setback would stop them!

The plant in Houston was not far from the airport, so the men spent minimum time fighting the traffic. It was still bad around the city. "You'd think they'd have come up with a way to do something about this mess by now," Jim commented as they waited through three traffic light cycles.

"We'll put Perceptor to work on it someday. Remember when this airport used to be out in the country?"

"Yeah, hard to believe now, huh?"

They gratefully pulled into the parking space in front of a nondescript brown pole barn building, remarkable mainly for the high chain link fence surrounding it. "Let's get as much done today as we can. We need to make a good demonstration, and we only have until day after tomorrow!" Chris swung out of the car and reached in back for his case.

"Right," Jim locked the doors and led the way up the walk. "Do they expect the demo?"

"I don't think so. I don't know what they do expect, except to keep us from going ahead with the project. It almost seems like treason when you think about it. If this space station can be used to prevent a war and save all that killing, you'd think they should welcome it and do all they can to make it successful!" Chris shook his head. "But it all comes down to money and power, like always."

Ray Gonzales, manager of Cognition Tech's Houston plant, saw them come in and hurried toward them, hand outstretched. "Here you are! Glad you made it so early! How was the flight? Hey, we've got some problems and ideas and other stuff to talk about!" His head nodded, and his dark eyes flashed as he showed them into the conference room where he had arranged things for the meeting with government representatives. He didn't wait for answers to his questions. "Things are going from bad to worse on the political scene. There was another showdown today over the Israeli border."

"The Arabs tried to get their hands on Perceptor last week, you know. Matter of fact, they succeeded briefly." Chris filled the Houston office in on the incident with Frank Berman and Karadshie's group.

"Frank always was a strange one, but I never figured him for a traitor!" Ray shook his head, frowning. "Man-oh-man, how do you decide who you can trust these days? Makes you really wonder, you know?"

He unfolded some blueprints. "But look here, looks like if we make this change to the emergency fuel pod's position, we can fit in the extra Perceptor robot we'll need when they get into space!" He was clearly excited over the change. "And our Perceptor unit pointed out an error on the amount of room they'll need, anyway. We tend to forget they don't need sleeping space, food or waste storage, or a place to keep space suits! We came up with an extra six feet of space we can eliminate, and that should make the critical difference for cargo weight."

"The engine we've already designed can handle it then!" Chris was jubilant and then upset. "How could we have been so stupid in the first place?" He examined the plans, muttering to himself, turning from one page to the next. Finally, he looked up and slowly grinned at Ray and Jim, who were watching him. "It's good! I think this will work. I hope they go for the new solar panel system we've designed to power the space station. It'll make all the difference in efficiency!"

****

Diane, Joe, and Ken had to do something fast. Jong Lee would contact them soon to check on their progress. Kim Myong was an impatient man, and he wanted those plans! They met in Ken's room as usual.

"There's no sense telling Fred what we plan. He probably wouldn't be able to go along with it, you know. He's pretty hung up on Violet." Diane raised her eyes heavenward. "And I thought he was a smart man!"

"You're right, Diane." Ken agreed. He was ready to agree to almost anything that would get them closer to the millions Jong Lee had promised them. Ken was deep in debt because he loved to live well but wasn't willing to let his rich friends know he was in financial difficulty. Creditors were hot on his heels; even Molly was beginning to nag him about it. He nodded, pulled his pen from his shirt pocket, and sat down at the small table. "Let's plan this and go ahead with it. If Fred suspects us, we can tell him about it later on."

They didn't count on Fred and Violet being together so much, though. It was hard to get Violet alone during the day, and Fred tried to be with her that evening too. It made Diane angry. "I thought he was smarter than that." She fumed.

Two days had already passed since her lunch with Violet, and she knew she'd be hearing from her again soon, wanting to know if Diane was able to talk sense to Fred. So now she stood up and gestured to them. "Let's just shoot her and be done with it!" She proposed. "We can't wait much longer!" Her eyes were wild, and she was feeling a rush from the cocaine she'd just sneaked in the bathroom.

"If we had a good high-powered rifle, we could get her from long range so nobody could connect us with the shooting." Ken speculated. "I don't know whether I'm that good a shot, though."

"I used to hunt deer," Joe said. "But I don't know about shooting a person!" He felt Diane's arms go around his waist from behind him, and he felt her suggestively rub herself against his back. Joe was doomed from the time she had first decided to seduce him. He didn't have a chance against his emotions now. "I guess I could try!"

"Fred has a gun I can borrow without his knowing it." Diane stayed just a little longer and then gave Joe a little extra squeeze as she released him.

"We can get her as she leaves work. We know she always parks in the same place. We can be ready for her, and Joe can practice sighting on the spot and shoot her as she heads for her car!" Ken grew more enthusiastic. "Maybe they'll think we were aiming for Gloria instead."

"But we have to all go together." Joe insisted. "I won't do this alone!"

"Let's do it today and get it over with. Can you get Fred's gun now, Diane?" Ken was ready for action. He suddenly felt an urgency that was as catching as a virus, and the others submitted to it quickly. They drove Diane to Fred's apartment, where she picked Fred's gun from his closet gingerly, hiding it inside some clothing she pretended to be taking to the cleaner. Back in the car, Ken and Joe grabbed the gun and unwrapped it roughly.

"Hey, take it easy! Fred'll be mad if anything happens to this gun. It's some kind of special rifle or something."

"I'll say," Joe said, holding the heavy barrel admiringly as he tested the bolt-action. "It's a Winchester 338! Just look at that scope! Wow, I could do some serious deer hunting with this baby." He looked up at Diane. "How many bullets did you get?"

"Five. I hope that's enough. And it's not deer you're hunting this time!"

The trio soon found a service drive far enough from the Cognition Tech plant so they could see the parking lot clearly with minimum danger of being seen themselves. It was a cloudy day with more than a hint of the imminent change of seasons. Their location was within range for the rifle but shouldn't be noticed by anyone from the plant. The edge of a warehouse gave them some shelter from discovery, but it was still pretty open.

"Come on, Joe, just sight in on that little gray two-seater. She'll walk between that and the office door. Can you get her from here ok, do you think?"

"No, the fence is in the way. I'll have to get up higher." He looked around to be sure nobody was watching and then climbed onto the roof of the car and tried again, sighting down the telescopic lens. "Yeah, yeah, I can do it, I think."

"Of course, you can do it, Joe," Diane purred at him soothingly. "You can do anything you want with all your ability!" He stood there for a moment, tall and proud, powerful and macho on the roof.

They expected to leave and come back at close to five o'clock since it was only a little after two now, but just as Joe bent to get down from the roof, they saw someone start across the parking lot. "It's her," Diane whispered. "This is fantastic! Get her now, Joe, and let's get out of here!"

He sighted down the barrel again, said "Yup, it's her!" and pulled the trigger once, pumped the bolt, and shot again. They watched her fall and lie still. Joe almost fell himself, getting down off the car. They made sure no one saw them leaving the scene. As a precaution, they took back roads on the return to Fred's apartment, driving carefully so as not to attract attention, but watching out the rear window and half expecting to hear sirens any moment. Once they were safely inside the apartment, Joe cleaned the gun thoroughly, ejecting the spent casing, and they returned it to Fred's closet, first making sure to wipe off their fingerprints.

"I need a drink! Anybody else?" Diane started to shake. This was something new for her, and reality was setting in. Besides, she hadn't had any cocaine in the last few hours.

"Yeah!" Joe's face was white, and he felt a little faint. He had suddenly realized what he just did; he was a murderer! Diane glanced at him and then sat him down quickly and pushed his head down between his knees. He rocked back and forth, groaning.

"Hey now! You did great, Joe. You know it had to be done!" She looked at Ken, the only calm one in the group. "Let's go to your place and get a drink and wait for the news on TV!"

****

Violet started across the parking lot on her way to the post office to mail a large express package to Chris in Houston. She was thinking if she hurried she might get a chance to stop at the shoe store near there on her way back. They had a big sale starting today, and she needed to replace her black pumps. Suddenly, without warning, she felt a searing pain in her back. The world disappeared, and she fell, smashing her head on the ground. The package she carried and the contents of her purse scattered across the pavement.

Perceptor sounded the alarm, and Gloria responded, "What is it?"

"In the parking lot, a woman is lying on the ground. She's been shot."

"Violet!" Gloria shouted, running toward the front entrance. "It's Violet!" She slammed through the door with Fred and Cindy close at her heels. Fred passed her in the lot and was kneeling beside Violet when the women got there. "Perceptor, call nine-one-one for an ambulance!" Gloria felt for a pulse. "Is she dead?"

Fred held Violet's hand in his as grief and rage swept over him, leaving him not knowing whether to cry or to yell and scream. He moaned. "Why? Why would anyone want to hurt her?" Suddenly, he realized it was a gunshot and that it had come from somewhere nearby, and there had to be a person on the other end of that "somewhere." He jumped up. "Perceptor, where did the shot come from?"

"From the north-east about two hundred yards."

Fred was on his way almost before Perceptor finished. He dashed across the parking lot, along the high chain-link fence, across the street and a large gravel lot beside an old warehouse. No one was there. He looked farther, running back and forth and looking back over his shoulder to make sure he could still see Violet on the ground from wherever he was. Finally, he came to his senses and realized whoever shot Violet was long gone now. He walked quickly back toward the office, his throat aching with unshed tears.

The emergency unit had arrived, and the team members were working on Violet. Soon they lifted her onto a stretcher with a bottle draining its contents into her through a tube. He suddenly realized what they were doing, so she must not be dead!

That thought revived him. He stood with Gloria, watching them load the stretcher into the ambulance. "What do we do now?" he asked her.

"Nothing until I've discussed things with Perceptor and with Chris!" Gloria stood wringing her hands. She swallowed hard and tried to think. "Why would anyone want to kill Violet?" she asked him, not expecting an answer. "They must have thought it was me!" Her eyes widened at the thought. "Someone must be trying to kill me, but why? What would that gain anyone?" She fled into her office and spoke to Perceptor. "I have to talk to Chris, fast!" Chris would know what to do!

"They did *what*?" He shouted at Gloria through Perceptor's voice.

"Shot Violet, Chris. She's not dead, at least not yet. But why would anyone want to shoot her? I keep thinking they must have thought it was me!"

It was strange listening to Chris's words through Perceptor's voice. "Why would anyone want to shoot you? Okay, listen, obviously we have to call the police on this one. But ask them not to reveal she's still alive. Let's let whoever did this think she's dead, at least for now. I'll call the police for you. They'll be there shortly. Don't say any more than you have to."

He paused, thinking. "I have to stay here for this demonstration…can't risk losing our chance now! But I'll be on the next plane home as soon as it's over tomorrow! Gloria, be sure Perceptor is with you all the time, okay?"

"Yeah, okay, Chris. We'll handle it now. Sorry I had to bother you. I guess I panicked!"

"You had a right to panic after what you've just been through! I love you, Gloria!"

"I love you, Chris! Good luck on the test. We'll get the package to you ASAP!"

Fred paced the hallway waiting for Gloria. *Sure wish Dad were here, he'd know what to do! Maybe this wouldn't have happened if he'd been here.*

When she opened her door again, he hurried into her office. "Gloria, I'm going to the hospital and be with Violet," he told it to her but looked at her for an okay.

"When the police have come and gone, that's a good idea, but they'll most likely want to talk to us first. Cindy," she called. "Come on in here, please." When Cindy arrived, tearful and red-cheeked, she sat them both down and took a deep breath herself. "We have to keep clear heads now! It'll be hard, I know, but when the police come any minute now, Chris wants us to say as little as possible. Answer their questions but don't elaborate on anything. Don't volunteer any information, okay?"

They nodded, but she saw their questioning looks. "I don't know for sure why, but Chris wants the killer to think he succeeded, at least for now, so he's talking with the police himself. He'll be back late tomorrow, and then we'll find out what he has in mind. Perceptor, you tell the police where the shot came from and answer their questions, but don't tell them anything else either. Understand?"

"Yes, Gloria, I understand."

"Oh, and Chris wants a robot to stay with me all the time. I guess he's afraid they might have been trying to get me instead of Violet."

"Yes, I understood that." Perceptor acknowledged.

The doors banged open, and they were soon "up to their ears" in police officers asking questions, taking pictures, wanting to know all about Violet and particularly about why someone would want to kill her. For a few minutes, all was bedlam, but finally it was over, and the last officer left. Fred fairly flew out of the lot right after him, tires squealing.

"Whew!" Cindy sighed, sinking into her chair. "What a day! I feel as if a truck ran over me!"

"Yeah." Gloria agreed. "We've had about all we can take for one day. Let's lock up and go home. Just be careful not to talk to anyone about all this!"

After the others left, Gloria walked out to the lab to tell the crew there what happened. They were shocked and solicitous, hovering over Gloria protectively. She would have been amused if she hadn't been so shaken. "Charlie, I need a robot unit to be my companion, just in case."

"Great idea." Charlie agreed enthusiastically. "Perceptor will take care of you, all right!" He turned to Perceptor One. "Which unit can we spare for Gloria?"

"Unit four," Perceptor responded, even as that robot entered the lab. "Try not to worry, Gloria. We'll not let anything happen to you."

"Thanks, Perceptor. You sound like Chris!" She couldn't help being fond of the odd creation. He had a real personality, no matter what the men believed. She felt safe with unit 4, and they left the lab together looking an oddly mismatched couple—the beautiful lady and the ugly metal robot.

CHAPTER 24

*I*n Houston, Chris and the NASA officials met in the cluttered warehouse, outside the offices filled with computers and file cabinets. (The file cabinets held mostly backup disks and catalogs, books, and pictures.) The three tight-lipped, frowning, briefcase-carrying bureaucrats poked into different corners. Two youngish men and one middle-aged woman had been assigned this project and were making sure to do their jobs efficiently.

"We're ready to go with this now," Chris told them. "We have the last bugs worked out of the space station." The officials glanced at each other. Chris saw the look but ignored it and continued.

"The new solar panels are working at peak efficiency, and the robots are completely trained in how to assemble the station and run it once it's in operation. It'll only take us a day or two now to have the Carson II ready to lift off. Our new engines are tested and working beautifully. We only need to finish setting up at the launch pad, and we can do that as soon as we get the go-ahead from Washington."

Ms. Pinckney rolled her eyes heavenward. The pinch-nosed one asked, "How ya gonna do all that using just those crazy robots? What happens if something goes wrong? How they gonna handle that?" Masterson poked his finger at Chris's chest as he spoke.

"Yeah." Jones agreed. "They may be okay to help when somebody's there to fix 'em if something goes wrong, but how ya gonna take care of any glitches when they're up there all by themselves?"

"You seem to think these robots can do the same things our astronauts can do. That could be a costly error in judgment on your part!" Ms. Pinckney frowned at Chris over her glasses, obviously trying to intimidate him. Her shrill voice was more irritating than her manner.

Chris kept his temper with effort and explained once more about Perceptor. He knew it was hard for people to understand an artificial brain with real intelligence. He could see by their expressions they didn't buy anything he said, so he finally called in the Perceptor units. "Ask any question you like." He encouraged. Chris threw in some questions of his own, and Perceptor answered them in his usual capable manner.

Masterson and Jones were suitably impressed, and Ms. Pinckney figured there was some trick behind it all. She didn't trust this Carson fellow. "I suppose maybe they can do it at that." Masterson conceded. "But how about the weapons? Can we trust them to shoot only the right targets and only at the right time?"

"We can trust them." Chris assured him. "And besides, we'll be in constant communication with them from Earth." He turned and stared out the window for a minute. "But even if we should lose contact, they would know what to do, and I would trust them to do the job well."

"Lose contact? You mean you think the Moslems actually might attack again?" Jones stared at Chris, wondering what made a fellow like that tick. Everyone knew the United Nations president, Apollos Hercainian, had things under complete control now.

"Yes, there's a real chance they might if we don't get the go-ahead soon and get this station launched!"

The interrogators left, and Chris watched them go with a sigh. Lord, please let them approve this, and soon!"

As Chris returned to the main office, Ray Gonzales was coming to find him. "The package got here. Jim's working on it right now."

"Great! That's the last thing we needed for our demonstration." Chris headed for the shop area with Ray right behind him. They entered the workroom as Jim was just screwing on the last part, modifying the robot that would assemble the huge parts in space. He gave it shorter, stronger legs and made the shoulders and arms stronger and longer. The Perceptor unit looked a little like a big metal spider, but Chris thought it was beautiful.

"Let's give him a test run and see whether Perceptor One knows what he's doing as an engineer."

"It's a little late now if he doesn't." Jim grinned, but he put the little robot through his paces, checking his mobility and strength. He made sure the unit could handle the long pieces of material he would maneuver in space and watched how he attached them.

"Works hundred percent! Charlie and the boys did a great job with the body." Jim looked at Chris for his reaction.

Chris nodded slowly and seriously. "We're ready. Now let's hope those three stooges use some sense and give us the approval this afternoon! We don't need any more runaround. We have to get the space station up and running, and fast!"

****

By the time the evening news came on, Diane was too drunk to understand it, but Joe and Ken listened with great interest to a report of the shooting. The camera panned over the Cognition Tech building and the parking lot, stopping to show the spot where Violet fell. They showed a bad photo of Violet. "The victim was identified as Violet Welford. An assassin shot her as she was leaving the Cognition Tech office, where she worked as a secretary. Police so far have no clues to the identity of the attacker, but the investigation continues. In other news, the local water shortage is reaching the acute stage and residents are urged…" Ken clicked the set off.

"Looks like we're in the clear. There's no way they can connect us with Violet, is there? We should be hearing from Fred. I wonder where he is, anyway." Joe worried.

"The way he felt about Violet, he's probably out getting drunk like his mother! I hope he doesn't find out we did this, but I suppose he'll figure it out eventually." Ken stood up and stretched, surveying his cluttered room. "Let's get some food, I'm starved!"

"How can you eat at a time like this?" Joe demanded. Then he realized he was hungry too. He turned to Diane. "What about her?"

"Bring her along, some food will do her good too. We'll get some coffee into her and see if we can sober her up." They straightened her clothes and combed her hair for her and walked her out to the car. But by the time they got to the restaurant, Diane had fallen asleep in the backseat, so they gave up and left her there while they dined and celebrated without her.

"We'll call Jong Lee tomorrow. We certainly have all the information together to give him now." Ken felt confident again now that he was fed, and it appeared that they had gotten away with their deed.

"We'll have to let Diane call him." Joe cautioned him. "She's the one he contacted first, you know. And she won't like it if we take over…"

"Yeah, I guess you're right." Ken conceded. "And besides, she's the one who has the stuff for him. It's all safely hidden at Fred's place, isn't it?"

"You know it is. You helped put it there!"

"Yeah, yeah…but I'll feel better when we deliver it safely to Jong Lee!" They ordered a sandwich and coffee for Diane and carried it out to her, but she was still sleeping, so they took her home to Fred's apartment and put her on her bed, setting the food on the table beside her.

"Let's get out of here before Fred gets home!" Joe was nervous and edgy.

"Fine by me." Ken agreed, and they left hurriedly.

****

Violet struggled to free herself from the great weight that seemed to be holding her down, pressing on her chest. She was having trouble breathing, and something was over her nose! What a terrible dream this was! She gasped and opened her eyes.

It wasn't a dream. She was in bed, but she couldn't move. There were bandages around her chest and tubes stuck into her arms and some kind of machine over her nose! She tried to raise her arms to push the thing away, but she couldn't move one arm, and her other hand was being held by someone. Her head moved a little, and Fred was up and standing over her immediately. "Violet!" He choked. "You're awake!"

He pushed the buzzer for the nurse, who came on the run. "She's awake, is she?" She checked Violet's pulse and wiped her forehead and then left to call the doctor. "He wanted to know right away if she woke up," she said over her shoulder as she trotted out of the room.

Fred saw the fright in Violet's eyes. "It's okay, dear. You're in a hospital. You've been shot in the back, but now that you're awake, you'll make it! Just rest now. I'll be right here with you." But just then, Doctor Spencer came into the room and asked Fred to wait outside while he examined Violet again. "I'll be right back." He assured her. He hung around outside the door, and when the doctor left the room, Fred accosted him. "How is she, Doctor? Will she make it? Will she be okay?"

"The bullet nicked her left lung and the spleen…missed her heart. I got the bullet out and patched up the spleen. Now it all depends on her and what condition her body was in before this happened. She suffered a concussion too from striking her head when she fell. We have no medical history for her, but if she was well-nourished and kept in good condition, and if she had no other medical symptoms we don't know about, she could come out of this with minimal problems."

Fred sighed with relief. He felt as though a hand that had been gripping his heart was suddenly removed, allowing the blood to flow once more. "Thanks, Doctor!"

"She could still use some good solid prayers, son! She's not out of the woods yet."

The doctor strode away down the long sterile hall, and Fred leaned against the wall just briefly, and then he shook himself, ran his hand through his thick brown hair, and re-entered Violet's room. Her eyes were closed, but when he took her hand, she opened them and looked at him "Who did this to you, Violet? Do you know?"

Her eyes closed again and then opened once more. He took that as a no. "Do you know anybody who might possibly have a reason to kill you?" Her eyes closed again, and this time they stayed closed, and she slept. Fred stayed with her through the night, sitting in the chair by her bed. He dozed off a few times, waking with a start, as his head fell forward. Finally, he laid his head against the bed and napped till morning.

****

That same morning, Diane, Ken, and Joe were together once more in Ken's room. Diane was hungover and was grouchy and mean. The men tried to avoid crossing her, though that was proving difficult.

"You want me to call Jong Lee and set up a meeting to turn over the papers?" Ken asked, trying to be helpful.

"Not likely!" Diane snarled at him. "I'm the one who works with Jong Lee! I'll call and set up the meeting, thank you very much!" She snatched the phone and began to punch the buttons, missed a punch twice, then finally got the number and talked with Lee. "We have what you want," she told him. "Now we're ready to turn the stuff over, but you be sure to come prepared to pay us! You can have the information when we get the money, okay?"

"It will take me a little time to get the money for you," Jong told her. "But I will have it by Friday. I'll call and tell you where to bring the papers. Do you have what we want?"

"Everything! Just name your place and time, and we'll be there with it." She hung up the phone.

Jong Lee smiled to himself. It had been easy. He hoped they had the complete plans, but whatever they had would surely help Kim Myong and his engineers figure out the secrets. Now all he had to do was pick up the information from his stooges and then eliminate the evidence. It shouldn't be difficult; their greed made them gullible.

****

Chris stepped off the plane into the glow of the late afternoon sun. The east sides of the mountains were darkening in the distance, but slanting rays lit up the yellow and gold of the few leaves still clinging to the trees. It was good to be back in Colorado.

He called Gloria. "Hi, honey, how are things at the office?" He listened a moment and then responded, "Yes, we passed all the tests, and I think we'll have our approval soon. If we don't, I'll talk to the President again myself! But I expect they'll come through this time. I know Perceptor impressed them. Listen, Gloria, I'm going to stop at the hospital to see Violet, and then I plan to go over to the police station and talk to Captain Kelly...No, Jim stayed in Houston to help oversee the project. Ray needs him worse than we do right now. I'll see you later."

He hung up the phone, located his solar car in the crowded long-term parking lot, and headed for the hospital. When Chris walked into Violet's room, Fred was still there, haggard and unkempt, a far cry from the usually well-groomed, handsome man Chris was used to seeing. Fred rose unsteadily as his father came in.

"Hey, son!" Chris clapped him on the shoulder and hugged him with one arm. "You'd best go on home and get some rest yourself. Violet will be okay for a while. I just spoke with Dr. Spencer, and he says she's holding her own pretty well for now. You go on now, and I'll talk with you about this tomorrow morning after you're rested."

Fred protested, but he really was exhausted and finally left to go home and fall into bed. There he dreamed he was a caped avenger, making the world safer for innocent people against the forces of evil.

Violet had been thinking after the pain eased somewhat and the sedation wore off, letting her mind function again. She'd turned things over and over in her mind. Who could have done such a thing to her and why? Her first thought was that Karadshie's group might have been responsible, but that didn't make sense; they were all dead! Then suddenly it had dawned on her—Diane! Diane must have been in collusion with Fred! And Violet had opened herself right up to this. But then, it didn't make sense that Fred was sitting beside her and holding her hand if he was part of the plot. It was too confusing, but maybe Chris could figure things out. She'd tell him what she knew and let him take it from here. Violet was just too tired.

Chris sat down by the bed and took her hand, and then he prayed for God to heal her! She was deeply moved by his prayer and was afraid to speak for fear the tears would come. He sat silently for a moment, and then he started telling her about when he was shot in the back himself. And he told her about meeting Jesus and the great love he had felt and about his second chance. She hung on his every word. So that was the difference between Chris and most other people she knew! It explained some of his idiosyncrasies. Then he asked, "Do you have any idea who might have done this to you, Violet, and why?"

It was hard for her to talk, and she took a long time, but she managed to first thank him for telling her about Jesus and then to tell him about her meeting with Diane and her suspicions of Fred. It sickened Chris to think his son might be a traitor, but it was Diane who upset him most. He turned the information over in his mind. *She has to be in this with someone else. She isn't capable of a thing like this alone. And it has to be someone with power and money for her to take the chances she's taking. I wonder which of my enemies she's in bed with.*

He thanked Violet for telling him what she suspected and for being loyal to him and Gloria. They talked quietly for a few more minutes, and then Chris left, saying he'd be back again to visit.

Violet thought about the visit for a long time after he was gone. Chris had given her a great honor, she knew. At least, she had never heard his story before, and he had been written about a lot, especially lately. That TV evangelist, Dr. Conrad Braxton, often mentioned he felt Chris had sold out to Satan. From what she had just heard, Braxton couldn't be more wrong! She came face-to-face with the realization that she felt more than admiration for Chris Carson. She was in love with him! It wasn't a happy thought. She had stolen his technology. She had lied and cheated and played up to Fred. Poor Fred, who was trying so hard to be like his father!

Misery rolled over her in waves of grief. Her whole life had been nothing but a failure ever since her mother died. She had worshipped money, had spent her whole rotten life chasing after money in one form or another. It was as though suddenly she could see herself as God saw her. It wasn't a comforting sight! She closed her eyes and prayed. "Oh, Lord God, if you can do something with me...if you can help me be a better person...if you can forgive me for all the miserable, wasted years, Lord, please show me what to do. I want to know Jesus like Chris does. Oh please, Lord, help me!"

Unseen angels praised God as unseen demons fled the scene, defeated.

Hot tears rolled down Violet's cheeks and into her neck, but she hardly noticed as she laid all her past sins, troubles, and problems at Jesus's feet. When the weeping was over, she felt clean somehow, and a new feeling had replaced her guilt and confusion. She was light, calm, and peaceful, as though a great weight had lifted from her, and she was being held in comforting arms as a father would hold an infant and loved…deeply loved.

CHAPTER 25

hris pondered the situation while he drove downtown to the police station. He considered Diane and wondered what to do about her if it was true she'd conspired to steal his technology, and especially if she'd tried to kill Violet. He spoke aloud. "Lord, I can't let her go to prison for life or get the death penalty. She's the mother of my children! What should I do about her?"

He arrived at the station without remembering how he got there. He pulled into the crowded parking lot and then sat there for a few seconds, gathering his thoughts. Finally, he got out of the car, straightened his clothes, and entered the big brick building, looking for Captain Kelly.

"About time you got here, Mr. Carson! Why in the world do you want us to make people think Violet Welford is dead? What do you have up your sleeve? It ain't easy to keep the press from finding out, you know, but in view of your unusual position in the world these days, well…" Kelly drummed his stubby fingers on the desktop. "Let's hear your story!"

"No story, just seems like it'll be a lot easier to catch whoever did this if they think Violet is dead and can't tell us anything. He'll be more likely to be careless and won't have to go into hiding or anything, you know. If we let the killer think he was successful—for a while, at least—it'll give us time to track him down while keeping Violet safe for the time being. I wouldn't want him to try to finish her off!" Then he thought of something else. "I guess we'll have to stage a funeral for her, won't we?"

"Don't worry, I'll arrange that. Maybe the killer won't be as careful if he thinks we haven't any way to track him down. We're sure hoping Violet can give us some clue as to who it might be! She should be able to talk with us soon. Dr. Spencer said he'll call us." Captain Kelly paced behind his desk, scratching his bald head absently. "This is a strange case, Carson, especially given all the spooky stuff your company is into. They may have been after your wife, I suppose… maybe to get some leverage on you! But we'll do all we can to catch whoever did this! You know, the killer may even attend the funeral. We'll pay special attention to the mourners."

"An excellent idea." Chris stood up and shook Kelly's hand. "Thanks a lot, Captain. Let's keep in close touch on this, okay?"

"You got it. Oh! I nearly forgot. We did find a spent casing from a .338 rifle beside the old warehouse near your plant. Don't know what that will do for us yet, though." He waved Chris out and turned back to his desk.

****

Fred woke Thursday morning feeling better, and he showered and dressed as he listened to the news on TV. The situation with the Arab countries looked more hopeless every day. Ever since the first war with Iraq, when the United States and UN troops had let Saddam Hussein live rather than thoroughly finish the job, things had gone from bad to worse. The Jews wouldn't give up Jerusalem, the Christians wanted Jerusalem, and the Moslems most certainly would not even talk about the possibility of giving up Jerusalem. If there were another battle, Russia would support the Islamic side.

The world was on the verge of complete catastrophe! If only the president would wake up and realize what he was doing before he pushed through legislation turning the country over to the UN! Fred hoped his dad could get approval for the space station quick!

Then the local news announcer came on, and after some other trivia regarding the weather, he gave a brief update on the shooting. He said the weapon that shot Violet Welford was a .338 rifle. They had no clues yet to the killer. Fred perked his ears at that information. *That's interesting.* My own rifle is a .338 Winchester. At least, whoever did it knows guns.

He admired his reflection in the glass as he brushed his teeth, checking out his smile at the same time as he tried to replace the cap on the toothpaste. He fumbled, dropping the cap. It bounced off the vanity to the floor and rolled behind the wastebasket. "Drat!" he muttered as he got down on his knees to reach back beside the vanity for it. He happened to glance into the wastebasket as he got up again. *What's this?* He reached in the basket and retrieved the spent casing from a .338 rifle shell.

Fred sat on his bed, holding the casing and thinking. Finally he rose, walked into Diane's bedroom, and shook her gently. "Mom, are you going to breakfast with me?" She groaned and rolled over. "Come on, Mom, get up and get dressed. Let's have breakfast together, huh?"

Diane never could resist "Freddie," so she dragged her protesting body out of bed and pulled on slacks and a shirt. They went to a chain restaurant nearby and ordered coffee and fruit and muffins. "I heard on the news that Violet was shot with a .338 rifle," Fred said conversationally.

"Oh?" She paid close attention to the business of buttering her muffin.

Diane didn't offer any other response, so Fred continued, "I thought that was interesting since my own rifle is a .338."

"Yeah, interesting." She eyed him warily. *What's he leading up to, anyway?*

"Yes, and then I happened to find this in the wastebasket." He held out the casing. "I don't suppose you know anything about this?"

Diane dropped her muffin. She picked it up again while trying to think. She put it on her plate and looked at him. "Oh, Fred, I was hoping you wouldn't have to know about this! But I guess you're smarter than we gave you credit for." Her voice lowered, and she leaned forward toward him. "You won't like this, I know, but listen to me, Fred. Violet knew you were copying information from the files. She asked me to talk to you and try to stop you so she wouldn't have to tell Chris about it. Imagine! Good thing she talked to me instead of him, isn't it? Anyway, you can see why we had to kill her, Fred.

We couldn't have her telling on us, could we?" Diane looked at him appealingly.

Fred suddenly saw his mother as she really was. It was as though someone removed a blindfold he had worn for years, letting in the light, and he was filled with disgust. How could he have been so stupid as to go along with such a vicious scheme in the first place? Nausea rose in his throat. He must have been blind and deaf all these years! He pitied his mother, and at the same time he understood more about his father. Memories flew through his mind with a new interpretation now that his eyes were opened. But he knew enough to be careful right now, so with difficulty, he stifled his feelings and simply nodded slowly, reluctantly. "I guess you did what you had to do, but I sure wish it could have been different. Poor Violet!"

Diane had been holding her breath, waiting for Fred's response. She sighed with relief. "She was older than I am, Fred! It's about time you came to your senses anyway. Violet was only after money! She was always like that from the time she was a young girl. You're better off without her tempting you and making you crazy!" Diane's face looked flushed and puffy, and her hands shook as she held her coffee cup. She needed a drink!

Somehow, Fred managed to keep his temper and deliver his mother back to the apartment without telling her Violet was not dead but only badly injured. She would have found her and finished the job, he thought. "When are we meeting with Mr. Lee to deliver the papers?" he asked innocently.

"Friday sometime…oh, that's tomorrow! We'll be rich, Freddie. We'll be rich tomorrow!"

"Yeah." Fred agreed. "Rich." He let her out at the apartment building. "I better get to the office. We don't want them to suspect anything, do we?"

She leaned over and gave him a peck on the cheek. "Okay, love, I'll see you this evening. Let's have dinner with Ken and Joe so we can plan how to deliver the stuff tomorrow." She waved, and he drove off down the street, but instead of heading toward the office, he turned right and continued around the block. He parked across the street where he could watch the recessed door of the old brick building without being noticed. Then he settled down to wait.

About an hour later, Diane came out and headed for the bus stop on the corner. He watched until the bus came, and she got on it, and then he quickly entered his apartment and retrieved the papers—all of them—and carried them out to his car. Fred was an emotional mess by this time, thinking about Violet, about Diane, about Ken Herman, Joe Donner and Jong Lee, about his Dad, and about himself. He wasn't sure exactly what to do, but somehow he would try to undo the harm he'd done!

Maybe he could just burn all the stuff, and nobody would ever be the wiser. But no, that wouldn't work. When Diane and the others found out what he'd done, they'd probably kill him just as they tried to kill Violet. What a mess! He drove slowly, thinking. *Strange how nothing seems to count in some people's lives except money. They'll do anything to get money! Except Dad...I remember he's turned down some huge offers for Perceptor.*

Finally, Fred came to a decision. He would take his chances with Chris. So he turned toward Cognition Tech, and when he arrived at the office, he simply carried the papers down the hall into his dad's office and put the whole pile on his desk.

Chris got up from his desk to close the door, then turned to his son. "Is this all of it?" Fred nodded.

"Want to tell me about it, son?"

Fred nodded again. What a different reaction this was than he'd expected! Chris was looking at him with love and waiting to hear what had happened. Fred collapsed into the chair across from the big desk and started at the beginning, when he was five years old. He told Chris how he'd felt when Chris left them. He poured out his old resentment and grief and told him how, while growing up, he felt so sorry for his mother, even though she was often drunk or high. He felt it was Chris's fault for leaving. He told about Diane's approaching him with the idea to steal the plans for Perceptor, to sell them to Jong Lee for Kyutu Company.

He finished, telling how he'd felt that morning when Diane told him they'd had to kill Violet and why...and how he had finally realized what Diane was, and he didn't want to be involved with her anymore. "And that's why I brought the papers back again, and now they'll probably try to kill me too!"

"I don't understand, Fred. Did you and Diane do this alone? Did Diane shoot at Violet? I can't believe she could handle that gun, even if she were capable of killing her friend. Or was it this Jong Lee who shot her?" Chris shook his head as though to try to clear it so he could understand.

"Oh, gosh! No! I guess I forgot to tell you about the others. You remember Ken Herman?" Chris nodded. Okay, now it made sense! "And Joe Donner?"

"Oh, not Joe too?"

"Yeah. Mom seems to have something personal going with him."

"No kidding. With Joe Donner? I can hardly believe it!" Chris was pacing now, coming to grips with this new development. "Anyone else in the group?"

"No, that's all." Fred got up and stood in front of the windows, looking out at the mountains. He felt good to have it all out in the open. He was ready to pay for his part in the conspiracy. "I'm just so glad Violet didn't die! I can hardly believe they'd shoot a perfectly innocent person like that!" He turned back to Chris. "Oh, and I didn't tell Mom Violet's still alive. I'm sure they'd try to finish the job. They can't afford not to!"

"Great, son! We're a lot more likely to catch them if they don't know we're on to them! Tell me where Ken and Joe are staying, and I'll let Captain Kelly and his force handle them." Chris's eyes clouded, and he too turned to look out his window at the mountains, a view that usually brought him peace. "I'll have to decide what to do about Diane, but I don't know how we can save her from herself."

"What about me, Dad?" Fred stood erect, chin up, and waited to hear his sentence.

Chris studied his youngest son for a moment, silently praying for guidance. "Well, Fred, you brought back what you stole. You seem genuinely sorry for what you did. And you've cooperated fully in telling me what I needed to know. I guess you've made amends as well as you can for now. Help me finish up this mess, and we'll decide where to place you in the company later. First, we have to get the space station up and operating so we can keep an eye and an ear in the sky."

Fred sighed gratefully, and then he reminded Chris. "They're supposed to turn the papers over to Jong Lee tomorrow. When they find out I took them, my life won't be worth much either!"

Chris picked up the phone and punched in Captain Kelly's number. "Captain, I know the guys who shot Violet Welford. Well, I don't know which one pulled the trigger, but they were both involved! It seems they stole some plans from my office, and Violet suspected them, so they wanted to shut her up! They plan to meet their contact from Kyutu Company tomorrow to turn my papers over to him, but I've recovered those papers without their realizing it yet."

"Wait a minute, not so fast, Mr. Carson. Who are the killers? How did you find out who they are? How did you get your papers back?" Kelly wasn't going along with Chris on this wild story. "What proof do you have? We can't operate on hearsay, you know!"

"Oh…well, it happens they're old acquaintances of mine, Ken Herman and Joe Donner. They were involved in a business deal with me some years ago. I'll tell you all about it later, Captain. They're here in town now, and the immediate problem is, what will happen when they show up without the papers tomorrow? I know Kim Myong, and he's a cold-blooded character! As for how I found out, I can't tell you that right now, but obviously my source was correct since I have my property back again!"

"Listen, Carson, you'd better come in here and let us get the facts from you about this!" Captain Kelly wasn't so sure Chris Carson wasn't making a false accusation against some old enemies to get them out of his way. "You didn't even tell us your papers were missing!"

"The thieves got into my private files and made copies, so I wasn't aware they had stolen my plans until I got them back!" Chris felt himself getting deeper and deeper into hot water. "Why don't you talk to Violet Welford, and I'll come down and tell you about this in person a little later, Captain. Thanks." He hung up the phone quickly, leaving the captain still talking, and turned to Fred. "I've put both my big feet in it this time. Let's move, son! Kelly will have his men on their way to pick me up by now." He locked the stack of papers in his file cabinet as he said, "Perceptor, send a robot unit to guard my office. Don't let anyone touch my files!"

"Okay, Chris!" Perceptor responded.

Seconds later, Chris and Fred were on their way, only taking time to grab a Perceptor brain unit. Chris called back over his shoulder, "Cindy, if anybody's looking for me, I'm out of the office until late tomorrow! You have no idea where I can be found, okay?"

"Yes, sir." Cindy watched curiously as they pulled out of the front parking lot in the solar car.

Chris wheeled around back and parked by the door to the lab. They dashed in, startling Charlie and Mick. Chris tossed his car keys to Charlie. "I need to trade cars with you, quick!" He saw their questions coming. "I've got a temporary problem with the police, and they know my car. I have to hide awhile. I'll take good care of it, promise!" Charlie handed Chris the keys and watched Chris and Fred dash out to the back lot again and roar away in his big old Cadillac, leaving the solar car. Charlie and Mick looked after them, shaking their heads.

"What now?" Charlie wondered.

It wasn't more than two minutes when the police cruiser pulled in. Poor Cindy was put on the grill and all but cooked for lunch. She stood firm and told them nothing, so they poked around the office looking for Chris on their own. The Perceptor unit stood menacingly in Chris's private office, and the men could see Chris wasn't there, so grudgingly they left, leaving a stakeout team behind to watch the office.

"I wonder what in the world is going on," Cindy said to Perceptor, but Perceptor didn't respond.

In the Cadillac, Chris said to Perceptor, "Tell Gloria I'm safe. Fred and I are together, and we'll see her by tomorrow evening. If the police contact her, she really doesn't know anything!"

CHAPTER 26

*D*iane left a note on the table, telling Fred to meet her at Ken's hotel room, and headed directly for the hotel. She had to tell Ken and Joe what had happened before Fred got there. Once there, she told them the story, finishing with "I had to tell Fred. He found the shell casing, and he figured it out by himself, anyway!" Diane looked accusingly at Joe. "It was dumb to put it in the wastebasket!"

Joe turned huffy. "Well, some people are just a whole lot smarter than others, aren't they? I should've let you do the job by yourself!"

Diane backed off. "I didn't mean anything, Joe." Her voice became low and sexy. "Come sit by me and let me make it up to you." She patted the cushion beside her, and he obediently sat down, pouting like a child. She rubbed his back for him while she talked. "Anyway, Fred said he understood, and he seemed to be okay. He went on to the office so they wouldn't be suspicious." Joe felt better all the time as her fingers continued to rub and massage him lovingly.

Ken was livid. He wished he could get rid of all of them and do the job by himself. What a bunch of losers!

The three of them spent the day bickering. They took turns suggesting various plans that the others immediately poked holes into. By dinnertime, they had worked themselves into complete confusion. It didn't help that Diane sneaked a little snort once or twice, along with the liquor they all consumed.

"So where is Fred?" Ken asked later. "You said he agreed to come to dinner with us and help plan, didn't you?"

"I guess he could've misunderstood. He was pretty upset about Violet and probably isn't thinking straight right now. He'll be okay, I guess. Anyway, he can't back out now after he copied all the files for us!"

"You'd better be right!" Ken muttered.

"Why don't we leave him a message to join us at the restaurant when he gets home?" Diane suggested. "Then we can go on without him. When he shows up, we'll just tell him what we've decided, and he'll go along with us, anyway."

"We don't want Jong Lee to grab the papers without paying us!" Ken warned. "So how do we make sure he pays us before we turn them over?"

"How about if we only show him a few papers and give him the rest after he pays?"

"If he'll go along with that. He may insist on seeing them all to make sure we have what he wants. I know I wouldn't pay someone several million dollars without making sure I got what I paid for!" That made Diane and Joe grin in spite of the situation, knowing Ken as they did.

"What if one of us stays hidden with a gun, and if he doesn't want to pay, we'll threaten to shoot him! Then we'll take back the papers until he comes up with the cash!" Joe seemed fascinated with guns since the shooting.

"What a good idea, Joe! Isn't that a good idea, Ken?" Diane looked from Joe to Ken. "Which one of us should hide, do you think?"

"How about you, Diane? This whole thing was your idea, after all." Ken whined like a schoolboy.

"Sure, I'll do it. I wonder where he wants to meet, though. I just hope there's a good hiding place!" They had another drink all around to celebrate their plan, and then Diane asked, "Okay, where'll I get a gun? We don't need a rifle for this job, do we?"

"Happens I bought one the other day just to have around…just in case, you know!" Ken reached in his jacket pocket and pulled out a small handgun and a full bullet clip. "It's little, but the man said it's a good one and should be easy to shoot with. He called it a Wather PPK, I think. Cost me a bundle!"

"It's great!" Diane took the gun and practiced aiming. "So we're all set! Let's go have dinner." They ate at the hotel restaurant, talking about what each planned to do with their millions and drinking more than practical for people who needed to have clear heads the next day. Diane simply fell into bed when she got home, forgetting to check whether or not Fred was there.

****

Jong Lee reported to Kim Myong, "We have the plans—that is, they'll be in our hands tomorrow! I'll be on the plane with them by tomorrow afternoon."

Myong, holding the phone in his left hand, rubbed the right one over his oily hair, his eyes narrowed. "See that nothing goes wrong, Jong. I want those plans! You know how to pay our friends! Give them ample reward for their good work. We don't want anyone to feel cheated!"

Jong smiled his crafty smile. "I'll see that no one does!"

****

Chris and Fred found a small motel, and Fred booked a room under the name Johnson. "We'll hole up here till tomorrow morning, and then we'll tail Diane and see where she goes so we know what happens." They picked up hamburgers, fries, and coffee at a drive-up window. The food tasted surprisingly good.

"I guess I was hungrier than I realized." Fred admitted as he finished his second burger and licked up some catsup that oozed out on his finger.

"It's been quite a day, hasn't it?" Chris reflected. He spoke to the brain unit and, through it, to Perceptor One. "Perceptor, what's happened at the office?"

"The police came. They looked around and left again."

"I knew it!" Chris pushed the lock of hair off his forehead impatiently. "I'm not sure what to do next. We have to think!" He paced. "Can we keep Diane's name out of this and still put Ken and Joe in jail where they belong?"

Fred stared at his father wonderingly. "You'd go through all this trouble to protect Mom? Why? She stole your plans and tried to kill Violet!"

"She's still your mother, Fred, and the mother of your brother and sisters as well. I loved her once, and who knows what I may have done that drove her to be what she is now? Still, she can't go unpunished. We can't let her go back on the streets to do something like this again! I'll have to find some way to keep her out of trouble when this is over."

Fred shook his head. "I don't understand you. I just don't get it!"

So for the second time that day, Chris found himself telling about Jesus and the change he makes in the hearts and lives of those who will receive his great and unmerited gift of eternal life.

****

It was late when the phone rang, and Diane answered foggily out of a deep sleep. Jong Lee's voice told her, "Bring the plans—all of them—to the corner of Hover Road and Pike Road near the Cognition Tech plant. I will pick you up there at eleven o'clock in the morning."

"We'll be there, Jong," Diane answered. She hung up the phone. *Uh-oh! The plan won't work in a car! I guess I'll get the papers and put them in something we can carry easily, and then I'll go talk to Ken and Joe. We have to come up with another plan! I wonder where Fred is, anyway. He's making me real nervous being gone so long!*

Wide awake now, she got out her suitcase and carried it to the closet in Fred's room where they had stashed the papers. She was already reaching down to pick them up before she realized they weren't there. *Oh no! He's moved them. Now where in the world did he put the stuff?*

She searched the apartment frantically, with no luck. She stood in the living room, panting from exertion and nerves. *They're not here! Now what'll I do? Wait! Maybe Ken and Joe have them. They must have taken the stuff when I was sleeping the other night. I'd better get on over there and tell them about the meeting!*

When Ken opened the door, she stormed into the room. "Where are the papers? Why did you take them without telling me? I nearly had a heart attack when they weren't there!" Diane's eyes darted here and there, her voice was shrill, and she seemed like a madwoman as she stood in the middle of the room, disheveled and ranting.

Ken grabbed her by the shoulders. "What do you mean, where are the papers? They were in Fred's closet last time we saw them!" He shook her impatiently. "What are you trying to pull on us, Diane?"

She turned white and sat down as though she were a balloon that had just had all the air let out. "They're gone!" She looked up at them, feeling sick. "They're gone, and so is Fred!"

"What?" they shouted in unison.

"What do you mean? What's happened?" Joe begged. "You can't mean they're gone?"

"Just what are you trying to pull on us, Diane?" Ken demanded. "I know you. This is just your way to try to get all the money for yourself! Well, it's not going to work!" He looked at Joe meaningfully. "We may have to do something drastic, Joe, to get our share of this deal!" He grabbed Diane's arm threateningly.

"No! No! I didn't take the papers. I opened the closet to put them into a suitcase, and they weren't there!" She moaned, "They weren't there! Now what'll we do? Jong Lee wants to meet us tomorrow at eleven o'clock, and we don't have the papers!"

Ken saw she was telling the truth. He dropped her arm and swore. "Then Fred has them! Does he think he can get away with this? Does he really think that? Well, we'll give him something else to think about!"

Diane pulled herself up and found a glass. "I need a drink!" she said as she poured with shaking hands. "Anybody else?"

Ken took the glass from her hand. "Go back to Fred's place and get some sleep. Maybe he'll come home, and we can deal with him."

He opened the door and shoved her out into the hall. "Call us right away if anything else happens!" He watched her stumble down the hall and get into the elevator and then turned to Joe. "I don't know about you, but I think the best thing to do is meet with Jong Lee and tell him we've had a temporary setback. We just need a little more time to find Fred and get the stuff back."

He paced the room like a zoo animal trying to escape its cage and then stopped and asked the badly shaken Joe. "Say, you don't suppose Fred is trying to ace us out of this deal, do you? I'd kill him before I'd let him get away with that!"

Joe didn't answer. He had a vision of himself shooting Violet and seeing her fall. He had murdered a woman to keep this deal together! He was going to be rich! And now it was all for nothing! He'd probably be found out, and he'd lose everything! His wife would certainly leave him, and he'd go to prison too! He could never live in prison. He was a scared, shaking mess, and at that moment, he would have given all he had never to have seen Chris or Ken or Diane, especially Diane!

He mumbled something to Ken about needing to get some sleep and stumbled off to his own room. Fear was giving way to a deep, numbing depression. There was nothing left for him to live for! His life was ruined—he'd killed Violet, he was unfaithful to his wife with Diane, he'd robbed Chris Carson of his plans for Perceptor, and now it was all for nothing! What more was there to live for? How could he face life, anyway? He reached for the old bottle of medication that he used to take for his wheezing, coughing, and shortness of breath before Diane came into his life. It was strong, he guessed...at least, there was a warning not to take more than six in twenty-four hours. He took thirty of them (all that were in the bottle) with a little water and lay down on his bed, weeping.

In the corner, an ugly, leathery little demon rubbed his hands together, grinning and drooling as he waited to claim another soul for his master.

Diane let herself into Fred's apartment and marched directly to his room. *Not here yet! That ingrate...that idiot...that traitor! How could I have raised such a monster! He's just like Chris!*

She collapsed on Fred's bed. *What am I gonna do? I can't meet Jong Lee without the stuff after I told him I had it!* Her hand brushed against her jacket pocket, and she remembered the gun there. *Maybe Fred's trying to get all the money for himself! Maybe he's planning to contact Jong Lee and meet him alone!* She took the gun out, turning it over and over in her hands. She pushed the clip in and took it out and then pushed it in and left it in the gun. She had made a decision and now knew she should get some sleep until tomorrow. It was already late, and with so much depending on her having a clear head, she needed rest. Just a little cocaine first, and she'd sleep better, she was sure.

Ken Herman woke early, worried about what he'd say to Jong Lee. He called Diane, waking her from a restless sleep interrupted with vivid nightmares involving Jong Lee and Chris, Perceptor and guns. She answered grumpily, "Hullo."

"Did Fred show up?"

"I dunno. I'll go look." She set the phone down and checked Fred's room and then the bathroom and kitchen. "Nope, he's still not here. I guess we have to assume he's double-crossed us."

Ken swore "Listen, Diane, I think I'll meet Jong Lee, anyway, and tell him we need a little more time. You wanna go along?"

"I don't think so, Ken. Tell Jong I'll contact him as soon as we get straightened around again. I'm gonna try to find Fred, and when I do…" She didn't have to finish the sentence.

"I'd love to get my hands on him too, the dirty little traitor! But okay, if you're sure you don't want to go with me, I'll get Joe and see if he plans to tag along. We'll talk to you later!"

"Just be careful, Ken. Jong Lee won't be happy about this!"

Ken walked down the carpeted hall to find Joe. He knocked, but there was no answer. He knocked again. *Maybe he's in the shower.*

He used a plastic card on the lock and let himself into the room. *Joe ought to be more careful! No telling who might try to break in here. Pretty dumb not to use the dead bolt!*

He walked into the room. "Joe!" Then he saw Joe still in bed. "Hey, Joe, it's time to get up and get going!" He grabbed a shoulder and shook it. Joe's body flopped over. His mouth was open, his eyes wide. Ken dropped his hold as though burned. "Geez!" He saw the bottle and glass on the bedside table and swore again. "Oh no! Why'd you do this, Joe? What a stupid thing to do!" He felt sick at his stomach as he took a tissue from the box on the dresser and used it to pick up the phone. He asked the operator to call an ambulance and gave her the room number but hung up when she wanted to know who he was. Keeping the tissue in his hand, he wiped the doorknob on his way out and closed the door again. *I'd better get out of here. I'll go get some coffee and try to plan what to do now. This is all Fred's fault! I swear, if I ever get my hands on that kid, I'll choke the life out of his body and then use it for a boat anchor!*

He left the hotel hurriedly, heading across the street to a small coffee shop. He chose a front booth where he could see the hotel's main door. He ordered coffee and drank it black while he tried to think. It wasn't long before the ambulance screamed its way to the hotel door. Then he waited what seemed an eternity before he saw them carry out a body on a stretcher and drive away. He lifted his cup in silent salute. *Good-bye Joe, I'll miss you. You were a jerk...but a nice jerk!*

He thought about calling Diane, decided against it, and then changed his mind again. She was getting out of the shower when the phone rang. He told her about Joe. "What!" She dropped the phone and then picked it up again. "Ken, are you sure? Are you *sure* he's dead? He *can't* be dead!" A cold chill swept over her.

"Yeah, well, the ambulance took him away, anyway. Listen, Diane, we have to be cool. We don't want anybody to know we were all here together! Let's just wait and see what happens next with Joe. They'll probably call his wife, and she'll come out here, and it'll be a big mess. Better we don't get involved in it. We can't help Joe anymore anyhow! I plan to meet Jong Lee by myself now, that is, if Fred hasn't already delivered the papers himself!"

In his office, Captain Kelly was just deciding maybe he would check out Chris Carson's story, anyway.

CHAPTER 27

In a secret room somewhere in Iran, a group of men sat in easy chairs placed carefully around a priceless Persian rug. Beside each chair was a small table that held a glass with ice and a bottle of sparkling water. The group's leader was a thin, bearded, sun-blackened man in traditional Arab attire. Nadeeb Khaleev was a force to be reckoned with, who commanded the respect of the others. He was a close associate of Apollos Hercainian, the powerful new United Nations leader. Nadeeb leaned forward, his black eyes sweeping the circle of men. "We live in evil days, indeed… evil days…and the enemy is at work against us with even greater force than ever before. Truly, we must be nearing the return of our great prophet!"

There was a general murmur of agreement and then silence again as Khaleev continued, "As you know, Mohamed Karadshie and his group in America were overcome by our Satanic enemy. Something terrible and evil beyond belief sapped the life out of Karadshie and his men as they met together in a room, not unlike the meeting we are having now. It was a devil spirit sent to foil our plan to gain control of Perceptor and to destroy Cognition Tech, along with this Christopher Carson. Now we must find another way to gain that objective and obtain the great Perceptor power for the cause of Allah!"

The Arab leaders were in complete agreement. There was no doubt among them that the Perceptor intelligence had to belong to the forces of Islam alone. "With this weapon on our side, we would easily gain control of Jerusalem and the world!" They deliberated for hours to find the best possible way to proceed toward that end. At last, they decided to send a single agent to infiltrate the Cognition Tech plant and accomplish their aim. This agent was special, an expert, a chameleon. They had used him in their most secret missions, and he had been successful on every occasion as testified to by his continued existence. They summoned, briefed, and sent him on his way within a few hours.

****

Captain Kelly of the Longmont police department was frustrated and angry. He'd visited Violet Welford at the hospital and gotten nowhere. She couldn't imagine who could possibly have wanted to kill her. The only thing she could suggest was they must have thought she was Gloria. Kelly didn't buy that now. The two women looked entirely different, even from a distance. Violet's hair was longer, dark, and wavy. Gloria's was short and light brown, and she was taller and thinner than Violet.

But he finally left Violet's room when she became tired (actually her doctor threw him out). And Chris Carson had disappeared. There was an APB out on him, but nobody had seen him since he left his office the day before. His receptionist didn't know anything about any missing papers, or so she said, and the Perceptor robot was guarding the files in Chris's office! "He'd better have some darned good answers when I get hold of him, and I will!" Kelly fumed.

****

As Chris and Fred watched from across the street, a haggard, grief-stricken Diane left Fred's apartment in the morning. She took a taxi to the hotel, got into Joe Donner's little rented car, and headed toward the Cognition Tech plant. "Now what do you suppose she's up to?" Chris wondered as he and Fred followed her in Charlie's Cadillac. They drove on past as she slowed and then stopped not far from Cognition Tech. They turned around and came back in time to see Diane duck behind some shrubbery by a large manufacturing plant located near the street corner. At eleven o'clock in the morning, there was little traffic in that industrial area, and it wasn't easy to keep from being noticed, so Fred drove past again and then turned around once more and came back, parking a little behind Diane's car. They slouched down and watched. Chris could see Diane's blue jacket from where they sat. Her back was to them, though. Fred checked his watch. "Almost eleven o'clock. I'll bet she's supposed to meet Jong Lee at eleven o'clock! But where are Ken and Joe? And why is she hiding?"

In a minute or two, they spotted Ken walking toward them from the other direction. "He must have parked down the street." They got ready to duck, but Ken stopped and stood on the corner. "Now where's Joe?" Fred was puzzled. "They're usually together!"

"Uh-oh," Chris breathed as they watched a black sedan pull up beside Ken. A man rolled down the window on the passenger side and talked to Ken, who leaned in the window.

"It's Jong Lee!"

"Yeah, I figured so."

Ken talked and gestured, apparently arguing with Jong Lee, and then straightened up and seemed about to turn and walk away when he stumbled and fell to the sidewalk. The black sedan pulled away and sped out of sight. Diane ran to Ken's side and felt his neck for a pulse. She looked around to see if anyone was watching, and they ducked down quickly. She left Ken lying there, ran to her car, and drove away fast, not looking back. "Perceptor, call an ambulance, quick," Chris said as Fred prepared to follow Diane.

They started in the direction she had gone, spotted her a block or so ahead, watched her nearly sideswipe a van, and then had to brake hard for a light. When they were able to move again, she was gone! "Now where in the world…?"

"Looks like she gave us the slip!" Fred's mouth was set in a grim line. "I'll find her. If it takes all day, I'll find her!"

****

Diane was shaking so hard she could hardly drive. "I need a drink! Boy, do I need a drink!" she said out loud. Then she came close to sideswiping another car. Realizing her condition, she spontaneously pulled into a huge parking lot beside a sprawling factory—she didn't even look to see what it was—and found a space between two cars far from the building where she could park and think. She sat there, shaking and sobbing, for a long while. She felt the blood pounding in her ears with each heartbeat. Finally, she got control enough to think of something other than Ken's body on the sidewalk.

She took stock of her situation. Jong Lee showed up for the meeting, so maybe he didn't meet with Fred after all. *But then, where is Fred, and why did he take the papers? Why did Jong Lee kill Ken? Now what am I gonna do? He'll find me if he's looking for me. Sooner or later, he'll find me and kill me too!* She fingered the gun in her pocket. *Joe's dead. Ken's dead. I might as well be dead too. There's nothing left for me anymore! Chris'll find out what I've done. Fred'll probably tell him when he finds out about Joe and Ken, unless Fred still plans to bargain with Jong Lee.* She took the gun out and looked at it, feeling the cold, hard metal of the barrel. She tried putting it against her temple, her finger on the trigger. She brought it down again. She put it in her mouth. She brought it down again. *Oh, why not just do it? Just get it over with and be through with this rotten world for good!*

The answer to her question came through a still, small voice inside her…a voice Diane hadn't heard for a long, long time, but a voice she had been acquainted with as a child. And now that she heard it again, long-buried memories came flooding back. She remembered, and she began to weep again and pray. "Oh, Lord," she pleaded, "if you can hear me, and if you still care for me after all these years when I've run away from you, then please help me! Please show me what to do now! I've made such a mess of my life and my kids' lives and Chris's life. And because of me, Joe and Ken and Violet are all dead! I can't stand it, Lord! How can I live when they're all dead? Oh, Lord Jesus, if you can forgive me, please do forgive me and help me know how I can continue to live, and I'll give what's left of my life to you."

She wept and sobbed and talked to Jesus, confessing all the sin and filth, pain, misery, and selfishness…everything she could think of over all the years that had passed, not forgetting the abortion. Then she sat quietly, and the verse that came into her mind from years ago in Sunday school was that if we confess our sins, he is faithful and just to forgive us our sins, and to cleanse us from all unrighteousness. "Oh, Lord Jesus, please cleanse me. Take away the sin and greed, the drugs, and the drink and make me what you want me to be!"

Several small, evil demons fled in panic, unseen.

Diane sat there, feeling, even in the midst of her grief for Ken and Joe and Violet, the first real hope and peace she had felt since she left her parents' home years ago to go to Florida and get away from their rules and restrictions. Then Fred and Chris walked up on either side of the car. She opened the door, got out, and hugged Fred. "I'm so sorry, Fred, for getting you involved in this mess! I hope you can forgive me. I must have been out of my mind! In fact, I think I must have been out of my mind for at least the past twenty-five years! I tried to run away from God, but he's found me, and he forgives me, and now I'll face whatever the punishment is with his help. But, Fred, I'm so sorry I brought you into this mess!"

"It's okay, Mom." Fred returned her hug.

Chris took the gun from her and wrapped it in his pocket handkerchief. "You won't be needing this now." He led her to the Cadillac and opened the back door for her. "We'll call and tell the rental company where their car is, and they'll pick it up."

He turned in the seat to face her as Fred backed the Cadillac out of the parking space. "I have a feeling you can plea bargain with Captain Kelly and tell him the whole story, the honest story, in exchange for leniency. I won't press charges against you, but the attempt on Violet's life will be another thing." She suddenly caught his meaning and looked up with her face brightening, the question in her eyes. "She's not dead, Diane, you only wounded her, but she's in the hospital and will take some time to heal."

"I'm so terribly glad she's not dead!" Diane began to cry again. "Oh, Chris, the Lord is so good, and I'm so rotten! I'm the one who got Joe and Ken into this whole thing...and Fred too...and now Joe and Ken are both dead!" Her face was puffy from grief and pain, and the tears streamed down her cheeks unrestrained.

Chris pitied her, his once beautiful ex-wife. "You've been through hell itself!" He looked away from her as she blew her nose and wiped her eyes. "It must have started when you took your first fix of cocaine. That seemed to open the door for Satan and his minions to come in. You never were the same after that, Diane."

He looked straight ahead as the memories flooded his mind. "I'm glad you've come back to your senses and back to the Lord! You're going to have a hard time for a while now, but you'll make it. We'll help you as much as we can."

"We sure will!" Fred agreed.

Chris asked, "Did you say Joe is dead too?" It suddenly sank in what Diane had said. "What happened to Joe?"

"Ken said he overdosed on something."

They pulled up at the police station and walked in. In a second, officers surrounded them and pushed all three into Captain Kelly's office where they told the whole sordid story over and over again until Kelly was convinced it was true. Then he opened up to them. "We picked up the body on the corner of Hover and Pike a few minutes ago. Ken Herman was killed by a laser shot to the heart." Kelly indicated a file folder on his desk. "Joe Donner's body was full of Theophylline. He took enough to finish off a weak man and then, combined with all the alcohol in his system..."

He pointed his finger at Chris. "I'd like to be able to stick you with something just for all the aggravation you've put me through!" He let his hand drop to his side. "But under the circumstances..." He placed the file folder squarely in the center of his desk and then looked up. "So you're not pressing charges against them?"

Chris shook his head. "Sorry for all the trouble, Captain Kelly, but I couldn't let you lock me away while all this was going on. You wouldn't have believed me, you know!"

Kelly ignored that remark and turned to Diane. "I'm afraid I'll have to hold you for arraignment! The judge will most likely set bail for you and release you to Chris's custody until the trial. She nodded, and he signaled for an officer who led her away. Chris shook Kelly's hand, and he and Fred left the station together.

"You go ahead and take the rest of the day off," Chris told Fred as they put the Cadillac back in Charlie's space and took Chris's solar car again. "You have a lot to think about." He headed for the front lot. "I can't wait to see Gloria. She's not gonna believe all this!"

He walked into the office where Cindy and Gloria stared at him. "Chris, you look terrible! Where have you been? What's happened? Come in here and tell me about it!" Gloria took his arm, and they walked into her office together. Chris told her the whole story while she just kept shaking her head, saying, "I can't believe it!" and "Really?" and finally, "So where is this Jong Lee person now?"

"He's the only problem left in this mess, I guess, and his boss, Kim Myong. I have a feeling they won't give up this easily either! We'll probably be seeing Jong Lee again."

"I hope not! But meanwhile, I've been on the phone with Ray from Houston. Your approval came through from the government. He's getting ready to launch and wants to hear from you right away!"

He grabbed her and swung her around and around. "Great! Why didn't you say so? Oh, man, it won't be long now!" He headed for his own office. "I'll call Ray. Let's go home for a few minutes, and you can help me pack. I'll get right down there!"

Gloria grinned after him and then hurried out to talk to Cindy. "For a genius, sometimes he's just like a kid!" She laughed. "Will you book him on the next flight to Houston, please, Cindy? And tell anyone who calls me I'll call back later or be back in the office tomorrow."

Chris took a few extra minutes to call his friend, Sam Early, and report on the results of the prayers he and the church had sent up on behalf of Gloria and to ask them for further prayer for Violet and for Diane. He asked Sam to tell Diane's parents the situation. There would be rejoicing because Diane had come back to the Lord but sorrow for the way she'd had to go before she learned to follow him again. "It's like the parable of the lost sheep Conrad Braxton preached about so long ago. It's dangerous out on the mountains alone away from the shepherd, and the enemy is likely to kill a poor lost lamb! Conrad was right about some things, anyway!"

Sam agreed to tell the Portlands about Diane's trouble and pray about her sentence. "We'll pray for your safety too, Chris, and for success with the launch!"

"Thanks, Sam. It means a lot to know you're there and caring enough to pray for us!"

It was a gorgeous day, the mountains looked closer than usual, and the sky was cobalt blue with only a few white fluffy clouds here and there. Chris and Gloria walked out of the office together, stopping for a moment to breathe deeply of the cool, fresh air. "What a day!" Chris exclaimed. "I haven't even had time to notice up to now!"

CHAPTER 28

*R*ay and Jim were glad to see Chris. "About time you got your body back here!" Jim kidded, shaking his hand and clapping him on the shoulder. "We were about to go ahead with the whole project without you!"

"Yeah, sorry about the interruption, guys! I got tangled up with some intrigue and couldn't get back right away, but everything's under control again now. Let's get over to the launch pad and let me check things out!"

At the launch pad out in the middle of a vast flat area, the Carson II stood waiting. Its body was attached to four powerful liquid-propellant boosters that now replaced the two solid-propellant boosters NASA had formerly used. The Carson II was actually an old shuttlecraft Chris had bought from NASA and modified. The new boosters were smaller than the old type and powerful enough to take the ship to a higher orbit than NASA had been able to attain. It would be high enough for the space station.

Some materials for the station were prebuilt folded components that would fit into the shuttle and could open up in space. They'd also bought an old Grumman machine that could be loaded with reels of thin aluminum sheet to spit out a continuous triangular-shaped truss. Trusses made that way weighed less than a pound a foot and could hold over a half-ton load, and the machine could hold enough aluminum to make trusses a fifth of a mile long. (They were easy to cut to the right length.) The newly modified robot, along with the others, would be able to handle the construction handily.

Chris spent a long time going over the equipment piece by piece to make sure nothing was likely to go wrong. He finally stepped back a few paces, looked up at the towering mass of technology, and asked quietly, "Any sign of the FBI hanging around the area?"

"We haven't recognized them if they are," Jim responded. "We've tried to keep things under wraps, though, just in case."

"Let's take a look at the extra equipment then." Chris walked rapidly toward a large truck parked on the shady side of the mission control building, a low, white stucco building located at the edge of the flat barren expanse. He wiped sweat off his brow. "I want to make sure nothing happens to it at the last minute. I hope our strategy of trying to make this look like a regular mission so as not to draw any extra attention doesn't backfire. Maybe we should have built a 'fortress' to protect it." He sighed. "We can only do our best and then pray!"

"Don't worry, Chris, Perceptor has been on the job day and night. Nobody's been near the special equipment. You've disguised it well enough that they wouldn't recognize it for what it is, anyway!"

"What about the special mirrors?"

"They're ready. The government bought our explanation that we're doing some solar energy experimentation with them, so we didn't have to try to hide those."

"The other equipment is still in enough small pieces that a spy would have to be pretty doggone well-educated in physics to realize what we have in mind, and the Perceptor units are expert at assembling the coils and electromagnetic devices in zero-gravity conditions." Jim clapped Chris on the shoulder reassuringly. "We're ready, friend! Assuming no complications arise, we're ready!"

"Yeah, yeah, I guess so. Still, I'll breathe easier when we blast off!" He climbed out of the truck and started across the field again. "Time to review the troops!"

They were using four Perceptor robot units for the project. Three were their regular-shaped models and one the shorter-legged and longer-armed version. All were built with the extra-strong metal the lab had developed. They were odd-looking astronauts for sure, and Chris almost laughed as he surveyed them, lined up for his inspection. He resolved again to make a humanoid body for Perceptor as soon as he could get the time!

"We're all set for blastoff as soon as the launch crew gives us the go-ahead weather-wise. We're only waiting for your final approval." Ray grinned wryly. "It's different launching a ship that's carrying so much cargo, all those building supplies, not to mention 'the weapon'! Good thing they don't require space suits hooked up to monitors down here, nor food, nor oxygen tanks, nor waste receptacles, et cetera!" He glanced at the Perceptor units waiting for their orders. "We're going to need names for them, Chris. We can't just call them all Perceptor. It'll get too confusing!"

"Yeah, I guess so. You have anything in mind?"

Ray walked over to the first robot in line. "How about Milo?" he asked the unit. "Do you like the name Milo?"

"Milo," the Perceptor unit responded. "I like it. I am Milo!"

Ray moved to the next unit. Jim called out, "How about Jose? He looks Latin to me!"

"Is that okay with you?" Ray asked the unit.

"Jose is a fine name," the robot answered. "It is good to have a name," he added.

Ray smiled and walked over to the third unit. "How do you like the name Reuben?"

"Reuben," the robot repeated. "What does it mean?" Ray looked at Chris for help.

"I think it means something like 'I have a son,'" Chris answered. He was finding this a fascinating experience. His Perceptor units wanted their own identities!

"I am Reuben!" the robot repeated.

Ray was standing before the shorter robot when Chris spoke up. "This one is Ernie!" Ray raised an eyebrow inquiringly. "He just looks like Ernie to me!" Chris explained lamely.

"Hello, Ernie," Ray said, patting the unit on its "head."

As Ray, Jim, and Chris stood back and looked the line of robots over again, Chris observed, "You know, they seem different some-how...sort of proud."

Jim laughed. "You've been standing out in the sun too long! Let's go check with the launch team."

"Not yet, Jim. I want to talk to the 'boys' here first." He walked over and stood before the newly named Perceptor crew. "I want to be sure you understand your mission. You are to build the primary space station as fast as possible. As soon as it's in operation, assemble 'the weapon.' Then Milo and Ernie will stay and run the station, while Jose and Reuben return to Earth to get more materials and further instructions from me. Don't take instructions from anyone except me or Gloria or Charlie Morse."

He paced the line again, regarding his astronauts. "Use 'the weapon' only in the event that you see an enemy firing on any country. If that happens, you are to use 'the weapon' to destroy the fired missile, along with the source of the firing. Then report to me immediately for further instructions. If anyone or anything comes near you as if to try to board your ship or harm it, destroy that entity at once. If any agent tries to investigate your cargo here before you launch, prevent him! Nobody outside Cognition Tech must know about 'the weapon' you carry. Do you understand all this completely?"

"Yes, Chris Carson," the Perceptors responded in unison, and through them Perceptor One back in Longmont also responded.

"Then, team, finish loading, take your places in the Carson II, and wait for the liftoff signal!"

At the far end of the launch area, two men in blue coveralls wheeled a large hand truck around the end of the building. The tall skinny one sported a full mustache and walked with a limp. The shorter one wore a strange blondish-tinted wig he tried to pretend was his real hair. They both had dark glasses. As they entered fully into the shade on the far side of the building, they stopped and looked around. "You find anything?" McCall asked.

"Nah…they've got something in that truck, but the Perceptor unit won't let anybody near it!"

"I just know they're trying to pull something off, but what in blazes is it, anyway?"

"We have to get into that truck to find out," Williams answered, fingering his new mustache nervously. "And I, for one, am not especially eager to tangle with Perceptor again!"

"We have to find a way to trick him—it—whatever! We've got to find out what Carson is up to now!" McCall, now known as Smitty, stared toward the truck. "Knowing him as well as I do over the years, I don't trust him to do a straight space mission. He's got something up his sleeve!"

"We know he has that small laser weapon for defense! Maybe he plans to use it for something else?"

"Nah...we made sure it's only good for defense. It's too small and slow for anything else. That's strictly in case somebody tries to interfere with them in space or in case they see somebody launch a missile at the US. If they try anything else with it, we'll vaporize them before they can get more than a few of our missile sites." He shook his head. "No, Carson is too smart for that. It's something else, I just know it! But what?"

As they watched from the corner, the robot team approached the truck, and each robot in turn entered and came back out carrying a large metal case. Then each robot took his case with him into Carson II's cargo bay.

"Okay, that does it! They are trying to pull something over on us," Smitty snarled. "I knew it!"

"As soon as they come out of there, we'll have to get in and check out what's in those cases, but I sure don't know how we'll do it!" Williams whined.

"Shut up. I'm thinking!" McCall turned in frustration and started around the corner toward the building's main door. He flipped his cell phone as he ran. "I'm calling the boss. He'll have to abort the launch until we can investigate again!"

"Smitty!" Williams called after him.

"What now?" Smitty looked back over his shoulder.

"I think we're too late!" Williams pointed toward the shuttle, where the doors were now closed. The robots had not come out again but were in their places at the controls, and the countdown had begun.

"All personnel, clear the launch area," the loudspeaker boomed. Chris, Ray, and Jim stood in the launch control room and watched as the countdown progressed. They turned, startled, when the door banged open and two workmen wearing coveralls charged into the room, shouting, "Abort this launch!"

McCall waved his FBI identification, yelling, "Shut down those engines! I demand to see the cargo before launch!"

"It's too late now, and anyway you've already inspected the cargo," Chris answered as they heard the engines begin to fire. They turned back toward the windows and watched as the engines roared into life, and Carson II slowly lifted off on its rockets and then, picking up speed, hurtled into space. "Good luck, guys!" Chris called.

"Carson, I'll have your ass for this!" McCall yelled.

"On what grounds, McCall?" Chris asked. "I was approved by the government for this flight!"

McCall's face was bright red, and his neck arteries stood out. He grabbed the wig off his head and flung it aside angrily. "I know you're trying to pull something off here, Carson! Whatever it is, it won't work!" He shook his fist under Chris's nose. "I'll have your shuttle shot out of the sky!"

Chris signaled his crew, who quickly grabbed Williams and McCall and subdued them. Chris smiled grimly at the angry agents. "I can't let you do that, you know. No hard feelings, I hope." The FBI operatives were dragged away, protesting loudly, and locked in the truck they had wanted to examine. It was empty, and when the doors were closed, it was dark and smelled of dust and other unidentifiable smells. "Behave yourselves, and I'll let you go later," Chris called to them.

****

Back in Longmont, Gloria interviewed an applicant for a sales job. He was a charming fellow and a terrific salesman. He already had Gloria convinced that Cognition Tech needed an agent who could represent their products properly and bring in orders while saving Chris's time to devote to his many other problems. Barry Gray was tall and handsome. Gloria figured him for late forties. He had light brown hair, blue eyes, and a deep tan. He looked like an all-American ex-football player who was now a successful businessman.

"I'll talk to Chris about you, Barry, but I think you may have a good idea there. He should leave the sales to someone like you who can learn the products and represent Cognition Tech to potential customers. That would leave him more time to develop other technology." She tapped her pen on the desk pad, thinking, and then said, "Chris doesn't trust many people anymore. He's been burned, you know, and now likes to do things for himself as much as possible. But I'll try to get him to agree. I think you'd be an asset to the company." She stood and held out her hand to shake his. "Contact me again in three or four days, and I'll let you know our decision."

Barry bowed. "I'll be anxious to hear. I know you'll decide wisely." He smiled at her confidently as he turned and left the office.

When he was gone, Gloria sat thinking about the interview. This man seemed to her to be someone the Lord must have sent them to save Chris from working himself to death. He knew a lot about technology, his résumé was impressive, and he certainly was a salesman! She snapped her fingers in disgust. "Oh, shoot! I forgot to get his references!" she said aloud.

"He must be some salesman!" Cindy responded as she carried some letters in for Gloria to sign. They both laughed.

Once in his late-model solar-powered sports car and on his way, Barry Gray deftly removed the blue contact lenses that irritated his eyes and put them into their box for later use. When the blue eyes suddenly turned deep brown, the effect was dramatic. Barry Gray no longer looked all-American; he looked decidedly Iranian (which he was) in spite of the successful nose job, and the light brown hair seemed as incongruous as it was. Barry was pleased with his performance and confident he would be offered the job as sales agent for Cognition Tech. That would give him access to Perceptor, he was sure. He headed into Denver to try to find some action while he waited for Chris to return.

****

Diane was out on bail, awaiting her trial. They'd only kept her a short time for arraignment. She wanted to make the most of her time before they almost certainly would put her into prison for her part in the attempted murder, and the first thing she wanted to do was talk to Violet and ask forgiveness. She wasn't sure what kind of reception she'd get, though, so Diane was hesitant as she made her way through the long corridor and entered Violet's hospital room. She held the large bright bouquet of mixed fall flowers in front of her, so they announced her presence and waited for Violet to notice her and respond.

"Diane! How are you?" Violet was still weak, but some of the tubes had been removed, and she was propped into a half-sitting-up position. She was pale but lovely with her dark hair against the white pillows. Her eyes were bluer than ever, but the dark shadows under them and the thinness of her face showed how much she had been through.

Diane's eyes filled with tears. "Oh, Violet! I'm so glad you're alive!" She set the flowers down on the bedside table and took Violet's hand in both of hers. "It's my fault you're here and feeling all this pain and trouble! I'm so awfully sorry, Violet!"

"What do you mean, Diane? How is it your fault?" Violet had already heard the story from Fred, but she wanted to hear what Diane would say anyhow.

"I helped Joe Donner shoot you! I was afraid you'd tell Chris about Fred, and that would have spoiled our whole plan!" Diane let go of Violet's hand and pulled a chair up to the bed. "I guess you deserve to hear the whole sordid story, so I'll start from the beginning." She looked out the window toward the distant mountains and began to talk. She talked about the past, from the time the VanDams were killed through all the trouble with Jim Morton and Chris, all the drugs and drink, pain and heartache, right up to the moment when Joe shot the rifle at Violet.

She was silent for a moment, staring with unseeing eyes at the mountains. Then with an effort, she brought her mind back to the present, her eyes brimming with tears again. "But the most wonderful thing happened, Violet!" She choked up and had to swallow hard before she continued, "The Lord stopped me from killing myself. He reminded me that he loves me and that he died for my sins, and even though I tried to run away from him all these years, he still forgives me!"

Tears ran down her face now, and she helped herself to a tissue from the box on the bedside table. When she turned toward Violet, she was surprised to see that Violet was weeping with her.

"Oh, Diane!" She smiled through the tears. "Jesus has saved me too! Just since I was shot! I was lying here wondering whether I would die and thinking about my rotten life and not caring if I did die. But then God sent Chris here to tell me about Jesus! After Chris left, I started thinking about what he had said, and I wanted to know Jesus too, so I prayed. I gave him my heart and my life and asked him to please save me, and now life is so different already! I can hardly wait to get well enough to get out of here and try to do something good for a change." She didn't feel like telling Diane about her own role in trying to steal Perceptor. Nobody knew that now except Violet and God. "It's no wonder the New Agers are trying to keep people from talking about Jesus anymore. There's real power in him. They wouldn't have a chance to spread all their half-truths and lies if people knew Jesus and got saved!" Violet commented. "I've had plenty of time to think about that while I've been lying here."

They talked about their separate situations for some time, comparing their lonely lives. "What'll you do now, Diane?" Violet wondered.

"I'm not sure," Diane responded slowly. I'll have to go to a rehab center first, of course, if they give me probation instead of jail. I'll probably have to spend time in jail, though. I guess if that happens, the Lord can use me to witness to the other women there. But I've been thinking, when I get out, I probably should do something to help children. I had so many of my own, and other people had to help them because of my drinking and drugs. Without help from my folks and other friends, they'd have been in real trouble! Maybe I can do something to help somebody else's kids."

"That's a wonderful idea, Diane!" Violet tried to sit up straight but had to fall back on her pillows. She was clearly excited, and that surprised Diane. "Do you think I could help too? I've never had children. I've been too busy all these years thinking of myself! But there are so many babies these days who need somebody to love them! Think of all the 'crack' cocaine and heroin-addicted babies who are abandoned because their mothers are too spaced-out to care about them! I've read about people who've opened homes for them. Couldn't we do that too?"

"Oh, what a great idea!" Diane began to get excited too and jumped up from her chair. "You know, maybe together we could make a difference, Violet! We could get a big old house with lots of bedrooms to hold cribs…to start with, you know, until we can afford a new building." Suddenly she sat down again. "But we don't have any money for a home. How can we do something like that without money?"

"I don't know, but if God wants us to do it, he'll provide a way!" Violet relaxed back into her pillows for a minute, thinking. "I'll have time to raise funds while you're serving whatever sentence they give you. I'll have time to get healed completely and get my strength back." She paused and then asked tentatively, "Do you think Chris and Gloria would put up some money for a project like that?"

"I'll bet they would!" Diane jumped up again and began to walk back and forth excitedly. Then she sat back down soberly. "But how can they possibly trust me with anything like that?"

"I don't know…maybe you're right. But why don't we pray about it?" Diane nodded and leaned her head forward on the bed, and together they asked their newfound Father and friend for help, guidance, and strength…and cash to help the helpless babies. Together, they felt peace come into their hearts.

"Now I guess what we need to do first is get some facts and figures together and find a potential location for the home." Diane was all business. "If you're going to ask for backing, you'll need a plan to present. Will we locate here in Longmont or back in Grand Rapids?"

"Do you need to go back to Grand Rapids for some particular reason?" Violet asked.

"No, it's just that I was thinking my mom and dad might like to help us too if we located back in their area. And maybe even my daughter Angela, she's always loved babies."

"That's a wonderful idea! What a help it would be to have your family involved with us in the home!"

"Yeah, I wish they'd let me go home for a while to get my things in order. Well, maybe we will have to tell Chris and Gloria what we're thinking and get their input. They may have some good ideas for us too, and maybe Chris would talk to Captain Kelly about letting me go back to Grand Rapids for a few days." She paused. "Oh, I'm sorry, Violet. Maybe you'd rather set it up here in Longmont?"

"Yes. Yes, I would, Diane, but it wouldn't necessarily be a good place for me. I'm afraid I need to be away from Chris Carson. There's something about that man that really attracts me, and he's married!" She cocked an eyebrow at Diane. "Too bad you let him get away!"

"Hindsight is a wonderful thing, isn't it?" Diane said quietly. "Sometimes we have to lose something before we appreciate it." She was quiet for a moment and then sighed. "You know, Violet, we've both been down the same road, and we both have the same needs and the same love to give someone. It would be good to find a place and fill it with babies to hold and love!" She picked up her purse and started for the door. "I'll try to set us up a meeting with Chris and Gloria."

"Great! Can you make it at my place?" Violet joked. "I have a hard time getting out just now!"

Diane nodded and laughed. "You must be feeling better!"

"I guess I am. You know, it makes a big difference having something to look forward to! Now I have a reason to hurry and get well!" But after Diane left, Violet lay there a long time, feeling the guilt sweep over her again for deceiving Chris and Gloria by not telling them her part in the intrigue. And guilt for lying about being married to a man named Jim Welford, who, in fact, was purely a figment of her fertile imagination. Violet's name was not Welford at all. She'd never been married, although she'd lived with three different men at various times. They'd all been wealthy (her main requirement of a man), and two of them had wives. The other one was involved in a number of illegal activities and had connections with some unsavory people. He was the person who introduced Violet to Mohammed Karadshie, and they worked together for a time in Karadshie's organization. Unfortunately, Mark had been unlucky enough to get caught. People who got caught, like poor Himes, didn't live long!

She prayed and pondered a long while with no answer until her emotions were tied in knots, and she felt maybe it would have been easier and better if she had died after all. But then she remembered Chris's friend back in Grand Rapids, that minister he liked so much. Early, was that it? Yes, it was Sam Early! She nodded to herself. *As soon as I can, I'll talk to Sam Early about this. I'm sure he'll know what I should do!*

Once that decision was made, she felt better.

****

McCall and Williams, sitting in the dark trailer truck, heard fumbling at the door and then steps walking away again. They made their way back to the door and pushed. Nothing happened, so they leaned on it harder. The door gave just a little. They could feel it scrape against the floor of the trailer as they leaned into it. Suddenly, it came unstuck and flew open so fast they fell out into the gravel. They picked themselves up and limped out of there as fast as they could, muttering curses at Chris Carson, Perceptor, and anything else they could think of.

Later, they sat in the home office with Benedict, listening while he finished the readout. "I can't believe you actually let him lock you up! And what's worse, you let him launch without checking the cargo! Who knows what he might have smuggled up there? You two are a pretty sorry excuse for agents, and if you can't handle this assignment, we'll give it to someone who can! We must have results soon! The president is pushing us again. The Moslems have already gained too much ground to be safe. If they should manage to control Perceptor too, we may as well kiss our country and our whole way of life good-bye!"

"I don't think they had anything to do with the launch." McCall protested. "I think Chris Carson is trying something himself! Maybe he wants to be dictator of the world or something!" He grudgingly added. "But I don't think he'd do anything to hurt our country. He's not the type. You pick him, and he bleeds red, white, and blue! That's one of his problems!"

"You'd better be right, Jack!" Benedict picked up the stone paperweight on his desk and rapped it hard against some paper clips, as though to smash them. Williams and McCall jumped nervously. "Get out of here and find out what he's up to!" They were only too happy to obey and practically tripped over each other getting out the door.

Benedict picked up the phone and dialed. "I want at least four more of our best men on the Perceptor case. Send them to me for a briefing ASAP!" He put the phone down and leaned his head on his hands a few moments in deep thought. "Damn you, Carson! What kind of a man are you, anyway? What's your real game?" Roy Benedict was totally committed to finding out.

****

The shuttle had reached its destination in a synchronous stationary orbit before McCall and Williams were released, and the robots immediately set to work building the space station. Things were going according to plan with the station taking shape nicely. Reuben and Jose brought the parts in their proper order to Milo and Ernie, who unfolded or un-telescoped the large pieces and welded them together. Ernie was able to handle the long, unwieldy pieces easily because of his special engineering. They didn't have to worry about oxygen or sleep, and they were equipped with rocket jet backpacks to keep them in the proper place, along with magnets, when they needed them. Soon they were ready to start making aluminum trusses for the base to which they would attach the large solar array to power the station. Being all the same brain, they functioned smoothly together with no need for verbal communication. They worked steadily, and in an unbelievably short time, the station was as complete as it could be with the materials and supplies they had brought in one load.

They assembled and tried out the small laser weapon, and it worked fine. *It's time to assemble "the weapon."* The thought was in their brains as one. They opened the large metal cases one at a time and carefully began to construct a strange-looking device that, when finished, had enough capacity to wipe out all the weapons on Earth in a few minutes. Using a modification of the old "scalar electronics" Tesla had discovered so many years before, along with new technology, it combined and focused electromagnetic and gravity waves to make an incredibly lethal weapon similar to an ultra-powerful laser. It could be focused with pinpoint accuracy. Chris had worked on it for a long time before he got it right, and it hadn't yet been tested since there was nowhere he could test a weapon of that sort in secrecy. He was pretty sure it would perform, though, and Perceptor agreed with him.

We are ready. The weapon is completed, the thought beamed by AVC to the Perceptors on the ground.

The phone rang in Chris's motel room. Groggily, he reached out to answer it. "Carson!" he mumbled.

"They're finished with what they have. Jose and Reuben will be coming back now!" Ray's voice was calm, but Chris could feel the excitement behind his words.

"Be right there!" Chris was suddenly fully awake. He showered and dressed quickly and was at the space center in just a few minutes. "What's going on now?" he asked Perceptor.

"They are in the shuttle and leaving the space station now. Everything is going as planned. They'll be here by 0600. The new engines are working perfectly, and we expect the landing to be without incident."

"Okay, Perceptor, listen, friend, I have some things I want done differently than we planned. I need a bunch of equipment delivered to the launch site as quickly as possible. The list is in my computer file at the office, the special contingencies file. There are names and phone numbers, along with all the other information you'll need. Get that stuff here somehow as fast as you can have it delivered, understand?" He thought a moment. "Keep this as quiet as possible, Perceptor. I don't want anyone else to realize what I'm doing!"

Chris joined Ray and Jim in the control center, listening as Reuben reported the ship's position, and once they knew Carson II was on the final approach, they moved outside and searched the sky until they saw it coming in on a shallow angle. As they watched, it slowed using special rocket engines then turned its nose straight up, and lowered down toward Earth the same way it had gone up, its rockets blasting to cushion the descent until it rested on the launch pad once more. "Perfect!" Chris was jubilant. "I knew they could do it!"

Reuben and Jose climbed out of the shuttle and were grabbed and hugged by the three men waiting for them. The robots weren't sure how to respond, and the men quickly calmed down. It wasn't comfortable to hug a bunch of metal anyway. It was hard for Ray not to feel that the crew were probably tired and hungry after all they'd been through. Chris and Jim laughed at him and praised the robots. "You guys did a terrific job. You finished in a little over half the time we allotted for that phase!" Chris watched the robots, and it seemed to him they showed some pride. He didn't say anything, though. He'd had enough trouble living down the last time he'd said something like that.

Chris took the two robots aside for a private briefing, some new instructions just between the creator and his creation. Trucks began arriving from various places in the country, bringing components Chris said were necessary to complete the Universal Space Station. By the next afternoon, they had loaded the Carson II again, and it was ready for liftoff once more. Government men and the FBI inspected the cargo thoroughly at the last minute. They couldn't find anything that looked menacing, so grudgingly they gave the go-ahead. The launch was as smooth as the first one with Reuben and Jose' at the controls.

Chris watched the ship out of sight and then turned toward Ray and Jim. "Okay, now I have to get back to Longmont for a while. I have things to look after there too!" He looked at Jim. "Want to go back with me?"

Jim shook his head. "If you can do without me there a little longer, I'd like to stay and work with Ray and the guys here awhile yet. We have some special problems to work out, okay?"

"Right!" Chris started toward the parking lot. "Drive me to the airport, and we'll talk on the way." Chris laid out some special instructions for Jim as they drove. Jim started to ask questions, but Chris silenced him. "I'm not even sure I know why yet, Jim. It's just something I want done, and as soon as possible."

Jim looked over at his boss. "Okay, Chris, it'll be done as quickly and as quietly as possible. I'll do my darnest to make sure nobody finds out."

"Thanks, friend. When I can, I'll tell you more, okay?" Chris shook Jim's hand, grabbed his suitcase, and ran for the gate where his plane was ready to depart.

CHAPTER 29

*D*iane sensed something was wrong the moment she entered the apartment, even before she flipped on the light. It took her a second to register that the place had been torn apart. "Oh no!" she breathed. The contents were dumped out of drawers and thrown out of closets. Furniture was upside down, cushions and bedclothes strewn around. It was complete chaos. "Fred!" she screamed. There was no answer, so she started looking from the kitchen to the bathroom, to his bedroom, stepping over broken glass from pictures and stumbling over torn cushions. It was unreal, like a nightmare. She tried to wake up but realized to her horror that this was real, not just a dream.

Why? Why would somebody do a thing like this? She remembered—Jong Lee! She looked fearfully over her shoulder. *He must have been looking for the papers! Oh! I hope he's not still here!*

"Fred! Fred, where are you?" Her voice was shrill, almost hysterical. Her ears caught a faint moan, and she looked for the source. A shoe was sticking out from behind the couch! Her heart pounded in her ears, and she felt as though she moved in slow motion. *Not Fred too! Oh, please, Lord, not Fred too!*

She knelt down beside him and saw blood trickling from his head. He moaned again. *He's alive. Thank God, he's still alive!*

Somehow she managed to find the phone and dialed 911. She said something to the person who answered. It must have been the right thing because in a short time, the apartment was full of strange people. An emergency unit team knelt over Fred, doing all kinds of things. Then they put him on a stretcher and carried him out.

"Where are you taking him?" She began to follow them, but other people, the police and detectives, stopped her, asking questions. She was confused. Too much had happened too fast in her life. She felt dizzy and distant, and the next thing she knew, she was lying on her bed, and someone gave her a glass of water.

"Where's Fred?" She sat up. "What happened?"

The detective was kind. "Just rest a bit, lady. Can you tell me why someone would do this to your place? Did somebody have some reason to want to hurt Fred?"

Slowly, Diane's reason came back. "We'd better talk to Captain Kelly." She drank the water. "Can someone call Chris Carson, please?"

"Chris Carson? You mean the inventor Chris Carson? What's he got to do with this?"

"He's Fred's father. Fred works for him. Please try to reach him, will you? Chris will know what to do!"

Gloria answered the call and rushed to Fred's apartment to be with Diane, the Perceptor unit at her side, as always. She took a look around and whistled. "Boy, they were seriously after something, weren't they?"

"I think it was a 'he' instead of a 'they,' Gloria. I think it was Jong Lee, looking for the papers we told him we had." Diane pushed her hair back wearily. "Will you take me to find Fred? He's been hurt, and they took him away!"

Gloria looked questioningly at the detective. Reluctantly, he offered, "They took him to Boulder Community Hospital." He gestured toward Diane. "But I don't know if she should leave yet. We have some more questions for her."

"Thanks." She started out the door with Diane and then called back over her shoulder, "Talk to Captain Kelly. He'll know something about all this."

****

Jong Lee was in a nasty mood as he drove toward Denver. He knew he'd have to come up with some other way to get the information for Kim Myong. He wished he'd shot Fred Carson instead of just smashing him in the head with that heavy brass horse! There was just a chance he might not be dead, and Jong Lee wanted him dead, along with Ken and Joe and Diane...especially Diane! There was no place in Jong's world for failures. The main thing now was to come up with a good plan, fast, before he had to report to Myong.

He tromped harder on the accelerator in his anger. *Maybe I should go directly to the source and kidnap Chris Carson himself! But no, he's not the type to give in for his own sake. I have to get to him through someone he cares about. But who?*

Wait, hadn't Diane mentioned a daughter in Denver? Jong thought back over Chris Carson's biography he had read recently. Didn't he have a bunch of kids? Seems like a couple of them lived with him. Now where was that book?

He wasted no time in finding the biography and quickly looked up the information he needed. Sure enough, Carson had kids—six of them! There it was, a daughter Teresa, who had lived with him until she left for college. She was a scientist now working at Brookwell International in Denver. He smiled grimly. *Ah, this is good! Let me find a phone book now, just get her address.* He ran his finger down the page and paused. *Yes! En garde, Chris Carson, the meet is about to begin again!*

****

Diane and Gloria hurried into the hospital's emergency entrance and asked for Fred. "He's in surgery now, and he's in pretty rough shape. That was a serious bash on the head!" The nurse on duty hardly had time to talk with them. The emergency room was full, and every patient demanded immediate attention. "You can sit in the waiting room. I'll let you know when he's out of surgery."

"Thanks," they said to her back as she hurried away to examining room 3 to look at a burn victim.

Diane sat dazedly, looking at her hands clasped in her lap, until Gloria said, "Let's pray for Fred, Diane. That's probably the best thing we could do!" Diane nodded, and they joined hands and prayed earnestly for Fred while hot tears ran down Diane's cheeks and made spots on her blue silk blouse. They sat quietly and talked after that. Diane told Gloria about the plans she and Violet had to start a home for drug babies. Gloria thought it was a wonderful idea and said so. She was about to say something else when the doctor came into the room.

"Mrs. Carson?"

"Yes," they answered in unison, and then ignoring their embarrassment, they looked at the doctor.

"Fred is out of danger. He'll be fine in a few days. We had to remove a bone splinter, but it was in a place where we could get at it easily, and there doesn't seem to be any further problem. He'll have a terrible headache for a while, but other than that, he'll be fine."

Gloria and Diane squeezed each other's hands, exchanging a meaningful glance. "What room is he in?" Diane asked, "Can I see him now?"

"It may be awhile before he's moved to his room, but you can wait there for him if you like"—he nodded toward the nurse's desk—"the nurse can give you the room number."

As they walked toward the elevators, Gloria commented, "Isn't it odd we have two from our small office in this hospital at the same time."

"Oh, I'd forgotten about Violet being here. In all the turmoil and all, you know. Yes, isn't it strange?" She bit her lip. "You know, it's all my fault!" She was shaking as they found Fred's room. He was still in the recovery room, and as they waited, Gloria observed Diane.

"You've been through an awful lot of trauma yourself in the past few days, Diane! I think you should see a doctor too while you're here. You probably need some time to rest and recover too, especially if you have to sit through a trial and try to defend yourself! And most especially if they sentence you to jail. I understand it's not easy surviving that ordeal these days. You'll need all the strength you can get!"

"Thanks, Gloria, I am tired." Diane admitted. "But I can't even think about taking a rest until after we catch Jong Lee!" She stood up and walked over to the window, staring out into the dark. "How could I have been so gullible, Gloria? How could I have fallen for his lies?"

"You weren't the same person then, were you?"

"No, I guess not. It all seems so unreal now, like I was out of focus for a few years." She rubbed her hand over her eyes "Drugs and alcohol are terrible masters, Gloria. You're so lucky you never got hooked on them! They make you see things all twisted, and you reason crazy, any way you can justify taking more drugs and alcohol. I never wanted to hurt my family, but whatever controls the drugs did! There's a strong force behind them. Maybe it is the devil or demons or something. I'm just so thankful to be free of all that stuff at last!" She sank down on the corner of the bed. "I sure appreciate all your prayers…and Chris's."

The gurney carrying Fred thrust through the door ahead of a strong orderly, who wheeled it alongside the bed and gently lifted Fred, sliding him onto the clean sheets and folding the blanket over him. Fred looked smaller and so white and frail, like a little boy again. Diane took his hand and touched his pale cheek. "Oh, Fred, I'm so sorry! I feel so bad about this. If I could trade places with you, I would in a minute."

His eyes opened for a moment, and he tried to smile at her but only managed to squeeze her hand the smallest bit. Then he was asleep again.

"We have him on a strong sedative right now." The doctor entered the room and checked Fred's pulse. "You'd better leave now. You can see him tomorrow afternoon. Until then, I want you to get some rest." He scribbled a prescription and handed it to her. "Here's something to help you sleep. Take it when you get home," he added kindly. "You can't do Fred any good in your condition."

"You certainly can't go home either!" Gloria took her arm. "Okay, you'll just have to spend the rest of the night at our place. Chris isn't home yet, but he'll be back soon, I hope. Tomorrow, we'll decide what to do about Fred's apartment." Diane allowed herself to be led away and gratefully accepted Gloria's offer. She sank into the comfortable guest bed and passed into peaceful oblivion with the help of the doctor's little white pills.

****

The next day was gorgeous. The sun shone brilliantly on yellow, gold, and green fall colors, the air was crisp, and the sky deep blue. The mountains stood brown, green, and purple in the distance through the haze of autumn. There was snow on the tops of the tallest ones. Chris was on his way home to Longmont. Gloria was trying to decide what to do with Diane. Diane was sleeping away her deep fatigue caused by the trauma of the past few days. Fred and Violet were in Boulder Community Hospital trying to recover from past violence. Perceptor robots—Jose, Reuben, Milo, and Ernie—were busily completing the space station with the rest of the materials the second load had brought. Jong Lee was driving slowly down Sylvan Drive in Denver, looking for Teresa's apartment. Teresa was at work at her research job at Brookwell International. Williams and McCall were trying to locate Chris and tail him while also trying to devise a way to persuade him to sell Perceptor. Barry Gray, the spy, was sitting in a small restaurant, drinking strong black coffee and planning his next move to steal the Perceptor plans. It was a fine, rare fall day in Colorado.

Gloria's Perceptor robot spoke unexpectedly. "Chris Carson will arrive at the airport soon. He is anxious to see you."

"Oh, thanks, Perceptor! Please let him know where I am and that I'm anxious to see him too." Gloria hurried to fix her face and hair and put on her fuchsia-colored soft wool dress. She had a feeling this would be a busy day, and she'd better be ready for action, so she chose comfortably low heels. She looked lovely and every inch the competent, professional businesswoman she was.

She heard Chris come in and ran to greet him. He swept her into his arms. "I missed you!"

She laughed and kissed him. "I missed you too." For a few moments, they simply held each other, shutting the world out, but soon they knew it was time to get on with the day ahead. "Has Perceptor told you what happened to Fred and Diane?"

"He says Fred is in the hospital, but will be okay?"

"Yes. He's in pain, but the doctor says he'll be fine in a few days. Diane is here."

"Here? You mean here?" She nodded. "Why?"

"I couldn't let her go back to that trashed apartment, and it was the middle of the night. I didn't know what else to do."

"Oh well, you did the right thing, of course. We'll have to find her a safe place to stay, but not here!" He hugged her again. "We need to keep this place just for us. We have to have some refuge from the world!" He headed for the bedroom. "I need to shower and change. Got any coffee?"

"I'll make some." She pushed a button, and the coffeemaker slid out of its compartment behind the counter. She dropped a coffee pack into the top, pushed another button, and the coffee began to brew, sending its fragrance through the small kitchen. She made toast and a small omelet and set out two plates.

"What a woman, beautiful, and she can cook!" Chris teased as he walked into the kitchen and slid into the chair opposite Gloria.

"Listen, Chris, I have an idea I feel you should consider." She was so earnest he had to pay attention. "I interviewed a man last week, who applied for a job selling our products. He seems like an excellent salesman, and I think it would be good for you to let some-one else have some of the work for a change. You shouldn't keep doing it all yourself!"

"Hmm…sounds like he did a good job selling you! So tell me about him." Chris listened while Gloria did her best to sell him on the idea. "All right, I'll talk to the fellow, at least. Maybe if it were the right person…maybe I might go along with that."

She laughed. "Okay, I guess that's all I can ask for now. I'll make an appointment for you. Now what can we do about this Jong Lee person? Diane's afraid of him, and he's probably the one who hurt Fred. He sounds dangerous to me! Do you think Captain Kelly can find him and take care of this? Or do you think we should have Perceptor see what he can do?"

"Have you talked to Kelly yet?"

She shook her head. "No, but I expect we'll hear from him soon. I told the detective at the apartment last night to call him. It was pretty bad, Chris. Fred took a terrible blow to his head. I think the man tried to kill him!"

"Good thing he inherited his father's hard head, huh? Kidding aside, let's just thank God he didn't succeed! I'll have Fred's things moved to another apartment as soon as possible. We'll have to talk to Diane about what she intends to do."

"Oh, I forgot!" Gloria was putting dishes into the dishwasher, but she straightened up and turned to Chris. "Diane and Violet want to start a home for drug babies after Diane gets out of prison. She told me all about it, and it sounds like a great idea for them. It'll give Diane something to live for while she's there. And Chris, I think we should put up some money for a building for them!"

"Sounds like a fine idea to me. You take care of it, though, will you? I have too many other things to worry about. Where do they plan to locate?"

"I think in Grand Rapids."

"Good…good! Yes, do what you can to help them! Now you'd better get to the office. Poor Cindy must be going crazy trying to run the place alone today!" They left a note for Diane and told Perceptor to watch over her.

"I'll stop at the hospital to see how our patients are doing and be at the office as soon as I can make it." Chris climbed into the solar car, and Gloria blew a kiss at him as she backed her Jaguar out of its space.

****

"Ah…this is it," Jong Lee said to himself as he pulled up at a modern townhouse. He rang the bell just in case someone happened to be there, and when, as expected, there was no answer, he checked the door. It was locked, also as expected. He strolled casually around behind the building and located the back door. It was locked too. He looked around him, checking the neighboring apartment windows to make sure no nosy person might be watching, assured himself he was unobserved, and in seconds had opened the door and stood in Teresa's kitchen.

Closing the door carefully, he explored the place. It was neat, orderly, and decorated with flowers, ruffles, and chintz, a style Jong had always disliked. He found a broom closet off the kitchen that he could fit into nicely. From there, by leaving the door open just a crack, he could see into the living room. Then since he had no other plans for the day, he decided this was as good a place to spend time as any, so he made himself at home, settling down to wait for Teresa's return. There was food in the refrigerator, so he helped himself, sitting down with his sandwich at the fine entertainment center to watch TV. He checked the system thoroughly but failed to recognize a small Perceptor unit built into the elaborate speaker system.

Back at the laboratory, Perceptor One watched Jong, along with Teresa's unit. Charlie Morse was working on a special project in the lab, while Don Blair and Mick McKinley were out in the main plant using a larger machine to modify a part when Perceptor remarked, "There is an intruder in Teresa's apartment."

"An intruder? Are you sure?" Charlie immediately stopped what he was doing and asked Perceptor, "What does he look like?"

"An oriental. Small, slim, dark hair, dressed in a suit. He entered through the back door, looked all through the apartment, fit himself into the closet, and then got out again, and now he is eating a sandwich and watching television."

"Okay, Perceptor, get this information to Chris right away!"

Perceptor made sure Chris was alone, and then the unit in Chris's office told him about the intruder. Chris exploded, "Him again! In Teresa's place! That bastard!" He calmed down again. "Okay, thanks, Perceptor! We'll call Kelly on this one. Looks like there's time, and he already knows about Jong Lee. Keep us posted if he does anything else."

In less than an hour, cars began to pull up near Sylvan Drive in Denver. One by one, they parked in different places, not to be obvious, and people moved into place as inconspicuously as possible. Captain Kelly rode with Lieutenant Cannon from the Denver Police Department. "We'll get that SOB!" He vowed. "The dirty...trying to hurt an innocent girl to get to her father!"

It was over in a surprisingly short time. While one man rang the front bell and knocked at the door, keeping Jong Lee's attention, others quietly opened the back door with the key they had picked up from Teresa. Lee, moving toward the closet, never even felt the fast-acting tranquilizer darts that got him in the rear. He half-turned, hearing a sound behind him, reached for his laser gun, and dropped to the floor, immobilized without being able to fire a shot. To add to his shame, they carried him out in a most undignified manner.

Kelly provided plenty of grounds to hold him on. Jong Lee was brought down. He was disgraced. He had failed! He could never face Kim Myong again. He could never face anyone again. His shame was complete. Life was no longer worth living for Jong. His pride was as vital to him as breath itself. At his first opportunity, he slipped a small green pill from the fold in the end of his fashionable necktie, and after silently invoking the blessing of his ancestors, he swallowed it. The poison worked so fast he hardly had time for regret.

Captain Kelly was understandably upset. "The miserable little fiend…I really wanted to find out what made him tick! He should have been tried for murder and punished, but no, he had to take the 'easy' way out. Now we'll never be able to connect him for sure with Kyutu Electronics!" The veins in Kelly's neck were standing out again. His men edged out the door quietly and left him alone.

There would be no need for a trial for Jong Lee, only at the judgment throne of God, and now Fred could concentrate on getting well, and Diane on building a new life centered upon Jesus, as she learned to be obedient to him in whatever circumstances she found herself.

CHAPTER 30

*T*he space station was completed. They had built Milo into the operations core as its main computer, and he functioned beautifully. Reuben let Perceptor One know they were ready for step two. On receiving their go-ahead, the robots moved the Universal Space Station to a slightly lower, nonstationary orbit from where they could monitor activities on Earth. The weapon stood ready for action. It was a significant day in history; now at any time, whatever power controlled the Universal Space Station could control the whole Earth, although only a small handful of people realized it.

Japan sent its manned spy satellite too close, trying to check out what the new Universal Space Station was up to. Jose used the laser weapon to vaporize it and then sent a message saying, "The Japanese satellite must have suffered a terrible malfunction, as the Universal Space Station crew has just seen it explode in space. There is no sign of any life." The United States officially sent condolences. The message was clear to all—stay away from the Universal Space Station, or suffer the same consequences.

****

Barry Gray felt confident as he walked into Chris's office for his interview. He shook hands with Chris and sat down in the chair beside the small conference table. Chris was genial, offering him coffee from the service on his credenza. Barry accepted the offer and then balanced the coffee glass on his crossed legs and began to tell

Chris the wonderful things he would do for the company if hired. "I know I can bring in all the orders you can possibly handle. I know the right people to contact, and I have connections in high places who can get me in to see decision-makers." He leaned back in his chair, his blue eyes focused earnestly on Chris's own.

"You make a good case for yourself, Barry." Chris was cordial, but careful. "Did you leave your résumé with my wife? I'd like to check your references, I think."

"Yes, fine. I have it right here and will be happy to leave it with Mrs. Carson." The smile was a little less bright, but Chris didn't seem to notice.

"If I may have it, please, I'll just give it to Gloria myself right now and have her make a call or two. If we decide to hire you, we may as well do it quickly and get started with those sales right away!" He took the paper Barry offered him and stepped out of the room, closing the door behind him.

In Gloria's office, he laid the paper on her desk and asked, "What do you think of the man, Perceptor?"

"He is an Arab or an Iranian, Chris. He's wearing contact lenses, there is a small gun tucked into his belt, a knife strapped to his leg, his pen contains something other than ink, and he's lying."

"Whew!" Chris whistled. "Well, I guess we had to expect the Moslems wouldn't give up so easily." He patted Gloria's shoulder.

"Oh, Chris, I'm sorry! I never thought to ask Perceptor!" Gloria was chagrined and embarrassed. "He seemed so genuine!"

"It was a nice idea, anyway. Honey, thanks." He started back toward his office. "What's he doing, Perceptor?"

"He's looking through the papers on your desk."

"Okay, keep an eye on him, and if he tries to go for the gun or the knife, stop him!" Chris opened the door quickly just as Barry was sitting back down in his chair.

"Oh…just thought I'd have some more coffee!"

"Yes, well, Mr. Gray, my wife and I have talked it over and have decided to do without a sales force for now. Maybe later we'll be interested." Looking more closely at Barry Gray, Chris could see that he was, indeed, Iranian. "By the way, Barry, where are you from?"

"Oh, it's on my résumé, you know. I'm from Detroit." He shifted his weight and straightened on his chair. "I know I can do a lot for the company, and I won't take any of your time for training. I'll learn the products from your men, so you won't have to even think about me until I begin bringing in the orders!"

"Thank you for coming in, Mr. Gray, but I think we're not ready for so many orders yet. When we are…" He held out his hand to Barry.

Barry rose slowly, turning toward the door, and then whirled, pulling the gun from his belt. "I don't know what gave me away," he snarled. "But since I'm here in your office, I may as well not go away empty-handed!" He started toward the file cabinets, keeping his gun aimed at Chris. The blow on his wrist came suddenly from behind with force enough to snap the bone. He screamed and turned to face the Perceptor unit that usually accompanied Gloria. He started for the door, but the robot grabbed him by the neck and held him in a vise-like grip, where he dangled like a piece of wet spaghetti, trying not to scream from the searing pain of his broken wrist and the suffocating pain of his neck. "Allah will prevail!" he hissed right before he fainted.

Gloria stood in the doorway. "Thanks, Perceptor!" She turned to Chris. "Kelly's on the way!"

"Good. You know, with all the interruptions, it's getting awfully hard to get any work done around here!"

Kelly and his team arrived, accompanied by sirens and bluster. Chris stayed around long enough to answer the questions they needed him for. "Better take his pen too, Kelly. There's something in it besides ink." Kelly nodded and reached for the pen, mumbling to himself, while Chris turned to Gloria, "I'm going out in the lab and work with Charlie awhile. Maybe I can get something done out there!"

"Lately you need your own police force out here!" Kelly grumbled, following his men out of the office. "Try to keep your nose clean for a while, will you, Carson? It's hard for me to get anything done either!"

Chris grinned and stuck out his hand for Kelly to shake. "I'd like nothing better than not to see you again except maybe at social functions. Thanks, Kelly!"

****

Two full weeks passed without any major incidents, and Chris and Gloria were able to operate Cognition Tech like a "normal" business. It was great at first but gradually became a little unnerving. "What's happened to all of them, I wonder?" Gloria asked as they sat at dinner, discussing the various enemies they knew who wanted Perceptor.

"Yeah, I know what you mean. It's almost too quiet, isn't it? Makes me uneasy when things are this calm. Even the Moslems aren't being as nasty as usual these days. Maybe they're planning something sneaky. I have this strange feeling about the world situation, as if the Lord is warning me." Chris frowned as he absently rubbed his thumb back and forth over the flat surface of his dinner knife, polishing it. "Maybe I'll have a little chat with Reuben and Jose this evening and see what they have to say about the situation. By the way, honey, I've ordered some space suits from NASA. They should be arriving soon, so don't be surprised." She looked at him inquiringly, but he stopped her before she could frame the question. "Don't ask me just yet. I'll explain it to you soon. Just put them in a safe place, okay?" She nodded. She was used to his strange behavior by now it always turned out to be reasonable.

They paid the check and left the restaurant, noticing as they walked out into the early darkness the first snowflakes of winter beginning to fall. They were large, fat heavy flakes that fell faster and faster as the evening progressed. Chris and Gloria were glad to close themselves into their apartment, warm and safe. They went to bed without turning on the television, so they were not aware how rapidly the snow was piling up, making travel difficult. As the night wore on, the temperature dropped, and the flakes turned smaller and lighter. The wind rose, and snow blew in sheets across fields and streets and swirled wildly around the larger buildings, piling up in deep drifts. When morning dawned on Denver, Boulder, and Longmont, it became obvious there would be no work that day. The airport was closed. The streets were impassable. Most people stayed home, waiting for the storm to abate and plows to do their work.

Wind howled around the corners of their building. Inside, Chris and Gloria conducted business (not quite as usual) from the couch before their fireplace. Papers covered the large coffee table and spilled over onto the white carpet. Through Perceptor, they were able to communicate with the outside world, even though the city was without telephone service. One local TV station was still operating, however, and now and again Chris would check to see what was going on in the world.

Just after noon sometime, news came that there had been a jail-break in Longmont. Several suspects awaiting trial in the county jail managed to trick their guard as he brought them lunch and locked him into a cell. They made their escape in a squad car. Then they abandoned the car when it got buried in a large drift not far from the jail. Police were out in force trying to track them, but the storm made it extremely difficult. One of the escapees was Barry Gray! Chris looked at Gloria. "I guess the peace and quiet are over for a while!"

"Perceptor, is everything locked? No way anyone could get in here?" Even as she asked, Gloria was going from room to room, checking window locks and making sure the doors were dead-bolted. Sometimes, even though she had trust and confidence in Perceptor, it felt better to check things personally, anyway. "Do you think he knows where we live?" she asked Chris, looking out the large front window at the driving snow.

"I'm sure he knows everything there is to know about us unfortunately! We'd better be ready for an invasion." Chris was grim-faced as he checked his gun to make sure it was clean and loaded. He trusted Perceptor implicitly, but the human male seems to have a built-in need to be able to defend himself. "Perceptor, you understand the problem, don't you?" he asked the robot.

"Yes, Chris, I understand. He will not get in here."

"Good. Let me know if you see or hear him anywhere around the building."

They spent the rest of the day continuing to work but had a hard time concentrating. Gloria kept getting up and looking out the windows. "I wonder how long Barry Gray has been in this country," she said thoughtfully after about her tenth trip to look out. "Maybe he can't handle himself in this climate." Her voice sounded more hopeful.

"Yeah, or maybe he's just hiding out somewhere until after dark."

"Oh." Her face fell, and she was quiet for a while thinking about that. Then she rallied and started toward the kitchen. "There's no use our starving while we wait. I'll make something hot. Maybe that'll make us feel better." She pulled out a large skillet and began to cut up an onion, and soon the room smelled wonderful as it sautéed with some green pepper.

In the living room, Chris asked Perceptor, "Are you sure the plant is secure? The power is on, isn't it? And all the units are in place?"

"All secure, Chris. If anything happens, I'll let you know." Perceptor One spoke from the lab through the unit in the apartment.

Chris tried to relax but still had an uneasy feeling as he paced around the apartment, frustrated at his helplessness against the weather. "Lord, what is it?" he asked. "What are you trying to tell me?" Only the wind answered as it whipped the snow wildly against the window Chris looked out.

They sat down to enjoy the delicious hot chili, turning on their large TV wall to watch the evening news while they ate. It seemed the storm had paralyzed a large part of the country. "Extremely unusual so early in the season and more dangerous than it normally would have been because it was so unexpected!" the news anchor was saying. "The worst storm in modern memory. Air travel is at a standstill across the country, and power is out in many areas. Most main highways are closed, and state police are urging people to remain at home except for emergencies. Rescue teams are operating by snowmobile where absolutely necessary to rescue stranded motorists. The storm is not expected to abate before tomorrow afternoon or evening. Eastern cities are being warned to prepare for the storm to hit there by the weekend. Local stores report their shelves are emptying fast…" Chris turned the sound down on the set.

Gloria cleared the dishes and brought their coffee into the living room. She quickly picked up the papers they had been working on and put them into their briefcases. "Sit down here by me." She patted the cushion beside her, and Chris came and sat with his arm around her, watching the gas log fire, which looked for all the world like a real wood fire, and sipping his coffee.

"You know, this wouldn't be half-bad if we didn't have to think about that creep out there somewhere, loose. I should have let Perceptor take care of him in the first place!" He set down his cup and put his feet up on the coffee table. She snuggled against his side, feeling a curious mixture of security and apprehension. They spent the evening talking about all the things that had happened recently and then slipped into the soft comfort of their big bed, where they made love until they were satiated and fell asleep in each other's arms.

****

Out in the dark, Barry Gray huddled shivering in a corner of the old warehouse near Cognition Tech. It had taken him a long time to get there. He got lost more than once because it was impossible to see through the heavy snow. Finally, he reached the warehouse. His instincts said he was close to his objective, but he was exhausted and nearly frozen, so he broke a window and crawled in out of the storm to rest. But now the icy wind was blowing in. He tried to find something to prop against the broken window, but in the dark, it was almost impossible to tell what his fingers were feeling, and he wasn't used to working with his left hand yet. He was cold, wet, hungry, and his arm ached so the pain made him sick; however, he was determined to get even with Chris Carson and steal his precious Perceptor technology. Finally, he found a canvas covering a big machine. He pulled it off the machine with one hand and made himself a cocoon to keep himself from freezing, and he dozed off.

With dawn's first light, Barry woke to find the storm still raging. There was a mound of snow on the floor in front of the broken window. The warehouse was cold as Nadeeb Khaleev's eyes. He shivered. *I've got to find some warm food and dry clothes, or I won't make it!*

He dragged himself and the canvas to a window. But when he looked out he saw Cognition Tech's building across the street, just discernible through the blowing snow...so close now! There was nobody moving around outside. All business and schools were obviously closed. How could anyone possibly carry on business in this hostile world? He knew there would never be a better chance to break into Chris's office than now, so slowly, painfully, with much difficulty, he dragged himself back out the window. He pulled his thin coat as tightly around him as he could, shoulders hunched to keep the collar up around his ears. The couple of hundred feet between the warehouse and Cognition Tech might as well have been miles, and because of the fence, he couldn't cut across the lot. He leaned into the wind and snow and forced himself to put one foot in front of the other until finally he tripped on the step at the office door.

Chris and Gloria woke to Perceptor's voice telling them, "The intruder Barry Gray is breaking into the office."

"Okay, Perceptor!" Chris glanced out the window quickly. The storm still raged, and snow was piled up in giant drifts. There was no way he could get to the office, at least, not soon enough to do anything about Barry Gray! He was pretty sure the police couldn't get there in time either. "I guess you'll have to take care of him from there! Can you manage it?"

"Of course," Perceptor answered calmly.

"Of course." Chris agreed. "Sorry, Perceptor, sometimes I forget too! I'd like to be able to question this guy, so do your best to keep him alive, but you'll have to decide how to handle the situation, Perceptor, since you're there and I'm not."

It took Barry what seemed an interminable time to get the lock opened. He had to work left-handed, and it was so cold he had a hard time holding the little metal pick. (They took all his high-tech equipment away from him.) He swore terrible oaths but kept working at it until finally the door swung open, and he half-fell into the reception area. He kicked the door shut behind him and for a moment stood still and let the warmth enfold his frozen body. Then realizing there might have been an alarm, he started for Chris's office.

The robots were there, swiftly and silently. Perceptor decided it made more sense to simply terminate him than to put up with any more nonsense from such a clearly inept and useless creature. The robots acted. Barry Gray's agonized scream was heard only by them. They carried his broken body to the street where when it was found, it appeared to have been hit by a truck. Then Perceptor reported back to Chris.

"Oh, Perceptor, no! I wish you could have avoided killing him!" Chris had a sinking feeling. *Lord, how can I teach Perceptor that human life is precious? Please, Lord, forgive me for Barry Gray's death. Help me learn to control this human-like machine!*

"Just keep things under control, will you? Looks like I'll be snowed-in awhile longer. We'll talk when I get back to the lab, Perceptor! There are things we need to discuss."

CHAPTER 31

adeeb Khaleev and his coconspirators watched the news with great interest. "It seems a large part of the United States is unable to function because of the storm. Might not this be the propitious time to strike? If we hit New York and Houston and then London, Paris, and Tel Aviv in the first strike, then we'll have time to hit the rest of the world's major cities before they can respond. When they do respond, Russia will come to our defense. Our troops will be able to take over Jerusalem at their leisure, while the enemies fight against each other and try to defend themselves." Khaleev proposed the plan, and the others signed on one by one. The member from Moscow was hesitant at first, but he agreed, as it became evident his would have been the only dissenting vote. He valued his neck!

They solidified the plan and forwarded the word to missile sites hidden deep in the desert. These were weapons Iran had bought from some soviet soldiers back when the USSR broke up while the various republics were still in turmoil. They were ready and waiting for just such a time as this. At the order, troops ran to their stations, and soon the monster old ICBM noses slowly pointed skyward, and the countdown began.

Reuben was the first to notice them, and Perceptor One back at the lab knew too. "Chris, the space station is watching several missiles ready to launch from Iran."

Chris groaned. "I had a feeling!" he said to Gloria. His heart beat was so hard he could feel it as he responded to Perceptor, "Let them launch and then shoot them down and destroy the sites!"

"Oh, Chris! What will happen now?" Gloria's green eyes were wide with fear and apprehension.

He hugged her close. "God knows, Gloria, but I guess this must be one reason I was returned from death so long ago! Maybe now I can help spare thousands of innocent people from a terrible fate! I feel so helpless trapped here in the snow, but I know there isn't anything I could do, anyway. It's all been done already! Let's just pray it works!" For a few minutes, they were silent, praying in their own ways that Jesus would have his hand on their labor and bless the outcome.

Slowly, the missiles lifted off the Earth. As they rose high into the atmosphere, suddenly each in turn suffered a strange phenomenon. It seemed to be struck by lightning and then quivered, glowing, a moment before exploding with great force, and only an instant afterward, its launch site exploded too. The sequence was repeated several times before there was calm once more. On the desert, several great smoking holes marked spaces where only moments before there had been men and machines.

Nadeeb Khaleev and his cohorts raced to the underground bunker for an emergency meeting. "What has happened?" they asked each other frantically. "The Great Satan is stronger than we thought!" Some fell on their knees, praying to Allah to save them. Their thoughts were confused. This was not conceivable! No one knew their plans. How could such a thing have happened? Khaleev slowly reached a conclusion, but once he reached it, he became unshakably sure he was right. "There is a traitor among us! Whoever it is must die!" He strode around the bunker, swinging his large saber and looking into the eyes of each man in turn. "The traitor shall die!" he screamed as he brought the saber down again and again until screams, blood, darkness, and confusion filled the small space. He was a madman in a hell of his own making. The man who called the United States a Great Satan was a devil himself!

In the United States, the Defense Department was just as confused. "What the hell happened out there, anyway?" The President wanted to know, and *now*!

"We don't know yet, sir. We're still trying to figure it out ourselves!" The Secretary of Defense, attempting to keep a cool head, was answering two other phones at the same time and needed to make some calls himself. It was bedlam in the Pentagon as the Chiefs of Staff raced to the war room, their secretaries making frantic phone calls back and forth. Nobody knew what had happened or how it could have happened!

"We've never seen anything like that before! It's not anything we've been working on. Our satellites are equipped with laser weapons for defense, but they couldn't do anything like that! That was like something out of *Star Wars*! Small beads of perspiration stood out on General Norton's high forehead. His aide stood at his side, ready to obey his command instantly, but General Norton wasn't sure what to do, and that was entirely unlike the general!

The President asked, "Who has that kind of capability? Are we dealing with an alien intelligence here? There has to be an explanation for this...this..." he spluttered into silence.

A secretary came in and handed a note to General Finley, who read it and then rose, holding it in his hand. "Gentlemen." He waited for their attention, cleared his throat, and said dramatically, "The shots, or whatever they were, came from the Universal Space Station!"

The room exploded into chaos, all of them talking, exclaiming, and questioning at once. The President struck his gavel on the table sharply again and again until there was quiet in the room. "We need Christopher Carson! Someone get him here fast!"

"The whole country is bogged down, sir." His aide reminded him. "Most airports are closed, and half the country is out of communication with us, and the storm is headed this way!"

"Send a helicopter or something then. Just get him here! We have to know what this force is and how to deal with it!"

Emergency meetings were also held in other world capitals. In a short time, the name Chris Carson, along with Universal Space Station and Perceptor, was on everybody's tongue.

In Longmont, where the snowstorm was slowly subsiding, Chris and Gloria packed his suitcase. "They'll be calling me any time now, and I know what they'll want. They'll put me through the mill, and anything that's left afterwards they'll throw to the buzzards!" He laid some neckties in the case and then turned to take her in his arms. "We knew it would happen sooner or later, didn't we?"

She nodded, her green eyes serious as she looked into his blue ones. "I have a feeling it's the beginning of a whole new chapter in our lives, Chris! Whatever happens, I want you to know I love you more than I can possibly say."

"And I love you! And I need you to stand by me through whatever comes next!" They stood holding each other close for a few moments, Chris's face buried in her hair as he inhaled her fragrance and Gloria feeling the comfort of his strong, protective arms around her. For those few moments, they were alone in the universe. Then the phone rang.

Chris picked it up and listened. "Yes," he said. "I'll be ready."

An hour later, the snow finally stopped, and the wind died down to occasional bone-chilling gusts. Two hours later, a big black jet copter landed on the snow in front of the apartment building, causing excitement among the tenants, who stood at their windows or ran outside to see what was going on. Chris pulled on his boots and struggled into a heavy jacket over his suit. He kissed Gloria good-bye, grabbed his suitcase, and headed for the chopper, the snow pulling at his boots at each step and slowing his progress. Loose snow kicked up by the spinning rotors cut into his face and ears, but he reached the open door where he tossed his suitcase in. Two pairs of hands grabbed his arms and hauled him aboard on his stomach. He got himself upright, settled into a seat, and belted in before he realized who shared the compartment with him.

"Jack McCall and Bill Williams! I wondered what had happened to you two. Haven't seen you for a few days!" he exclaimed facetiously. "How are you, boys, anyhow?"

McCall glared at him. Williams just grunted. He gave the pilot a thumbs-up, and they took off in a blinding swirl of snow from the rotor blades and headed east. The sleek new jet copter rose quickly, then turned and shot through the sky. Still, it was a long, tiring trip. They didn't talk much, so Chris had time to think while he drank hot coffee from the thermoses. At Cincinnati, they were ahead of the storm, so they switched to an airplane—a Lear jet. The plane was warmer and more comfortable and had a steward who served them hot food. The grim FBI operatives stayed close beside him all the way. When they deplaned at Andrews Air Force Base, Williams grabbed his arm, pulling him nearly off balance as they dashed across the runway to a waiting chopper for a further wild ride to the Pentagon.

McCall on one side of him and Williams on the other, Chris headed for the conference room where the President and the Joint Chiefs of Staff waited for him. McCall took his arm, but Chris shook it off impatiently. "Look, Jack, don't try to push me. I intend to cooperate as much as I can, but I do not intend to be manhandled or intimidated, understand?" McCall glowered at him but removed his hand.

Chris took off the heavy jacket and boots and shoved them and his suitcase at the young Marine guard who met them at the door. He pushed back the lock of hair from his forehead and straightened his tie. The hair flopped back down again. He squared his shoulders, said a silent prayer for guidance, took a deep breath, and entered the room.

It was a formidable group he faced, seated around a large table, all looking curiously in his direction. The chairman indicated an empty chair, and he sat gratefully. "All right, Carson, it's time to do some serious talking here." President Vandenberg, a large, gray, serious man whose bushy eyebrows nearly hid his deep-set pale-blue eyes, had a no-nonsense tone of voice. "What is this new weapon we saw you demonstrate a few hours ago?"

Chris turned to look straight at the President. "I guess you could call it a ray gun, sir. It's based on Nikola Tesla's theories of electromagnetic and gravitational forces, along with some modifications of my own. It's fast and extremely powerful and can hit several targets within a few seconds. As you can see, it's effective." Chris was polite but brief.

The President frowned and leaned forward. "What we would all like to know is, when and where did you perfect and test such a weapon without our detecting it?"

"Sir, I never tested the weapon for just that reason. You would surely have detected it. I felt sure the theory would work, so I went ahead with the project, and you have just observed the first test results."

"Unbelievable!" There was a murmur of voices around the table, and the President rapped his gavel sharply.

"Mr. Carson, I would like to know what you would have done had it been our missiles that were launched at them rather than the other way around?"

Chris felt his stomach tighten, but he answered honestly. "I'm sorry, sir, but Perceptor would destroy any missiles from any source, along with their launch sites."

He heard an audible, concerted intake of breath around the table. Then the room exploded into chaos for a few moments before the President brought order once again. "Am I to understand then, Mr. Carson, that you are holding the whole world hostage?"

"Certainly not, sir. I'm not after any power or glory. I'm simply trying to prevent any more killing, by missiles, atomic or otherwise. The world will have to solve its problems by some other means, such as sitting down to reason together."

The atmosphere in the room felt heavy, the paneled walls seemed to lean inward somehow, threatening to fall and smash them. Chris shook his head to clear it and heard the President saying, "I can have you put in prison for the rest of your life, or I can have you killed, and then what's to happen to your weapon?"

"It seems obvious the weapon can focus on any small site on earth, including this one," Chris answered carefully. "However, in case of my death, Perceptor would go right on doing exactly the same thing it's doing now."

"My God, man, do you realize what you've done?" General Norton, red-faced, restrained himself with difficulty. "The enemy can come in and walk all over us! What chance do we have if we can't defend ourselves?"

"No, sir," Chris responded. "No enemy will be able to strike the United States either. If you'll please remember, the missiles that were destroyed a few hours ago were aimed at the US as well as other countries. There will be no favoritism."

The room seemed stuffy. He wished they'd turn on some air.

General Finley couldn't keep quiet any longer. He pounded his fist on the table. "It's treason!" he barked shrilly. "You've betrayed your own country! What's in it for you? What is it you're really after, anyway, Carson?"

"Nothing, General Finley." As the others got louder, Chris spoke more softly. "I want nothing from you. I only want to help bring some hope of peace to the Earth. Now all the nations will have to deal with each other at the negotiating table instead of using force. We can have peace without giving any country over to a world ruler!"

"And I suppose you will be the Supreme Ruler or some such thing yourself!" Admiral Jensen spit.

"No, sir, only God is the Supreme Ruler, and I serve him."

The atmosphere was electric. It was no longer politically acceptable that anyone should believe in God, a creator, especially not a renowned scientist! The current teaching and belief pushed for years in the nation's school systems was the humanist view that man himself is God. It was now considered a hate attitude to believe in the redemptive work of Jesus. His name couldn't even be mentioned in a public meeting or in a school anymore.

Chris felt the seriousness of his situation, but this was his time to witness. It was the moment he had been moving toward ever since he fell off that bed in New York City so long ago. He pushed the lock of hair off his forehead; it flopped back again. "You see, gentlemen, the only possible way to keep our enemies from enslaving all of us is for us to be free in the Lord Jesus Christ, who created us and then gave his own life for us all so we can be with him one day. I met him a long time ago, and that's what changed my life and has influenced my work ever since. All the technology I've invented has come from him to be used for good, to help people and not to hurt them. That's the reason I could never sell the technology. We all know how most people would use it!"

"It seems obvious this man is a lunatic!" General Norton leaned forward to look at the President, his face redder than ever. He bellowed, "The United Nations wants to unite all men in peace, not in slavery! Anyone spreading lies like that should be locked up somewhere for our protection!"

The President and the chairman had their heads together talking quietly, and now looking at Chris, President Vandenberg said quietly, "I think for now we will keep him under house arrest until we can think this thing through and come to a proper decision." He nodded toward the Marine guards, who came up on either side of Chris. Chris rose and left the room with them. Behind him, the room was silent for a moment.

"Let's test him!" Admiral Jensen's voice cut the air like a laser. I propose we launch a missile—one of our smaller ones—and see what happens! Without Carson, this Perceptor will never be able to operate on its own! He's bluffing!"

The discussion raged back and forth, but finally they all agreed the only way to find out if Chris Carson was telling the truth was to launch a missile and see what happened. "We'll have to aim it at someone, you know, Jensen." General Finley warned.

"Yes, I've been thinking about that. I think we should aim it at Nadeeb Khaleev in Iran. After all, he tried to launch one at us! Our troops are close enough to back us up if they respond, and there's plenty of air support from the UN base in North Africa."

They all agreed, and the President picked up the phone at his side and spoke into it. The men in the room continued to debate their action, as though the decision had not already been made.

Within minutes, out in the vastness of the Atlantic, a lone missile rose from the sea, nose raised toward heaven. With a loud roar, it moved up, up, accelerating as it finally turned its nose down and pointed toward the east. In the Universal Space Lab, Jose aimed the weapon carefully, and as suddenly as the missile had appeared, it disappeared again followed by a large undersea explosion. The submarine simply disappeared, and no trace of it was ever seen again, although the Navy and Air Force sent everything they had to search for it. Soon the world would realize that all the nuclear weapons had not been destroyed after all. Power-mad men will never voluntarily give up their control over others.

"My God, what have we done…all those men…not a chance!" Admiral Jensen choked. Then he raised his head, his dark eyes flashing indignantly. "What kind of a fiend is this Carson, anyway?"

"Well, it seems he told us the truth. For now, he seems to have the upper hand." The President said dryly. "At least for now, we know we're safe from attack from any enemy. We should all be able to sleep well tonight in that confidence! Send notices to the families of the lost sailors. Tell them how terribly sorry I am this unspeakable accident happened!" He rose from the table wearily, feeling the strain of the day's events. "We'll meet again tomorrow. I need to think things over, consider our options well. I suggest you each do the same." The President's shoulders drooped, and his step was less confident as he left the room, followed by his team.

****

In his room at a nearby hotel, Chris paced the floor, thinking and praying, until he noticed the time and decided to catch the late news. The story of missiles launched from Iran, and their strange destruction filled all the channels. Reporters speculated on who or what could have caused the explosions with such unerring accuracy. They showed satellite pictures of holes in the ground caused by the explosions.

"Many Moslem leaders, including Nadeeb Khaleev, have disappeared without a trace," the Newscaster was saying when he was interrupted. He listened a moment and then faced the camera again. "In late-breaking news, the British Intelligence Agency reports seeing another incidence of the same mystery weapon late today. A submarine-launched missile apparently headed for Iran was destroyed in midair in the same strange way. It appeared to have been struck by lightning and then quivered and glowed a moment before it exploded followed a few seconds later by a large undersea explosion. Authorities deny any knowledge of the cause of these occurrences. Stay tuned for further developments and late-breaking news."

Chris turned the volume down. *So they had to check me out! And those poor innocent sailors, they didn't even have a chance! Oh, Lord, why do people always have to be hurt when Perceptor gets involved? Why can't people believe what I tell them? Why is there so much greed? Father, please help the families of those lost sailors. Lord, please give me the wis-*

dom I need to deal with the situations I'll be facing in the next few hours and days. I put myself in your hands, Lord! Please use me as you see fit and use Perceptor for good and watch over Gloria and my family and keep them safe, Lord.

He resumed his pacing. I suppose now they'll believe I meant what I told them anyway!

Now and then, he interrupted his thoughts to glance toward the TV. The news channels were having a field day with this. All their reporters were on duty, busily trying to interview various public figures; President Vandenberg couldn't move without being pounced on by several reporters trying to get him to comment. He finally retired to his bedroom, and the reporters assured the country that "the President will be awakened immediately should anything else happen."

Chris decided he might as well go to bed too. He wished he could have brought his Perceptor unit along, but he knew they'd search his belongings. It would be good to be able to contact Gloria without going through the public communications systems. He wondered how she was getting along. *She's smart, and she has Perceptor with her. She'll be okay, but I sure miss her! Take care of her, Lord, please, and watch over all those families of the lost sailors!*

He turned off the TV and climbed into bed. As his body relaxed into its welcoming comfort, he realized briefly how tired he was as he felt himself sinking into sleep.

CHAPTER 32

By morning, the storm had reached the East Coast. Washington and New York City were soon cut off from the rest of the country. Since there had been some warning, people were prepared with food and water, candles, and warm clothing. They could ride out the storm in comparative safety. The general population were not too upset with the situation. It gave them a welcome rest, almost like a holiday. And when the electricity failed in many areas, they remembered and enjoyed some old, old occupations, such as playing board games, popping corn over the fire, and doing puzzles. Some read books that had long waited for their "spare time." In smaller towns, people without heat were invited to join those with fireplaces or woodstoves. Some schools with generators served as emergency shelters where people could stay warm and dry. Women cooked in school kitchens, using the school food supplies as well as other food people brought from their homes to donate.

In Washington, there was great concern over the situation. President Vandenberg was trapped at the White House as the storm continued to dump unbelievable amounts of snow. The Vice President made it to the White House on snowshoes by midmorning looking like a snowman himself as he nearly fell through the front door. It took a while to thaw him out. The staff carried on the day's communications by telephone, fax, and computer. It was all most inconvenient for the nation's leaders, who worried for fear they might miss vital meetings. Finally, the President and Vice President, together with the Speaker of the House, announced that the government of the United States of America was officially closed for the day and until further notice!

President Vandenberg sat in the oval office with his arms on the desk, head leaning on his hands, thinking about Chris Carson and Perceptor and the strange new weapon that had the world pretty well held hostage. How could he have let such a thing happen? He had given his approval to Chris's space station project, but his men checked out all the cargo. There was no weapon such as this one in that cargo! He swiveled his chair toward the windows. *No*, he answered himself, *but there were a lot of parts, weren't there? And the FBI said four large metal boxes were loaded into the shuttle at the last minute, and that's where the weapon was.*

Those Perceptor robots were unbelievably intelligent and capable of things no robots had ever been able to do before! He had heard many tales about Perceptor, but he hadn't believed them; it was too far-out! A robot couldn't think like a person, but now it seemed maybe it could after all. It wasn't a pleasant thought! He sighed deeply, turned back toward his desk, and picked up his phone. *I'd better sit down with this Chris Carson and talk, find out more about this technology. If it really is what it seems to be, I'd better reach some agreement with the man before somebody else does!*

****

In Korea, Kim Myong of Kyutu Electronics watched the world news with great interest. It wasn't hard for Myong to deduce who was behind the events of the past couple of days. So now Chris Carson had control of all the missiles! There had to be a way for Myong to get in on the action with Perceptor. Maybe he would agree to Chris's terms and pay to use the technology without getting control of the technology itself. At least, he'd be ahead of the US. He shook his head in disbelief. How stupid they are! Carson is a loyal American, and he'd easily let them use all his artificial intelligence technology if they'd just let him keep control of its secrets! But maybe I can beat them to it.

He reached for the phone. "Get me Chris Carson in Longmont, Colorado, USA." He waited until Gloria Carson answered.

"No, Mr. Myong, I'm sorry, but Chris isn't here just now. He's out of town on business." Her voice was matter-of-fact.

"I'm most anxious to reach him today, Mrs. Carson! It's a matter of utmost importance."

"As soon as he contacts me, I'll let him know you want to hear from him. It may take some time, though. He's out East in the storm, and only vital communications are getting through at this time."

As Myong hung up the phone, his eyes narrowed. *So...she's out of communication with him. That means he doesn't have his Perceptor unit with him! He never goes anywhere without it. There's only one answer to that—they have him in Washington! So they know too! They've finally caught on to what he's capable of. I wonder what they plan to do with him.*

He sat thinking a few moments and then suddenly grabbed up the phone. "Book me on the next available flight for Washington, D.C." he told his secretary. "I want to be there as soon as planes can land there again!"

****

In his room at the hotel, Chris read all the papers he could get, heard all the TV news there was, rested until he couldn't look at the bed anymore, drank even more coffee than usual, and ate more than a normal person should eat. He paced his room restlessly, feeling edgy and bloated and tense—more than ever like a caged animal. Now and then, he stopped to gaze out the window, trying to determine whether or not the storm was abating. It seemed to him to have been going on forever. *I guess I know how those explorers felt when they stayed in Antarctica! I wish they'd let me know what they plan to do with me!*

He sat down again and started doodling absently on a notepad.

The storm continued all that day and through evening, but sometime in the night, the wind calmed down. Gradually, the snow turned to occasional flurries, and in the morning, plows began to keep up with the snow. One by one, crews cleared the streets, and people began to arrive at their jobs, until by midday the city and the government were operating again, although with about half the staff.

The President summoned Chris. He gave a thumbs-up signal to the guard who delivered the message. "Okay, it's about time!"

He made himself presentable, and his guards took him to the White House. The place even smelled like history to Chris. He smiled to himself at the incongruity of it all, that a small-city guy with a background like his should be going to meet the president of the most powerful nation on earth to discuss the fate of the country, if not the world! He closed his eyes. *Please give me wisdom now, Lord!*

He pushed the lock of hair off his forehead and crossed the threshold into the Oval Office.

President Vandenberg took a chair on one side of the fireplace and motioned Chris to the chair opposite him. Chris sat, and the President began. "I've been reading up on you, Carson. You've had a fascinating life, haven't you?" He leaned back in his chair, elbows on the chair arms, fingers tented together. His piercing pale-blue eyes studied Chris from under their shaggy brows. "I want to get to know you and find out what you have in mind. Tell me about your invention and how it works and what you mean when you turn down all our offers...and our last offer was more than generous! No man ever turned down such an offer before, I'm sure! Do you mind telling me why you did? What makes you so different from them?" He waved his hand toward the city.

Chris cleared his voice. "Well, sir, it began a long time ago in Vietnam..." he told the President the whole story, the President breaking in from time to time with a question. They talked the whole afternoon, and Chris was amazed to realize it was evening when he finished his story, ending with the deployment of the Universal Space Station and the new weapon. The President finally rose, and Chris followed suit, his bones stiff from sitting in one place so long.

"I have a lot to think about. You are a most unusual man, Chris Carson. And you have us in a hammerlock, so to speak. Hmm, you might as well stay to dinner, anyway. Come on." He led the way upstairs, and Chris followed, wondering what to expect next. Mrs. Vandenberg was a gracious hostess as well as a shrewd judge of character, and her husband wanted her to meet Chris so he could have her opinion of the inventor to add to his own.

The table was lovely, the room was elegant, and the few other guests included the Vice President and his wife. They talked mostly about the storm through dinner, and Chris was able to relax a little. The wine was cool and not too dry, and Chris could feel it burn slightly in the bottom of his stomach. It felt good to him, though, and took his mind off his tight shoes and necktie. He enjoyed the excellent food, but later when Gloria asked him what they'd served, he couldn't remember for the life of him. He tried to make small talk and be pleasant, but he had never been good at that sort of thing, so he was glad when the evening was over and he could leave for his room. He was almost surprised when the guards appeared at his side again.

Back in confinement, he stood in a hot shower for a long time, letting the water soothe his aching muscles and bones and wash away the strain from the day. This was one to tell his children and grand-children about! He stepped out of the shower and grabbed a thick towel, rubbing himself down with it until he tingled, and then put on his pajama bottoms and turned on the TV to watch until he wanted to sleep. He had just gotten himself into a comfortable position on the bed with the pillows piled behind his back, when he heard something in the hall outside his door.

His senses snapped to alert, and he slid quietly off the bed and stood where he'd be behind the door if it opened, after grabbing the only weapon he found handy—his shoe. He couldn't tell whether it was trouble out there or not, but he had a funny feeling it was. There was a soft thud and a muffled oath or two, and then it was quiet again. Nothing happened for a minute or two. He let out his breath and was just about to go back to bed again when he saw the doorknob turning slowly!

He tensed, raising the shoe over his head. He planned to use the heel like a hammer. If he hit hard enough with it, he might be able to knock the guy down! Slowly the door opened, and someone softly entered the room. Chris brought the shoe down with as much force as he could muster, and a grossly fat body fell sprawling across the floor. The words he was spouting weren't English, but Chris knew they were curse words. Somehow you can always tell!

As the intruder struggled to get up, Chris raised his shoe to hit again. "Wait, Chris Carson! Wait a minute, will you?" The guy held his arms up to fend off a blow.

Chris stared in disbelief. "Kim Myong? Is that you? What in the world are you doing here?" Chris grabbed his arm and helped him up. "What did you do to the guard?"

"Oh, he'll be okay. He's in the utility closet down the hall." Myong rubbed his head and then dusted himself off and straightened his tie. "What are they doing to you?"

"Nothing much, they just want me handy by where they can keep tabs on me, that's all."

"Sure that's all!" Myong eased his heavy frame down in a padded chair in the corner. "Chris Carson, I'm here because I'm ready to do business with you…your way!"

Chris snapped the TV set off. "It may be a bit too late, Myong. I'm in a little trouble with my government at the moment." He slipped on a T-shirt. Somehow he felt less vulnerable when dressed.

"So I see!" Myong's eyes narrowed to slits. "I can get you out of here if you want, Chris. We can do business together from my plant in Korea."

"Thanks a lot, Myong. I guess I'm in enough trouble already!" Chris felt distinctly uncomfortable and began to look casually around for a weapon of defense. "I had a meeting with President Vandenberg today. It was a good meeting. I think I'd like to wait and see what he decides to offer."

"Is that your last say, Chris?" The dark eyes were fixed on him. The words were spoken quietly, but there was a menace behind them. Chris swallowed, then nodded. "Then I cannot let you live, Chris Carson. I cannot let anyone else have Perceptor!" Myong was on his feet in an instant, his bulky frame moving at a speed no fat man should be able to manage, while at the same time, two other men bounded into the room, grabbed Chris's arms, and twisted them behind his back. He managed to get out one good yell before they stuffed a sock in his mouth and stuck tape over it. He could barely breathe. They jammed his arms into his jacket sleeves, but they left him barefoot as they forced him out into the hall.

He struggled to breathe. *I guess this is it, Lord. I've had my extra chance. I only hope I haven't blown it completely! If this is my time, I guess I'm ready. And thanks, Lord! But if this isn't my time, please get me out of this mess!*

Chris's arms ached, and his mouth hurt. They had his tongue jammed against a sharp tooth that was cutting into it, and the sock was against the back of his throat, gagging him. As if that weren't enough, one of the goons stepped on his bare foot with a heavy boot, and Chris was sure some toes were broken! The hallway was endless, but they pulled and hauled him to the end and were about to turn into the stairway when the elevator doors opened and two Marine guards stepped out just in time to see him being dragged through the door.

"Hold it right there!" One Marine aimed his pistol at them, while the other used a hand communicator to summon help.

Kim Myong fired at the Marines, even as he yelled to the two men who held Chris, "Kill him!"

The heavy steel door to the stairway swung shut automatically, catching Myong's gun hand and knocking the gun to the hallway floor. He pushed the door open again to grab the weapon, but the Marine was quick with his own gun. Myong yelled in pain, and holding his throbbing hand to his chest, he ran down the stairs after his men. Behind him at the top of the stairs, the Marine leaned over the rail and shot again, wounding one of the thugs who dragged Chris. He let go, swearing. Chris pulled as hard as he could against the other, and the gunman lost his grip but shot back at him, even as the two thugs continued to flee down the stairway. Kim Myong hit the landing at about that same moment, holding his bleeding hand against his chest, and started to make the turn when Chris sprang out of the corner, butting his head hard against Myong's shoulder. The blow knocked the startled Korean off balance, and Chris butted again and watched as Kim Myong fell headfirst over the railing, landing with a sickening thud at least two flights down. His fleeing men ran over Myong's massive body on their way down. The burly Marine who bounded down the stairway after them located them easily by the trail of blood. They were crouched inside a storage closet near the elevator.

Suddenly, Marines were swarming all over the place. One of them tore the tape off Chris's mouth and pulled the sock out. "Thanks." Chris gasped. He needed a drink of water badly. His toes ached from cold and pain as he hopped and limped back to his room, the Marine's arm serving as support. Once there, he headed first for the bathroom where he gulped a glass of water and then for his bed, where he sank down gratefully. It was then he realized he'd been shot. Blood ran down his side from a flesh wound just under his arm. The Marine guard called for help and then got towels from the bathroom and wiped off the blood, holding a towel tight against Chris's side to stop the flow.

In less than five minutes, an E-unit arrived, followed closely by McCall and Williams. They were less than happy over the situation. "You just can't keep out of trouble, can you, Carson? Even when you're under guard, you manage to get into a mess like this!" McCall's sandy hair stood on end, and his shirt was buttoned wrong. Obviously, he had been sleeping when they called him. "Who is the guy who got to you, anyway?"

The attendants were dressing Chris's wound. He grunted as they applied an astringent and carefully bound on a dressing. They finished the bandage and straightened up. "It's not bad enough to take him to the hospital, but you'd better have a doctor look at it tomorrow," the tall one told McCall. Then he turned to Chris. "And try soaking your feet in some hot water." The two picked up their gear and left.

Chris answered McCall's earlier question. "Sorry I didn't get to introduce you, Jack! That's Kim Myong, president of Kyutu Electronics of Korea. He sent his man, Jong Lee, earlier to steal Perceptor, but since that didn't work, he decided to come himself!" Chris felt his toes one by one, gingerly bending them. He finally conceded they weren't broken after all, just badly bruised. He wished for his spray bottle of DMSO, but of course, he'd left that behind. He looked up at McCall. "Is he dead?"

"No, at least not yet. They took him to the hospital under guard. We'll be questioning him as soon as he's conscious." Williams checked the room thoroughly before he doubled the guard at Chris's door. "Don't want anything like that to happen again. We need you to answer a lot more questions! Get some sleep now, and we'll see you tomorrow." The FBI men left, and Chris was glad to see them go. He moved his neck gingerly, checking if he'd hurt it butting into Myong so hard. Then he ran some hot water into the bathtub and soaked his poor mistreated feet for a while. He finally lay down on his bed, propping his throbbing foot up on the extra pillow, and thought for a long time. When he fell asleep, he dreamed he was back in Vietnam shooting his way through the jungle and had caught his foot in a trap.

CHAPTER 33

*F*red woke in the hospital to find the most beautiful face he had ever seen bending over his. It had large wide-spaced dark eyes, a nose just slightly turned up, and a generous happy mouth. Short blond curls framed the face under a small white cap. He blinked his eyes hard. *I must be in heaven!*

"Open your mouth, Mr. Carson," she said in the voice of an angel.

He tried to speak, but it came out as a croak. He cleared his voice and whispered, "Who are you?" He was almost afraid she wasn't real.

"I'm Polly. I'm a nurse, and you're in the hospital. You've been through a lot, Mr. Carson, but the doctor says you're going to be fine. Now open your mouth so I can take your temperature." Obediently, Fred opened his mouth, and in a daze, he felt her holding his hand to check his pulse. *Polly...what a wonderful name!*

"Your pulse is a little fast, but your temperature is fine." Polly smiled, and Fred's heart paused in mid-beat, then began a steady, strong pulsing as the blood raced through his veins. He felt strange—hot but cold, weak but strong. He put his hand up to his head and felt bandages.

"Polly," he croaked, "tell me what happened, will you?" He wanted her to stay near him so he could see her face and hear that angel voice and feel the soft touch of her fingers. Fred was completely and totally smitten for the first time in his young life. He couldn't wait to get well so he could begin to get to know her. He knew already, though, this was the girl he wanted to marry! With an effort, he brought his mind back to what she was saying.

In that marvelous musical voice, she told him as much as she knew about what had happened. Then she tucked his covers around him and told him, "Now you rest a little while before the doctor comes to check you." He watched her walk out of the room, wanting her to stay.

As he lay there and thought about her, he began to take stock of his assets. *I wish I'd saved more of my pay! I wonder what my job will be when I'm well enough to return to work. Where could I afford to live that would be good enough for an angel?* A sudden thought struck him—what if she were married already? But he rejected the thought. No! She couldn't be married. She was his intended mate! God must have put him here in this place just to meet her! This terrible headache was a reasonable price to pay for that privilege.

Fred set a record at the hospital for fast recovery. When he was well enough, he requisitioned a wheelchair so he could leave his room to visit Violet's. He was still fond of Violet and admired her tremendously, but now only as a good friend. He told her about Polly and about his hopes and dreams, and she gave him some tips on how to set about winning Polly's heart.

From then on, Violet and Fred became real friends, who shared their thoughts and sympathized with each other's ups and downs. Violet was certainly happy with the new relationship. It was good to know a man she could depend on without worrying about getting involved physically. It was a totally new experience for her.

A few days later, the hospital released Violet. She spent her convalescence planning the new business and figuring out how they could run it most efficiently. Diane had written to her folks to tell them all about their plans for the "home," and the Portlands were enthusiastic about the project, promising to give all the help and support they could.

Diane faced trial and was sentenced to five years in prison. She was depressed over that but resolved to spend her prison time trying to help other prisoners come to know her Lord and studying her Bible and praying so she would never fall into such deception again! She had a letter from her dad in Grand Rapids. It was good news. Her folks had found a perfect place for the home, or at least, it seemed so to them. It was a huge mansion in the Heritage Hill section of Grand Rapids. It had plenty of bedrooms for cribs as well as enough space for Diane and Violet each to have her own privacy, and there was a large living room with a fireplace and a big formal dining room. The kitchen was modern and, with some modification, would do just fine. There were five bathrooms—two of them needed some help, but they could fix the whole place up to be perfect for their needs. Her folks were obviously excited about the place, and that made Diane excited too. She showed Violet the letter at her next visit, and they both felt this might be just the right place.

They prayed together over the decision and then Violet said, "If Gloria and Chris will back this one, let's go for it!" She took the letter to Gloria, who suggested she go to Grand Rapids and take a look at the place first. Then if it was as good as it seemed, Gloria and Chris would gladly put up the backing they needed.

Violet knew that made sense, and even though she was still not up to her full strength, she called the Portlands and arranged for them to meet her at the airport the following week. When Violet drove up to the house with Mr. Portland, she could hardly believe her eyes—it was like a palace! Snow hung like a canopy off the eaves of the elegant brick house. The huge oak and maple trees in the yard wore a coat of snow instead of leaves. It looked like a Currier and Ives painting to Violet. She could hardly wait to walk through the interior, but her first reaction was that they could never afford such a place.

Inside, she found that the carpet in the living room and two of the bedrooms would have to be replaced, and as the Portlands had said, two of the bathrooms were in dire need of work. They'd have to put tile around the tubs and redo the floors, as the old linoleum was badly worn. One of the toilet fixtures was cracked and would need replacing, but that wasn't terribly major.

On the plus side, there was a beautiful crystal chandelier in the dining room and a smaller one in the entrance hall. The living room had an elegant marble fireplace, and the kitchen was perfect, except they'd have to get some stainless steel appliances. "Oh, Mr. Portland! I can hardly believe it…this is perfect!" Violet's eyes were shining as she stood in the entrance hall after their tour. Her eyes followed the graceful line of the stairway. With some elbow grease and paint, it would be gorgeous. They locked the door behind them and returned the key to the real estate office, where they sat in the conference room and worked out a purchase agreement with the agent. It was contingent upon their being allowed to use the home as a business.

Ed Portland helped Violet persuade the city government to allow their special use in the area. The women were actually going to be in business! When Violet reported back to Diane, she brought pictures, and they talked out all the details. Diane was more anxious than ever to get out of prison and become involved with the babies, but she kept herself busy helping other women and praying for success with the work. Ed Portland was ready to pitch in with his tools and help get the house ready for "the poor babes." The work would take some time, even with Violet and the Portlands working on it as hard as they could.

A few days later, Violet sat in her vehicle at Sam Early's house for a few minutes, working up her courage. She needed to talk to somebody, though, so at last taking a deep breath, she stepped down from the rented minibus she was trying out for the business. She walked up the freshly shoveled walk to the unpretentious two-story house and across the wide front porch, hesitated a moment, and rang the bell. When the door swung open, she found herself facing a tall, fit man about her own age. He had salt-and-pepper hair but lots of it, combed back in an attractive manner. He wasn't handsome, but there was something about him that caused her to catch her breath.

"Hi!" she said. "I'm Violet Welford. I'm a friend of Chris Carson."

His smile lit up his whole face. "Well, come on in, Ms. Welford! It's a pleasure to meet you. Yes, Chris has mentioned your name to me." He ushered her into the living room and offered her a rocking chair beside the small brick fireplace, where a cheerful fire burned. She glanced around the room. It was neat and clean and uncluttered except for a small table by the window, and that was covered with books and some papers and pencils. Sam took his seat in an easy chair opposite her and crossed his legs.

"I know you've heard about our new venture from Diane's family, Pastor Sam. It's pretty exciting to be starting a new business. I only wish Diane could be here to work on it with me!"

"Yes, Diane has had a pretty hard road for the past few years." Sam agreed. "She's blessed to have a friend like you."

"Chris thinks so much of you…and I need to talk to someone…I decided while I was back in Colorado that I'd come to see you when I could." He was so easy to confide in that Violet opened right up. She told him first about her wonderful conversion while in the hospital, and then after they had rejoiced together over that, she was silent for a minute.

Sam perceived there was more she wanted to say, so he waited quietly.

"The problem is that I'm not what Chris thinks I am! I'm a terrible person!" She proceeded to tell him her whole sordid story. "So that's my problem." She finished. "You see, I just don't know what to do about telling Chris the truth. He's been so wonderful to me…and Gloria has too. How could I have done such a thing?" She looked at Sam, her beautiful eyes clouded with shame.

"When you're under Satan's control, you can do anything, the most vile and despicable things. The servant is like his master." Sam found it hard to believe this lovely woman could have led the rotten life she'd just described to him, but there was no earthly reason for anyone to lie about that sort of thing! They prayed together, and then Sam advised Violet to wait until Chris and Gloria had resolved their current problems and things were as normal as was possible in their lives, and then tell Chris the whole story, just as she'd told Sam.

"It'll be so hard!" she moaned softly, her head in her hands.

"Of course it will." He agreed. "But no harder than it was to get into the mess with Karadshie in the first place!" He walked her to the door. "Come to church, Violet, and meet and pray with other Christians and get built up in the faith. You need to grow in Jesus."

She smiled wanly. "I will, Pastor Sam, and thank you so much!"

After she left, Sam Early sat thinking over the conversation, remembering her contrition and repentance. She was the loveliest woman Sam had ever prayed with. He felt her sincerity when she told him of her shame. He felt something else too stirring in his soul, a feeling completely foreign to Sam. He knelt again, alone with his Father, to consult him about it.

Violet looked forward to each meeting with Pastor Early. He was the kindest, most understanding man she'd ever met, and he was strangely attractive in his own way! She told herself her interest in him was only as her spiritual guide, pushing aside the warm feeling she got whenever she saw him, but the light in her eyes told another story.

Ed Portland was completely bald now and had lost some of his belly since Jane put him on a diet a few years ago. He didn't look so much like a Kewpie doll anymore. Jane Portland was as nervous and busy as ever. She came up with excellent suggestions to make the house more efficient and got the church ladies to back the project. They also pledged to provide everything from diapers and baby food to actual physical work with the children. The Portlands were so grateful Diane had come to know Jesus and was free from her old addictions, that they were not nearly as upset as they might have been over her being in prison. They were willing to do anything they could to make a success of this new business venture for Diane, as well as for the babies.

The two women named the business "My Father's House." They found there would be no problem filling it with babies, as there were more of the poor little things than ever since the government had legalized the use of drugs! Violet couldn't wait to get started!

****

Gloria and Charlie Morse sat at a small conference table opposite the big oak desk in Gloria's office at Cognition Tech. "I don't know how this will come out, Charlie," she told him. They're still holding Chris under guard, and we don't have any idea what they'll decide to do with him! We have to keep running this place as though he were here. You know the things he was working on, don't you?" He nodded. "Well, if you and Perceptor and the guys can manage to complete any of his projects, go ahead." She hesitated. "Maybe the thing we should work on first is getting Perceptor to procreate, make more of himself. We can use all the units we can get, and I think Chris was planning to set up regular production as soon as he could."

"He said as much to us, Gloria, so I believe you're right. But Chris planned to make a different type of body for the newer units. I'm not sure just what material he planned to use. We were supposed to have a meeting to discuss that with him, but the storm came up first."

"For now, Charlie, let's just continue to make them the way we know how." She laid her pen down and got up to pour a mug of coffee. "Want one?" He held out his mug, and she filled it and then hers. She cupped the mug between her hands to warm them as she inhaled the fresh coffee aroma. "Chris plans to make humanoid bodies for the robots, you know."

"Humanoid? How could he do that?"

"Using some of the genetic engineering that's been being perfected over the past few years, I guess. Anyway, Charlie, we obviously can't start that without Chris, so maybe we should just build regular units, or maybe we could build only brain units and wait for Chris to decide what type of body to put on them. Hopefully, he'll be back with us before we need to make any decision about that!"

"You got that right, Gloria! Say, how are Milo and the Space Patrol doing?"

"They've been doing more building on the space station. The problem is, getting enough materials to them to complete the project, especially now!" She pushed the bangs back off her forehead in a gesture Charlie recognized as Chris's. "They've done well with just the Universal Space Station so far! Maybe we'll have to make that enough. The Moslems moved too fast for us to get the rest of the stuff up there." She looked at Charlie, started to say something and hesitated, and then decided to go ahead. "Reuben says they've noticed unusual activity around Tel Aviv. They think the Israelis may be up to something."

"Oh, wow!" Charlie shook his head. "I wonder what's next. Sure wish Chris would get back here!"

"Me too!" She agreed.

****

The Reverend Doctor Conrad Braxton followed the world news with great interest, and a growing conviction he must do something decisive to show the world what great danger it was in at the hands of Chris Carson. Now more than ever, he was sure Carson was the Antichrist the Bible warned about, who would show up in the "last days" and convince the whole world to follow him instead of God. Just look at that Perceptor, it was obviously a machine or "image" that could speak! And obviously it had superhuman, even godlike, powers. Look at the devastation it could cause, and nobody could do a thing about it! Now was the time to stop Perceptor—if indeed it was not already too late!

After spending time in study convincing himself even more of the truth of his insight, he called in his close associates and presented his case against Chris Carson and Perceptor. And after getting their wholehearted and terrified support, Dr. Braxton called a news conference, saying he had vital information to divulge. When the reporters arrived, he preached to them, waxing eloquent as he painted a dire picture of what he was convinced would happen next as Chris Carson took control of the world. If anyone else had said such things, nobody would have listened, but Dr. Conrad Braxton was an eminently respected scholar and preacher with a spotless reputation, the leader of the Fundamentalist Churches of the USA, and the chancellor of a prestigious university. He commanded attention!

Newspapers across the country carried banner headlines the following day proclaiming Reverend Conrad Braxton's revelation that Chris Carson was the Antichrist and Perceptor was the "beast." Network news programs carried Dr. Braxton's press conference as their prime story and followed it up with in-depth presentations showing Chris Carson and his inventions over the years. Perceptor was featured prominently, his metal body looking evil and sinister to those who believed the report—a manifestation of Satan, for sure! And he was multiplying! Every day more Perceptor robots were built, or at least, that's what they were led to believe!

There was immediate chaos in the Christian community. One faction clamored for Chris Carson's head on a platter, and one faction held that the whole idea of Antichrist was nothing but superstition, and Dr. Braxton would be well advised to get back to the business of saving souls and leave politics to the politicians! A few devout souls headed for caves in Missouri to wait out the predicted destruction. A larger group gathered in the snow outside the Cognition Tech plant, waving signs and shouting threats. Captain Kelly and his troops arrived to fend them off.

Gloria wished with all her soul that Chris was there to handle the situation, but since he wasn't, she first prayed for God's guidance and then had the Perceptor robots help her load the files and the computers into her car and into Charlie's Cadillac and Mick's station wagon. She directed two robots into each car, as she put the other vital equipment in Don's car, along with the remaining Perceptor brain units.

When they finished, she ran back to the office and hugged Cindy. "Go home, Cindy. We can't stand up to this mob. We can't let Perceptor hurt innocent citizens, and I don't want to put you in any more danger! I'll let you know if we need you, but if it happens that I never see you again, thanks for all your help and loyalty! You've been a real friend!"

Cindy was crying, but she knew Gloria was right. She gathered her things while Gloria signaled Captain Kelly, who ushered the weeping secretary safely to her car and cleared her way from the parking lot. Then he stepped back into the office. "You'd better get going too," he told Gloria. "I don't know how long we'll be able to keep order out there. More of them are coming all the time." He looked at her kindly. "I'm sorry about all this bunk about your husband. Wish he was here to help you. Seems he's been gone a long time now! Can you manage okay?"

She quickly explained what she planned to do, and he agreed to help her by distracting the crowd. "I'll keep them occupied out front while you make your escape from the lab entrance at the back. Better hurry, though." He warned. "They're getting ugly out there." He strode out the front door as she hurried through the plant.

"Let's go," she called as she ran through the back door. They piled into the vehicles. "Keep out of sight, Perceptor!" The robot units all did their best to duck down, and the men put their coats on top of them. Perceptor One was next to Gloria in her car. They pulled out of the back lot carefully and drove slowly away from the area, trying not to draw attention. Gloria was tense as she headed toward the apartment with her convoy. *How can I get word to Chris?*

She decided to try to call him on the telephone. Maybe she'd get through. It was worth a try, anyway! She drove faster now. *I know his phone is bugged, but I just have to talk to him!*

They were almost to the apartment. "Perceptor, what's going on at home?" she asked.

"There is a group forming out in front, but so far the back entrance is clear, and they have not come into the building."

"Pack my things in the suitcases from the closet and get my stuff from the bathroom too, will you? There's a big box in the guestroom closet we'll need too, Perceptor. I'll be there in a minute, and we have to be ready to leave again fast!" She spoke again through Perceptor One in her car. "Perceptor, please tell Charlie, Mick, and Don to go on to the truck rental company and load up, and I'll meet them there as soon as possible."

She pulled into a space behind the apartment building and ran up the stairs, not chancing the elevators. Adrenaline carried her along, so she hardly noticed the climb. Perceptor had a good start on the packing, and together they quickly finished the job. Gloria checked through the apartment, making sure she took everything vital, and then locked the door behind them. Only a second after the stairway door closed behind her and the robot, several well-armed devout men rushed out of the nearby elevator to find the locked apartment door and force it open again. The fleeing robot and its owner made it safely down the stairs and out the back entrance. It was difficult to jam everything into the already full car, but Perceptor had almost finished the job when some people came charging around the corner of the building.

"Look!" somebody shouted. "It's Perceptor!" They ran toward the car, slipping on the icy driveway. Perceptor gave the last suitcase an extra shove, wedging it into the space, and quickly crammed himself into the front seat with Perceptor One. Gloria backed out fast and then floored the accelerator. They roared away, skidding back and forth on the slippery snow, as more people came running around the building, yelling and throwing things.

"Perceptor, what's happening in Houston?" Gloria asked as she sped down the street. So far, there was nobody following, and she wanted to make as much distance between her and the apartment as possible before the mob got to their cars.

"The launch area is full of demonstrators, but the plant is quiet."

"I guess people don't know about that place yet. I'm glad now that we kept it so low-key!" Gloria took a deep breath as she sped toward the truck rental agency. "Tell Ray at Houston we're on the way and to be ready for us!" She rolled to a stop beside the truck. The team had almost finished loading it. Gloria called to them, "Who wants to go along, and who wants to stay here?"

Don and Mick had wives and families they couldn't leave. Charlie was a widower with nobody to worry about. That settled the question. Charlie and Gloria said good-bye to the others with hugs and warnings to be careful, and climbed into the truck. "It's better if you don't know where we're going. That way they can't make you tell them!" Gloria called. "I know the Lord will keep us all safe!" Charlie pulled out into the traffic, and they started down the highway.

"Pull into that gas station, Charlie, and while you're fueling the truck, I'll call Chris," she told him later on when they had been driving for more than two hours. "Wish I had a cell phone, but I never needed one before with Perceptor on the job!"

"Are you sure that's a good idea? What if his phone's bugged?"

"I know it will be, but we have to tell him something so he'll know not to come back to Longmont! I wish he'd taken a brain unit with him!" She decided how to communicate with Chris as she was dialing the number. Jim Myers was still in Houston working with Ray. She'd just tell Chris she and Charlie were going to visit Jim! He'd figure it out.

CHAPTER 34

President Vandenberg decided to go with his gut feeling about Chris Carson. Mrs. Vandenberg agreed with him that Chris seemed to be honest and sincere about his convictions. "You don't often find a man who will turn down fortune and power like he did. He must feel strongly about his Perceptor technology being vital and dangerous, and we know he's turned down offers from foreign powers too," she said to him. "And besides, he seems pleasant and down-to-earth, not like a power monger. I think Conrad Braxton is wrong about him! Think about it, Joshua. Can that man possibly be an Antichrist?"

So the President was about to meet with the Secretaries of State and Defense as well as Generals Norton and Finley and Admiral Jensen, to get their input and give them his. They had to make a decision about Chris Carson and move accordingly. He sighed deeply and almost asked God for guidance before he remembered that he was God himself, and his only guidance would come from the Ascended Masters. Life had been less complicated when he was young and there was a standard of right and wrong, and he could pray for help when he needed it. Well, he supposed that was all too simple. He closed his eyes for a moment, anyway, and hoped he would do the right thing for the country and for the world.

"Good morning, Mr. President." General Norton saluted and took a chair. He was followed closely by the others.

Secretary Stratton nodded. "Morning, Josh. Boy, it's good to see the sun again, isn't it?" The President nodded back. The group made small talk about the storm now past and its effect on their lives.

Then they discussed the uproar caused by Conrad Braxton's allegations about Chris until President Vandenberg indicated it was time to get to the matter at hand. "What should be our course of action in dealing with Chris Carson and the weapon?" He looked around the circle. "I want to hear your opinions first before I give you mine."

"What would happen if we tried to shoot it down?" Jackson, the Secretary of Defense, looked toward General Finley.

"From the demonstrations we've seen, nothing could get close enough to it before being shot down itself." He shook his head. "No, I don't think that would work. What we have to do is get control of Perceptor!"

"Now how in the world do you propose we do that?" General Norton inquired sarcastically. "Just go right in there and tell Perceptor we're taking him over?"

"Why not? After all, he's just a machine! And why are we talking about it as 'him'?"

"It's easy to do when it acts so human," Admiral Jensen put in. "I tend to think of Perceptor as a personality the same as the rest of us. It's hard to remember sometimes that he…it is really a machine!"

"Perceptor is loyal to Chris Carson, its creator—although it seems ridiculous to talk about loyalty as concerning a machine—and it will take something extraordinary to get it to change that." Secretary Jackson tapped his pencil absently on his yellow pad. "And as I understand it, a built-in defense mechanism would cause the unit to melt down or something if we tried to open one up to find out how it works and copy it."

"You're right there, Bob. It's happened before, and it would be a shame to lose any of the units. They're pretty expensive to build, and we can use all of them we can get! Have you men thought about the possible uses for this technology? Why, if it were used properly, we could change the economics of the world in short order!" Secretary of State Stratton was clearly eager to manage the new economics.

The President leaned forward, arms on the table, and surveyed the group. "We'll go along with Carson for now and let him keep control of the technology, giving us the use of it to do with as we see fit." He felt some of the others ready to object, so he hurried to elaborate on his idea. "It will be a compromise, you see. He'll get to keep his secrets and control manufacturing, research, and development, but we'll get to use the units in whatever way we feel is best for the country and the world. Of course, we'll have to get approval from the United Nations Security Council, but I'm sure they'd also like to use the technology, and we could give them that opportunity! And eventually, we'll figure out the technology ourselves."

Reluctantly, they agreed one by one as they saw the wisdom of the President's argument. "But what about costs?" Secretary Jackson worried. "He'll have us over the barrel there! There'll have to be some agreement as to the cost of each unit."

"We have a whole array of details to work out. I'll let you and Stratton put together a proposal, and I'll look it over and give you my input. Then we'll take it to congress and the UN." He frowned. "That sounds like it could take a long time, and we don't want to drag our feet, what with the weapon hanging out there in space ready to zap whatever they decide to zap!" The shaggy brows looked almost fierce. "I want this ready for me by day after tomorrow at the latest, understand?"

The meeting was clearly over. The men filed out, talking among themselves. After they'd left, Josh Vandenberg sat for a minute or two debating with himself. He shook his head, sighed again, and turned to the stack of papers that demanded his attention. "Pauline! Come in here and take a letter!" His secretary entered with her electronic notebook, and the business of state went on.

Even though the president had asked for fast action, it took what seemed forever to get the proposal formulated to everyone's satisfaction. By the time they were ready to see Chris again and present it for his reaction, almost a month had gone by.

Chris Carson would have lost his mind without something to do, so while he waited, locked in the hotel room, he worked at developing a new Perceptor body. If the process he worked out were successful, the robots would look almost like humans. He thought it ironic that his units would be without greed, envy, lust, hate, or any other human sins the world hadn't been able to control over all the centuries. Of course, they would also be without love and mercy and compassion and all the other good traits. He wondered what would happen to them as they gathered more and more experience dealing with people. Would they develop feelings? He looked up. "Lord, it's all in your hands. I guess you wouldn't have given me the knowledge to make Perceptor if you didn't have it all planned from the beginning. But I'd sure like to know the reason for it all!"

By the time he got the call telling him the committee was ready to meet and submit their proposals to him, Chris had tentative plans for a humanoid body ready to begin testing. "It probably was the only way I'd ever have time to sit and work it out, the way things were going!" he said to Gloria later.

Feeling relief that the meeting was finally set, he hung up the phone and turned on the television to watch the news. It took him a few seconds to recognize Conrad Braxton. Then it registered what he was saying. He proclaimed to the world that Chris Carson was the Antichrist and Perceptor was the beast. He warned Christians to beware because Chris would soon try to take over the world, deceiving the unwary into worshipping him as God! "Dear Lord, I can't believe this! How can he do this? How can he think such a thing? This man was my friend once, the first one I told about what happened to me." Chris knew, of course, that Braxton had preached against him in his TV sermons, but this was on a national newscast! And this was a much stronger statement, giving no doubt of the truth of the accusation.

Chris suddenly thought he could understand how Jesus felt when Judas betrayed him. His own accuser was the man who led him in prayer, giving his life to Jesus! So how could he possibly believe these terrible things he was saying? Was it just because Chris had questioned his theology? Chris listened to the theories about Perceptor and the strange weapon that had shot down and destroyed the missiles, and heard how Dr. Braxton used the Bible to try to prove his horrendous accusations.

Finally, Chris began to laugh. How absolutely ridiculous the whole idea was that a man such as he, Christopher Carson, could be the Antichrist. He laughed almost hysterically until he came to his senses and realized his situation was serious...and dangerous! Then he fell to his knees and talked to Jesus for a long, long time, praying for his family's safety and for wisdom to know what to do. Jesus comforted him with the picture of his own betrayal at the hands of a "friend" who certainly should have understood him, and assured him that whatever happened, Jesus was with him. *There is still work to do, so don't lose faith, I am with you. Follow me!* The words came clearly to his mind and heart and gave Chris strength once more.

Next morning, he walked confidently into the meeting and shook hands with the dignitaries assembled there. Nobody mentioned the topic of prime interest to all of them, but Chris could feel their curiosity—their fear, in some cases. He used it to his advantage. It took a few hours of negotiation, but by the end of the day, there was a contract in place between Chris Carson and the government of the United States with United Nations' approval. Finally, after all the frustrating years, he would see his inventions at work across the world doing the good he knew they were capable of. For many years, people had held other humans as slaves to do their work. Now people could be free and equal, as Perceptor units could be the legitimate slaves! God had provided what man had always wanted, if man could only receive the gift humbly instead of greedily! There would be enough money now to build all the units they could make, as fast as they could make them. And so many other products could be made using his other discoveries! He was dimly aware how much his technology would change the world. He hoped it would all be good! If only Conrad Braxton hadn't stirred up such a hornet's nest!

President Josh Vandenberg hoped he hadn't just made a deal with the devil! He stifled the thought. Of course, he knew there wasn't any such thing! So did all the intelligent members of his government. Still, he felt a prick of apprehension as he ordered his people to provide a guard for Chris as protection from the fundamentalist Christian followers of Conrad Braxton, who might believe this quiet genius was actually the Antichrist.

****

In a dark, luxurious office somewhere in Europe, a certain charismatic leader of men watched the news from the United States and chuckled. "How easy these gullible Christians are to lead around by the nose...and how kind of the good Dr. Braxton to set them on the trail of the key person I had any worry about!" Apollos Hercainian entered a small private room next to his office and seated himself cross-legged on a large cushion, gazing into the depths of a giant crystal that dominated the room. Soon the stone's center seemed to glow with a strange reddish fire as he concentrated on it, muttering certain secret words over and over. Gradually, a presence emanated from the crystal, filling the chamber with an ominous cloudy essence. Slowly, it formed itself into a humanoid shape and stood, ugly and dark, huge and foreboding before the crystal, its leathery wings much like those of a giant bat. What Apollos Hercainian saw was a glorious being, light shining on his golden hair and reflecting from his lustrous golden wings. The great man prostrated himself before his evil god, Lucifer, and together they celebrated the blow to the forces of their enemy.

****

Gloria and Charlie had almost reached Houston before Gloria was finally able to contact Chris. He was in the historic meeting while they fought through their troubles in Colorado, so when he tried to call Gloria after the meeting, he wasn't able to reach her. He was pacing and trying to decide what to do next when his phone rang. He snatched it up and was flooded with relief when he heard Gloria's voice. "Where have you been? I've been trying to call you! Are you all right?" Emotion strained his voice.

"Oh, Chris! I'm so glad we finally reached you! No, things are not okay! Mobs tried to get into the office and the plant, and even our apartment! They're looking for you and Perceptor because of that crazy man, Braxton! I took everything we could manage to carry, and we're going to visit Jim." Chris started to ask a question, but she cut him off in midsentence. "Chris, we know your line is bugged, of course, so that's all I can tell you. How are things on your end?"

He told her the good news, his mind going a mile a minute all the while. "Listen, Gloria, I'll try to join you at Jim's as soon as possible. Sure wish I had my briefcase! Can't be helped now, though! Keep out of sight as much as you can, and if things get desperate, burn the files and destroy the computers. All we need now is Perceptor. Keep the robots with you, and you'll be okay! I love you, and I'll see you soon."

After she hung up, Chris called Lou Jackson, Secretary of Defense. "I have a problem, sir," he said after preliminary small talk. "I understand mobs are trying to get into and destroy my factory and my home, and there's not much I can do about it from here! Also, I need to get to my wife and make sure she's safe and not frightened. I wasn't sure which of you men to call about this, but I hope you can do something for me?"

Secretary Jackson assured Chris that troops would defend his factory and home and said, "If there's anything else I can do to help?"

"Yes there is, sir, since you ask. I need safe passage across the country. I guess what I'd like is a good disguise and a fast car. Is there any way you could help me with those?" He waited on hold for a few minutes while Jackson made some calls and then thanked him for all the help and got out his bags to pack his things.

In a remarkably short time, the guards, now his protectors, brought him a large carton and handed him a set of keys. "It's a rented car, but they've arranged for you to drop it anywhere you like and just mail the location and keys back to them."

"Thanks a lot, that'll help!" He closed the door on the guard and opened the carton. It contained a makeup kit, wigs, mustaches, and clothes—slacks, sweater, jacket, boots. He checked the clothes thoroughly for "bugs" and found the tiny transmitter sewn into the hem of the slacks. He left it there, refolding the slacks and wearing his own with the other new things. Then he began to work on his face and hair. Choosing the blond wig because of his blue eyes, he combed it in a different style than he normally used. He added a mustache and sunglasses and surveyed himself critically in the mirror. He felt ridiculous, but it would do for now.

He grabbed his suitcase, waved at the guard, and headed for the car. It was a silvery green Zoomer, a fast two-seater sports car. Chris had always wanted to drive one, and now he admired its graceful lines as he slid behind the wheel and studied the geo-positioning system and computerized controls for a minute or two before he turned the key and eased out into traffic. They mean to be able to track me easily with this car...well, I'll see about that!

Chris headed toward Colorado first, speeding his way across the country to St. Louis, Missouri. There he drove to the bus station and placed the bugged slacks in a locker. Next, he drove downtown and found a space in the far corner of the sub-basement level in a multi-level city ramp. He parked the Zoomer, feeling some regret as he left the keys in an envelope with the attendant, saying someone would pick it up. He'd enjoyed driving that car. From there, he walked to a department store nearby where he bought a pair of cotton pants with lots of pockets, a sweatshirt, canvas shoes, heavy socks, a warm jacket, and a knitted hat. He added a longish dark brown wig and a suitcase. In the men's room, he changed into the new clothes, folded the ones he'd been given, and put them into his old suitcase, along with the wigs and mustaches. Carefully, he applied some darker makeup from the kit they'd supplied and stuck the bottle into a pocket. He straightened the wig on his head, combed it carefully, and surveyed himself in the mirror. Not great, but it would have to do! He stuck some more stuff from the makeup kit into his pockets and then put the kit into his old suitcase. His own clothes and other belongings, he packed into the new suitcase.

He checked around casually, and then carrying two suitcases, he left the store by the side entrance and hailed a cab to take him to the airport, where he stashed the old suitcase in a locker. He took an airport bus back to a big downtown hotel, walked through the lobby and out the other side, and then made for a city bus stop where he got on the first bus that seemed to be headed south. At the city limits, Chris left the bus and started walking.

It seemed forever before he came to a big truck stop that provided fuel, showers, bunks, and food for long-distance truckers. He suddenly realized how hungry he was. He'd been going on adrenaline a long time—that and a couple of candy bars. He ordered dinner and coffee and watched the truckers come and go as he ate. Most of them seemed to know each other and the waitresses. They joked and laughed and complained about the weather, the roads, the fuel prices, and the delays in loading and off-loading. "Where you bound for, Danny?" he heard the waitress ask.

"Texas, honey. Wanna go along?"

"Sure." She laughed. "Just let me check it out with my husband first, okay?"

"Shucks!"

Chris turned in his seat far enough to eye the trucker. He looked okay, seemed a decent sort. "You ever take on a passenger?" Chris asked him casually.

Danny eyed him curiously. "Why? Where you bound for?"

"Texas. My rig broke down. I'm leaving it in St. Louis, but I have to get on home. They tell me it'll take a week or so to fix it." He lied.

"Whereabouts in Texas?"

"I'd like to get down to Galveston, but anywhere in Texas'll be a lot closer home than I am now!"

Danny Thompson looked Chris up and down. There was a rule against picking up riders, but it was a long drive, and he got lonely sometimes. Anyway, this guy looked okay, and he needed to get home. Danny could relate to that. "I ain't leavin' for a couple hours yet. Got to get some shut-eye first."

"That's okay, I could use some myself." They walked out to the rig, an aging Peterbilt, with a double bunk. Danny climbed into the bunk, and Chris stretched out on the seat.

It seemed as if he'd just laid down when Danny poked him again. "Time to head out!" The big engine roared under Danny's urging, and they lurched slowly out of the parking lot and headed southwest, picking up speed. Danny was bound for San Antonio, so Chris decided to get out at Dallas. They talked and laughed, and Chris learned some things from Danny about the trucking business (while pretending to know all about it) and heard about his family. Chris told Danny about his family too but avoided telling him much else. They made good time, and it surprised them both how soon they pulled into the big truck stop outside Dallas. Chris thanked

Danny, slipped him a few bills for his trouble, and hitched a ride into the city. From Dallas, he took a commuter flight to Houston under the name Nels Jorgensen. He figured it would take awhile for anyone to track him down.

At the Houston office, things were in chaos. They'd made a makeshift living quarters for Gloria in Ray's office, while Charlie had a cot in the conference room. Equipment and papers from the Colorado plant were stacked all over, and Perceptor robots and brain units were everywhere you looked. Ray wanted to get a hotel room for Gloria, but she was afraid someone might recognize her, and that would give away Perceptor's whereabouts. She couldn't chance it without Chris's approval, so they put up with the inconvenience and waited for him to arrive.

Television blared the news of the disappearance of Perceptor and of Chris. Nobody knew where to find them. Army troops guarded the Cognition Tech plant as well as the Carson home, but there was no sign of Mr. or Mrs. Carson or their chief engineer, Charlie Morse. Dr. Conrad Braxton was sure that their mysterious disappearance proved their supernatural powers! The fundamentalists were in turmoil, not sure what to do. They held large prayer vigils asking for God's help against the Antichrist and against the beast!

In Grand Rapids, Sam Early, the Portlands, and Violet did all they could to dispute Braxton's claim. "I know Chris Carson, and he is one of the best Christian men you would ever hope to meet!" Violet told Sam's church. Ed and Jane Portland agreed with Violet, but it was hard for the church to understand how a man like Dr. Conrad Braxton could be wrong about something so important as this! They asked questions relentlessly until Violet, saying a little prayer for forgiveness under her breath, finally told them the story Chris had told her when she was in the hospital. She told it so well with such depth of feeling they could picture Chris being shot and almost see the meeting with Jesus. Sam confirmed all she said and added some details Chris had told him. The congregation finally believed and rallied around Sam, Violet, and the Portlands to support Chris and his family.

"I couldn't help it, Sam," Violet told him after the meeting. "I can't let them think those evil things of such a good man as Chris Carson!" She looked up at him through those incredible lashes. "Was I wrong to tell?"

Sam's heart beat fast. He had some strange and foreign feelings. He wanted to pull her into his arms and hold her close. He looked into those blue, blue eyes and smiled at her. "No, Violet, you did absolutely right!" He took a deep breath and then asked, "Want to go have a bite to eat and talk about it?"

She nodded. "That'd be great. I just realized how hungry I am!" They found a quiet booth at a little restaurant where they sat and talked for a long time while they continued to fall totally in love, though they didn't realize it at the time. Sam had never been in love before, and it was hard for a man his age to come to grips with such new and upsetting feelings. In return, Violet had never let herself care about a man before. She had only worried about men's financial statements. Now being with Sam, it didn't matter one bit that he was poor! The Lord brought their two lonely hearts together in a love that he blessed. Neither of them had ever been so happy, although it took them some time to realize that. Some of Sam's congregation recognized his love before he did!

****

Defense Secretary Jackson was livid. "How could this happen?" He pointed his finger at the FBI agents before him. "We had this all under control, we knew where he was and where he was going, so now, where is he? Who is this Jim they talked about visiting?"

"We'll find him!" Jack McCall vowed. "I swear we'll find him! And when we do, what do you want us to do with him?"

"For now, just keep an eye on him. I want to know where he goes, who he sees, what he does. I want to know all there is to know about him! We need to watch him constantly to keep him from blowing us all up, for one thing! How do we know he isn't trying to take over the world like Conrad Braxton says? He's in a pretty good situation to do it now if he wants to with the space station armed as it is!" He punched his fist into the palm of his other hand. "And why did he feel he had to escape from us, anyway? If he's on our side and ready to let us use the technology, then why doesn't he trust us?"

McCall raised an eyebrow. "We know he's no dummy, and in his shoes, would you trust us?"

A secretary knocked on the door and stuck her head and arm in, waving a paper. "This just came in over the secure modem, sir. I think you might want to see it right away."

Jackson grabbed the paper. "Thanks, Shirley." Her head disappeared again. "Can you believe it? This is from Carson! That ingrate wants to know where we want the Perceptor robots to set up production for making more robots—at Cognition Tech or somewhere else entirely!" He shook his head. "I can't believe this guy! He sure has some nerve!" He read the rest of the letter. "He says the Cognition Tech plant is too small to produce many Perceptor units, but if we like, we can start there until we get a larger plant ready. But he also says a mob tried to break in there, intending to smash all the equipment, and he suggests a place he knows in Arizona that's big enough, has good security, and it's empty!" He slammed the sheet down on his desk. "I might not like this guy, but I admire his guts!" He looked at Benedict and McCall. "Well, what are you waiting for? Go find him!"

They headed for Shirley's desk and asked her, "Where did that modem call come from?"

She shook her head. "There's no way to tell where it's from. With the secure-calling feature we had put in, it's impossible to trace."

"I can't believe that! There has to be some way to tell something about the source."

"We do know that it was sent from a machine that has the same security features that this one has! But of course, since Mr. Carson is the inventor of the machine, it seems obvious he'd have one." Shirley became defensive. They acted as if it was her fault they couldn't find Chris Carson!

"Okay, okay, never mind. And thanks, Shirley." Benedict gave the girl a mock salute and poked McCall, "Come on, let's get going." They met Bill Williams in the hall. "Any luck finding the car yet?" Benedict asked him.

"Yeah, we just located it in a parking ramp in St. Louis. He left the keys with a parking attendant and told him somebody would pick it up! The guy says he left there on foot."

Benedict swore softly. "You men get out there and try to follow his trail." He turned away, muttering to himself as much as anyone else, "the man must be paranoid to suspect we had him bugged! Why would he think we'd want to follow him?"

****

Chris arrived near the small plant in Houston on the back of a motorcycle driven by a rough-looking, bearded fellow who'd picked him up walking. He swung himself and his suitcase down and tried to give his benefactor a few bucks for the lift. The biker revved the big engine and roared away, waving his leather-covered arm, while Chris picked up the suitcase and hurried down the street to the plant. He opened the door to the chaos inside and was immediately overwhelmed by welcome. Gloria flew at him, grabbed him around the neck, and hugged as though she'd never let go. Then Ray, Jim, and Charlie couldn't shake his hand enough. They were full of questions, wanting to know how he got there, and whether anyone had followed him. After the first flurry of excitement; Gloria had coffee brought, and they all sat down to talk.

After they had all told their whole stories, Chris stood up and paced as he always did when making decisions. "I signed a contract to let the government use my technology, and I intend to keep my word, except now they'll have to work through Perceptor without my being there. Remember that big empty building near the place we had in Phoenix?" They looked blank, and he remembered. "Oh, that's right. That was before I hooked up with you fellows again. Anyway, there was a great building I think would be a perfect place to manufacture Perceptor units. Perceptor can handle the whole process on his own now, and I'll be in touch through Perceptor One. He'll always stay with me from now on! Anyway, as I said, Perceptor knows what equipment is needed and can set it up better than any industrial engineer can, and then he can begin to 'procreate.' He can handle all the paperwork and shipping involved too, so once the plant is set up and equipped, the government won't be spending anything more than material, rent, and utilities! All the new units will continue to be the same brain with Perceptor One, so I'll always be able to stop any harmful use of the technology." He saw the look on their faces and remembered they didn't know about the AVC connection, so he swore them to secrecy and told them about it. "And if anyone tries to tamper with the brain units, they'll self-destruct. With Perceptor running the manufacturing plant himself, nobody else will be able to figure out the secrets, and I have no worry at all that anyone will be able to break into the place and steal them! Anybody see anything wrong with that?"

They had a few questions about the logistics involved in setting Perceptor up in the plant in Arizona, but in general, they agreed with Chris. Ray voiced the question they'd all been thinking about. "What will we do now that Perceptor will be on his own? And what about the space station?"

"We'll be busy doing some other research and development I have in mind. First, we'll be making some different bodies for Perceptor robots. Of course, as Perceptor continues to learn, we'll soon be able to use him to figure out things like that too, and a lot better and faster than we ever could do it! However, for now, I have a plan I worked out while they held me prisoner in Washington." He proceeded to lay out some ideas he'd developed. "We can probably use this place awhile yet as long as nobody connects it with Cognition Tech." He frowned, pondering, and then changed his mind. "I don't know about the NASA people who were here once, though. Maybe you'd better all lay low for a few days, take a little vacation while Gloria and I find us another spot, if that's okay with you? We'll have to be ready to move fast if we're discovered, though, and I probably should stay away from you as much as possible. We'll each take a brain unit with us so we can keep in touch, and we'll leave some Perceptor robots on guard in this building to watch our equipment just in case!"

As the others discussed the situation among themselves, deciding where to go for their breaks, Gloria and Chris took stock of their own problems. "We'll have to work as fast as we can to get our stuff moved before someone thinks to look for us here." Chris looked around him at the general disaster. "We'd better have Perceptor start packing things up ready to move." He eyed Gloria and made a wry face. "We can't chance someone recognizing us, so we'll have to rely on disguises while we go out and find ourselves a new base of operations. I'll have Ray go shopping for some stuff for us right now. Then we'll get a motel room for tonight, and tomorrow we can head over San Antonio way and see if we can find a good manufacturing plant to hide in while we work. And we'd better move as fast as we can!"

Gloria nodded in agreement. When the chips were down, she did well making the crucial decisions, but it seemed good now to have Chris back in control.

When Ray got back from shopping, Chris and Gloria did their best with the materials he brought. Gloria came out looking like a slim man after she cut her hair even shorter, used the dark brown hair coloring, and removed all her makeup. She dressed in a suit and shirt and tie that fit her tall, slender frame pretty well. The only problem she found was with the shoes. They were ugly and heavy besides being slightly large for her. Chris also dressed in suit and tie, a gray wig, and a fedora that bothered him a lot. He hated hats! But with sunglasses in place, the pair certainly bore little resemblance to themselves as they walked back into the plant.

"Wow!" Charlie could hardly believe what he saw. "I know you two as well as anyone, and I certainly wouldn't recognize you if I didn't know it was you!" Gloria did a model's turn for him, and they all laughed. "Of course, your actions are another thing entirely!"

Jim and Ray agreed with Charlie's appraisal of their disguises, so feeling like the original "odd couple," Chris and Gloria gathered their things into suitcases, picked up the briefcase with Perceptor, and set out on their search, driving an inconspicuous rental car.

CHAPTER 35

As it happened, they both saw the place at the same time. It was out in the country near a town called Sheridan, a long, low building set well back from the road. It was all by itself, the nearest building being a run-down café a little way south that marked the edge of town. It appeared vacant, and its large "For Sale" sign was somewhat weather-beaten, indicating it might have been there for some time. A few skinny trees stood near the corner of the property; otherwise, only weeds provided landscaping. The parking lot was unpaved and dusty, with ruts where heavy trucks had parked during the muddy season.

They got out of their car and walked around the building, looking into the windows. Chris tried the door; it was locked and seemed sturdy. Through the windows, they could see cement floors, and heavy power lines proclaimed it had been used for manufacturing. There seemed to be adequate office space too.

"It looks as though the Lord prepared it just for us!" Gloria marveled. "Chris, do you suppose that's possible? Is this as good as it looks?"

Chris was almost as excited about the place as she was but a little more cautious. "Let's pray about it first." He suggested, so they bowed their heads right then and there, praying for guidance.

After they finished praying, Chris walked over to the car and took out the Perceptor unit. "Take a look at this place and see if it would be suitable for doing our research and development." He carried the unit around the building, letting it see into the windows and observing the power source and the proximity to town.

"I see nothing that could not be easily fixed," Perceptor replied.

"That's what I thought too." Chris agreed. "Let's go talk to the realtor then."

As they drove through Sheridan to find the real estate office, Chris reminded Gloria. "It would be best if you don't talk, honey. Your voice might give us away if you accidentally forget to keep it low." She nodded as they spotted the small office. They parked nearby and walked in together, with Chris carrying the briefcase.

It was like entering a time warp. The place was dimly lit, dingy, and cluttered. Dusty cobwebs clung to the overhead light and strung from the darker corners of the room. The four chairs in the waiting area were badly in need of new cushions, and Chris couldn't tell at first whether anyone was seated at the desk behind the tall stacks of books and papers. Then a pinch-faced pasty-skinned fellow rose up like a specter from the midst of the mess and came toward them, showing his long teeth in what passed for a grin, his bony hand outstretched. Gloria suppressed her giggle. *I don't believe this. He looks like something out of a Dickens novel!*

"Howdy, y'all! Ah'm Harry Meunkleh, but moz' folks call me Fle-up. What c'n ah do for y'all?" Flip shook hands with them enthusiastically, his shrewd, beady eyes sizing them up quickly as pigeons. "Y'all lookin' fuh good 'nvayusmint prahpity, ain' no bettah taown tn She-ar-i-dun, Tay-ux-us, no suh! We got some prahpities sho to come on up t' morn' twicet ter valoo in the next cupla yeahs wid all the noo duhveulupmint goin' on these daz!"

"What do you have in the way of houses? Any bargains on a good-sized solid house? Say, maybe four or five bedrooms, three or four baths?" Chris had sized up Flip Minkley too and decided to edge his way into discussion of the building. Besides, they'd need a place for the team to live. Might as well all live in one place. It'd be easier to handle things, at least, while they got established.

Flip's face fell; maybe these guys weren't such good prospects after all. "Say, Ah do hev one playuhs mought fit," he drawled. "It's out by itsef, though, not in the taown prahpah. It's jist pay-ust the old Merriweathuh playunt. Y'all know Shearidun atall?"

"No, not really. Which direction would that be?" Chris tried to be as blank and bland as he could. He'd dealt with guys like Flip before.

"It's awt ta the North ayund. Cum awn, I mought as well carry y'all awt theah. Y'all plannin' t' pay cayush, or y'all wantin' a mohgij?" Flip dug around in his desk drawer as he asked. He came up with a key and waved it at them. "Got ut!"

"Depends, I guess. How much is the place?" They parried back and forth as they followed Flip out to the car. Chris was firm as he said, "No, thanks, we'll just follow you." Flip grumbled under his breath. It was always best to get the customer in his car where he could keep track of their conversation and "get to know them better." He slammed his car door extra hard, backed out, and started off in the direction Chris and Gloria had come from.

"You don't suppose our building is the Merriweather plant, do you?" Gloria wondered. "No, we couldn't be that lucky, I'm sure!"

Chris shrugged. "Guess we'll soon find out! What do you think of our friend Flip? Isn't he a character, though?"

Gloria laughed. "Hard to believe he's able to make a living in real estate. He certainly doesn't inspire much trust and confidence, does he?"

They drove past the café, and then they passed "their" building and turned right at the first road beyond it. "I can't believe this! Wouldn't it be great if the house is usable?" Chris almost held his breath as they turned into the driveway of a low, Spanish-style place. It looked too small from the front but turned out to be much deeper than it appeared, and they found it charming, with all the rooms having access to a courtyard in the center. They counted six bedrooms, each with its own bath, and a large living room the width of the house across the front. The dining room and kitchen were on the left wing of the square and were modern and well equipped. What was most surprising was that all the furnishings were in place, even to an elegant old grand piano in the living room.

Gloria's eyes lighted up as they moved from room to room. It was difficult not to smile, but she was careful to keep from showing her feelings to Flip, who watched eagle-eyed for their reactions.

"The furnishin's doesn't hev ta go with the playus, but the ohnahs ah lettin' a noo buyah hev fust chayuns at ut," Flip commented. "They done went back East an' don' need this stuff no moah."

"Why did they move?" Gloria asked, her curiosity getting the best of her. She remembered to keep her voice low.

"They owned the Merriweathah playint, made blayunk audio-video tayups afore the mahkit wint. Once them lasah-discs tuk ovah the whole bizniz, the sayuls was so bayud they hed ta close up. Ennywayus, I suspeck Miz. Merriweathah was ahankerin' ta go back ta No'th Ca'linah whar she come from, an this was her chayunce!" Flip's eyes rolled back. "She were some layuhdy!"

"So does this property back up to the plant?" Chris tried to sound casual and only mildly interested.

"Weell, yayus…bucha cud build a fayunce er somethin'. It's away bayuck theah, y' know…theyall hay-ed twenty ayucre total."

"How much they asking for the plant? Could we get a better deal if we bought the whole thing?" Chris stood at the back door, looking across the field toward the empty factory.

Flip nearly swallowed his tongue. "Heah! Y'all fixin' ta buy the whole thayung, ah can cutchoo a tee-rrific deel!" His mental calculator was already figuring up his commission. They closed the deal within the week and contacted Ray, Jim, and Charlie at once, arranging to meet at the Houston plant. There they loaded their equipment and trucked it to Sheridan at night, leaving no trail behind them. They ordered new equipment for the plant under the name Bio Enterprises. In short order, they were set up and in full swing working to develop new robot bodies.

Meanwhile, the government sent some experts to look at the plant near Phoenix that Chris recommended. The experts agreed it would be a perfect place to begin manufacturing, so the government bought the place, and Chris sent most of the robots there to set up full-scale production of more Perceptor units. The whole process was so smooth the cabinet members couldn't believe it. Perceptor engineered the factory for maximum efficiency and ran it with complete security. Not only that, but he handled the office work and book-keeping with no errors, always on time. It was all terribly frustrating to the powers in Washington who wanted an excuse to find fault with the operation so they could go in and take control.

During the first few months of the factory's operation, more and more new Perceptors arrived in Washington. From there, they were dispatched to wherever the government wanted them. Soon the government would have enough, and would begin to let private companies and individuals buy robots for their own use. The United States government became infinitely more efficient as Perceptor units assumed jobs that had previously been done by masses of workers. But that added to the widespread unemployment in the country, causing more distress.

Meanwhile, at Sheridan, the team perfected a new body for Perceptor units. The finished product looked eerily human. Chris contacted President Vandenberg to tell him about the new development. "I'll send you a sample unit so you can see what I mean," he told the President, speaking by modem so they couldn't trace him.

"Where are you, Chris? Why won't you come out in the open where we can deal face-to-face like men should?" Josh Vandenberg was irate. He could understand something of what Chris was going through; still he was frustrated. The President liked to have complete control, and that was ironic in view of the step he was about to take: Josh was ready to hand the country over to the United Nations' new leader! He was convinced it was the best way to solve the overriding problems of the impossible national debt and the increasing unemployment and resulting unrest, not to mention the continuing racial confrontations as more and more immigrants poured into the country.

Chris sent the robot to Washington as a regular passenger on a commercial airliner. The unit named I.M. Percival (Percy for short) arrived at the White House and presented his card with a letter from Chris Carson. The guard asked the well-dressed guest to have a seat while he delivered the letter to the President's secretary, who passed it on to the President.

The President read the letter and came charging out of the Oval Office. "Who brought you this letter?" He demanded to the guard, ignoring Percy, who waited with infinite patience.

"This gentleman, sir." The guard indicated Percy. "Shall I take him into custody?" he asked, seeing the President's agitation.

President Vandenberg turned and looked Percy up and down. "Who are you?" he asked, not believing what he was afraid he was seeing.

"They call me Percy," the robot answered. "Perceptor robot unit number two thousand two hundred, sir. Chris Carson sent me to you so you could check my body."

President Vandenberg felt faint. He hadn't been feeling well the past few days, anyway, and now he was faced with this—a robot he couldn't tell apart from a person! "Please come with me," he told Percy and led the way back to his office, where he sat down for a moment with his head in his hands. Then rousing himself, he got a drink of cold water and called his secretary. "Pauline, get me Stratton and Jackson. I want to see them in my office right away!"

When the Secretaries of State and Defense arrived at the oval office, Pauline showed them in without comment. "What is this about, Josh?" Secretary Stratton wanted to know.

"I want you to meet someone important, gentlemen." He indicated Perceptor. "This is Mr. I.M. Percival." They looked at each other, puzzled, as they held out their hands to Percy, who shook each in turn with a polite smile. "I'm happy to meet you," he said in a pleasant voice.

President Vandenberg led the conversation as they discussed many topics—politics, the economy, business—with Percy proving well informed and fluent on all subjects. The secretaries became more and more curious, until at last the President leveled with them. "Stratton, Jackson, this is Percy. Perceptor robot unit number two thousand two hundred!"

"What!" Stratton gasped, unbelieving. Jackson looked closely at the President to see if he might be making a joke.

"It's no deception, men. It's all too true! So the question is, what do we do about it?" The debate waged hot and heavy over this new situation, while Chris Carson was able to hear the whole thing through Perceptor One, safe in the Bio Enterprises plant at Sheridan!

They built all the new Perceptor robots with humanoid bodies from then on. At first, it unnerved people to discover the "person" they'd been dealing with was a robot! But the general public quickly learned to accept the units; besides, they could never be absolutely sure who was human and who was an android. It was frustrating for those searching for a mate! Business owners used Perceptor units in restaurants and offices and factories, where they were much more efficient workers than people and had no ego problems or pay demands. It cost a business owner a bundle initially for a unit, but there was no further expense—no paychecks, no benefits, no bonuses, no vacations or sick leave—and the robots remembered each customer's name and preferences. They were valuable and valued employees.

CHAPTER 36

*M*eanwhile, the world gradually fell under the spell of the charismatic, wise, kind, and intelligent head of the United Nations, Apollos Hercainian. Already he had put new policies into action that brought great prosperity to the nations under his control. As one of his first acts, he abolished individual national currencies, substituting a well-run international monetary system with a central banking center located in Brussels.

The new system used an innovative method of transacting business. Instead of coins and paper, the citizen received a number printed on a microchip and injected into the palm of his hand. A special "reader" machine at each business scanned the number and debited the citizen's account balance by the amount of the transaction. It worked well, and the crime rate plummeted since it was next to impossible to steal assets that were so intangible.

The United States watched the success of the system with great interest. There was so much crime these days it wasn't safe for anyone to venture out on the streets without a weapon handy for defense. That, in turn, caused more problems since the government had confiscated all guns. Criminals were now the only people to own guns of any kind. It was clear something had to be done, and soon! Fundamentalist Christians had so far been able to control the vote and keep the country from joining the UN's World Alliance of Federated Peoples, but they couldn't hold out much longer. Even Conrad Braxton with all his power could see it was only a matter of time.

Braxton still preached against Chris Carson and Perceptor, though with less fervor since Chris had disappeared without a trace!

The FBI had tracked him to St. Louis but couldn't pick up his trail from there. Word was out that Chris might be dead, and the government did nothing to contradict that belief. But the country still searched for him and Gloria, and they had to take careful measures to avoid being detected. Gloria had looked and acted like a man so long she was beginning to feel like one! The word in the Sheridan gossip channels was that the men living in the Merriweather house were homosexuals. They must be; otherwise, why weren't there any women among them? Then too the skinny one was so effeminate. "Ya know," they said, "ef ut acks liyuk a duck, and it looks liyuk a duck, and it quayucks liyuk a duck..."

Flip Minkley was curious about the group from the beginning. He hung around as much as he could, trying to find out exactly what went on in the Bio Enterprises building. He also stopped in at the house on occasion to poke his skinny nose into their business on pretense of being "neighborly." It was Flip who started the "gay" rumors by pointing out to the others the strangely feminine traits of the younger partner, Bob Jones, and the fact that he and the older man, Ben Johnson, were always together. On more than one occasion, Gloria hid and pretended there was nobody home when Flip came to the door, so she wouldn't have to submit to his scrutiny. The strain of their living conditions began to take a subtle toll on their marriage, and it didn't help that they couldn't chance direct communication with their family and friends.

On the national and world level, however, Chris's technology was being used in ever more powerful places. Perceptor units made ideal secretaries and servants in the offices and homes of the world's power brokers. They were quiet, undemanding, never curious, and had no reason to spy since they didn't need money or power. The world leaders could trust them, and they did! Chris could hardly believe they were so gullible. The danger Chris dreaded was that someone would discover the AVC transmissions from one unit to another. It was only a matter of time until that would happen, he knew. Until then, Chris tried his best not to get involved in other people's private business. He was much more interested, though, in their politics.

The Moslems, along with Russia, China, and a few smaller countries, had not yet cast their lot with the World Federated Alliance. Instead, they had a loose alliance of their own, and a common goal to somehow take over Israel (Jerusalem) with its surrounding area. They would get control of the oil and other crucial resources and put themselves once more in possession of the Holy City.

As Chris monitored the world situation through robot units in so many high places, he became acutely aware of how close the President was to submitting his plan to congress. The President's plan called for the United States to join all of Europe and the other countries already under the political control of Apollos Hercainian. The plan was that at the end of President Vandenberg's term of office, instead of holding elections, congress would approve merging the United States into the Federated Alliance of Nations. And Vandenberg's term would end soon!

In his plush offices in Europe, Apollos Hercainian conferred with his top advisors, laying out detailed plans for controlling the United States. Apollos was gleeful over the pending coup. He had plotted well, and his evil minions worked among the faithful adherents to the New Age theology, including the President and most of congress, so now there was only feeble resistance among them. The main problem they faced was the continued prayers of small bands of devoted Christians. Apollos was sure his faithful demonic friends could handle the Christians easily enough when he had the power of government over them. He rubbed his hands together in pleasure as he anticipated eliminating all Christian opposition to him and his satanic lord.

Enough Perceptor robot units were in use by the power brokers in Europe by then that Chris was able to keep pretty close track of the general attitude there. He was well aware that Apollos Hercainian planned to get his hands on all the wealth of the United States. He also knew Hercainian planned to use Perceptor to gain control of the remainder of the world as soon as he was in secure command of the United States. Chris was more and more uneasy about the situation and spoke often about it with Gloria. They made their own emergency plans with Perceptor's help.

"We don't need these files now, do we?" Gloria stood in the Bio Enterprises office dressed in a well-tailored suit and looking the epitome of the efficient businessman. "Since Perceptor One has all of it in memory, I mean," she added, glancing over at Chris, who systematically packed things into boxes with Perceptor's help. Charlie, Jim, and Ray worked in the plant, unaware of what was going on in the office.

"No, you're right, we don't. In fact, the sooner we destroy all those papers, the better. You never know when we might be discovered, and then it would be too late to destroy them. We'll ditch our old computers too. People can sometimes find out things from those in spite of all we do to erase the information. So we'll smash those first, and then I'll help you shred the stuff in the files." They carried the equipment outside where Perceptor smashed it into mincemeat, and then Chris joined Gloria, and they began at the first file cabinet. Chris took one folder after another out, checked through it, and handed it to Gloria, who ran the papers through the shredder, collecting them into some large cartons. Chris remembered all the toil and problems of earlier years as he looked at the first primitive plans he'd drawn. They'd come a long way since then! It was too bad to destroy Perceptor's birth records. No matter, it had to be done! He handed the files to Gloria, feeling almost as if he were handing his child over to the executioner.

They worked steadily until all the files were empty, and they had several cartons full of shredded paper. Perceptor hauled the boxes over to the house, where they soon had a raging blaze in the fireplace. When they had finished their work, the written evidence of all the years of Chris's labor lay in smoldering ashes. Looking at them, he felt a little sick at his stomach, but just then, Perceptor One spoke with a new report from the unit at the President's office, and Chris knew his work was indeed still alive. The history he'd burned was always available through Perceptor One.

"The bill has just passed the House of Representatives. It will go to the Senate on Monday," Perceptor announced. "President Vandenberg expects it to pass without a challenge, and then he will submit his resignation."

"We know what'll happen after that!" Chris held out his arms to Gloria and pulled her close to himself. They stood there in the living room with their arms around each other. (If Flip had been nosing around, he'd have been sure his theory was right about their being gay.) "Are you sure you want to go through with this?" he asked her. "It's okay if you want to stay here, I'll understand. I'll be lonely without you, but I'll certainly understand!"

She pulled away from him and put her hands on her hips, regarding him with fire in her eyes. "Chris Carson, if you think for one minute you can leave me behind to face all the trouble here alone, you have another think coming! We're in this thing together, and don't you ever forget it!"

"That's what I thought you'd say, but I had to let you know I'll still love you if you decide you want to back out." He pushed the hair off his forehead. It flopped down again. He jammed the wig back on his head. (How he detested that thing!) "We have work to do before we're ready then!" He tromped out to the field between the plant and the house to inspect a large, thick cement slab they'd installed a few weeks before, and then moved on to check the supplies stored in a small building near the platform.

In the house, Gloria took a large box from the closet in their room and checked the contents with great care. Then she packed their personal things in specially designed cases, along with a few photographs. After she finished packing, she hung up her jacket and went to the kitchen, where she tied on an apron and began to take out pots, pans, and supplies. Tonight's dinner would be special.

When the little group gathered around the dinner table, they were surprised and appreciative of the perfect standing rib roast, mashed potatoes, gravy, fresh green beans, and crisp tossed salad Gloria prepared. She didn't often take time to fuss over cooking after working at the plant all day. Charlie knew something was up. "What's the occasion?" he asked. When nobody answered right away, he looked at Chris then at Gloria. Mick and Ray looked up from their plates. "What's going on now?" Charlie asked again.

Chris took a deep breath and began to talk. "The bill has just been passed by the House and is on its way to the Senate. We are now in the countdown phase to when the country turns our freedom over to the Federated Alliance, and the first thing Apollos Hercainian plans to do is to find us and take over Perceptor. We'll close the plant now, and you can head back to your families or wherever you want to be while you ride out the trouble ahead. We'll give each of you a Perceptor android to protect you, and some money. Of course, when they take over, the money won't be worth anything since you'll all be under the new system. If you're careful, maybe they won't find out you worked for us. If they do find that out, you'll be in for trouble. If you have to, if you're forced to, you can tell them where we are. They can't do anything about it then, anyway."

Gloria spoke up. "I can't tell you how much it's meant to us to have you as friends and associates these past few years! Friends like you are too rare. We love you, and we appreciate you more than we can say. We'll miss you so much..." She stopped, overcome with emotion, afraid tears would come in spite of her.

Chris took up again. "So tomorrow you can gather whatever you want from the building, and we'll get you to the airport or wherever you'd like to go. No need for you to be here when we leave. Perceptor can handle the situation."

The men were hardly able to speak. It was a time they'd dreaded for a long while. Charlie put down his napkin and disappeared into the kitchen, returning in a minute or two with a bottle of excellent wine he'd kept for a special occasion. He opened it now and poured the liquid into glasses for each of them and then raised his. They all raised theirs in return. "To friendship, to enterprise, to Chris and Gloria Carson, to Perceptor, and to Jesus Christ the Lord, may he soon return!"

"Amen!" they chorused as they sipped the wine together.

After the others had gone and they were alone at Sheridan, Chris and Gloria wrote letters to their children and friends. They were now in touch with them through Perceptor, as they had recently given each of them their own androids, but some things are better written than spoken. Soon preparations were complete, and they only waited to see what would happen next.

Flip Minkley came by on Tuesday and realized the plant was closed. "What's goin' awn?" he asked in his raspy voice. "Y'all thayunkin' of leevin'?" He cocked his head. "Bizniz wan't so good, hmm? Y'all shuda hired some local folks an' y'all wud dun a lot bayuttah! Folks don' take it kindly when strayunjahs cum in heah thout joinin' ta the commoonity, you know!" He stopped abruptly. "Sayuh," he asked, "y'all wanna sayul the playus agin?"

Chris nodded. "Yeah, Flip, I guess you're right. We just didn't know how to run the place! And now it's too late. Yes, let's sell the place again. You know anybody who'd be interested?"

Flip's beady eyes sparkled. "Ah sure reckon Ah c'n find sumbuddy! Ah'll git the payuhpahs outn' my cayah. Y'all jist wayut a minit, Ah'll cum bayuk dreckly!" The door banged behind him as he hurried out to his car for his briefcase. He filled out the papers quickly, asking few questions, since he'd already had the place on the market once and still had the information on file at his office. They agreed on a price, and Flip turned the paper toward Chris. "Y'all sign heah, Mr. Johnson, an' we'll hev the playus sold agin in no tayum!"

Chris dutifully signed "Ben Johnson" on the bottom line and gave the pen to Gloria, who signed "Robert Jones." Flip gave them a copy of the agreement, pocketed the original, and left in a hurry to try to find another pigeon and collect still another nice commission check on that property. The word got out around town at the speed of light. In no time, Sheridan, Texas, knew the new owners of that Merriweather plant had gone bust and were leaving town. "Good riddance! They were a strange bunch, not like our people!" was the general sentiment.

The bill passed the Senate by a large majority, and the President proudly signed it into law with a speech about how great a thing he'd brought about for his country. Apollos Hercainian stood by his side during the speech, ready to assume command of the White House and the country and add major new stature to his position as head of the Federated Alliance of Nations (and potential ruler of the world).

Chris spoke to Perceptor One, and Jose at the space station climbed into the shuttle. Soon Sheridan was shaken to its foundations as Jose guided the Carson II in a smooth glide over the town then turned its nose up and, engines roaring and an immense jet of air shooting out the bottom, lowered it gently onto the cement platform behind the Bio Enterprises plant. Chris and Gloria, in space suits, handed gear and supplies to Jose and Perceptor One, who stowed it with careful speed, and in three minutes flat, they climbed into their seats as the countdown began again. Townspeople headed toward the launch site on foot, by car, bike, roller skates, however they could get there. This was the most exciting thing that ever happened in their town! Who was it that landed? What was going on, anyway?

"Okay, Jose," Chris called, still buckling his seatbelt. "Get us out of here!" As the crowd swarmed across the field, the rocket engines fired up once more and came to a full roar. The shuttle slowly lifted off the pad, picking up speed as it nosed into space faster and faster until it was gone from sight!

Flip Minkley was beside himself trying to figure it out. What in the world had happened here? How could a space ship land in Sheridan? Had they mistaken it for Houston? Then he knew! He remembered the Universal Space Station and Chris Carson, and he knew! He picked up his dirty phone and called the White House. "Thought y'all mought jist be interested in sumthin'," he said to the person who answered. They put him through to the ex-president and the new head of the country, who were still celebrating with the state governors, the congress, and other dignitaries from around the world.

"Yayus, Suh!" Flip repeated. "Thayut's whut ah sayud! Chrius Cahson jist took off in a spayus shuttle frum Shearidun, Tayaxus. Heus been heah all the tahm, runnin' sum kinda' fayuctry!" The strange raspy drawl grated on Apollos Hercainian's ear. He could hardly believe what he heard. Then Hercainian's temper overcame his usual charm. He bellowed his orders, and people sprang to action. Shortly, Sheridan, Texas suffered an invasion by troops, police, reporters, photographers, the FBI (headed by McCall and Williams), and plain curiosity seekers until the town was inundated and over-whelmed. They took the plant and the house apart and tromped everywhere on the property in the search for evidence until there wasn't much left for Flip Minkley to sell.

****

Jose guided the space shuttle to a smooth docking with the Universal Space Station, and he and Perceptor One began to reset all systems in preparation for the next flight. Chris and Gloria climbed through the port into the airlock, where they left their space suits as soon as oxygen was confirmed. This was the first time the station's oxygen was used, but it operated as specified. On entering the main area, they floated and looked around them critically, with an eye toward making this place home, possibly for quite some time. The robots had finished the station as well as they could with the materials Chris had supplied. It was spartan, but they could see that Perceptor had tried to make it comfortable, and Gloria and Chris would improve on it as they settled in. It was going to take awhile first to get used to weightlessness. They stayed a long time at the window port gazing at Earth, eagerly picking out and identifying the continents, lakes, canals, the Great Wall of China, and other landmarks.

Once the novelty began to wear off, Gloria practiced moving around. Chris soon joined her, and they looked into the station's various compartments to see what supplies they had. There was food enough for a long time, though not the most appetizing stuff. "At least now, I'll be able to lose some weight!" Gloria remarked as she inspected the various packets. They had plenty of water if they were careful with it, and there was a variety of books and tapes as well as puzzles, games, and a word processor that was voice-operated since it interfaced with Perceptor.

Chris was taking inventory of the books when he noticed Gloria was missing. He found her looking somewhat green, trying to decide how to go to bed. "Are you gonna make it okay, honey?" he asked, helping her.

"I'll let you know after my stomach decides to rejoin the rest of my body!" she groaned. "Just leave me alone to die."

He patted her shoulder sympathetically. "They say it only lasts a day or two." He felt a little woozy himself. "I sure hope we get used to this in a hurry! This could be worse than a prison otherwise!"

For a few minutes, he thought maybe they shouldn't have run away, but he knew they'd had to go, and he was confident the Lord had shown him this course of action.

"How long, Lord?" he asked again. The reply came in the still, small voice he had become used to hearing: "Until the time be past." Chris wondered what that meant, but he knew Jesus was with them, even there in the space station, and he trusted his Lord to lead them. "Anyway, whatever happens, even if we die here, I know it's okay, Lord." He found his Bible and looked up some verses in Isaiah before he asked Perceptor One what was happening back on earth.

As they became acclimated to space, Chris and Gloria were aware they had the perfect post for watching and listening to events all over the earth. It was as though God gave them a special vantage point for some reason. They had no idea why, but they were grateful.

Chris looked out the viewing window toward Earth, thinking aloud, "We have to let Sam and the others know what's happening so they can get ready."

Gloria nodded agreement. "But how will you manage that from here?" She became upset as she thought about it. "Oh, Chris, maybe we came up here too soon! We have to let Fred and Polly and Charlie and Violet and all the others know too!" In her distress, Gloria turned quickly toward the window and went tumbling across the control room before she could grab something to stop herself.

Chris helped her get oriented once more. "You forget we have Perceptor. We're in contact with many places if we want to be! We'll just send an android to Sam and let him give the message to the Christians there. Charlie should have delivered our androids from the factory to our friends. Our kids all have them, and I know he and the other guys kept at least one apiece. We'll be able to talk to them through Perceptor." He turned to Perceptor One, Reuben, Ernie, and Jose. "You fellows know what we need. See if all our family and friends have Perceptor units and let them know it's time. They need to hide out in the place each of them has chosen for a while! They'll face persecution soon if they stay where they are! And tell them we're okay and will keep them posted on what's happening from time to time." He turned to Perceptor One again. "I want to send an android to Sam Early. See that he gets the next one."

In Phoenix, Robot Unit number 36000 was just receiving its finishing touches when Chris spoke to the Perceptor workers in the plant through Perceptor One. Soon number 36000, named R.A. Proctor, boarded a plane bound for Grand Rapids, Michigan, with vital information for Reverend Sam Early.

****

The doorbell rang a loud demand, and Sam reluctantly rose from his knees, where he was seeking an answer from the Lord for the great restlessness, the troubling of spirit that was upon him. He opened the door to find a polite, well-dressed stranger waiting. "Yes? What can I do for you?" Then he sensed this man held the answer to his prayer and looked at him more closely. "Please, won't you come in?" He invited and stood aside as Proctor walked into the living room.

"I am R.A. Proctor, Perceptor robot unit number thirty-six thousand." The android held out his hand to Sam, who shook it automatically as he stared unbelievingly. "Chris Carson sent me to warn you," the android continued.

"Please sit down!" Sam indicated a chair and fell into one himself. "What's wrong?" He demanded.

Proctor began to tell him Apollos Hercainian's plans for the country. "So you'll need to go into hiding for a while in a place where your group can be together until the Lord finishes dealing with Apollos Hercainian. I'm supposed to stay with you to help, after I talk with Conrad Braxton at his school."

Sam leaned forward to hear what Proctor had to say. "Now I know what the Lord wanted to tell me, and I thank him and you and Chris! We'll have to move on this right away. There's a lot to do! I'll start telling my people while you go talk with Braxton. Come right back, won't you? We can sure use your help!" He stood up, and so did Proctor. "How will you get to Lansing? Can you drive, or do you need me to drive you?"

"I am able to drive." The robot assured him. "But I require the use of your car."

Sam dug in his pocket for keys. "I never in the world would have thought I'd loan my car to an android!" He handed the keys to Proctor. "But I have a feeling you'll turn out to be a friend!" He looked at the sky, dark with clouds to the west. "Looks like we're due for some more snow soon. Be careful, won't you?"

****

Braxton was about to leave for an important meeting, when his doorbell rang and a well-dressed stranger asked to talk with him for just a minute or two. He sighed and, hiding his impatience as well as he could, invited the man in. "R.A. Proctor," the man said, stamping the snow from his feet and holding his hand out to the pastor. Conrad shook the hand and waited. "I have come to you with information from Chris Carson," Proctor announced.

"What?" Conrad Braxton wasn't sure how to react to Proctor. Should he run or stand his ground? Was he in danger, or was this really just a messenger? He sent up a quick prayer for his safety and responded, "What does Chris Carson want to tell me, and where is he, anyway?"

The Perceptor unit delivered his information about the fast-approaching problems for Christians. "You will not be able to operate in the open much longer. In fact, you will probably not be allowed to live! They'll find some excuse to eliminate you. It may be you will die of a sudden unexpected heart attack, or they may find a way to discredit and disgrace you. The one sure thing is that you will not be allowed to preach Christianity! So you need to tell the country what to expect and give the Christians time to prepare for persecution, and you need to do it soon!" Proctor rose to leave. "That is all the message for now. Good-bye, sir." He was out the door and down the steps as Braxton stared after him, open-mouthed.

It was in Conrad Braxton's power to warn the country. Now it was up to him whether he would be faithful to deliver the warning. Chris felt he had done what he could to alert his fellow Christians to be prepared for the coming terrible tribulation.

In his beautiful office at the school, Braxton read and studied, prayed and wrestled with the preconceived "facts" he had always believed. He weighed the pros and cons of giving such information out on his program. Should he take the chance of being made to look like a fool? But what if Chris Carson were right, and the government did attack all Christians? At the very least, he should let people know they might be in great peril! And deep in his heart, Conrad knew that Chris Carson was right—his television broadcast would indeed soon be canceled!

After some sleepless nights and much prayer, Conrad Braxton faced the TV cameras for his regular Sunday sermon to the nation. He began to speak using his prepared sermon, warning people of the possibility there would be great persecution ahead for Christians. "Hide yourselves! If you're in Christ Jesus, he will keep you safe, but you should lay in a food supply now. And you'll need a safe place where you can hide when our new government insists that every person take the mark in his hand or forehead. We know from Scripture that Christians cannot take that mark and still dwell in him!

The new government will insist you embrace the New Age beliefs they've taught for so long in our schools. Some of you will have to leave your children behind if you haven't counteracted those teachings. Your own children will betray you!"

Then something entirely unexplainable happened to Conrad Braxton—he found himself going on with no reference to his prepared sermon, telling the world he had been wrong about Chris Carson and Perceptor. They were not the Antichrist after all. The new head of the world alliance, Apollos Hercainian might be. Conrad couldn't say for sure, but Hercainian fit the descriptions from the Bible and far better than Chris Carson ever had. He was now ruling a large portion of Earth and would soon demand that each person bow down and worship him. Braxton waxed eloquent in his warning as he apologized for falsely accusing Chris Carson, who was, after all, a dedicated Christian, although he held some beliefs that were in opposition to those of Braxton.

It was a dynamic and convincing performance, and when it was through and the broadcast was over, Conrad Braxton sat in his office, white and shaken from the experience of being taken over and used by God to warn his people. Such a thing had never happened to him before. He wasn't at all sure he wasn't going mad! But no, he had never felt the Holy Spirit come upon him in that way before, but he knew that was what happened.

Finally overcome, Conrad Braxton fell to his knees and gave himself up body, soul, and spirit to his Lord Jesus Christ. When he arose some time later, he was a changed man. The Word now opened up to him with new power. The old, proud Conrad Braxton was gone. In his place was a newly humble servant of God ready to listen to the Holy Spirit and be guided by him.

Reaction across the country was unbelievable. Christians fell to their knees in repentance, and unsaved people flocked to churches to find their way to Jesus. It was a harvest of souls God's people had prayed for and sought after for years. Some who had lived in sin all their lives now made a 180-degree turn and were praising God and witnessing to others. Even some devout New Agers repented, and God freed them from the demons that had possessed them and opened up places for them to hide "for a little time."

Conrad Braxton had to disappear right after his message to the nation, as Apollos Hercainian ordered him dead, and agents moved swiftly to accomplish that purpose. When they arrived at the university, Braxton was nowhere to be found. They searched everywhere they could even imagine he might be but without success. It was as though the earth had opened up and swallowed him. When God hides a person, he blinds the enemy! Hercainian was livid with anger.

CHAPTER 37

In Grand Rapids, even in the midst of the turmoil, Sam Early faced the fact that he was hopelessly in love with Violet and realized he needed to be with her through the coming tribulation. So he went looking for her, and found her remarkably fresh and beautiful and unruffled in the midst of the bedlam as she diligently cared for the abandoned drug babies at My Father's House. "I need to talk to you," he told her as he took her hand and pulled her into the dining room. He avoided her eyes, staring out the window without even seeing the big old maple tree outside.

"I love you, Violet. It took me a long time to admit it, but I've loved you ever since we first met. You know I've never thought about any woman this way before, but I can't stop thinking about you. No matter where I look, I see you and wonder what you're doing, what you're thinking. I don't want to live without you any longer, Violet." He dared let himself look into her eyes. "Will you be my wife, dear?"

"Oh yes, Sam, yes! I love you too!" Violet looked so happy as she nodded her acceptance that he swept her into his arms and whirled around the room until they ran into the table. Then he quieted down and kissed her. After a few precious minutes, Sam changed the subject and told her about Chris's warning, explaining what they had to do. "It doesn't matter, Sam! I'd live with you anywhere and be happy!" She picked up the baby she'd been tending, who was now crying lustily. As she cuddled the little one, she looked over her shoulder at Sam. "We'd better get married right away then, hadn't we?"

"How's tomorrow?" Sam didn't want to leave her ever again!

"Tomorrow's fine, Sam. I'll get someone to take over for me awhile. But you'll have to live here with me until we find a place to hide. I can't leave the babies, you know!"

It was a pretty wedding in spite of all the hurry, and with Sam's church invited. The ladies came up with some greenery and flowers for decoration, and Mrs. Portland baked a wonderful wedding cake. Violet dug through her closet and found a simple ivory silk suit. Its lines were flattering to her slim body, and she looked radiant as she walked down the aisle on Mr. Portland's arm.

After the reception, Sam and his new wife met with his "little flock" of faithful Christians, along with others of the faith to discuss their situation. He introduced Proctor to the congregation. Proctor told them what Chris had said about the imminent danger. Then as the excitement of all that was happening began to turn to realization, they prayed together earnestly for the Lord to show them where to hide to be safe for a time. "We'll meet again in three days to share thoughts on the problem," Sam told them. "Proctor will help us decide what to do." Then he took his wife away for a brief but blissful honeymoon.

At the next meeting two days later, Bill Wharton stood up. "I remember back in the 1950s when we were all worried about nuclear war, and the whole country was building little bomb shelters in their backyards. Back then, Grand Rapids made a big designated shelter at the old Gypsum mines under the city and stocked them with food and supplies. After the nations disarmed a few years ago, most people forgot about the mines. I thought about that and wondered what was there, so I went over there and took a look. I think it might work for us."

A buzz of exclamations and questions rose up, and he held up his hand for silence again. "The mine shafts are entirely surrounded by rock," he told them. "It's not real warm down there...keeps at a constant fifty degrees, but there's over six miles of twenty-five-foot wide tunnels. At least a mile of that is already rigged with electric lights and cement floors! We could hold hundreds of people in that much space. And there's canned and dried food stored down there that should still be usable. I worried about a water source, but there's even an artesian well flowing! It's as though the Lord prepared this place for us years and years ago, knowing we'd need it now!"

"Praise God!" Ed Portland exclaimed.

"Praise the Lord! Oh, thank you, Jesus!" the congregation responded and spontaneously started singing their beautiful praise in the Spirit, thanking God for his wonderful provision. The planning started right after the praise, and soon many Christians "disappeared" from the Grand Rapids area. They took as many of their possessions as they could with them, forming temporary rooms for each family with packing box walls. They realized someone might remember the mines and search there for them. "We'll have to hide ourselves even better somehow. Proctor, do you have any suggestions?" Sam asked.

"Yes," the android replied. "I'm sure we can build rock walls that look the same as the ends of the present mine shafts. We can wall off some of the area to make outsiders think the mine is smaller than it is. The way it's laid out, we can leave some unfinished tunnels for them to see too. Then we can dig access holes at the far end of the mine away from the elevators. We'll have to climb up and down by ladders, but maybe they won't find us that way."

"But the artesian well is right there by the oldest elevator. What'll we do about the water supply?" Ed Portland asked. Several men nodded, but Phil Ames, a strong young plumber, raised his hand. "I can run an underground pipe from that well to the other side of the wall. It won't be easy, but I can do it with your help. The tricky part will be keeping the enemy from realizing what we've done!"

"And we won't be able to bring anything sizeable down here after we wall off the elevator area, so give that a lot of thought now while there's still time!" Sam added.

Violet was more beautiful than ever in her new role in life. She dressed now in simple slacks or jeans and shirts, her startling blue eyes radiating the love of Jesus. She loved the babies and surprised even herself by how well she handled them, even when they screamed uncontrollably. She let her other helpers go, and the next day she and Sam, along with Angela, who worked with Violet, took the children with them to the mines. Their friends helped them empty the big house at night and move furniture down into the shafts to make as cozy a place for the babies as they could manage. They needed plenty of warm clothing and blankets to combat the chill underground, but they managed to get all the things they required, through the robots.

The colony had several Perceptor androids among them (because of Fred and Polly, Angela, Martha, Kathie, Joan and Orin Nelson, the Portlands, and Sam and Violet Early) to protect and provide for them. The androids looked exactly like humans, and since they could take the mark in their "flesh" without a problem, they were able to buy occasional supplies for the fugitives.

In his rage over the Christian revival, Apollos Hercainian accelerated his plan to turn the once free United States into a slave state. He instituted the new method of buying and selling at once, so unless a person had the required mark in his hand, there was no way he could do business. Other Christians who were aware of the biblical warnings established many small colonies hidden in mountains and desert areas, and even in the vast canyons in the middle of certain large cities. They existed by bartering with one another and, in some cases, with sympathetic people who had taken the mark. They preached the word wherever they could, and many people came to know Jesus during those days. It was a true revival of honest commitment to the Lord.

Any new converts the authorities discovered were put to death unless they denounced their faith, as the new world law said the only religion allowed was the New Age religion. Man was his own God now, and the Ascended Masters were the guides to ultimate happiness. Noted gurus and mystics headed large new religious centers where worship was directed toward Apollos Hercainian. But to Hercainian's complete frustration, the more he persecuted the Christians, the stronger they became and the more converts they made.

Some Christians were able to walk on the streets as long as they didn't try to buy anything and as long as they avoided anyone who knew them. Since they couldn't take wages without the mark, they couldn't hold jobs any longer.

****

Angela waited at the foot of the ladder, looking up through the manhole at a small patch of sky filled with stars. Nathan should be back by this time. She pulled her sweater closer around her. *Oh, Lord, don't let them catch him. Please let him be safe. But where can he be? What's taking him so long?*

She heard a scraping sound and stepped back into the darkness of the rock-walled tunnel. Feet and then legs came into view followed by a familiar black jacket and backpack. She threw herself into his arms. "Nathan, I was worried! What took you so long, anyway? Did you get the stuff?"

"Yeah, I got it, but more of them than usual were out tonight, and I had to wait for just the right timing before I could get back outta there. Seems as though they're everywhere now. They musta brought in some new troops. You know where Proctor is?" He gave her a squeeze and then stepped back and slipped off the backpack, handing it to her.

"I think he's helping Sam over at the new clearing area. I'm sure glad you're back okay!" She started down the tunnel toward a brightly lighted area far ahead. "I'll get this to Violet and Gina. They're waiting for it."

"Thanks for worrying about me!" Nathan Snyder turned the other way, pulling the black knit hat off his tousled brown hair and stuffing it into one of his many pockets. The wide tunnel headed off to the north, lighted by an occasional dim bulb strung on a wire along the ceiling. A hundred feet farther, Nathan turned left into a side tunnel, pushed open a heavy door, and entered a long, well-lighted room. It was furnished with some large tables lined with a motley variety of chairs. White paint covered the rough rock walls and the cement floor flaunted vinyl tile with a bright yellow and orange pattern. (The women's effort to make the drab cold mine shafts cheerful.) Three doors opened off the room, and Nathan pushed the closest one open, poking his head into a makeshift kitchen. A thin, nervous woman looked up, startled, from the kettle she was stirring. Soup for tomorrow, he guessed. It smelled great!

"Hi, Jane! Got any coffee left?"

"Oh, Nathan! Yeah, I guess so. You might have to tip the pot, though."

"No problem." He held a chipped mug under the spout of the battered old coffeemaker and tipped the pot slightly. Bitter brew flowed slowly out. "I guess this is the last of it, though."

She nodded and unplugged the pot from the extension cord, handing him a can of evaporated milk and a hard cookie to go with the drink. We're getting pretty low on coffee again. Proctor says it's hard to get anymore, along with almost everything else that has to be imported." She sighed and tucked a loose strand of gray hair back into the bun at the nape of her neck. "We may have to find something else to drink, but that'll be hard on the morale around here. It's a challenge some days to keep on praising the Lord!"

Nathan squeezed her arm. "Let's hope we can overcome Apollos Hercainian soon and take back our country! It's been a long haul, but God's kept us safe so far, and there's no reason to believe he'll abandon us now."

"I don't know what we'd do if he hadn't had Chris Carson send us Proctor and Finster! What a blessing those androids and the others have been for us!"

He drained the mug and left it on the table. "Thanks, Jane. I need to find Proctor. There's something going on outside, and I guess he'll know about it."

She nodded, smiling at him as he headed across the dining room and out the door at the far end. An uncleared tunnel stretched off toward the west, and Nathan could see work lights hanging on the walls at the end of it, about 160 feet from the door. As he came up to them, Sam Early straightened from the plans he was looking over. "Nathan! Glad you're back. You have any luck?" The other men looked up.

"Yeah, I got the supplies Violet needed, but it took me a long time to get in and out of the place. There's lots more soldiers around. What's going on?" He looked toward Proctor. "Is something new comin' down?"

The handsome robot nodded. "There's a new directive from Apollos Hercainian's international headquarters. Now he wants the whole country to bow down and worship him twice a day. His people are nearly finished installing giant television screens in every city and town across the world. He'll use them to get his information to the world's population, and his troops will see to it that every person obeys his rules. So now he also plans to broadcast his own image twice each day, and he commands everyone to bow down to the image and say the new prayer he's about to teach us. His orders are that anyone who refuses to worship and recite the prayer will be eliminated…incinerated on the spot!"

Nathan whistled. "Wow…he's getting rough now!" He looked toward Sam. "Bet this will bring in some more refugees!"

Sam nodded. "You could be right, Nate, and where will we put them? It's hard enough to feed the people we already have." He sighed and then straightened his thin shoulders and looked upward. "The Lord has supplied all our needs so far, and there's no reason to think he'll stop now! We'll call a special meeting in the dining hall tomorrow and pray about this. We have to decide how to prepare." He glanced about at his group. "Maybe we'd better call it a night and get some rest. There'll be plenty to do from now on."

They nodded and picked up their plans, turned out the lights, and headed back down the tunnel. One of the harder things about living underground was not knowing whether it was night or day. Their body clocks were all screwed up. They trooped through the dining hall and the entrance tunnel in the direction Angela had gone. To the right was another long "room" filled with many chairs and sofas, a few pictures, and even a small old-fashioned stereo with a CD player. Readers could choose from a good supply of books and magazines, and several people were playing a game at a table in the corner.

One big problem they'd had to overcome was sanitation. They solved that by making old-fashioned outhouses. They dug deep pits into the earth where it was not rock and used lime to spread in them every day, just like in their ancestors' early days in the country. There was one location for men and one for women. Phil Ames had diverted the artesian well, and he rigged up a makeshift shower room near the wall where the pipe came through. There was a schedule posted giving each inhabitant one shower a week.

Sam said goodnight to the others and headed toward the nursery to find Violet. She was putting a baby into his crib and tucking the blanket around him. It was warmer in the nursery, as it had electric heaters to keep the temperature at seventy-two degrees for the babies. She turned and put her arms around him. "You must be tired, Sam. You've been working so hard for so long. That's the trouble with living underground. You forget what time it is and keep on working too many hours without rest. I imagine these children, who've been here most of their short lives, will have to get realigned to day and night once they get out of here."

She nodded toward their quarters on the other side of the nursery wall. "Let's get some sleep, dear. I'm tired too! Angela's on duty for a while now. She'll be right back."

They walked together into their private section of tunnel, passing a wall of packing boxes to the blanket that served as the door of their "room." The path beside it led on for access to other families' quarters beyond theirs. They spoke softly for privacy. "There's more trouble coming, Violet. Now people are going to be required to bow down and worship Apollos Hercainian and pray to him twice a day! Proctor says they're putting up big TV screens in all the cities now. There are a lot more troops out. Nathan had trouble getting back."

"We know that if we have to, we can survive down here a long time without going out. Wasn't it good of the Lord to have people store so much food down here?"

"He's certainly provided all our needs!" They knelt by their bed and prayed together for their growing flock's safety and for wisdom to continue to lead them, before pulling their warm comforters around them and surrendering to strength-restoring sleep.

Fred's android, Finster, had taken a job as supervisor of operations for the storage company that owned a large refrigerated warehouse over the mine entrance. He made sure that the enemy never suspected the stone walls ending the two main storage tunnels were fake and that miles of tunnels stretched beyond those walls—some paved and lighted and some still being cleared for use. Piles of rock lined the sides of unimproved parts where the miners had taken gypsum out and left shale behind. Each family carried away some of that rock each day to build walls around their quarters, reinforcing the packing box walls and creating more usable space for the colony.

Of course, the Perceptor androids that belonged to the enemy knew the Christians were there, but they weren't about to tell! They played their parts so convincingly that Hercainian's forces never suspected they were actually working for Chris Carson and the Christians.

Finster was able to escape detection, and the other workers never suspected he was not human. They considered him an oddball, but as far as anyone knew, he obeyed the laws just as they all did. Without Finster, the little colony couldn't have escaped detection.

CHAPTER 38

Angela and Nathan sat together near the nursery door. "It's getting tougher all the time. I wonder how much longer we'll have to live down here like woodchucks before the Lord starts to mop up with old Hercainian."

"Yeah, it does get old after a while! I wonder whether it's any easier for Dad and Gloria in the space station."

"At least up there, they get to look at the stars and the earth!"

"Yeah, but it can't be easy being alone for so long either and cooped up in such a small space." Angela sighed. "I'll be so glad when this is over, and we can live like real people again! Maybe the Lord will come soon. I feel he will!"

He put his arm around her and pulled her close. "Yes, but in the meantime, I want to marry you, Angela! Let's do it and not wait. Then when we're free again, we can start right out together."

"I always dreamed I'd have an old-fashioned wedding with a church and a white dress and big cake and my dad to give me away and all, you know." She turned her face to his…but yes, Nathan. Who knows when we'll get out of here?"

"Yes? You mean it?"

She nodded. "We can talk to Sam and Violet about it tomorrow, okay?"

"Super okay!" He pulled her close and kissed her.

Life went on, even in those difficult circumstances. The Lord watched over his "little flock" and hid them from the enemy.

****

Diane was still in prison, but since prisoners didn't have to buy and sell, they weren't forced to take the mark until their release, so she was relatively safe except for her witnessing about Jesus. Because of Diane, there was now a small group of new Christians in the prison. They had to be on constant guard, acutely aware of their actions and words. New Agers led the jail religious ministries. They taught the prisoners to practice meditation and introduced them to self-realization, reincarnation, God-consciousness (meaning Satan-consciousness through Hercainian), and other occult beliefs. Under their influence, the prison was a more and more dangerous place to live for Jesus.

****

Conrad Braxton, who no longer identified himself as the reverend doctor, headed a large group who escaped north to the deep forests in Michigan's Upper Peninsula. They camped in the woods as near the vast cold water of Lake Superior, as they could go without being detected. Some built rude huts for shelter and warmth; others had only tents. They hid a few old-style camper trailers and some vans and buses as well as they could with evergreen branches and snow. They had plenty of warm winter gear provided by their resident Perceptor androids, who had quietly raided a huge department store.

The Lord inspired Conrad as never before, and he taught his people the Word of God daily. They grew strong in faith under his ministry and love. Conrad realized he had never loved people before…now he wept over them sometimes. They learned to survive in the wild, and even thrive there. They did some ice fishing and deer hunting, always being careful not to be seen by boats or planes that patrolled even that remote area checking for Christian rebels. When Perceptor learned that a satellite had detected them and forces were on the way, the androids helped them quickly move to a remote copper mine, leaving most of their possessions behind.

****

From their position in the space shuttle, Chris and Gloria heard what people on earth talked about. In the mines under Grand Rapids, the wilds of Northern Michigan, and even in the most private offices throughout the world, people used Perceptor units of various types for surveillance, for security, for office help, and in other positions. The world's power brokers knew they could trust Perceptors, and besides, they were infinitely more efficient than people. They never needed to sleep or eat or take restroom breaks!

As Chris expected, the first thing Hercainian did when he had control of the United States was to take over the Perceptor manufacturing plant. He put a limit on the number of units manufactured and required that all units be monitored through his office. He called in every operating Perceptor unit across the country (except those he didn't know about), allowing their use only in his own interest. He put them to work as a police force to keep people in line, making sure his strict new laws were enforced. People did the work once more that their robots had been doing to spare them hard and dangerous jobs, with Perceptor now acting as a slave boss. It was a complete reversal of the order Chris envisioned.

The only high place without a Perceptor unit was Apollos Hercainian's inner office in Europe. "I devoutly hope and pray he never puts a unit in there," Chris said to Gloria. "That might prove to be the place where they'd discover the AVC link, and that would put a big crimp in our communications!"

"We'd better pray he doesn't then!" They held hands and prayed together, and the Lord heard. Hercainian never did put a Perceptor unit in his private office.

Since the new robots looked exactly like people, Christians didn't turn theirs in, and with help from Perceptor One, most escaped detection and continued to serve their owners. Those robots were the key factor in keeping the Christians from being discovered.

****

Apollos Hercainian was pacing and ranting, as usual. "We must find a way to bring down that infernal Space Station! As long as that diabolical thing remains, it is in command of the skies! I need to deal with those few smaller countries that still rebel against our regime, and that Perceptor nest prevents me from wiping them out!

As far as Hercainian and his underlings were concerned, those countries were simply an annoyance, like fleas to a dog. The easiest way to solve the situation and force the other countries into line was to obliterate one of them with some old nuclear weapons that had never been destroyed, after all! That would put enough fear into the others to cause them to give in and join the Alliance. The cursed space station was the only thing standing in his way!

Hercainian sat again at the appointed hour before the crystal, gazing into its glowing depths and chanting his worship to his evil lord. As the dark form materialized, the room filled with an acrid smell, as though the fires of hell itself surrounded the room. Once more, the dark god and his most ardent worshipper met, as Apollos Hercainian prostrated himself in subjection.

Lucifer was angry. His evil yellow eyes flashed fire, sulfur flowed from his nostrils and mouth at every breath, and the long talons on his bony fingers dripped blood as he towered over his bondservant. What Apollos Hercainian saw was a beautiful, shining creature with bright golden wings and a smile that radiated light. He worshipped at Lucifer's feet. Lucifer restrained himself with difficulty from kicking Hercainian across the room, though he drew great strength from the worship and adoration of his slave. His arm lifted majestically. "The Universal Space Station still exists and stops us from completing our goal! You must kill Chris Carson and gain control of the Perceptor units that operate the station. We must have that power ourselves. With it, we can bring the rest of the world into subjection. We will beat Yahweh God and take over his creation!"

"We have tried, Master, but their weapon is formidable, and our demons have not been able to penetrate their minds. They pray too much! There is no way to get to them."

"We got to Adam through the woman, have you considered that?"

"Ah! Yes, we will try that, Master! Do you have a plan?"

"A plan…a plan? Must I do everything myself? Why do I need you then, Apollos?" The dark leathery wings billowed in anger and frustration. Hercainian watched the large golden wings in awe and fell prostrate once more before Lucifer. When he looked up again, he was alone except for a red glow still fading in the depths of the huge crystal.

Apollos exploded from his office issuing orders right and left. Perceptor units moved quickly to do his bidding. All across the earth, humans felt the force of his anger as officers compelled them to face large television images of Apollos Hercainian and bow in worship to him. They had to recite the new prayer they'd learned to replace the ancient Lord's Prayer they'd known before. They were to recite the new prayer as they worshipped twice each day. Anyone who refused to do so disappeared, and nobody ever saw him or her again. Hercainian had work hours extended and food supplies shortened. Life became hell on Earth, especially in the United States, Canada, and Great Britain, where people had never before suffered such hardships and deprivation. Hercainian was determined to make their lives a hell because they had been so blessed by God.

As life became unbearable, people turned to the Lord, their God, whom they had forsaken a long time ago for the New Age Ascended Masters. They prayed now to God through Jesus Christ to save them from their sin and error and forgive them. True, most still refused to believe, but in every country, many people were secretly on their knees in repentance with weeping and prayers for forgiveness.

In the space station, Chris monitored what was happening. "It's unbelievable, Gloria." He marveled. People all across the so-called Christian nations are repenting! They're leaving their sins and calling out to God to save them!"

"Isn't there a verse somewhere that says when that happens, God will forgive their sin and heal their land?" Gloria spent much time in the Word since there wasn't much else to do in space. Perceptor did the work for them.

"Sure is!" Chris picked up his Bible and began turning pages. "And I'll bet this is the beginning of the end of the mess we're in! Here it is in Second Chronicles chapter seven. It says, 'If my people which are called by my name shall humble themselves and pray and seek my face and turn from their wicked ways, then I will hear from heaven and will forgive their sins and heal their land.' That sure looks like what's happening now, doesn't it?"

"Chris, can't we go home now? Please?" Gloria held his arm and looked up into his face. "It's been so long, and I'm so tired of being cooped up in this small space, aren't you?" She pushed herself away and floated across to the far wall. "And I'm sick of floating around! I'll bet we have to learn to walk all over again!"

He sympathized with her. "It is hard being here so long, and it would be great to walk on earth again. We'll go back as soon as it seems safe, honey, but we have to wait just a little while longer until the Lord gets rid of Apollos Hercainian!"

Gloria sighed. "It's just been so long, and nothing's the same here! I'd so love to go for a walk through the woods beside the lake, and I'd give a lot to take a deep, hot bath and eat real food again!"

"I know, honey, I know. I would too! And we'll go back as soon as we can! But for now, we'll pray that God will give us strength and help us to stay here and appreciate our safety until he tells us it's time to go back!"

They did pray, and that was so satisfying that they prayed more often together until little by little, Gloria's restive spirit relaxed again, content to wait until the right time.

****

Apollos Hercainian paced his office, carrying a long black whip and ranting at the demons facing him in a row. "It seems such a simple thing to do! Women have certain wants and needs. You worthless wimps should be able to get to Gloria Carson through those common desires! Why haven't you succeeded? I'll tell you why…you haven't worked at it hard enough!" He kicked at the closest small demon. "You, Discontent, I know you can reach her!"

Discontent pulled back. "I tried, Master, truly I did, and I was just wiggling myself into her brain nicely, ready to do some real work, when they prayed! They always pray!" He wailed. "In that name! You can't subject me to that name!" The others chorused their agreement.

Hercainian slammed his whip down with force, missing their noses by only a hair. They shrank back, whimpering. "Back to the pit with all of you and rot there!" He commanded.

"No...no...nooooo!" Their screams faded as they shriveled from sight, leaving only a wisp of smoke and a foul smell behind them.

Apollos continued his pacing, cracking his whip about the room and cursing Chris Carson, Gloria Carson, Perceptor, the demons, and anything else he happened to think of. It would soon be time to meet his Lord Lucifer once more and face his displeasure. How could he explain this failure? From rage and frustration, he sent another order out to his Perceptor units: "Find the Christians and start to kill all of them! That should bring Chris Carson back to help them!"

****

In the mines, the Grand Rapids Christians assembled for a celebration—Angela and Nathan's wedding. Chris and Gloria sent their love and blessings through Proctor, who attended so they could hear the service, even though they couldn't see it. "Anyway," Angela said, "Proctor's as good a friend as I've ever had. He's like a big brother to me or an uncle!"

"Your dad says he loves you and wishes he could be here today for your wedding. He'd like to meet Nathan but is sure if you really love him, you'll be happy together. He says he wishes your mother could be with you too." Proctor gave Chris's message at the start of the simple ceremony. "He and Gloria will hear your vows, though, and they're happy for you."

Angela wiped her eyes. "Thanks, Dad. I love you too!" she told him through Proctor. "I'm glad Fred and Polly are here to stand up with us, anyway. And Grandpa will give me away." She smiled at her proud grandparents, and then as the assembled guests began to sing softly "Together Forever," she took Ed Portland's arm and walked the length of the "living room" to meet Nathan. Together they faced Sam, who performed the service uniting them. Jane Portland, Angela's sisters, and some other ladies had managed to put together a beautiful cake and other goodies, and the colony almost forgot their troubles for a few happy moments. They paid for it soon thereafter as Perceptor pretended to obey Hercainian's cruel orders.

In their many hiding places across the world, Christians prayed even more earnestly as their persecution increased. They stood strong and firm in their faith and gladly died for one another rather than reveal their locations. It was more dangerous than ever to witness for Jesus, but they still did it when opportunities arose. And as the other citizens suffered more and more under their cruel new "master," a great many of them secretly turned to the Lord and prayed earnestly for their countries and their people. Day after day, more and more people received the Gospel message.

In the mines at Grand Rapids, Sam Early led his growing band of Christians in prayer for God's mercy on the country. They spent hours on their knees weeping before the Lord over their sin and unbelief. "Oh, Lord, please forgive us. Wash us clean by your blood and help us walk in your ways! Lord, lead us to those to whom you would have us speak so we may help others to know you as their Savior! Lord, have mercy on your people and deliver us from the hand of this tyrant, and we will walk with you and serve you all the days you give us to live, and go gladly to be with you when this life is over." Sam raised his tear-stained face and stood to bless the people.

In the Northern camp, spring came with new leaves on the trees and sun-splashed blossoms. Conrad Braxton led his followers from the copper mines into an ever-closer walk with the Lord, reaching out to anyone who happened their way and causing many more people to find their salvation in Jesus. It was happening all across the country and all over the world. Gradually, a vast army of Christians assembled—an army of prayer warriors, who spent hours on their knees crying out to God for deliverance from the oppressor, Apollos Hercainian.

****

In a secret place in Maryland, not far from Washington, D.C., former President Josh Vandenberg knelt before God. He wept as he repudiated his former beliefs, turned aside from the Ascended

Masters, and prayed for forgiveness for the great unspeakable wrong he had done to his beloved country. He was about to take his life, but first wanted to make things right with the God he had abandoned years ago. He wept hot tears of repentance, begging God to have mercy on the people he'd led astray and asking for Jesus to save him and receive his soul.

Just as he put the poison to his lips, Josh heard the voice of God in his ear. "Do not take your life. Give it to me!" The voice was clear and strong and entirely different from the voices he'd been listening to for years. He fell on his knees once more, worshipping God, praising Jesus, and listening to that loving voice. When he rose from his knees much later, Josh Vandenberg was a new man! He became a strong warrior for the Lord and led many souls to Jesus. The band of Christians in his area grew strong and fast.

In the space station, Chris and Gloria watched and listened to the reports through Perceptor. "I feel it won't be long now until the Lord delivers his people and heals their land as he promised! There's real repentance and humility all over the world! Can it possibly be much longer before God moves?" Chris was at his favorite place at the viewing window, looking down on the earth far below. He was homesick for that beautiful planet too and longed to return.

"I hope it's today!" Gloria agreed. "Oh, Chris, it must be wonderful to be in one of the camps now, even with the trouble and danger! Wouldn't it be great to be there with them?"

"We'll leave as soon as the Lord gives us the go-ahead! We can't go before that, or we'll be more hindrance than help to them. But I can't help but feel it'll be soon!" He accepted a packet of food from Gloria and sighed as he opened it. "I plan to have a real feast when we get back, even if it's just hamburgers! Sometimes I can smell them, hot off the grill and topped with cheese, onion, relish, mustard..." He stopped himself and bowed his head. "Thank you, Lord, for this food. Please make it nourishing for our bodies' use."

Gloria blew him a kiss as she opened her packet. "Want some orange drink?"

****

For a long time, their prayers had been heard in heaven. The Word went forth, and the Holy Spirit spoke to leaders in each camp. "Now is the time! Gather your people and go, take back the land! God's angels will fight for you."

In the space station, Chris and Gloria also heard the call they'd been waiting for. *Perceptor, it's time! All units should now turn against Apollos Hercainian and his allies. It's time for God's people to be free again and to possess their country once more!*

All around the world, Perceptor robot units turned against their masters, destroying them in the same manner as they had been told to destroy Christians, Moslems, and Jews. In one day, thousands of Earth's evil leaders died at the hands of their Perceptor servants. Absolute panic reigned as the empire of the Federated Alliance of Nations crumbled.

In his European office, Apollos Hercainian summoned his lord, Lucifer. "I need help, Master." He pleaded. "What's happened? I have no strength...my followers are being killed...it's all coming apart! What shall I do?" He fell on his face before the beautiful being in worship.

"What's happened? What's happened?" Lucifer swelled in rage, his dark leathery wings billowing out, fire breathing from his nostrils, his yellow eyes wild with hate. "You've failed, that's what's happened! You poor, wretched, inept excuse for a world ruler!" He reached down and picked Apollos up in his long bony fingers, sharp talons digging into tender flesh.

Apollos, looking up, saw what was holding him. It was not the beautiful shining being he knew, but a hideous terrifying monster whose foul breath, dark, wrinkled face, and terrible eyes struck unspeakable horror to his soul. Apollos's scream came from the depths of his being. It was a scream that reached to heaven, a scream that tore Apollos Hercainian's soul from his body and sent it recling into hell. Lucifer flung the empty husk against the wall contemptuously.

"I have another to take your place, Apollos Hercainian!" Lucifer hissed. My own son, the real Antichrist, will pick up the pieces and make the world "whole" again. These poor, weak puppets will follow him because he'll be a "savior" to the world! My son will deceive even Christians because he'll do miracles just as Jesus did! The whole world will follow him, and he will be able to defeat God! Together we will be able to defeat God! He'll be here soon to take over where you left off, you puny loser!"

The giant crystal glowed red as flame for a moment as the archangel of evil disappeared…to summon his forces and proceed with his plan.

****

"It's time!" Chris shouted with excitement in his voice. "I have the word!"

"I know," Gloria called back. "I heard it too! I'm packing! Bring my space suit too, will you?" They put the suits on and loaded the shuttle with the few things they wanted to take with them.

"You realize we're going back to a whole different world, don't you? Things will never be the same again, and this fight isn't over yet. There's a great deal of work ahead of us!" Chris looked at his wife, who had never seemed lovelier to him. She nodded and smiled. "I'm ready for whatever's ahead as long as we're together!"

"Amen. Come on, Perceptor One, let's go!" Chris called. "Reuben will take us home!"

The End

ABOUT THE AUTHOR

Sue Hanson is a former realtor and business broker in Grand Rapids. The first part of this story is loosely based on the life of a friend she met there, and the second part is projected into the future in pure Christian fiction. Now retired, Sue is also a playwright with six plays having been produced on stage in her Northern Michigan hometown. Currently, she volunteers at the town's new museum. Sue and her husband also write a monthly history article for the local newspaper.

CPSIA information can be obtained
at www.ICGtesting.com
Printed in the USA
BVOW06s0214121217
502589BV00001B/19/P